THE COWBOY'S BANDANA

Eight Long Years

BOOK 11
HOME ON THE RANGE SERIES

Rosie Bosse lives and writes on a ranch in northeast Kansas with her best friend and husband of many years. Her books intertwine history with fiction as she creates stories of the Old West. May you enjoy this visit with all of your "friends" and maybe even make some new ones in this final novel in Rosie's Home on the Range series.

THE COWBOY'S BANDANA

BANDANA

Eight Long Years

Brenda ~
May you enjoy
this finale to the
series - it was so much
fun to write!
Rosie

Rosie Bosse

Cover illustrated by Cynthia Martin

POST ROCK
PUBLISHING

The Cowboy's Bandana
Copyright © 2024 by Rosie Bosse

ISBN: Soft Cover – 978-1-958227-35-0
ISBN: eBook – 978-1-958227-36-7

POST ROCK PUBLISHING

Post Rock Publishing
17055 Day Rd.
Onaga, KS 66521
www.rosiebosse.com

This book is dedicated to the ranchers and farmers of this great nation. Thank you for your love of what you do—for your care of the land and animals that provide our food and fiber.

Home on the Range
Community of Families and Friends

Badger and Martha McCune
Parents, Grandparents, and Friends to All
Owners of Mule

Children and Ages	1884	1888
Lance and Molly Brewster Rankin		
Sam *(Samuel and Josephine Mosier's son)*	20	24
Paul	16	20
Abigail "Abbie"	12	16
Henry "Badger"	11	15
Olivia "Livvy"	9	13
Paul "Rowdy" and Beth Williams Rankin		
Rudy *(John and Marlene Hatch's son)*	23	27
Maribelle "Mari"	17	21
(John and Marlene Hatch's daughter)		
Twins: Ellie Elizabeth and Eli August	14	18
Pauline	8	12
Emmalene	6	10
Betsy	--	4
Fred "Fritz"	--	2 ½
Callie	--	1

Children and Ages	1884	1888
Levi and Sadie Hayes Crandall Parker		
Leo Strauss *(Orphan Train)*	22	26
Levi "Slim" *(Slim Crandall's son)*	12	16
Rose	8	12
Martha "Marty"	5	9
Reuben "Doc" and Josie Crandall Williams		
Charlene	5	9
Ruby	1	5
Jonah	--	2
Gabe and Merina Montero Hawkins		
Nate *(Gabe's younger brother)*	19	23
Rollie *(youngest Hawkins brother)*	10	14
Emilia *(youngest Montero sister)*	9	13
Grace	4	8
Elena	2	6
Merina Pregnant	--	*
Mule "adopted" Merina, 1879		
George "Spur" and Clare Childs Braxton Beckler Spurlach		
Nora *(Clare's niece)*	11	15
Annie *(Rock Beckler's daughter)*	10	14
Zeke *(Clare's son)*	10	14
Chas *(Clare and Rock's son)*	4	8
Jackson David "Beaner" Boyce *(Alice and David Boyce's son)*	4	8
Eddie	1½	5½

Children and Ages	1884	1888
Steve "Stub" and Adeline "Kit" Saunders Jackson		
Isaac "Tuff" *(Stub's younger brother)*	18	22
Savanah "Stevie"	4	8
Kathleen "Kate"	1	5
Jasper and Evelyn Jackson Claining Merrill		
Isabelle "Izzy" *(Ira Claining's daughter)*	19	22
Jorge "Angel" and Anna Whitman Montero		
Zach *(Dan and Mary Morton's son)*	10	14
Mandie *(Dan and Mary Morton's daughter)*	7	11
Consuella	4	8
Georgia	--	3
Wade "Tex" and Flory Whitman Montero Doolan		
Miguel	2	6
Jacob	--	3
Rusty and Laurel "Larry" Evans Dugan O'Brian		
Twins: Oscar James and Lorena Mae	5	9
Larry pregnant	*	
Beuford Porterhouse "Tiny" and Annie Small		
Beau—Stillborn, 1880		
Joey *(Rosann Linder's son)*	4	8
Lizzie *(Rosann Linder's daughter)*	9	13
John "Frieder" and Dorothy "Dot" Doolan Frieder		
No children		

PROLOGUE

This book, *The Cowboy's Bandana, Eight Long Years*, is number eleven in my Home on the Range series and is set in the heart of Nebraska's Sandhills.

This series closes with some of the children you have come to know moving into adulthood. Like many of you, I will miss "our friends." However, I do plan to create a new series that follows the lives of our young friends—and some of those ideas are already percolating.

As Nebraska's population moved north and west, more counties were divided and named. Until that time, the open areas were often designated as "Unorganized Territory." Grant, Arthur, Hooker, and McPherson Counties in west central Nebraska were originally part of that designation. All were created between 1887 and 1889. Kieth County, where Ogallala is located, was organized in 1873. Its early growth was a result of the growing cattle industry and the railroad. These five counties are where my story begins.

Nebraska Sandhills, the Last Prairie

"The ranchman understood and loved the land the way he found it—grass side up. He knew, even as the Indian knew, that much of it could not be profitably farmed, that to break its thin, root-bound skin would deface and ruin it for years to come." Nellie Snyder Yost, Writer and Historian (1905-1992)

The Sandhills, or Sand Hills as it is sometimes written, cover over one fourth of north and west central Nebraska. They consist of 19,300 square miles of sand dunes and stretch over 265 miles. Stabilized by the prairie grasses, the Sandhills are the largest dune formations in the Western Hemisphere and are one of the largest grass-stabilized dune regions in the world. Annual rainfall averages 17 to 23 inches per year with the lesser amount on the western side. Numerous lakes and subirrigated bottoms are scattered through the hills.

Livestock grazing is still the most common use of the land. Over 535,500 beef cows call the Sandhills their home. In fact, Nebraska is one of nine states in the United States where cattle are more plentiful than people!

Three Toes, the Killer Wolf

Three Toes was said to be a Great Plains or buffalo wolf, a subspecies of gray wolf, which made him larger and stronger than the typical timber wolves which at one time inhabited the river areas of western South Dakota. He roamed freely on those plains in the early 1900s, particularly in Harding County. According to "sagebrush philosopher" Archie Gilfillan (1886-1955), a sheepherder and writer, "Three Toes for 13 years laughed at poison, traps and guns, lived in and off enemy country with the hand of every man against him, a cunning, bloodthirsty killer, a super wolf among wolves and the most destructive single animal of which there is any record anywhere."

The wily wolf earned his name when he lost a toe from his front paw in a trap as a young wolf. In his prime, he was over 6 feet long and likely weighed around 150 pounds. (There are no records of his live weight. However, he was an extremely large wolf. At the time of his death, he was past his prime and weighed about 80 pounds.)

Three Toes was likely born around 1907 somewhere north of Camp Crook, South Dakota. Some believed he had been captured as a cub since he was unafraid of humans. According to local legend, he often sat and watched lighted ranch homes long into the night.

By 1912, Three Toes had established his reputation as a bloodthirsty killer. It is estimated that during his adult lifetime (between 1909 and 1925), his kills exceeded $50,000 in sheep and cattle—a market value of nearly $1,000,000 today. Some estimates show him killing over a 1000 head of cattle and even larger numbers of sheep in addition to horses and other livestock. The peak of his destruction was in the 1920s.

Three Toes was said to kill for the pure joy of killing. On one occasion, he attacked three ranches in one night. He easily leaped over the seven-foot-tall stockades where sheep were kept at night and killed six sheep or lambs at each. However, he only ate the liver of one lamb. While he killed cattle, horses, hogs, and sheep, his favorite prey were the small ones—calves, colts, and lambs.

The wily wolf was unstoppable. He seemed to know how to avoid traps as well as bullets, and once jumped a 30-foot ravine to elude his hunters. Coyote packs followed Three Toes to eat his kills. Their tracks blended with his, aiding in his escape.

After years of attempts to catch Three Toes by local ranchers and thousands of dollars in lost revenue, the United States Department of Agriculture sent their master wolfer, Clyde F. Briggs, to catch the killer wolf.

Briggs arrived in Harding County, South Dakota, on July 6, 1925. He talked to local ranchers, scouted the wolf's most often used territory, and finally determined where to place his traps.

Three Toes was captured on July 23, 1925, using special traps in sets of two. The old wolf's injuries were superficial, but he died while being transported to the county seat of Buffalo 19 days after Briggs began his quest.

Just off Highway 85 in Buffalo, South Dakota, a statue of a wolf can be seen, a tribute to Three Toes, the terror of the plains, a despised but respected wolf in South Dakota history.

While Three Toes ranged from South and North Dakota into Montana, I found no records of him hunting as far south as Nebraska. His walk through history was also later than my timeline in this novel. However, I was intrigued by his story and made him part of this adventure.

Ogallala, Nebraska: Queen of the Cow Towns and Gateway to the Northern Plains

Ogallala received its name from the Ogala Sioux Indians who pronounced it "Oklada." Their word means "scatter" or "to scatter one's own."

The tiny settlement went from a water stop for the railroad's steam engines to a shipping and trading point for cattle in a short amount of time. Built on the north side of the Platte River, Ogallala soon became known as the wildest town in Nebraska.

From 1870 to 1885, the small town's population swelled with the influx of cattle and the men who handled them. Ranchers from Wyoming and Montana Territories met in Ogallala to purchase breeding stock brought up the Texas or Western Trail. Other cattle were purchased in Ellsworth, Kansas, and were contracted for delivery in Ogallala. Many herds had already been sold by the time they arrived in Ogallala. In 1874, the Union Pacific Railroad completed its stockyards in Ogallala which made the new town the northernmost shipping point for cattle headed east.

The town site was platted in 1875, and a free lot was given to anyone willing to build a business. Ogallala's early businesses were south of the railroad tracks. They faced Railroad Street and the Texas Trail which led to the Platte River. The railroad depot and section house were located on the north side of the tracks along with brothels and residential homes.

The town remained quiet through the winter and early spring, but that all changed when the Texas herds began to arrive in June. Wild and rowdy cowboys filled the town until the end of August when those who had no riding jobs began to drift south.

To add to the chaos and fighting, United States Calvary soldiers were plentiful and an unwelcome sight to the southern cowboys. The Civil War was still fresh on everyone's mind. During the 10 years that Ogallala professed to be the end of the Texas or Western Trail, 17 violent deaths took place in the tiny town.

In 1875, Samuel and Harriet Gast opened the Ogallala House. It was a large hotel and restaurant along Railroad Street where Harriet was known for her excellent cooking. Two new saloons were added as well, the Crystal Palace and the OK Saloon. The OK Saloon was quickly sold and renamed The Cow Boy's Rest. The Spofford House soon opened on the north side of the tracks and was even more luxurious than the Ogallala House.

By 1880, Ogallala boasted a courthouse, a school, a hotel, two residential homes, and 25 permanent residents. It was the bustling nerve center for Nebraska's western ranchers.

Texas Fever

Texas cattle fever arrived in Ogallala in July of 1884. It was believed to have been brought in by Texas longhorn cattle shipped north via the Union Pacific Railroad. The disease spread rapidly through much of western Nebraska's native cattle herds causing heavy losses.

Some of the smaller ranchers who lost cattle levied lawsuits against the big cattlemen, especially the Rankin Livestock Company. It was believed the large outfit, headquartered in the Sandhills, had shipped in the infected Texas cattle. Longhorns were immune to the tick-carried illness, but native breeds were highly susceptible. Cattlemen who had introduced purebred bulls to their herds joined the cry to stop the Texas cattle from being trailed or transported through their area.

Trailing cattle north for better markets came to an end in 1885, 20 years after the long drives began. It was a huge blow to the Texas cattlemen and was the end of Ogallala's reign as a cow town. A few herds still managed to push their way through to the Platte River despite quarantine laws as well as angry farmers and ranchers. However, the days of the large cattle drives were over.

Valentine: Cherry County, Nebraska

Valentine was named for Edward K. Valentine, a popular congressman from 1883 to 1885 who worked to promote western Nebraska. It is a beautiful little town located in a small valley created by the Niobrara River, a tributary of the Missouri River. Valentine is surrounded by huge rock cliffs and pine trees. The largest waterfall in Nebraska, Snake River Falls, is also located near there. The town itself is located ten miles from the South Dakota border.

In its early days, Valentine was just a one-room log house beside the Niobrara River. Early explorers did not think the Sandhills were habitable, so settlement was slow. The Homestead Act encouraged farming there, but the early pioneers quickly learned that much of the area was not suitable for farming. Thousands left, never to return. However, the plentiful grass drew in cattlemen. By 1882, Valentine boasted grocery and hardware stores, harness shops, five livery stables, five saloons, and a few churches.

The railroad completed a wooden trestle bridge over the Niobrara River at Valentine in 1883. The first train arrived in late March of that year and provided a way for local ranchers to ship their beef east. Valentine was incorporated as a town in 1884.

Like many western towns, Valentine was wild in its early days. Outlaws sought refuge in the isolated hills, and the lack of law officers meant defensive actions were often required of the local citizens.

Dancing the Two Step

It's hard to say when exactly the Two Step was created. It is a dance mixture of the Foxtrot and the One Step—two early dances that were popular for many years. Both of those dances had their roots in the age-old waltzes—lilting dances that today still have dancers gliding across the floor.

The Two Step has gone through many changes over the years. Its early popularity is sometimes credited to John Phillip Sousa, who wrote a song called the "Washington Post March" in 1889. The beat of the music moved people out of the flowing waltz to a different style of dance. The French called the new two-beat dance "valse a deux temps," but that name did not fit the dance that was popular in 1800-era American saloons and dance halls. The name was soon shortened to the Two Step.

The Cowboy Bandana

Bandanas have been a necessary part of cowboy garb for many years. The first bandanas were cut from flour sacks. The 30 × 30-inch cotton squares were tied around the neck. There they became protection against wind and weather of all kinds. Most early shirts did not have collars, so the knotted bandana added a barrier of warmth in the winter and sun protection in the summer. They were also handy to use as bandages for both horses and men as well as hot pan holders and dish rags. They could even be used as temporary saddle riggings if one of the metal rings that held the girth was lost or broken—wet cotton is extremely strong. Once silk became available, it quickly gained popularity because of its moisture-wicking ability in all seasons, and its warmth in the winter.

The paisley pattern often seen on bandanas or handkerchiefs today was created hundreds of years ago in Kasmir, a part of the Persian empire. Traders took it to India where the textile makers there used "bandhani," their traditional process of tie-dying, to create brightly colored cotton and silk scarves.

The first bandana to be produced in America was allegedly created by John Hewson for President George Washington. Hewson was a printmaker in the early years of the American Revolution and was an associate of Benjamen Franklin.

Washington's bandana contained four flags and showed an image of Washington seated on a horse while surrounded by military symbols. Although no records are available, Martha Washington likely designed and commissioned the bandana to honor her husband. An interesting sidenote: one of the flags is the Gadsden Flag. It pictures a coiled rattlesnake with the words, "DON'T TREAD UPON ME."

The words in the center of the handkerchief, around the figure of Washington, read: "GEORGE WASHINGTON, ESQ. FOUNDATOR, AND PROTECTOR OF AMERICA'S LIBERTY, AND INDEPENDENCY."

Large silk and synthetic bandanas are called wild rags today and are still popular cowboy garb.

Bloodsuckers and Barber Poles

Using leeches for medicinal purposes has been documented as far back as the pyramids. Tombs of Egyptian pharaohs even contain pictures of them. Leeches were so popular in the eighteenth and nineteenth centuries that there was a shortage of them in Europe. France alone imported 40 million leeches per year by the mid-1800s.

While European doctors reduced their use of leeches by the late 1800s, American physicians continued to use them. This was partially due to the seemingly endless supply available. Even in the 1900s, jars of leeches could be found in many saloons, bars, and barber shops.

In the West, the barber was commonly the local doctor. In fact, the red, white, and blue stripes rotating around a pole outside a barber shop were originally a sign of the services offered inside. The red represented blood and bloodletting while the white was for setting bones, tooth extraction, and bandages. And the blue? Some say the blue was unique to the United States since it completed our national colors. Others say it represented the veins.

Even the barber pole had significance. A stave or piece of wood was originally given to the patient to grip during the chosen procedure since there was often no way to deaden the pain. Besides, gripping the pole made the patient's veins more visible. (Of course, some patients resorted to drunkenness and passed out. It was easier for them when they did not have to see *or* feel.) Once the "doctor" finished, the bandages were rinsed, wrapped around the pole to dry, and the pole was set outside. The bandages were never completely clean, so the pole always had a striped appearance.

And why were leeches found in saloons? It was for their bloodletting and anticoagulation abilities. There were lots of fights in saloons, some with guns or knives, and some with fists. A leech attached to the puffy skin around a blackening eye or a wound would take the swelling down by drawing out the loose blood.

Leeches were also used to successfully treat frostbite. In severe frostbite, ice crystals are formed due to the freezing of tissues, and this can cause the affected cells to die. Typically, hands and feet are the most affected. Leeches helped this condition by reducing the swelling with their intake of excess fluids. They also reduced the itching and inflammation and thus enhanced the healing process. Careful removal of the leeches was important if they were to be used again. However, leeches will release on their own when they are full.

Since they only ate every six months, those who kept leeches rotated them carefully. Habitat was also important, and care was taken to mimic the conditions where they naturally lived.

The Simple Shovel—For Work and For Play

The earliest examples of shovel use have been documented between 10,000 and 4500 BC. Ancient shovels have been found throughout the Middle East and northern Europe. Those early shovels were made by attaching a large animal's shoulder blade to a piece of wood with leather straps and were primarily used for building or searching for food. It is interesting that the early shovels found, regardless of location, all used the shoulder blade as their digging tool. In America, Native Americans were using the bone shovels until the early settlers arrived with their iron tools.

Shovel designs stayed mostly the same until the early 1800s. Railroads inspired some of this change since much dirt and rock had to be moved to build the ever-growing rail system. The shovel is a simple tool, but one that helped to build many civilizations.

If you have never ridden a shovel in the snow pulled by a horse, try it! The longer the rope, the wilder the ride. New shovels work the best because they are smooth and slide easily. However, that same thought process can cause a lot of angst if the farmer or rancher who owns the shovel sees you riding it without his permission—at least it did with our father!

Bucker Plow

The Bucker plow, a wooden wedge plow, was developed by early railroads to clear snow and was available by the 1840s. The smooth surface allowed the snow to slide over the plow face instead of accumulating in front. The vertical and horizontal wedges pushed the snow to the sides and dropped it on top of the drifts beside the tracks.

This method of snow removal requires much force due to the weight and density of the packed snow. Early plows usually required multiple locomotives to provide enough force and speed. They were noisy and involved much backing up and pushing forward. However, the simple design worked and is still in use in some places today.

The Big Die-Up

The summer of 1886 was dry from Montana south into Texas. This reduced the growth of prairie grass which ranchers counted on to sustain their livestock through the cold winters. In addition, stocking rates were not fully understood, and the ranges were often over-populated with livestock.

The winter of 1886-1887 was devastating to Wyoming's cattle industry. On November 13, 1886, it started to snow and snowed for a month. However, in mid-December, a chinook (warming weather pattern) caused the snow to partially melt. This slush was frozen solid when the temperature dropped into the -30s by late December, and the prairie became a sheet of ice. January of 1887 was the coldest month in Wyoming history and included one blizzard that lasted three days.

Cattle keep their tails to the wind which means they usually drift south in a winter storm. They are only stopped by rivers, fences, or some other kind of barrier. If left on their own, open range cattle could drift up to one hundred miles in a storm. Drift fences were built to keep cattle from wandering too far or into dangerous areas. However, a drift fence in a blizzard could have disastrous consequences.

Andy Adams in his 1907 novel, *Reed Anthony, a Cowman,* described that 1887 blizzard. "We were powerless to relieve the drifting cattle. The morning after the great storm, with others, I rode to a south string of fence on a divide, and found thousands of our cattle huddled against it, many frozen to death, partially through and hanging on the wire. We cut the fences in order to allow them to drift on to shelter, but the legs of many of them were so badly frozen that, when they moved, the skin cracked open and their hoofs dropped off. Hundreds of young steers were wandering aimlessly around on hoofless stumps, while their tails cracked and broke like icicles…"

Teddy Blue Abbott, a storytelling cowboy of the time, described the range conditions. "It was all so slow, plunging after them (the cattle) through the deep snow…The horses' feet were cut and bleeding from the heavy crust, the cattle had the hair and hide wore off their legs to the knees and hocks. It was surely hell to see big four-year-old steers just able to stagger along. It was the same all over Wyoming, Montana, and Colorado, western Nebraska, and western Kansas."

By the time the snow began to melt in the spring, the prairie was nearly bare of grass and life. However, it was full of dead animal carcasses. To make matters even worse, the terrible winter was followed by prolonged summer droughts in parts of the country. Many ranchers went broke. Eastern livestock investors began to withdraw from the cattle business, and foreign ranchers left the country.

Losses of both cattle and sheep were high. However, sheep seemed to endure the terrible weather better. Smaller ranchers also fared better than many of the larger ones.

Some ranchers sold out at a loss while others fought through and attempted to recover. Many ranches changed hands during this time. Ranchers lost from 15 to 25 percent of their cattle herds with losses in some locations as high as 50 percent.

Fires and Firefighting in Early Cheyenne

Early towns were mostly constructed of wood—after all the tents were replaced. Wood burns easily and with little in the way of fire-fighting equipment, as well as limited water, fires were always a concern.

Cheyenne's first threat of fire took place in 1867, shortly after the town was settled. Residents fought the prairie fire with wet burlap bags and managed to save their new town. In 1868, another fire burned half a city block. It caused more than $50,000 in losses and damage.

After the 1868 fire, the Pioneer Hook and Ladder Company was formed to fight fires on a more organized basis. Still, fires had to be fought with bucket brigades. With the help of the Union Pacific Railroad (which had a vested interest in keeping its depot, shops, and rails operating), the Thomas C. Durant Engine Company was formed. The town quickly ordered a $10,000 steam fire engine from the East. It was the first steam fire engine west of the Missouri River, and the residents of Cheyenne were proud of their investment.

The new steam engine was not all Cheyenne had hoped it would be though. The high cost was a drain on the city's residents and financial coffers. The Wyoming Territorial Legislature had to authorize special taxes three times to cover the mortgage and the many necessary repairs.

In addition, high pressure was necessary to operate the steam engine's pump. Lighter material was to be kept in the firebox so the fire could be started quickly and pressure built while the horses were hitched and driven to the fire. Unfortunately, pressure took longer to achieve, and the fires were often out of control or over by the time the necessary pressure was reached.

In 1870, another fire burned two city blocks in Cheyenne including Barney Ford's brick building. This fire caused between $150,000 and $200,000 in damage. A third fire took place in 1874. It burned McDaniel's theatre and a butcher shop.

By the 1880s, multiple volunteer companies were in operation. They had at their disposal one steam engine, chemical extinguishers, a hand pumper, two hook and ladder trucks, multiple hoses and hose carriages, as well as stored water supplies. The volunteers were consolidated into one department in the early 1900s, and Cheyenne's history of deadly fires was slowed.

The Tree Rock

On the Interstate 80 drive between Cheyenne and Laramie, Wyoming, if you stop at the right rest area, you will see a scrubby tree growing out of a boulder in the center of the median. There is even a sign there to tell you all about the old tree.

Tree Rock is a limber pine. Along with ponderosa pines, it is a common pine tree in the area. However, limber pines thrive in areas where many trees will not grow.

The small, twisted pine tree growing out of solid rock became part of history when the first rail system was built between Cheyenne and Laramie. In fact, the rail company diverted the tracks a little to bypass the tree—or maybe it was to avoid moving the huge rock. Those tracks were built across Sherman Mountain between 1867 and 1869. Some even say the train firemen (those who stoked the wood or coal for the steam engines) gave the little tree a drink as they passed by.

In 1913, the Lincoln Highway Association built their highway near Tree Rock. US 30 also passed by in the 1920s followed by Interstate 80 in the 1960s. The views of the mountains there are breathtaking. However, Tree Rock seemed to be the thing that most early travelers talked about.

The stunted and twisted little tree growing out of a huge boulder of pink granite is still worth the stop for those travelers who care enough to pay attention. While its age is unknown, limber pines can live up to 200 years. The lonely Tree Rock may be around for some years to come.

C.H. Hyer and the First Cowboy Boot

After the Civil War ended in 1865, rail lines exploded across the eastern half of the United States. As the rails moved west toward the vast plains of Kansas and beyond, Kansas City emerged as a commerce hub with boundless opportunities. Even before the Transcontinental Railroad was completed in 1869, larger cities like Saint Louis, Omaha, and Kansas City became gateways to the West.

C.H. Hyer, the son of a cobbler, was one of those individuals who embraced the new opportunities in front of him. He left Germany for the United States, arriving first in New York before traveling west with the railroad. He reached Kansas City in the mid-1860s. Tiring of his work with the railroad, Hyer decided to share his rich legacy of craftsmanship with a new generation.

In 1869, The Kansas School for the Deaf gave him that opportunity. However, Hyer did not want to just hire his students—he wanted to empower them with a worthy trade as well.

Originally known as the "Asylum for the Deaf and Dumb," the Kansas School for the Deaf emerged as a beacon of hope—hope not only for those struggling with speech impairments and deafness but hope for their families as well—a realization that their children would be able to support themselves. Still, the school grappled with meager funding and inadequate facilities, not to mention the "less than" attitude the students themselves had to contend with.

C.H. Hyer opened his cobbler shop in 1874. By 1875, he was employing eager students from the Kansas School for the Deaf where he taught shoe and last making. (The last was a wooden form created and shaped like a human foot. It was used to customize a shoe or boot to a specific size and shape.)

The railroad drew large numbers of cowboys who arrived at the stockyards with their herds to ship east. Those cowboys frequented C.H.

Hyer's cobbler shop in Olathe, Kansas, seeking the quality footwear he was known to make.

One day, an unnamed cowboy wandered into Hyer's shop. His Civil War-style boots had seen better days and he needed new footwear. However, he had some specific requests. The cowboy did not just want comfortable boots that could withstand his rugged lifestyle. He also wanted a toe shape that would slide into the stirrup along with a raised heel to hold it there. He also wanted a scalloped top that would allow his foot to slide in and out of the boot more easily.

Hyer had never made boots like the cowboy requested, but he willingly accepted the challenge. After several attempts, he finished a pair he thought would fulfill the needs of the footsore cowboy. He called his new creation the "Cow Boy Boot." (Cowboy was originally spelled as two words and was used as a derisive term to belittle the men who followed cattle for a living. However, it did not bother the wranglers and riders to whom it was applied. They adopted the name as their own, and those western riders began to call their friends cowboys. Throughout history, cowboy has been spelled as both one and two words. Today, one word is the accepted spelling.)

The pleased cowboy must have shown his fine boots to everyone he met because orders came in from all over for Hyer's functional and comfortable cow boy boots. Business exploded, and C.H. changed the name of his cobbler shop to Hyer Boot Company.

Cowboys trailing herds ordered their boots when they arrived in town and picked up their completed boots when they left or even on their next drive. The last Hyer created for each pair of boots allowed that individual's size and shape of foot to be labeled and saved.

Working cowboys were not the only ones to hear about the small boot company in Kansas. Cattlemen, rodeo performers, and dignitaries such as Teddy Roosevelt and Calvin Coolidge were soon wearing Hyer boots. Buffalo Bill Cody was never one to be left behind when it came to style, and he was quick to purchase a pair of C.H. Hyer's custom boots as well. Even Jesse James ordered a pair. He hid out on the top floor of the factory while C.H. crafted a pair of boots for him! During World War I, the United States Military commissioned Hyer to make their boots. Later, movie stars such as Will Rogers and Marilyn Monroe became proud owners of Hyer boots.

History credits Hyer Boot Company with innovations beyond their popular cowboy boots though. They were the first to sell boots via mail order and the first to add a toe bug to their boots to allow for better flexion without the toe collapsing. They are also hailed for their invention of the fork construction for pull tabs. One historian even credited Hyer Boot Company with the first assembly line. For over 100 years, this family-owned boot company was at the forefront of manufacturing and innovation becoming the largest manufacturer of handmade boots in America.

The Kansas School for the Deaf is the oldest state educational institution in the state of Kansas, and it remained a part of Hyer Boots and its success. That association was a story of perseverance, partnership, and the pursuit of excellence.

Unfortunately, people's tastes changed, and the popular boot company sold in the 1970s due to financial difficulties. It sold again several more times. However, no one had the drive or the dedication the Hyer family had, and the once-famous boot company eventually closed.

The forgotten company became a glimmer of hope in 2018. After his grandfather died, Zach Lawless found an old picture in the basement that showed Calvin Coolidge dedicating Mount Rushmore…in Hyer boots. That was enough to stoke the fire that had been passed on to him.

Thanks to much work and persistence, Hyer Boots is back in business with its *original* trademark.

While the headquarters are in Overland Park, Kansas, Hyer Boots are now made in a small factory in León, Mexico, an area renowned for its exceptional bootmakers and leather goods. The legacy C.H. Hyer created now lives on through two great-great-grandsons, Zach Lawless and Cameron Boyle, fifth generation boot makers. Their mission is to champion the Western lifestyle through their customers—to provide boots that working cowboys and cowgirls can afford and wear with pride.

By the way, did you ever wonder about the origin of the hand signals that baseball players use? Some of those signals are the result of sign language used by deaf ball players like William "Dummy" Hoy. That connection highlights the ingenuity and adaptability of human nature to overcome all kinds of barriers.

May this story be a tribute to C.H. Hyer, a German immigrant who used his passion to teach a craft he loved. May it also highlight the accomplishments of the students he trained and inspired to reach new levels of pride and success.

Thank you for choosing to read my novels. Please follow me on Facebook: Rosie Bosse, Author. Your comments and reviews are welcome as well.

Additional novels may be purchased through my website below or through your local bookstore. Paper and digital copies are also available through various online suppliers. My books may be requested at your local library as well. Happy Reading!

Rosie Bosse, Author
Living and Writing on a Ranch in the Middle of Nowhere
rosiebosse.com

Feb 6, 1884
Unorganized Territory
Nebraska Sandhills

CHAPTER 1

BLOOD ON THE SNOW

THE TWO COWBOYS CRESTED THE SNOWY HILL. THE morning sun was just pushing through the clouds and the air was crisp and clean. They stopped as they stared down at the bloody scene below them. Five wolves were ripping apart the carcass of a dying cow, and the snow was covered in blood. The newborn calf had been dragged away, and two more wolves were fighting over the calf's small body.

Both men cursed as they pulled out their rifles.

"I was afraid this was what we'd find. The tracks say that's Three Toes' pack. Let's clean 'em out today," Sam growled.

They began firing. Two wolves went down, and the rest looked up in surprise. The large, black horse one of the cowboys was riding charged toward the snarling wolves, mouth open and screaming. It grabbed the closest wolf and threw it up in the air, kicking and whirling as it smashed through the pack.

The cowboy who was riding the angry horse slid off to give it more freedom. He dropped down beside the cow and began firing his pistol.

A large wolf darted by the kicking horse and sprang at the man on the ground, snarling loudly as it jumped. A rifle fired and the wolf fell. It knocked the struggling cowboy back as it landed on top of him. He rolled out from under it, pushing its open mouth away from his neck. He stood shakily.

"Sam, I'm glad you didn't talk while you were shooting that time. I reckon you saved my life."

Sam Rankin pushed back his hat and grinned.

"You need to keep old Demon there from rushin' into fights like this, Nate. We could have shot just as many if we'd stayed back on that hill."

Nate Hawkins walked slowly toward his horse, talking softly.

"Easy, Demonio. You're all right now. Let me take that bit out of your mouth and clean it off some. You have wolf hair and blood all over it."

The horse was trembling, but it allowed Nate to remove the bridle and bit. It rushed toward the downed wolves and checked each one before it returned to where the two men stood.

Nate chuckled as he cleaned the bit. He warmed it with his hands before he put it back in Demonio's mouth.

"You know Demon. He hasn't forgotten about the wolf that jumped us shortly after we took this job. He carries his mad around a long time. Old Cassidy told us he had a wolf problem when we took this job. I reckon it's five less of a problem now."

Sam pushed at the body of one of the wolves with his foot.

"Maybe more than five. This bitch has pups."

"We aren't too far from where old Windeater winters. Let's ride over there and tell him. Maybe he will send some of his youngsters out to track the two that got away. They can clean out their den. Maybe even capture a few of the little ones." Nate pointed at the large wolf that had attacked him.

"Look at the size of that thing. He's almost as long as me, and I'm over six foot."

Sam bent over the large wolf. He picked up one foot and grinned as he looked back at Nate.

"We got Three Toes. Windeater will be glad to hear that. Maybe he'll be able to keep the rest of his horses alive through the winter now."

CHAPTER 2

WINDEATER

THE TWO FRIENDS RODE SLOWLY TOWARD THE WINTER camp of Windeater. Both young men were tall with wide shoulders and the lean hips of riders. Heavy beards covered their faces and both needed haircuts.

Sam's hair was curly. The longer it was, the more pronounced his curls were, and after a long winter in the line shack, blond curls poked wildly from under his hat.

Nate's hair was shorter and was nearly black. His hair was curly as well, but he chopped it off before it became as long as Sam's.

Both men had blue eyes and smiled easily although Nate's smile broke slowly across his face while Sam grinned easily.

The old Indian chief stepped out of his tipi. He didn't come to greet them but watched silently as the two White men rode into his camp.

Sam spoke in the tongue of the Northern Sioux.

"We have come to tell you Three Toes has been shot. We killed him this morning along with four more wolves in his pack."

The old chief nodded somberly and replied in English.

"We heard many shots this morning." His eyes glinted with humor as he added, "Perhaps you did not shoot so straight. It took many shots to kill five small wolves."

Sam's eyebrows shot up and he started to respond. When the old chief grinned at him, Sam chuckled.

"Well, that could be true, but between our shootin' and Nate's horse, we got all but two of them." He pointed his finger at Demonio. "That horse has a strong dislike for wolves, and he was more than happy to help."

The chief nodded as he walked toward Demonio. He talked softly in his own language and held out his hand. The horse blew loudly and shook his head. Windeater laughed and spoke again in English.

"The great black horse is a warrior. I think he has killed before perhaps." He looked hard at Nate and the young man shrugged.

"Perhaps. Demonio was a gift from a man who died. Miguel Montero raised him. When Miguel died, his sister gave Demonio to me. Now we are one."

Windeater's eyes bored into Nate.

"I know this Montero. We called him Pequeño Tornado. You would say Small Tornado. He was not so big, but he could cause much damage. His brother too, I think. I have heard many stories." He touched Demonio's head again. "I remember this horse. He is calmer now."

Nate slowly nodded. "He is a good horse. We have been together for four years. In the beginning, he wasn't so sure he liked me. Now we are brothers, this horse and me."

Windeater watched Nate closely. He nodded behind him to where a woman was cooking.

"Come and eat with me. Let us talk of these fine wolf pelts you are going to give me." His dark eyes sparkled as he opened the flap of his tipi. "My young men were watching you. Our women have already left to bring the hides back."

When both Nate and Sam stared at him in surprise, the chief spoke seriously.

"This is our land. We only loan it to the man you call Stag Barrett. He brings his cattle here. We let them stay because we take a few to eat when the buffalo leave…when we are hungry." Windeater waved his hand at the land around him.

"The wolves are our brothers. We kill them sometimes, but we respect them too. Three Toes was not a normal wolf though. He did not respect anyone or anything.

"Three Toes was sly. He covered his tracks and hid from those who chased him. Even the coyotes helped him to escape. They were his brothers and they guarded the way for him when he was tired—when he was pursued as well—even if it cost them their lives. Three Toes killed for the pure love of killing. He killed even when he was not hungry.

"If the Great Spirit allowed you to kill him, you must have powerful medicine.

"Tonight, we will mourn the passing of a great warrior wolf, but we will celebrate too. Now our horses and our small children will be safe at night.

"We will celebrate his passing and we will thank the two men who had strong medicine, medicine strong enough to take Three Toes' life." He nodded at the woman who was working over the cooking pot outside the tipi before he looked again at Sam.

"My woman will make a fine blanket for you from his pelt. It will keep you warm, but it will keep you safe as well." His eyes moved to Nate.

"And for your horse, I will make him a necklace of wolf teeth. He will wear it with pride, and everyone who sees it will know your horse is a great protector. He is a warrior horse."

Nate and Sam were quiet as they followed the chief into his lodge.

CHAPTER 3

THE END OF A LONG WINTER

SAM AND NATE RODE SOUTH TOWARD THE RANCH headquarters. They each led a pack horse. Snow was still everywhere but the days were warming.

Nate's appaloosa didn't like the smell of the wolf pelts on his back. They'd had to reload them several times after he bolted and shook the pack loose. Even now he snorted and shied at every loud sound.

"Appy, you settle down. You keep that pack on this trip, and I promise I will never make you haul wolf pelts again." Nate's voice was soft as he talked to his horse.

Sam grinned at his friend.

"I sure am glad we made friends with old Windeater. He showed us where the wolves usually traveled and how to make snares. We have a fine load of pelts now to sell on top of our winter wages. Maybe old Cassidy will even give us a bonus for catching so many wolves."

Nate was quiet a moment before he answered. He finally looked over at his pardner.

"How do you suppose Windeater knew Miguel? I didn't think he was ever up this way."

Sam shrugged.

"Miguel moved around a lot. I don't think he always rode on the right side of the law either." He frowned slightly and added, "Deep down though, he was a good man.

"I reckon Miguel is pleased Flory married Tex. Tex will give her a good life. Shoot, they probably have a passel of little ones by now. We ain't been home for nigh on four years."

The two men rode in silence for a time.

Sam finally asked, "You ever goin' to mail those letters you keep a writin'? How's Mari s'posed to know you pine over her all the time if you never go home and you never mail 'em?"

Nate's face turned a darker red and he glared at his pardner.

"I'm not going home until I make something of myself. I have nothing to offer her yet. And I don't reckon I'll ever mail any of these letters. She'd probably laugh and read them to her friends. I'll send her one that's not so lovesick."

Sam snorted and Nate swung at him.

"Come on, Nate. You ain't hardly looked at another gal since we left Wyomin'. How do you even know Mari's the one if you don't spark any other women?"

Nate's face colored again but he answered coolly, "If I meet one that's as pretty and as smart as Mari—and as sweet, I'll think on it. I just ain't seen one yet is all. Besides, most gals ain't easy to talk to. Mari is."

Sam snorted again. "Speakin' of women makes me think of money. How much of this wolf money do I get to spend? You only let me keep $5 each month out of my wages, and that ain't much to court a gal on."

Nate grinned at his friend.

"We agreed when we became pards that I'd take care of our money. You'd blow it all, and we need to have something to show for our work. Besides, $5 a month for seven months is $35. That is a lot of money to drop in one town.

"And we'll do the same shares with the wolf money. I'm hoping they will be worth $5 per pelt, but they might not be worth that much. We might only get a dollar each, and that won't amount to much. Still, we have ten of them, so whatever we get will be more than we had."

Sam listened quietly as he watched his pardner. He finally shook his head.

"I think we'll get more than a dollar. Windeater's woman showed us how to scrape 'em and how to make 'em soft. We don't just have a pile of rough hides. We have soft pelts with heavy fur. That should account for somethin'."

Nate shrugged. "I guess we'll see. Let's pick up the pace. It's a three-day ride back to headquarters in good weather, and I don't want to spend any more time sleeping outside than necessary."

Sam laughed as he listened to his friend.

"Shoot, we don't even know what day it is. You *think* it's April 5 but we ain't sure. For all we know, we could get there before we even left!"

Nate glared at Sam again. "I swear, Sam. Sometimes you are mighty irritating. And keep a tight hand on that pack horse. I don't want to go three days without eating."

CHAPTER 4

THE BOSS' FRIENDS

IT WAS NEARLY DARK WHEN NATE AND SAM ARRIVED at the ranch headquarters. Both were tired and hungry from the long, cold ride. They had traded most of their grub the first night to a farmer for a night in his barn. The man offered the barn for free, but his was a hardscrabble operation. They knew the extra provisions would be appreciated. They left most of their food in the barn with a note of thanks. The second night, the two cowboys found a run-down line shack. There was no wood and they brought the horses inside since there was nowhere to pen them.

They looked around in surprise at the number of rigs tied in front of the house along with extra horses in the corral.

"The boss havin' himself a party?" Sam asked a cowboy who was tying his horse to the hitching rail.

"He built him a new barn down the road a piece. Thought he'd have a party whilst it was still clean. A barn dance an' the whole shebang. He said to tell you boys to go on up to the house if you made it in this evenin'." The cowboy studied them a moment before he shook his head. "I don't know how he does it, but the boss seems to know when winter riders are goin' to show up." The cowboy grinned as he continued.

"He has some friends visitin' from back East. Mighty good-lookin' daughter too. Too bad you fellers are lookin' so rough. You won't make much of an impression now. 'Course, that might make it easier on the rest of us since we ain't so purty as you two."

Nate and Sam stared at the man. They both rubbed their faces and looked down at their clothes.

Sam growled, "I ain't puttin' on a clean shirt till I take a bath an' shave…and I ain't doin' neither till I get paid."

"Come on, Nate. Let's get this deal over with. She probably ain't that good lookin' anyhow. Peters always stretches the truth some."

The two men dismounted stiffly. They led their horses to the barn, pulled off the saddles and packs, and dumped a little grain in the feed pans. Another rider followed them inside.

"I'll rub your horses down. The boss wants to see you right away."

Both men nodded. Nate called over his shoulder, "Don't mess with Demonio. I'll rub him down later. I don't want you to get kicked or bitten." As they turned toward the main house, his stomach growled loudly.

"I sure hope Cookie has some supper left. My stomach is so hungry it's chewin' on itself." He rapped on the door loudly and stepped back.

Mrs. Cassidy opened the door with a smile. Both men pulled off their hats.

"Peters said the boss wanted to see us tonight. We just got in."

Freda Cassidy stepped back with a smile.

"Yes, please come in. Bill is expecting you."

Bill Cassidy strode into the kitchen. He was a large man with a ruddy face and a loud voice. He was followed by another man. Both Sam and Nate looked from Cassidy to the man behind him. The contrast between their boss and his guest couldn't have been greater.

The smaller man wore his white shirt buttoned all the way up. A black string tie was knotted neatly around his neck. His black coat had long tails, and his boots were polished to a shine. The stranger stepped forward and put out his hand with a friendly smile.

"You must be the riders Bill was telling me about. He said you spent the winter out in the hills and wouldn't come back to the ranch until spring. It is the eighth of April and here you are.

"Did you keep a calendar or how did you know when to return?" Sam grinned at the man in front of him.

"We asked our horses, and they said it was time." His grin became larger as he added, "Besides, we were about out of grub." He put out his hand and encircled the older man's hand in his rough one.

"I'm Sam Rankin and my talkative pard here is Nate Hawkins. And you are?"

"Jasper Merrill. Bill and I met each other during the War for Southern Independence."

Bill laughed. "That's one way to put it. Jasper here led a company of fighting Rebs. He captured me and my soldiers at the end of that war. I had fifty men and he had twenty.

"He didn't turn any of us over when his brass was collecting prisoners though. He said the war was almost over and we all just needed to go home.

"He was right too. Several days later, the word came through that the South had surrendered. We all sat down and shared our vittles. Then we parted ways.

"Jasper and I try to get together at least once a year. We planned to have our kids marry one day. Poor deal that Freda and I never had any kids at all let alone any boys. Jasper's little Isabelle is a sweetheart."

Bill looked toward the room behind him.

"Evelyn! Isabelle! Come on out here and meet two of my riders. I reckon you'll see more of them if you move out this way."

CHAPTER 5

A Good-Looking Daughter

A YOUNG WOMAN WITH BLONDE HAIR AND LOTS OF curves hurried into the kitchen.

"Mother has a headache and is lying down." She smiled as she looked at the two cowboys standing inside the door.

"Hello! Uncle Bill was telling us about you. He said he asked you to hunt predators while you were out by yourselves all winter.

"I'm Isabelle. Which of you is Nate and which is Sam? Were you able to capture any wolves?"

For maybe the first time in his life, Sam was speechless. He stared at Isabelle and stuttered a little as he tried to talk. Nate finally stepped forward.

"We got some all right. Some shot and some trapped. An old Indian showed us how to set snares and they worked well." He waited briefly for Sam to speak before he added, "I'm Nate Hawkins and my pard here is Sam. Sam Rankin. It's a pleasure to meet you, Miss Merrill."

Sam still wasn't talking as he continued to stare at Isabelle. Nate poked him before he spoke again.

"We brought back some pelts, boss. We thought we'd take them on south with us unless you know of someone up this way who would like to buy them."

Jasper Merrill's face showed his interest.

"You have wolf pelts? May I see them? They are a hot commodity in the East right now but are rather hard to come by, especially ones of good quality." He looked directly at the two young men in front of him and asked, "They aren't mangy, are they? I'm only interested in high-quality pelts."

Cassidy waved his hands toward the door.

"Let's go look at them now. Freda, get me those two packets on my desk. These boys need to get paid so they can wash some of this winter dirt off."

As they stepped outside the door, Cassidy asked softly, "Did you see old Three Toes? He has been terrorizing folks north and south of the Niobrara River all winter."

"We did. Sam shot him. We got four of the wolves from his pack the same day, and some Indian boys cleaned out the rest. Old Windeater's woman skinned Three Toes and gave his pelt to Sam. That hide was so durn soft, we just wanted to cuddle up in it.

"We asked her how she did that. She just grinned but after we bothered her long enough, she showed us how to scrape and clean our pelts. It was quite the process. Before we left, Sam offered Three Toes' pelt to Windeater as a gift.

"Windeater offered to give Sam Three Toes' front foot since he was the one who shot him, but Sam said out of respect for the warrior wolf, that three-toed foot should stay with his hide. That old Indian was downright delighted. He offered Sam his best horse, and they both decided it was a good trade."

Just then, Isabelle hurried out the door. She carried two packets which she handed to Cassidy.

"Here are the packets you asked Freda to get. I told her I would give them to you. I want to see the pelts too."

Cassidy's steps slowed a little and he frowned at Jasper. The smaller man shrugged and laughed.

"Isabelle loves anything to do with animals. She even hunts rabbits with me. She can see them if she wants."

Nate dropped back so Isabelle could walk beside Sam. His friend had finally gotten his tongue back and as they walked toward the barn, Sam casually asked, "Are you visiting here long, Miss Merrill?"

"We are leaving the first part of next week, but Father is talking about buying a ranch out here. One of Mr. Cassidy's neighbors has one for sale."

Sam looked at Isabelle in surprise. He asked carefully, "Does your pa know anything about ranchin'? Runnin' cattle out here ain't all that easy."

Isabelle's blue eyes sparked, and she answered tartly, "My father runs cattle in Georgia. We have a large farming and ranching operation there. However, Atlanta is growing, and the city is crowding us. Father wants to sell. He wants to move someplace with fewer people."

"This area for sure has fewer people. An' there ain't no cities to crowd a feller neither. Still, I think it gets a mite colder here than in Georgia. Or so folks say. I ain't never been any farther east than Kansas City."

Isabelle didn't answer as she looked up at Sam. She started to speak but frowned instead and looked away.

CHAPTER 6

WOLF PELTS

NATE UNTIED THE PACK OF WOLF PELTS AND LAID them out on the hay. Isabelle reached over and touched one.

"Those are beautiful. Still, it makes me a little sad to think each of them was once a living wolf. Wolves are so enchanting."

Nate pointed to each hide as he talked.

"We took that one not long after its pack killed nearly twenty sheep." He pointed at two more pelts. "Those two had a couple of horses backed up against a creek bank when we shot them." His finger moved again. "We caught these four after they killed a cow that was birthing her calf. Killed the calf too." He pointed at the last three pelts. "Those we caught in snares.

"Wolves do what they were born to do and that is to kill. When they move from hunting elk and deer to killing our livestock, then we hunt them down.

"Some Indians call cattle 'slow elk,' and I reckon that's what wolves think of them too. They are for sure easier to kill than elk. Most of the cattle up here don't have much for horns.

"I admire them for their courage and their cunning, but I will never feel bad about hunting them. I've seen what they can do to livestock."

Isabelle listened as Nate talked but she didn't answer.

Jasper lifted each pelt and looked it over carefully.

"I'll give you $8 each for these."

Sam started to grin, but Nate shook his head.

"Those are prime pelts. We are asking $10 each. If you don't want them for that price, we'll take them down to Ogallala. That's where we're headed when we leave here. John Kirkham—"

"I know Kirkham. All right. $10 each. I'll pay you tomorrow morning." He turned around and stomped out of the barn still muttering about Kirkham under his breath. Isabelle hurried to catch her father. She took his arm as she smiled at him.

Nate looked after them in surprise and Cassidy laughed.

"Jasper and John Kirkham go round and round. Those two are both quite the horse traders, and they've locked horns on several deals." He grinned at the young men in front of him. "They are both my friends, but they don't like each other much." He winked at Nate and added with a chuckle, "You couldn't have dropped a better name to get the price you wanted."

Cassidy turned to walk out of the barn, still laughing. He called over his shoulder, "You boys had better get cleaned up. Tell Cookie to find you something to eat and meet us at the new barn in an hour. You ought to be ready to socialize a little after being gone all winter."

Sam threw his hat up in the air. He started to yell, and Nate punched him. He began to brush out Demonio's mane and tail.

"Don't make so durn much noise. We ain't been paid for those pelts yet." He grinned at his buddy. "$10 a pelt! I knew he wanted them though. If I'd known how much he disliked Kirkham, I'd have asked $15!"

Sam filled the feed pans again and the two visited until Nate finished. They looped their arms over each other's shoulders and did a little dance as they left the barn. Then Sam shoved his pardner as he hollered, "I get first water!" and Nate chased him toward the bunkhouse.

CHAPTER 7

A Dance and a Party

NATE WAITED NEARLY TEN MINUTES FOR SAM TO finish shaving. He looked at his friend curiously.

"I've never seen you take so long to get ready for a dance. You are usually the first one on your horse. Now here I am waiting on you."

Sam grinned at his buddy.

"I've never cared that much, but I need to look good for Miss Isabelle. Shoot, she'll have all the fellers after her. I'll have to figure out some way to make her notice me."

Nate eyed his friend and shook his head as he laughed. *Sam doesn't have to work too hard to be noticed by the girls. They all seemed to like his blond curls and ornery grin. Besides, he's just plumb likeable. He talks easy and makes each gal feel special. I reckon that doesn't hurt any either.*

"Just be yourself. That's enough. If she doesn't like you for you, she's not the gal you think she is. Now let's grab something to eat. I know someone will bring whiskey, and I don't want to drink on an empty stomach."

The dance was going full tilt by the time the two friends arrived. Nate strolled over to the punch table. He found a plate and began to fill it with the food that covered two tables.

"I forgot the women cook for these dances. Just look at all this food. When I'm done, I'll wipe this plate off, and Sam can use it."

As he walked away from the table, he heard a small girl complaining.

"My plate is gone, Mama. I only set it down for a little bit while I got my punch!" As the mother looked around, Nate hurried to the other side of the room.

"I found a loose plate," he whispered to Sam. "I'll wipe it off with my bread and you can use it. But stay away from the lady in the gray dress. It belongs to her little girl, and that mama might take it away from you!"

Sam looked around at Nate in surprise. He nodded as he grinned. Soon both had eaten. Sam left the dirty plate on a table near the woman and sauntered back across the room. The same little girl soon found it and began to wail.

"Someone dirtied my plate, Mama. They left their slobbers all over it! I don't want to use this dirty plate!" The mother tried to quiet her daughter as she glared around the room. Nate and Sam ducked behind some other cowboys and were soon in conversation with them.

Sam's eyes kept straying toward Isabelle. Nate nudged him.

"Just ask her to dance. The worst that can happen is she will tell you no. 'Course, she could yell it at you—or point and laugh." Nate was laughing by the time he finished. Sam glared at him. He fidgeted some more and finally strolled across the room.

Isabelle was just returning to her seat. Sam bowed as he put out his hand.

"May I have the pleasure of this dance, Miss Isabelle?"

Isabelle looked up at him in surprise.

"You know how to two-step?"

"I shore do. Waltz, polka, Texas two-step. I can even do the Mexican Hat Dance if I drink enough first." Sam grinned down at her. "Shall we?"

That dance led to three more and Isabelle finally begged to sit down.

"You dance so fast that you have worn me out. I need to rest a bit."

Sam looked over at the refreshment table. He frowned slightly before he looked back at Isabelle.

"I'd offer to get you something to drink but I don't see any extra cups. I guess we'll just have to talk." He dropped down in the chair next to her as he winked.

Isabelle laughed as she studied his face.

"I guess that means you didn't see a cup you could borrow. Like you did that small girl's plate?"

Sam stared at Isabelle, and his face slowly turned red.

"Now that was all Nate. I only returned it."

Isabelle laughed again. She leaned forward as she smiled.

"Tell me about you and Nate. Where are you from? Have you always been pals?"

Sam leaned back in his chair. He smiled as he watched Nate.

"Nate is the best pard a feller could have. We didn't grow up together though.

"We met when I was about fifteen. He was a little younger. His brother and him followed some cows up from Texas. They bought a place next to my pa's south of Cheyenne in the Wyomin' Territory.

"We hit it off right away 'cause we both like to fish. We've been friends ever since.

"We left Cheyenne about four years ago to help with a cattle drive. Now we're pards and I reckon we always will be."

Isabelle watched Sam as he talked. His eyes were animated, and he used his hands as he spoke. She smiled at him again.

"Do you plan to go home someday?"

Sam thought a moment before he shrugged his shoulders.

"I reckon so. I never did think about settlin' anywhere else. I have lots of family there. Little sisters and brothers as well as girl and boy cousins of all ages. I like it there. It's home so I reckon I'll go back someday." His eyes wandered toward Nate again.

"Nate will for sure. He's sweet on one of my cousins, but he says he won't go back till he has somethin' to offer her." Sam frowned. "He owns half his brother's ranch, but he won't claim it. He says his brother needs to have somethin' for his own kids." Sam's frown became bigger.

"I hadn't really thought on that before but he's right. And I have more younger brothers and sisters than Nate does." His frown changed to a grin. He looked back at Isabelle as he added, "'Course my folks are older, so they started sooner.

"That's enough talk about me. Let's dance again so you can tell me about you and your folks."

CHAPTER 8

SOMETHING TO PONDER ON

IT WAS AFTER MIDNIGHT WHEN THE DANCE FINALLY wound down. Sam wanted to ask Isabelle if he could ride with her back to the ranch, but her pa whisked her away.

He was quiet on the ride home which was certainly unusual. Nate waited for his friend to talk. When they were nearly back to the ranch headquarters, he looked over at Sam with a grin.

"Well?"

"Well, what?"

"Miss Merrill. What about you and Miss Merrill?"

Sam stopped his horse to stare through the darkness at Nate. The moon skipped in and out of the clouds giving just enough light for the two friends to see each other.

"I reckon she is the most wonderful gal I've ever met. I'm a gonna marry her, that's what I'm a gonna do. And if she don't move out here, I'll head back East to find her."

Nate stared at his buddy in surprise. He chuckled softly.

"And you think I'm pie-eyed over Mari? You only just met her!"

Sam shrugged. "I mean it.

"I talked to Beth some about women 'fore we left. Rowdy too. Beth said she knew Rowdy was the man for her the first time she met 'im." Sam's face was serious as he spoke.

"Rowdy just laughed. He told me later he felt the same way. He said Beth was so wonderful that he just lost his words. Besides, he didn't think he had anything to offer her. He was goin' to skip town right after he got to Cheyenne, but Pa's old pard, Slim, rode out to the ranch to get Pa.

"Pa didn't know Rowdy was still alive. He thought he'd died in that War Between the States. 'Course he called Rowdy by his given name of Paul. Pa rode back to Cheyenne with Slim that night and met his younger brother for the first time since he'd left Georgia at age fourteen." The two men rode in silence until they reached the barn. As they pulled their saddles off and began to rub their horses down, Sam spoke again.

"I like Rowdy. I reckon I like him almost as much as I do my own pa. Beth too. Her and Ma are just like sisters." He looked over at Nate and added softly, "If we ever get married, I hope our wives like each other like that. I hope we'll still be pards when we are old like Pa and Rowdy."

Nate was quiet as he brushed Demonio. *I hope so too. I hope we are pards forever.* He finally grinned at his friend.

"I reckon we will be unless you run off to Georgia after that gal. I don't intend to move East."

The two were quiet again as they walked toward the bunkhouse. That conversation made them both ponder a little.

As they pulled off their boots, Nate commented quietly, "Some of the fellers tonight were talking about a rodeo the local ranches are holding tomorrow afternoon. I figured you'd want to enter so I signed us up." His eyes twinkled as he added, "I would have asked you first, but I barely saw you tonight. Miss Isabelle's feet should be mighty tired as much as the two of you danced."

Sam looked up as he grinned.

"What all are we in?"

"I put you in bronc riding and calf roping. I'll head and you can heel in the two-man roping." His grin became bigger as he added, "I almost didn't sign us up for the shooting contest. I was afraid you'd lose track of where you were pointing your pistol if you caught sight of Isabelle. And I don't want to get shot."

Sam blushed and shook his head. "Now I ain't that bad. We can win that shootin' deal and you know it."

"You just focus on riding and roping. All-Around Cowboy gets a free saddle, courtesy of Cassidy and Valentine. If you win those two events and we place high in the other two, you might finally have a shot at that fancy saddle you've always wanted." Nate grinned at his friend before he laid back on his bunk.

"And I'm plumb tuckered out so don't try to talk to me all night."

CHAPTER 9

BECAUSE OF A WOMAN

THE CROWD OF COWBOYS WAS EXCITED AND ROWDY. Most of them knew each other, and the good-natured bantering was loud. Of course, women were a topic of their conversation too.

One cowhand looked around at the group in front of him and commented with a grin, "I think we need to up the ante a little. How about whoever wins the calf ropin' gits to sit with Miss Merrill durin' the picnic?"

The chorus of disagreement was loud, and Sam finally suggested, "How about the best of three events? Whoever scores the highest in at least three events combined gets the pleasure of her company."

The cowboys stared at Sam as they thought. Finally, a large group of them pushed their way out of the cluster of men.

"Guess we'd better sign up for more events. Dang. At a buck each, this rodeo is cuttin' into my beer money," one of the cowboys stated.

"It won't if you win. Winner in each event gets $5. 'Course you'll have to beat Sam in the ropin'…an' the only way that'll happen is if he falls off his horse," another cowboy commented.

Sam was grinning as he walked away. Nate frowned as he joined his friend.

"I'm not so sure that was a good idea. What if Miss Isabelle gets wind of this? She might not like being used as fodder among a bunch of cowboys. I don't know much about women, but I know Merina wouldn't like a deal like that."

Sam stared at Nate. A slow blush climbed up his neck. "Guess I'd better win then," he stated quietly.

The calf roping event had the most entries. Most of the cowboys caught their calves on the first throw, although some had to chase them farther before they roped them.

Finally, it was Sam's turn. He was riding Demonio. Nate and he had agreed in advance that Demonio was the fastest of their horses, and Sam figured he needed a break.

Their strategy worked. Sam won. He roped and tied his calf shortly after it was turned loose, beating the fastest roper.

Nate was sitting on his Appaloosa beside the fence. When he saw Isabelle, he rode toward her. He dropped down to the ground and tipped his hat.

"Howdy, Miss Isabelle. Enjoying the rodeo?"

"Oh, yes. I have never been to one before. Those cowboys certainly do know how to rope and ride."

Nate grinned and nodded. "Yep. 'Course most of those fellows were born into this way of life. And even if they weren't, it's still what they do every day. They get lots of practice."

They both watched as Sam took a long drag from the whiskey bottle he was handed.

Isabelle's voice was sarcastic when she spoke again.

"I think your friend is getting drunk."

Nate watched Sam for a moment before he shook his head.

"Naw. He ain't had enough to get drunk. He's just having fun."

"Is he always so cocky?"

Nate turned to look directly at Isabelle. He was almost irritated by her tone.

"Sam is one of the best cowboys around. He's the best bronc rider I've ever met, and he's one of the best ropers too. I guess if he's proud of that, well then, maybe he does show off a little.

"Notice how those other riders act around him though? He doesn't lord it over them. They are all his friends. See how he is showing that younger cowboy how to hold the rope on the bronc he is going to ride? Sam doesn't hog all the glory. He's always willing to help another feller get better.

"Nope, Sam is a stand-up fellow, and I'm proud to call him my pard."

Isabelle listened quietly but she didn't answer.

After Sam won the bronc riding, Nate cheered. As he clapped, he told Isabelle excitedly, "Sam just might have won himself that saddle. If we do well in the shooting competition, he'll have it!"

Isabelle smiled and clapped with the rest of the spectators.

Sam was in the middle of a bunch of cheering cowboys. He finally stood up on his horse. It was the one he had received as a gift from Windeater, and it pranced nervously as he stood there. He waved his hands and hollered until he had everyone's attention.

"Us riders want to thank all you good folks for comin' out today. We appreciate the prize money all the ranchers here put up. We're plumb tickled as well about the fancy saddle that Red Valentine with the Bell Ranch and Bill Cassidy of the CC are offerin' for All-Around Cowboy." He grinned around at the crowd and spun his horse as he scanned their faces. He didn't see Isabelle, but he saw Jasper. There wasn't a woman beside him though. *Jasper's missus must still be sick.* He grinned and added, "There's one more thing I'm a wonderin' though.

"Most of us cowboys want to have our own ranch someday, and I shore ain't no different. Now I have a question.

"I'm a lookin' for a ranch widow with a bad cough. If there's one here, maybe we could have us a little confab about me helpin' out for a time 'round yore place—maybe marryin' up durin' yore last years." Sam's grin was wide as he scanned the crowd.

A woman in front of him gasped and stepped back. "Why I declare! You are an impudent young man. How dare you make such a suggestion!"

Sam jumped off his horse with a grin and strolled toward the woman. He pulled off his hat and bowed deeply.

"Yore a bit older than I'd hoped, but if yore willin' to talk, I'm all ears."

The cowboys behind him were whooping and slapping their legs with their hats. Some of the older men were openly laughing while others hid their smiles as they rubbed their chins or looked away.

Freda Cassidy laughed out loud, but most of the women were shocked. The woman whom Sam had addressed was appalled. Her face was pale, and she gasped several more times before her husband appeared to take her arm.

Sam stared from the woman to the man beside her. *What is Jasper Merrill doing beside this woman?* When it finally registered that the angry woman was Jasper's wife, Sam stopped grinning. His face turned pale, and he stuttered an apology.

"Mrs. Merrill, I'm sure sorry. I—I didn't mean to insult nobody. I—I was funnin' is all."

Jasper said nothing but Evelyn Merrill was still sputtering when she turned away. She gasped incoherently as he turned her around and led her toward the barn.

Sam looked toward Nate. When he saw Isabelle standing beside his friend, his face became even paler. He slowly walked toward the fence with his hat in his hand.

"Miss Isabelle? I'm sorry. I—I didn't mean to insult your ma. I was only teasin'."

Isabelle stared at Sam for a moment before she stepped away from the fence. She hurried after her mother and father.

CHAPTER 10

A Fine Mess

NATE WATCHED THEM GO BEFORE HE TURNED BACK to Sam. He was trying to contain his grin but it finally leaked out.

"Well, didn't you create a fine mess. And just when you were about to win the right to eat with Miss Isabelle too.

"I don't know that I've seen you step in it so bad in all the time I've known you—and with the woman of your dreams!"

The rest of the cowboys were still laughing, and Sam smacked Nate with his hat. Nate shoved him as he laughed.

"Get your rope, Romeo. It's time for the two-man roping. You sure you don't want me to heel this time? You might be too rattled to catch both back feet at the same time."

Sam glared at his friend as he jerked his hat down on his head.

"I reckon I could rope a buffalo right now if I wanted to." He stomped back to his horse, vaulted into the saddle, and hollered, "Let's get this dog an' pony show rollin'. I have whiskey to drink!"

Sam heeled his calf, but luck played a big part. His open loop landed under the belly of the steer. The animal danced a little before it finally dropped both back feet inside the circle of rope. Sam pulled the rope tight, and they stretched the steer out. Sam wheeled his horse to face

Demonio and time was called. They weren't the fastest, but they did come in third.

"If we get first in the shootin' competition, I can still win that saddle."

"Huh-uh. You're mad, and when you're mad, you get reckless. One of us will get hurt. We are dropping out."

Sam glared at his best friend.

"I'll find someone else who will shoot with me."

Nate jerked Sam around. His eyes were a deep blue as he growled at his friend.

"No, you won't. That competition requires shooting in front of each other at targets on each side while the horses are running. It requires skill *and* a cool head.

"Go ahead and get a drink if you want, but you aren't firing a gun when you're this mad."

When Sam began to cuss, Nate asked softly, "You want to fight me over this? That would be a fine way to end an enjoyable afternoon. If you want to fight though, go ahead. You throw the first punch."

Sam stared at his friend for a moment. He finally shook his head and turned away. He stomped to the other side of the corral and climbed up on the fence. Nate joined him and the two sat side by side as they watched the shooting competition.

When it was over, Sam commented softly, "We could have won that."

Nate shrugged his shoulders. "Probably. But Shorty and Tooley won. They entered every event. Now at least they have most of their entry fees back so they can have a few beers before they go back to work tomorrow."

When the winners were announced, Shorty and Tooley had also won the team roping. Shorty had placed in the bronc riding as well.

Nate added the scores in his head. It looked like there might be a tie for All-Around Cowboy.

The judges were the foremen from the surrounding ranches. They huddled together as they compared notes. When they finished, one addressed the crowd.

"We have a tie for All-Around Cowboy. Sam Rankin with the CC Ranch and Shorty Stout with the Rocking Chair are the top two cowboys." He paused to wait for the cheering to end before he continued.

"We decided to have our top cowboys do a little sorting. The one who can get the ten head we choose sorted out of a herd of cattle the fastest wins. Each of you fellows can pick who you want to run the gate for you. Otherwise, no one else will be in inside the fence."

Nate was already stepping away from the fence when Sam looked over at him. He sauntered toward his pardner and slapped him on the back.

"Now I don't intend to break a gate or get myself killed trying to stop the whole herd. Do this easy." He grinned at Sam before he strode across the corral to position himself behind the heavy gate.

Before long, a group of cowboys drove in fifty head of cattle. The two contestants flipped a coin to see who went first and Shorty won. Nate climbed over the fence and Tooley took his place.

Shorty sorted off the first nine with no trouble. However, the last calf refused to leave the herd. Finally, he brought all the cattle down to the bottom end of the corral. All but two were cut off. The rest raced to the other end.

As he started the two calves toward the gate, Shorty hollered at Tooley, "Hold the back one! Don't let it through!"

Tooley was almost run over by the first calf. He caught the second calf's head as he jerked the gate shut. The calf pulled back and the judges called time. It had taken Shorty just under nine minutes to sort off his ten head.

The penned cattle were released, and fifty more were brought in. The judges showed Sam which cattle he needed to cut out. The timekeeper watched the hands of his pocket watch and hollered, "Go!"

Sam moved his horse slowly toward the cattle. Four head lined up like he wanted, and he cut them out. He added two more and began to push them slowly toward the gate. Just before they reached the gate, Nate hollered, "Push them! The rest are coming!"

Nate pulled the gate open wide and slammed it after the sixth calf raced through. The last four head Sam wanted broke to the edge of the herd and Sam cut them out. He pushed them toward the gate. One broke back but three were turned out. He was down to one calf.

The cattle moved to the far end of the corral and Sam rode his horse slowly toward them. The calf he wanted dodged out of the herd and headed for the fence. Sam followed it. He ran the calf down the fence and pushed it toward the open gate. The calf ran through, kicking the gate hard. Nate dodged to the side as he slammed the wooden gate shut behind the running calf. The judge with the pocket watch hollered, "Time!" and the contest was over.

The crowd began to clap. Some cowboys tried to shake Sam's hand even before the judges announced their final results.

"Sam Rankin of the CC sorted his cattle in seven minutes. That makes him this year's All-Around Cowboy. Congratulations, Sam. Come on up here and get your saddle."

Sam and Nate rode toward the judges. Both men dismounted. Nate held their horses while Sam was presented with his saddle. The corral was soon full of cowboys. They hollered and slapped Sam on the back. When the judges handed Sam an additional $5, he looked at them in surprise.

"Jasper Merrill offered to sponsor the calf sorting if there was a tie. Congratulations, Sam."

Sam stared at the money for a moment. He pushed through the group of cheering cowboys and walked over to where Shorty was joking with his friends.

He put out his hand.

"Shorty, you gave me a run for it. Take this $5 and get your friends some beer."

As Shorty's friends gathered closer and began to talk excitedly, Sam added, "But don't ask me for the saddle. I'm keepin' it. My good nature only goes so far."

Shorty chuckled as he shook Sam's hand.

"I reckon that's the closest I'll ever come to a free saddle. Congratulations, Sam. You earned it."

He waved the $5 bill in the air and hollered at his friends, "The beer's on me, fellers! See you boys at the saloon!" A large group of cowboys was soon mounted and racing toward the only saloon for miles.

Nate looped his arm over Sam's shoulders.

"Well, you didn't win the girl, but you did get your saddle."

"Yet," Sam replied. "I didn't get her *yet*. I ain't givin' up though." He lifted the saddle in one hand and stared at it.

"That is a mighty fine-lookin' saddle though," he commented softly. The two cowboys strolled toward the big barn where the food was being served.

CHAPTER 11

A Talk with the Father

SAM WAS QUIET AS THEY WALKED INTO THE BARN. HE scanned the room and finally found Jasper Merrill. He walked slowly toward him. Mrs. Merrill was nowhere to be seen.

"Mr. Merrill, I want to apologize for upsettin' your wife. I was just havin' fun. I guess I got a little carried away." Sam had his hat in his hands and was twisting it as he talked.

Jasper's eyes glinted for a moment with what almost looked like humor before he nodded.

"Evelyn isn't used to the rough ways of the West. I think it will be a big change for her if we decide to move out here. She isn't for it at all right now, and today didn't help her attitude any." He smiled as he looked up at Sam.

"I hear you won the sorting competition. Congratulations on All-Around Cowboy."

Sam nodded. "I appreciate you sponsorin' that event. I've always wanted to win a fancy saddle, and now I have one."

Jasper smiled and nodded. When he spoke again, his voice was quiet, but it was hard.

"And Sam—don't ever use my daughter again as a trophy to be won in one of your games."

Sam turned a deep red and nodded.

"Yes, sir. I know that was wrong. I just wasn't thinking."

Jasper studied the young cowboy's face. His face was still hard, but he nodded.

"Well then. Let's get something to eat." His eyes glinted and his face relaxed as he waved toward a stack of plates on the table. "You don't even have to borrow one this time."

Jasper's back was to Sam so he couldn't see his face. Still, Sam could hear the humor in the older man's voice, and he grinned.

"I reckon findin' that plate was a lucky thing for Nate and me both. That food was durn good, especially after eatin' our own vittles all winter."

As the two men sat down, Jasper looked at Sam seriously.

"I knew a Rankin in the War for Southern Independence. He was a sharpshooter for the Rebs. Would he be any relation of yours?"

Sam nodded.

"That would be Rowdy. He's my uncle. His given name is Paul, but after that war, everybody called him Rowdy." Sam took a bite and chewed a moment before he continued.

"By the time Rowdy made it up to Cheyenne, I had a little brother by the name of Paul. Rowdy liked his nickname and it stuck."

"So you are the oldest in your family?"

"Yeah. I was born down in Kansas. My first folks were killed by some outlaws. Pa found me and my big sis shortly after that. Sissy was killed in a rockslide on the trip up to Cheyenne. I don't remember much about her or my first folks." Sam frowned slightly before he grinned again. "Molly and Lance Rankin took me in. I always wanted to be a cowboy, so I'm happy they did."

"Are you headed back home now? I know lots of riders hire on with outfits in the spring. I ask because Bill told me both you and Nate are moving on."

"We are headed south to work for John Kirkham for the summer. I'd like to head home after that. We left in the fall of '80 on a cattle drive, so we've been gone almost four years."

The two men ate quietly for a time before Sam asked, "How did you know my Uncle Rowdy? He has never talked much about that war. Some of our hands over the years have mentioned they fought with him. None of them will share any details though."

Jasper was quiet a moment before he answered. When he spoke, his voice was soft.

"Your uncle was a heck of a shot. The Yanks called him "One Shot" because he was deadly with that big gun of his.

"He had a hard job too because the sharpshooters had to shoot fellows from cover. It's not easy to kill a man, especially one you don't know. It's even harder to cut a man down unawares.

"Sergeant Rankin saved a lot of our boys though. He never did get captured that I know of. In fact, he didn't get hit hard until that last battle at Columbus, Georgia." Jasper rubbed his face and shook his head.

"I helped identify dead soldiers after some of those bloody battles. It was necessary but it was difficult.

"Reminders of that war are all over Georgia. Now with the towns growing up around us, I think I'd just like to make a clean start."

Sam was quiet a moment before he responded.

"My pa did that. Old Man McNary—he was the rancher Pa worked for—he talked Pa into going back home. He told Pa if he rebuilt the family plantation in Georgia and sold it that he'd have enough money to buy his own ranch.

"Pa said it took almost a year to get it all fixed up, but it worked out. He sold it for enough to buy Old Man McNary's ranch. That's the ranch we live on now.

"He met Ma on that trip too." Sam's blue eyes sparkled as he added, "Pa said marrying Ma was the best decision he ever made.

"I reckon it was. They sure like each other."

The board and barrel tables were filling quickly. A young mother near them with three small children scanned the tables looking for someplace to sit.

Sam quickly stood.

"Take my chair, ma'am. I'm almost done."

Jasper glanced at Sam's plate. It was nearly full. He smiled as he stood and stepped away from the table.

"Take my place too."

The young woman smiled. She wrangled her children and was finally able to seat all of them.

"Thank you, gentlemen. It is hard to keep track of these little ones, and it's nearly impossible if I can't seat them together."

Sam laughed.

"I have lots of little brothers and sisters, so I know how that is. We have messes at almost every meal too."

The two men moved away from the table, and Jasper put out his hand.

"Sam, it was a pleasure to visit with you. I hope we see more of you if we move down this way."

Sam's face turned a little pale, but he looked Jasper in the eyes.

"I hope so too, Mr. Merrill. In fact, I'd like to call on your daughter if that's all right with you."

Jasper's eyes twinkled as he looked at Sam. He chuckled.

"I don't try to pick my daughter's suitors, Sam. I just run off the ones I don't like. My gun isn't as big as your uncle's, but I can hit what I'm aiming at.

"Best of luck to you."

Sam watched as Jasper wove through the crowd. He had just turned to look for Nate when Isabelle appeared.

"Did you have a nice visit with my father? It looked like the two of you were in deep conversation."

"We sure did. I just asked him all kinds of questions about you—and about your suitors too. He's an obligin' sort of man." Sam grinned down at her as he spoke.

Isabelle cocked an eyebrow but before she could speak, Nate appeared. He tipped his hat to Isabelle before he faced Sam excitedly.

"Hurry up and eat. Some of the fellows are arm wrestling and those Rocking Chair cowboys think they have us CC riders whipped. We are going for the best of four sets, and we need more sober men on our side.

"Some old neighbor of Cassidy's has a still, and a bunch of the riders have been out there sampling his newest batch."

Sam looked from Isabelle to Nate. He was about to shake his head when Isabelle turned away.

"Go on and play with your friends. I have work to do."

Sam stared after her with a frown on his face until Nate grabbed his arm.

"Come on, Sam. We've been arm wrestlin' all winter. Let's see if we can do any good."

CHAPTER 12

A Long Ride and Good Conversation

The two cowboys rode south toward John Kirkham's in silence for a time. Sam finally looked over at Nate and glared.

"Dadgummit, Nate. If you hadn't interrupted me, I might have been able to talk Isabelle into sittin' down with me awhile. Now who knows when I will see her again."

Nate grinned at his friend.

"Shoot. If you had talked to her for too long, you would have just said something to make her mad. Now she can dream about you for a time." He studied his friend before he asked curiously, "What did you and Jasper talk about anyway? I was going to come over sooner, but it looked like the two of you were in some deep conversation."

Sam nodded as he looked over the rolling hills.

"He knew Rowdy in the war. We talked some about that." Sam's face colored slightly as he added, "I told him I'd like to call on Isabelle."

Nate stared at his friend before he laughed.

"When? When are you going to call on her? We are headed south, and she's headed east!"

"I didn't say when. I just said I'd like to. He didn't tell me no either. He said he doesn't pick her suitors—he just shoots the ones he doesn't like."

Nate's laugh became louder, and he snorted.

"You'd better hope her mother doesn't have a say in that. I don't think she likes you too much."

When Sam glared at him, Nate shook a bandana full of coins.

"We have a lot of work to do between now and when you see little Miss Isabelle again. And this money is what we have to show for last night.

"Lucky for us their biggest feller was too drunk to hold his arm up. I think he would have whipped me."

Sam was quiet as Nate talked. He finally looked over at his friend.

"When are we goin' home, Nate? Jasper asked me that last night and it set me to thinkin'. We are goin' to have to work another ten years 'fore we have money enough to buy our ranches—and that's if there's any land left. What are we doin'?"

Nate threw down the stem of grass he had been chewing on.

"I've been thinking on that too. Let's work through roundup for Kirkham and then decide. If Isabelle moves down here, we can go to work for Cassidy again next winter." A grin filled his face as he added, "'Course, you'll want to be closer to Isabelle than that. Shoot, you'll probably try to get hired on by her pa even if you have to be the stableboy." Nate looked over at his friend, and his voice was high and lilting as he spoke.

"Yes, ma'am, Miz Merrill. I'd be glad to slop those hogs an' milk yore cow if it means I cin talk to yore daughter. Wash the dishes too? Why yes. I'd be glad to. That would help me get the pig smell off my hands." Nate was trying not to laugh as he teased his friend.

His grin grew as he added, "And Miss Isabelle might not even come back out here. She probably has a fellow back in Georgia. She might be married off by fall."

Sam glared at his friend.

"You have a mean streak in you, Nate Hawkins. I don't even know why I put up with you.

"All right. It's a deal. We work for Kirkham through the fall. After that, we head north if Merrill moves out here." Sam's voice was soft as he added, "And if they don't, I'm headed east."

He glared at Nate. "And don't you say a word 'cause I know you'd choose Mari over me if you could only have one of us. Well, I'm makin' it easy for you."

Nate stared at Sam for a moment before he shook his head and growled, "Women. They cause trouble even when they aren't around."

The two rode in silence for a time. Before long though, they were discussing what the weather would be like in Georgia and who they would know on Kirkham's spread.

August 1, 1884
John Kirkham's
JK Connected Ranch
Kieth County, Nebraska

CHAPTER 13

An Opportunity

KIRKHAM SAT AT HIS DESK AND DRUMMED HIS fingers against the rough top. He pushed some papers aside as he frowned.

"I heard Merrill signed a contract back in April, but he didn't move down here right away. Word was they were originally going to rent for the summer. Something about letting his missus try living here before he bought. I didn't want to say anything until I knew for sure.

"Cassidy stopped by last week. He said it was a done deal." He looked up as his frown grew deeper.

"I know this means you fellows will be leaving. Can you stay through roundup?"

Nate nodded.

"We'll stay until that's done. After roundup, we'll head north." The three men visited a little more before Nate and Sam turned to leave.

Kirkham watched the two cowboys stride out of his office. His face changed and he hollered after them.

"Nate, come on back here. I've got a question for you."

Nate looked at Sam in surprise. He shrugged and turned back toward Kirkham. He called over his shoulder to Sam, "I'll see you in the bunkhouse."

The old man was smiling as he waved Nate toward a chair. He waited until the cowboy was seated before he spoke.

"I need to take a trip after roundup, Nate. I am invested in the railroad, and I have a meeting with some of the big wigs.

"I'd like you to come with me. If you like what you see, I'd like you to be my front man." He waved his hands toward the door.

"You know and I know if it works out for Sam, he will marry. Merrill has no sons so Sam could be running that ranch in five years.

"And where does that leave you? Stay and work with me. Get a taste of what's available in this country outside of ranching. Help me run the non-cow side of my business and put money in your pockets while you're at it."

Nate stared at John Kirkham in surprise.

"I don't know a thing about the railroad, Mr. Kirkham. All I have ever done—all I've ever wanted to do—is ranch and raise cattle. I like wide-open spaces. I don't want to be squashed down in a city."

"That's not what I'm talking about, Nate.

"The railroad is growing. It is expanding, and soon there will be lines everywhere.

"The rail engineers know the grade of land they need, but they don't understand the weather out here. They often don't know how to relate to the people either. You know both.

"Now, I know the big rail companies pretty much get to put rails wherever they want, but it would be easier for them if they had cooperation from the farmers and ranchers. It would be good too if someone could point out when a location is going to be a problem.

"They want me to be a sort of go-between." Kirkham frowned. "I'm an old man though. I don't want to galivant all over the country." His eyes were intense as he added, "It will pay well too, lots more than cowboying. It would give you that nest egg you want. Three to five years of working with the railroad and you'd have enough to make a start on your own." He put up his hand as Nate started to answer.

"You think on that. Talk it over with Sam but give it some serious thought.

"I'll leave shortly after roundup ends. I need to be on a train headed for Omaha October 6." He smiled at Nate as he put out his hand, "And I'd like to have you on that train with me."

Nate stood and shook Kirkham's hand. He was stunned at the suggestion, but it did sound interesting.

"I'll give it some thought, Mr. Kirkham. Sam and I will talk things over, and I'll let you know in the next day or two."

CHAPTER 14

A New Opportunity

SAM'S FACE SHOWED HIS SURPRISE AS HE STARED AT
Nate. "He wants you to do what?"

Nate grinned at his pardner and shrugged his shoulders. "I think it's because he liked trailing cattle with Gabe.

"It might not be so bad though. Kirkham's a good man. We all liked him when we rode with him.

"He'd like to keep us both around and you know it." Nate's grin became bigger as he added, "He thinks you are going to get married and ditch me anyhow."

Sam frowned as he looked away. When he looked back at Nate, his face was almost sad.

"This ain't how we planned to do things. We were goin' to be pards forever."

Nate looped a long arm around Sam's shoulders.

"That's life, Sam. Who knew you'd fall for a little gal up here instead of picking one back home."

"You know I can't marry a gal around Cheyenne. I'm related to just about every single gal back there," Sam growled.

Nate laughed. When he spoke, his voice was sincere.

"Me leaving don't mean we can't still be pards. Shoot, the train already runs from Cheyenne to Ogallala. We can still get our wives to be friends—if we ever marry!"

Sam finally grinned and banged Nate with his elbow.

"You help me win my gurl and then you can take off." Sam almost pouted as he added, "Sometimes she acts like she likes you better than me anyhow.

"And when you do leave, you'd better check in from time to time. I don't want to wait no ten years to hear from you like you are makin' Mari do."

"I write her letters. I've written her lots of letters. Besides, we have only been gone four years."

"And you only mailed one. It was a short one too, more like a note. You sent it after we finished that first drive and that was only six weeks after we left.

"I think you should mail those letters. Before long, you won't be able to fit any more of them in your saddlebags anyway." When Nate didn't answer, Sam frowned and shook his head.

"At least stop in and see 'er while you're out runnin' around. She could be married off by the time you make it back, and you won't even know it. Shoot, the weddin' could be the day you step off the train."

Nate glared at Sam as he shoved the letters tighter in his saddlebags.

"All right. I'll stop in and see her when I get up that way. I told you before though—I won't go home to stay until I have something to offer her. Now stop bothering me and let's make a plan to get you a job on Merrill's ranch."

CHAPTER 15

A Hard Roundup

ROUNDUP WAS LOTS OF WORK. COWBOYS FROM ALL the neighboring ranches worked together. Cattle were sorted in the open by ranch. The younger animals were branded, and the bull calves were castrated. It was dirty, exhausting work, but it was a social event too. Even though the hours were long, most of the men looked forward to this time of year.

The loss of cattle to the south because of tick fever caused concern among the ranchers and the riders as well. Everyone was on the lookout for cattle that acted weak or had trouble breathing.

In addition, the year before had been dry. The grass had been in short supply and the cattle were in poor condition when cold weather hit. To top it all off, the winter had been brutal. All those forces combined to make the loss of livestock high for nearly every ranch around.

Roundup almost finished when a group of cattle was driven up. The cowboys who drove them were from a ranch farther to the south. They had been late gathering and wanted to complete their own roundup before they headed north.

Sam watched the new cattle closely. When two of them stumbled, he hollered for Nate. They raced their horses toward the small herd.

"Stop them right there. Those cattle have the fever. See how they're tremblin' and breathin' hard?

"Who are you reppin' for? Your boss might want to go ahead and shoot any that are stumblin' around." Sam frowned as he studied the cattle. His voice was quiet as he added, "They all look sick to me."

The cowboys stared at Sam and they shook their heads.

"They ain't ours. The boss told us to bring them up here. They didn't act bad when we left, not like they are now. They belong to Murphy."

Nate rode back to where the men were gathered. He nodded over his shoulder as he spoke to Pog Murphy.

"Those fellers have a group of your cattle and they are sick. Said their boss told them to trail them up here. I'm not sure who their boss is—they just said they were from a ranch down south."

Murphy cursed as he threw down his cup.

"Those are my purebreds. I brought them in last summer. We didn't have the grass up here, so I left them with Cletus down on the Broken Arrow Ranch." He rode toward the small herd of cattle. His voice was bitter as he looked out over the red and white cattle that carried his brand.

"Those cattle are all I have left. The drought last summer burned up my grass. I moved my cattle to winter pasture early and had to keep moving them north when the grass ran out. My herd got caught in that Norther that blew through late. They piled up and I didn't find them until the snow melted."

He pointed at the group of Herefords clustered together with their heads down. "Between what we worked this week and those cattle there, that's all I have left. If those purebreds die, I have nothing."

Sam shook his head as he watched the cattle.

"I don't know what to tell you. Your cattle have tick fever. If you have any that are healthy, separate them from the sick ones. It might be too late but that's what I'd do.

"The winter will help you out some because the ticks can't tolerate real cold weather. That's a while off though, and those cattle are sick.

86

"And you need to burn any place they bedded down. In fact, we're a goin' to follow along and burn a swath of grass behind where they trailed." Sam's voice was soft when he spoke.

The rancher looked at his small herd of cattle. He pulled out his rifle. There were tears in his eyes and his voice caught as he hollered, "Shoot 'em, boys. They are all sick. Maybe the few head north of here we couldn't catch will survive the winter. Let's shoot these and burn them here."

Riders slowly circled the fifty head of mixed cattle. Most of the cows were breathing hard as they swayed on their feet. There were only a few with babies. Those calves were small and weak.

Sam hollered across to the cowboys who were riding toward the cattle, "Stay back as far as you can. Don't get any closer than necessary. We'll burn them all here. Maybe we can stop those ticks before they reach the rest of the cattle."

Murphy lifted his rifle and men began to fire. When it was over, everyone was quiet. Two cowboys turned their horses away. They gagged as they rode. Murphy threw down his rifle. He wiped his eyes as he turned his horse around.

There was just a little wood nearby. Several cowboys dragged a dead tree up from the creek. Several more began to gather dried cow chips while others dismounted to start grass fires. Fires were lit on three sides of the dead cattle. The wind whipped the fire and drove it quickly toward the gory scene. Cowboys began to backfire to keep the fire under control while others pulled blankets off the backs of their saddles to put out any small fires that got away.

The tired men fought to keep the fires under control for nearly three hours. By the time they quit, the dead cattle were smoldering and a long swath of burned grass led toward the southeast as far as the men could see.

Sam wiped his black face and shook his head. "I hate shootin' animals even if it is necessary." His hand was trembling as he pushed back his hat. He cursed quietly and jerked his hat down tightly.

"I'm goin' to tell Kirkham to throw some fence up. Maybe he can keep cattle off this area until he gets some heavy snow."

Nate nodded.

"You can bet the coyotes and wolves will be in here. They'll have a heyday with these carcasses. He'd better fence off more than just a little."

It was dark when the cowboys finally rode up to the camp site. Some didn't even eat. They just climbed into their blankets.

Nate and Sam rode down to small creek where a few cowboys were climbing out of the water. One hollered to them as he dried off.

"She's cold but you might be able to get a little of that black smoke off you." He stared from one man to the other before he asked, "When are you two headed out?"

"First thing tomorrow morning. We are riding back to the ranch tonight." Nate nodded to the north as he grinned.

"Sam thinks he's in love, so I have to help him win his girl." His grin became wider as he added, "I'm the smooth talker, you know."

Sam snorted and one of the cowboys who was drying off chuckled.

"I worked for Bill Cassidy for a time. One summer, he had a fellow he knew from the war out there for a visit. That man and his wife had a pretty little gal for a daughter.

"All us riders tried to get to know her, but her ma had her on a mighty short rope. She made it plenty clear that no cowboy was goin' to court her daughter. She had way bigger plans for her girl than the likes of us.

"I can't remember their names. That's been a couple of years ago. That little gal is probably married by now—probably to some uppity feller back East somewhere."

Sam just grinned and neither man answered. They both rinsed off quickly and were back in the saddle.

"We'll see you fellows around." Sam grinned as he called over his shoulder, "Maybe you can come to my weddin'."

CHAPTER 16

OLD MEMORIES

SAM AND NATE WERE PACKED AND READY TO RIDE OUT of the ranch yard by six in the morning on September 30. Kirkham had paid them out the night before when Nate told him he'd take the job. The old man came outside to see them off. He shook hands with both men.

"Good luck to you, Sam. If things don't work out, you always have a job with me.

"And, Nate, I'll see you at the train station in Ogallala on Monday morning. That is October 6. The eastbound leaves at six sharp. Don't be late."

Both cowboys nodded. They thanked Kirkham before they stopped at the bunkhouse to tell their friends goodbye.

Kirkham's daughter, Ann, came out to stand beside her father as the two cowboys pointed their horses north. She waved when Nate and Sam turned around in their saddles. Kirkham put his arm around his daughter as they walked back toward the house.

"Those two young men are climbing a new hill in their lives while I'm on the downhill side of a big mountain range."

Ann laughed as she hugged him.

"Now, Father. You are only old in body. Your mind is as sharp as it ever was."

The old man nodded as he chuckled.

"Maybe. I'm glad Nate accepted my offer though. I was impressed with his older brother when we trailed my cattle up here. Nate was just a sprout then, but he had the makings of a fine man.

"I never met their old man but one of my friends down in the Indian Territory knew him. In fact, he warned me away from doing business with Gabe when he heard his name was Hawkins." Kirkham frowned and shook his head. "Judging a man by the actions of his father isn't always a good thing.

"I liked Gabe as soon as I met him. Once I rode out to his camp and met his riders, I liked him even more. 'Course you did too when they reached Ogallala. In fact, you liked one of his riders so well that you married him! Old Tab has been a good husband too.

"Yep, I got to know those brothers well on that drive. Their dad may have been a poor example of a father and a man, but he sure had two fine boys." Kirkham's frown returned. "Three actually. Badger told me another little fellow showed up in Cheyenne, and Gabe took him in. Said he was the spitting image of those two older boys.

"Those Hawkins are fine men. I'm glad Nate is going to work with me." Kirkham patted Ann's hand and smiled softly.

"Times like these make me miss your mother though. I'm tired of being alone."

"Father, you aren't alone. You will always have me and the boys. Besides, you have always liked cattle better than most people anyway. You just won't admit it."

"That's true but your mother understood me. She laughed at me when I was grumpy. Oh, I'm sure there were times she wanted to send me down to the bunkhouse, but we always managed to get along.

"We never ran out of things to talk about either. I miss that. I miss her conversation. I even miss her waking me up at night to talk."

Ann kissed his cheek. She started to speak but they were swarmed by three little boys.

"Grampy, can you tell us a story? Tell us a story about one of your adventures. Tell us about Pa and how he was almost bit by a snake."

Kirkham let the children drag him to his big armchair. Ann smiled as her boys piled on top of their grandfather. She slowly backed out of the room. She leaned against the door as she whispered, "I miss you too, Mother. I'm sure you're smiling down about now though. You would have loved being a grandmother—and you would have loved watching Grampy tell stories to those little ones."

CHAPTER 17

NEW OWNERS ON THE ROCKING CHAIR RANCH

When Nate and Sam rode into the Rocking Chair headquarters, they looked around in surprise. The Merrills had made lots of improvements in the short time they'd been there.

Isabelle stopped in front of the house. She held a basket of clean, dry clothes she had just taken down from the clothesline. She stared at the two cowboys in surprise.

"Well, look who finally showed up. For a man who told my father he wanted to court me, you certainly took your time in making an appearance, Sam."

Sam opened his mouth to speak. He stuttered for a moment and growled under his breath as he tried to think of what to say.

Isabelle turned her back and quickly carried the basket into the house. Once inside, she dropped the clothes and rushed to her room. She pulled off her soiled dress and slipped on a clean one, working quickly to smooth her hair. She took a deep breath before she walked calmly back to the kitchen. She peeked out the window to see where the newcomers were.

The two cowboys had dismounted and were talking to some of the hands. Just then, Jasper rode into the yard. Nate and Sam were smiling as they walked toward him.

"Kirkham told us last month you'd bought this place. We finished roundup two days ago and headed on up. Thought we'd check to see if you needed any winter help." Sam's smile was big as he reached for Jasper's hand.

Jasper smiled as he dismounted.

"Come on up to the house. Let's have a glass of lemonade and talk. Evelyn is visiting Freda Cassidy, but she always keeps something to drink in the icehouse." He looked closely at the two young men.

"You boys hungry? Isabelle made fried chicken for dinner, and I think there are a few pieces left."

The three men walked toward the house. Nate and Sam slapped their hats against their legs to knock off some of the dust. They all washed their hands and faces in the horse tank before they stepped into the house. Isabelle was nowhere to be seen.

"Izzy! Come out here and get these boys something to eat. They rode up from Ogallala and they look like they ran short on vittles."

Isabelle appeared with a smile. "Of course. There are potatoes with gravy and a little fried chicken left. Give me just a bit and I will have it warmed."

Nate looked around with appreciation at the house. He could see where a new addition had been built on.

"You didn't waste any time fixing this place up, Jasper. Old Stag kind of let things go around here the last few years. It sure looks good now." Nate chuckled and added, "Stag was in his sixties when he bought this ranch. That's why he called it the Rocking Chair. That was nearly twenty years ago.

"Did Stag move to Valentine? I know it's a new town, but it seems to be growing,"

Isabelle set a plate down in front of each man. Her father's plate held a piece of plum pie. She sat down beside the men with a smile.

Sam stared at his plate almost reverently before he began to eat. He finally looked up and commented quietly, "This is mighty good chicken, Miss Isabelle. I reckon I haven't eaten chicken this tasty since I last had Ma's."

Isabelle smiled and leaned forward.

"Mr. Barrett did move to Valentine. He has a daughter who lives in Ohio though, and she wants him to move there."

When Sam and Nate both looked at her in surprise, she continued, "We were all surprised too. No one even knew Mr. Barrett, or Stag as you call him, was married. Evidentially, his daughter never visited him here and he never left this place.

"He said he was going to try Ohio for one year. He bought a little house in Valentine just in case he wants to come back."

"An old Lakota Indian told us the name Valentine means water or waterfall city. I thought it was named after some politician though." Nate's comment was offhand.

Both Isabelle and her father looked at him in surprise.

Sam nodded. "That Indian's name was Windeater. He's the one who showed us how to snare wolves. He showed us how to tan their hides too." He nodded toward the north.

"Windeater and his people winter north of here. I'm not sure if it is reservation land and they let Stag use it or if Stag lets them winter there. Either way, they all get along." He took another bite before he added, "Windeater's a good man. You should introduce yourself."

Jasper slowly nodded. Nate finished his meal first. He leaned back and rubbed his stomach.

"That was mighty fine eating, Miss Isabelle." His eyes twinkled as he added, "I might have to visit more often."

Isabelle smiled and all three men chuckled.

"How did the hides work out for you, Jasper? Some of your men could maybe work on getting more of those if you think you have a market." Nate's voice was sincere as looked at the older man.

"The hides were top quality and yes, I can market more of them." He frowned at Sam.

"I don't need two more men. I just hired my last man before roundup. I wish I had known you boys were looking for jobs. I assumed since you didn't come by earlier that you were happy where you were."

Sam tried to keep his disappointment off his face. He shrugged.

"I'll probably talk to Cassidy. He said he'd have a winter job for me again if I wanted one." He pointed toward his friend.

"Nate took a job with Kirkham on some railroad business, so I'll have to find me a new pardner though."

Isabelle was watching Sam closely. She finally looked over at her father.

"Perhaps we could use one more hand, Father. Mr. Barrett said the wolves were a problem last winter. Since Sam has experience catching them, he might be handy to have around."

Sam looked at Isabelle in surprise. The pure delight on his face was hard to miss.

Jasper looked from his daughter to Sam. "If Sam is willing," he commented dryly, "although he did say he had a winter job."

Sam grinned at Jasper.

"I'm mighty willing, Mr. Merrill. I'd like a job where I didn't have to stay out in a line shack all winter. I'll probably need a helper though. It ain't a good idea to track wolves alone." He added with a grin and a wink at Isabelle, "Then I could maybe have more of Miss Isabelle's chicken from time to time."

Isabelle blushed and Sam's grin became bigger. Nate laughed out loud, and Jasper shook his head.

"All right. You are hired, Sam—for the winter. Find a cot that's open in the bunkhouse. Nate, you are welcome to stay a while too unless you need to head south right away."

"I appreciate that, Mr. Merrill. I'll spend the night and head out tomorrow. I need to meet Kirkham in Ogallala on Monday morning."

Jasper pushed back his chair.

"Let's go for a ride. You boys can show me around up north—maybe introduce me to your Indian friend if we see him." He paused and looked over at his daughter.

"You want to come along, Izzy? You'd have to ride astride but I can have one of the hands saddle your horse if you want."

Isabelle slowly shook her head.

"Not today, Father. Mother should be home soon, and I will help her with supper." She looked at the two young men before she spoke, "Since Nate is only staying one night, why don't you both join us this evening? I'll have supper ready around six-thirty. It will be dark shortly after that, so you should be back by then."

The three men moved outside, talking as they walked toward the barn.

Isabelle patted her chest as she talked to herself.

"I'm sure I sounded overly eager, but I didn't want Sam to be gone all winter. How are we ever going to get to know each other if we don't get to spend any time together?

"Mother certainly won't be happy about him working here though. And she for sure won't want me to spend any time with him.

"I don't care though. I like Sam. I'm glad he took the wolf-hunting job.

"Too bad Nate is not going to be around. The two of them are like brothers. It will be hard for Sam—and Nate too—when Nate leaves tomorrow."

CHAPTER 18

AN AWKWARD MEAL

NATE AND SAM ENJOYED THEIR RIDE WITH JASPER. THE
man didn't say much but he knew cattle. He was willing to listen
too. Sam liked the looks of the cattle they saw.

Jasper waved his hand to the east as he spoke.

"I did see an Indian encampment before roundup. It was a distance
away and I wasn't sure who they were. I figured I'd have one of the hands
introduce me another time since I don't know what protocol they follow."

Sam nodded his head as he pointed. "Their summer camp is usually
right over there. They probably already moved north. They like to put
their winter camp close to water and where there is some shelter.

"I'll take you up there this week so you can meet Windeater. He's a
good man to have as a friend. His braves won't bother you either although
they will kill a few head of cattle if they run out of meat." He looked over
at Jasper. "Windeater's a proud man. He'll want to trade you something,
probably some wolf hides." Sam grinned and added, "Shoot, in another
year, you'll be such good friends that I'll be out of a job."

Supper was good but the mood was much tenser than it had been
earlier. Evelyn's dislike for Sam was thinly veiled. The young cowboy
tried to be courteous, but it didn't help. Jasper was even quiet. Isabelle

tried to keep the conversation going but the mood at the table was awkward. Once they finished eating, Sam and Nate thanked the women and quickly moved outside.

Nate shook his head as he looked at his pardner.

"This might be a long winter. That woman can't stand you."

Sam said nothing as they walked toward the bunkhouse.

Nate chuckled and bumped his friend.

"Most of the men thought your joke was funny. Too bad you picked Mrs. Merrill to address it to." When Sam growled, Nate laughed.

"The women we know back home around Cheyenne would have laughed at that comment. Why, Martha McCune might have fallen out of her chair. I think Isabelle's ma is just a sour old prune."

"I'm not going to answer you, Nate. That woman might be my mother-in-law someday, and I have to get her to like me. I just don't know how I'm going to do it though."

The men hollered greetings at the two cowboys as they entered the bunkhouse.

"You fellows have a job here this winter? I thought Merrill was done hiring."

Sam grinned as he looked around the room.

"I'm goin' to be Jasper's head wolfer. I do need a helper since Nate took a job with Kirkham. Any of you fellers good at trackin' and can shoot straight too?"

The men were quiet for a moment and then all eyes moved to a quiet man sitting on his bunk. One of the older riders nodded his head in that direction.

"Chancy Logan over there is the best in this outfit."

When Chancy looked up and grinned, Sam sauntered his way.

"Where are you from, Chancy?"

"I been all over but the closest thing to home was Kansas. Tay and me left there when we was thirteen to help trail a herd north. Ain't nothin' back there no more so we just ramble around now. Our last job was on a spread south of Cheyenne."

Sam perked up.

"That's where I'm from! Who'd you ride for?"

"Miguel Montero hired us." He pointed toward a grinning man on a bunk near him. "Tay there is my twin brother."

"We stuck around for a time after Miguel died but we both have itchy feet. We was goin' to head south when we ran into Belt over there in Cheyenne. He said Merrill was hirin' so we all three hired on here. Tay and me ain't sure we'll be around after this winter, but I reckon I can help track wolves if that's what you need." His grin became bigger as he added, "You don't want Tay to hunt no wolves 'cause he talks too much. I'm the quiet one."

Sam nodded. "I remember you now. We left shortly after you came north." He put out his hand.

"Pleased to see you again, Chancy. You too, Tay. I'm Sam Rankin. I want to take the boss up to meet Windeater, so we just as well do that tomorrow." He looked around the room at the men.

"What bunks are open? I'm ready to call it a night."

The men pointed at several bunks in the corner. They looked up at Nate. One rider grinned as he nodded at the cards in front of him.

"How about you? Want to play a little cards? We're all tryin' to win a little beer money."

Nate chuckled.

"I won't play for money, but I'll sit in a few games for fun." Nate pulled out a chair and sat down. The banter at the table was friendly and he enjoyed himself. Finally, after three games, he pushed his chair back.

"I'm going to call it a night. I'm headed south early tomorrow. I don't want to be late for my first day at my new job."

Belt, the rider who had done the most talking, nodded.

"Railroad job, huh? Shoot, you'll make so much money doin' that easy work, you won't never chase cows again."

Nate chuckled and shook his head.

"It's just a job to get me my own ranch. When I get enough money saved, I'm headed back to Cheyenne."

Nate lay back in his bunk and listened to the snoring of the men around him. *Yep, this job is just a means to get what I want, and that is to run cattle. I'll work until I have enough money to buy my own place and then I'm going home.* He drifted off to sleep, but the smile remained on his face as he dreamed about his own ranch.

CHAPTER 19

AN ANGRY MOTHER

EVELYN'S VOICE WAS ANGRY WHEN SHE SPOKE TO HER husband.

"I won't have it. I don't like that young man, and I don't want him working here. And I certainly don't want him spending any time with Isabelle." Evelyn's voice was strident as she argued with her husband.

Jasper's voice was soft as he replied.

"Give him a chance, Ev. He's a fine man and he comes from good stock. I liked him the first time I met him. I liked him even more after we visited last spring.

"I did some checking on his family. His folks are highly respected in their community. I think we are lucky that Izzy is interested in such a hard-working young man."

"You don't see what's coming. She is going to fall head-over-heels in love with that cowboy and marry him right away. She could have ten little babies by the time she's thirty-five."

Jasper smiled at his wife as he took her by the shoulders. "You mean fall in love fast like we did? And we would have had ten little ones if you had been able to get pregnant again after we lost our little boy. Now tell me what is really bothering you."

"I want Isabelle to go to college. I want her to see more of life than a cattle ranch in the middle of this prairie." Tears filled Evelyn's eyes as she whispered, "I'm afraid he will die young and leave her a widow with a small child like I was when you married me. I'm afraid she won't be able to support herself let alone her babies if she doesn't have an education." Evelyn was sobbing by the time she finished. Jasper wrapped her up in his arms.

"Shush now, sweetheart. You know and I know that Izzy will be provided for well if something happens to us. We have planned for that very thing."

Evelyn sniffed several times before she whispered. "That cowboy probably thinks we're wealthy. Maybe he is just after Isabelle's money."

"His father owns a big ranch south of Cheyenne. I don't think that is his motive. However, if you want Izzy to go to college, she will go.

"There is a fine college south of here in a town by the name of Manhattan. That's in the northeast part of Kansas. She can go there for at least two years. If she wants to come back to the ranch after two years, we will let her. Hopefully, by that time, she will see the value of education and will want to complete her degree."

He paused to clear his throat. "Of course, classes will have already started. She will need to leave tomorrow to be there by Monday morning."

Jasper slowly followed his wife as she rushed out of their bedroom. He helped her drag her large trunk into the living room. Their daughter's bedroom was quiet. Jasper tiptoed to the bedroom door and listened. He shook his head as he whispered to himself, "Izzy isn't going to like this at all. We could have a complete meltdown tomorrow morning—and then I have to send the two of them on a long trip together." He paused and held his stomach as he groaned softly. He hurried back across the room. His frown became deeper as he helped his wife open the trunk and push it up against a chair.

"You know I can't ride that far with my stomach problems, Ev, and I don't want to send you alone." Jasper's frown slowly turned to a smile. "Maybe Nate will escort the two of you to Ogallala. He is riding that way tomorrow anyway. He can make sure you get on the right train.

"Yes, that's what we'll do. And don't you be arguing with Izzy on the way down there. You know she is going to be upset about this idea when I tell her in the morning. I want that ride to be pleasant for all three of you."

CHAPTER 20

So Many Tears

ISABELLE HUGGED HER KNEES CLOSELY TO HER CHEST and tried not to cry.

"I don't want to go to college. I won't know a soul there and the girls will probably all be snooty. Mother has been trying to arrange my life for as long as I can remember. I just know she'll try to arrange my marriage to some stuffy man just because his family has a pedigree.

"Well, I don't care about that. I want to marry for love. I want to marry and have a family, and I don't need to go to college to do that. I'd rather spend my time riding with Father and learning to manage this ranch. Mother knows that.

"And why does she hate Sam so?" A sob slipped out of Isabelle's throat.

"I won't go. I'll refuse. I am going to stay right here. I'm not leaving until I'm good and ready.

"And if she tries to force me to go college, I *will* ride south with Nate. He can leave me in Ogallala. I will get a job there. We'll see how bad she wants me to leave then."

Isabelle slipped out of her room. She pulled her heavy coat on over her nightgown and rushed outside.

Nate pulled up his britches for the second time before he walked around the bunkhouse. "I drank too much lemonade tonight," he muttered. He heard someone running and he squinted through the darkness. He stared as Isabelle rushed toward the barn. He could hear her crying as she ran inside. A horse nickered as she slid through the stall door. Nate could hear her talking softly, and her voice was punctuated with sobs.

He scowled as he quietly opened the bunkhouse door. He felt his way through the dark until he found his bunk. He reached over and shook Sam's bunk. There was no response, so he kicked it.

"Wake up. We need to talk," he whispered.

"Now?"

"Right now. Get dressed."

Sam pulled on his pants and socks. He jerked on his hat and carried his shirt and boots to where Nate was waiting.

"Put on your shirt and boots. Then meet me outside."

Nate quietly opened the door and stepped outside. The barn was quiet except for an occasional sob.

Sam was glaring when he finally appeared, and his curls poked out in all directions from under his hat.

"I don't know what is so all-fired important that you not only wake me up, but you make me get dressed too—and in the middle of the dadgum night."

"Your gal just rushed out of the house crying. She's in the barn with her horse. I thought you ought to know.

"And Sam—she's in her nightgown. Keep that in mind if you decide to hug her." Nate pulled the bunkhouse door open and stepped inside.

Sam stood up straight as he stared from the bunkhouse door to the barn. He hurriedly buttoned his shirt and tucked it in while he strode toward the barn. As he slid through the partially open door, he called softly, "Isabelle? It's Sam. I'm comin' in."

There was a gasp from the back stall.

Sam stopped and spoke softly again. "Nate saw you run in here cryin'. I came in to talk to you. If you don't want me to come any closer, I won't."

Isabelle began to cry again, and Sam felt his way toward the sound of her voice. He stopped in the opening of the stall. "Isabelle?" he called softly.

"Mother is sending me away. She hates you and she doesn't want us to spend any time together," Isabelle sobbed.

Sam dropped down on the hay beside her.

"I heard Mother and Father arguing tonight. They rarely fight but Mother's voice was so loud that it woke me.

"She was angry with Father for hiring you. She doesn't want you on this ranch, and she doesn't want us together. She is sending me off to college tomorrow to keep us apart." Isabelle was sobbing and Sam put his arm around her shoulders.

"Well, I'll quit then. I can get a job on another ranch. I'll quit so you don't have to leave."

Isabelle looked up at him. Her hair was loose, and tear tracks showed on her face.

"But I want you to stay. I don't want either of us to leave. It's not right."

"Where does she want to send you?"

"To some college down south of here in Kansas. Manhattan, I think Father said. And I won't know anyone there. I don't want to go."

Sam stared down at Isabelle for a moment. He finally chuckled softly.

"Shoot, Isabelle. All the girls in my family will probably go there to college. In fact, the cousin Nate is sweet on is there now.

"Just look for the name Rankin—if they have that name, they are my cousins. And if they're from Cheyenne, they're friends." His white teeth gleamed as his grin became bigger. "Besides, Nate and his brother own a ranch just south of Manhattan. Gabe's partner, Rusty, runs that ranch. I can always get a ridin' job down there if you get too lonesome.

"'Course, if I stay here, I'll be around all summer when you come home." He squeezed her shoulders and added, "It will be all right. I think you'll like it there."

"You've been there?"

"Sure have. Nate and me stopped there once after we trailed a herd north. It was in the summer so there weren't many young folks around since school was out. It's a nice town though.

"Ma talks of it some. She wants all my sisters to go to college there."

"But, Sam, you won't be able to come and see me. I'll be too far away."

"I'll see you when you come home on holiday. A couple of times in nine months plus all summer. That's not so bad."

"Will you write me?"

Sam squirmed uncomfortably.

"I ain't so good at writin', but I'll for sure read anything you send me."

Isabelle smiled up at him and Sam felt squishy inside.

"Would it be all right if I kissed you, Isabelle? I'd sure like to kiss you right now."

Isabelle smiled at him again and Sam kissed her. He stared at her a moment before he stood.

"I need to leave, and you need to go back to the house. I don't want to be responsible for tarnishin' your reputation.

"We shouldn't be seen together in the middle of the night…and for sure not in the barn with you in your nightgown."

He put out his hand to help Isabelle up. His eyes were dark as he smiled down at her.

"I'd walk you to the house but that wouldn't be right so I'm leavin'. Right now. I'll see you in the mornin'." He stopped and looked over his shoulder as he spoke again.

"Maybe your pa will let Nate ride with you and your ma down to Ogallala. He knows the way. You can catch the train at Ogallala. You might have to go east a ways to catch a train south though.

"Shoot, yore pa will have the route planned out. You don't have a thing to worry about.

"Good night, Izzy."

Isabelle stayed where she was for several minutes. Sam was so quiet that she barely heard him leave. She touched her lips and smiled.

"I guess college won't be so bad after all." She was still smiling when she left the barn.

Jasper stepped back into the shadows as Isabelle hurried toward the house. He had followed her outside just in time to see Sam disappear into the barn. Anger almost overtook him, but he forced himself to stay calm as he slipped inside the barn. He heard Isabelle and Sam's conversation, and a flood of emotions poured through him.

"Sam's a stand-up fellow. I knew I liked that cowboy." He walked slowly back to the house and the shadow of a smile flickered across his face. He stared out the kitchen window for a moment before he turned toward the bedroom.

"Our little girl is in love, and she picked a man I approve of. I guess I won't have to use my gun after all."

CHAPTER 21

AN ORNERY PARD

JASPER BANGED ON THE DOOR OF THE BUNKHOUSE at five the next morning. Both Sam and Nate were gone, and he looked around in confusion.

Any riders who weren't up already dived out of their bunks at the sound of their boss' voice. Tired men were milling everywhere.

"Where are those two cowboys who rode in last night?"

One rider pointed toward the barn.

"They were up an hour ago. I think they're in the barn."

Jasper strode to the barn. He pushed the door open and stopped in surprise.

Nate's horses were saddled, and a pack was on the appaloosa. Sam was polishing the buggy as the two of them talked. They looked up in surprise as Jasper pushed through the door. He stared from one to the other before his eyes drilled into Nate.

"Nate, I'd like you to escort my wife and daughter down to Ogallala. I know it will take three full days to get there by buggy. I've given Evelyn the names of two ranches where you can spend the first two nights. I'd like you to arrange a room for them in the Spofford House when you arrive in Ogallala the third night." Jasper's face was serious as he added, "I'll pay you. I know this will slow you down."

"I will be glad to do it, Mr. Merrill, but I won't accept pay. I'm going that way anyhow. Will there be much baggage? I just need to know if we will need a buggy or a surrey."

Jasper looked from one cowboy to the other. Neither man gave any indication he knew why Jasper's family needed a ride. His eyes settled on Sam, and he spoke dryly.

"No need to act all innocent, Sam. I saw my daughter go into the barn last night…and I saw you follow her."

Sam turned red. He started to speak but Jasper put up his hand.

"I heard your conversation. If your intentions hadn't been honorable, I'd have shot you last night." Humor glinted in his eyes for a moment before he added, "Now hitch up that buggy you've been polishing and pull it up by the house. Izzy only has one trunk plus her saddle.

"And make it quick. I'm guessing Nate wants to be gone in an hour." He wheeled around when he finished speaking and hurried toward the house.

Sam stared after him. He looked bleakly at Nate.

"Isabelle's ma is goin' to hate me now for sure."

Nate pulled the girth strap tight on Demonio's saddle. He shook his head before he answered.

"I'm guessing the missus doesn't know. If she did, she'd have been down here with a shotgun last night.

"You might have scored some points with Isabelle's old man though."

Nate's face creased in a grin as he added, "Too bad you can't drive them down yourself. You could spend three days on a rough, dirty ride just to try and convince her ma that you are the right man for her daughter."

Sam threw the harness he had in his hands at Nate. His friend caught it as he laughed.

"Lucky for you I already have a little gal in mind. Otherwise, I might have to fight you for this one—and a three-day buggy ride would give me a lot of time to work on her!"

Sam stared at Nate. He cursed low and long at his friend.

"You have a mean streak, Nate Hawkins, and I've seen it twice now in just a few weeks. Mean is what you are. I can't believe my own pardner would say such a thing.

"Fine. You take advantage of these three days, but it had better be to soften her ma up. There had better not be any sweet talk takin' place between you and my gal.

"Now let's get these horses hitched so's I have a little more time to say goodbye."

Sam growled and grumbled as he harnessed the team. He glared at Nate several more times as he muttered about friendship and loyalty.

Nate finally laughed. "I was only funnin' you, Sam. I'll do the best I can to make Isabelle's ma like you. Now quit growling and put a smile on your face. I think Isabelle would like to see a happy man before she leaves."

The two men led the horses and team up to the house. Nate fiddled with the team's harness instead of helping load. He figured Sam needed to be the one who was "handy."

While Jasper was strapping down the luggage, Nate led Appy to the back of the buggy. He made sure to get in Jasper's way as he tied his horse, so Sam had time to help both women into the buggy.

"You ladies have a safe trip now," Sam drawled, "and I'll shore look forward to seein' you when you get back." He placed his hands around Isabelle's waist and lifted her into the buggy as he winked at her. Her mother was already seated, and Sam tipped his hat.

"Miz Merrill, Nate there is quite the talker so don't feel bad if you need to tell him to shut his mouth so's the two of you can have some peace." He grinned at Nate. He winked again at Isabelle when her mother turned her head to stare at Nate.

Jasper was quiet as he worked. He squeezed Evelyn's leg and patted Isabelle's before he spoke.

"I'll have a man waiting for you when you get back to Ogallala, Ev. He will be there on Wednesday morning so you can take a little time to enroll Izzy and familiarize yourself with Manhattan. You'll stay Sunday and Monday nights in Manhattan.

"You will leave for Ogallala Tuesday morning, and I'll make sure Herman is down there Wednesday morning to pick you up at the Spofford."

Jasper stepped back and waved as Nate wheeled the buggy around. Both women waved in return, but Jasper noticed that Isabelle's waving was mostly directed toward Sam. He was almost irritated.

Sam waved back and grinned. When Jasper glared at him, his face lost its smile. He turned toward the barn as he called back to Jasper, "I can be ready for work in no time, boss. I can help you and the boys, or we can ride up to Windeater's camp if you want."

He strode toward the barn and was out quickly with his saddled horse. He joined the other riders and waited for his orders.

CHAPTER 22

TO WIN OVER A MOTHER

NATE WAS QUIET FOR THE FIRST HALF MILE. HE FINALLY looked sideways at the two women.

"Ladies, we can ride quiet or we can talk, whichever you'd like to do.

"Sam and I have been up and down and all over this country. I can answer 'most any questions you might have."

Mrs. Merrill looked over at Nate and frowned slightly. She finally cleared her throat and asked, "How long have you known Sam? Did you grow up together?"

"We met in '79 when my older brother settled south of Cheyenne. We've been friends ever since."

Evelyn looked at Nate in surprise.

"You weren't born in Wyoming?"

"Naw. I was born down in Texas. My ma died when I was young, and my brother mostly raised me. His name's Gabe, and his ranch is about five miles from where the Rankins live.

"Sam grew up on the ranch his folks own south of Cheyenne." Nate smiled as he tapped the horses' backs with the lines. "He was the first friend I ever had my own age.

"I worked to support Ma and me before she died, so I never got to know many kids. After Ma passed, I followed Gabe around. I worked where he worked.

"He only took riding jobs on ranches where they'd take a kid. 'Course he was a top hand, so he didn't have much trouble finding work.

"He was trail boss on quite a few drives too. That's actually how we ended up in Wyoming."

"He—Sam, I mean—seems kind of wild." Evelyn's back was stiff as she spoke.

Nate frowned and shifted in his seat. He pushed down the irritation that was creeping up his neck. He looked over at Evelyn and spoke sincerely.

"Wild? Maybe a little. Most of us have a wild streak in us. Shoot. It's a rough country and folks have to be tough to survive. Sam is one of the finest men I have ever met though.

"I read one time that the West was settled by tough people because the weak ones died or turned back.

"It's not so easy to make a living in unsettled areas, and this part of the country was raw and untamed when the first White folks came. 'Course, things have calmed down some, but parts of it are still wild." Nate waved his buggy whip around the area they were riding through.

"This is beautiful country, but she can be hard. You'll see that. Winters in the Sandhills can be mighty mean.

"The people are what make this country great though. I think folks are kind of like cream. The weak ones stay on the bottom and the strong ones rise to the top.

"Sam's folks are like that. His pa is hard as nails, but he's a gentleman through and through. Some of our Indian friends call him 'Angry Eyes.' His eyes can drill right through you, and it's not a good feeling when he's glaring at you.

"I like him though. I like Sam's Uncle Rowdy, too.

"Rowdy and Beth live west of Sam about five miles." The two women were listening closely, and Nate paused to grin at them.

"Paul is Rowdy's given name. He lost his memory for a time after the War Between the States. He raised so much Cain during that time that he got the nickname of Rowdy.

"Rowdy's mighty tough but he's a fine man. His wife is real nice too. Ol' Rowdy just melts when she's around.

"Sam's ma is nice too. She grew up in Georgia on a big plantation. I've seen pictures of her when she was young. She was real pretty." Nate blushed as he added, "Folks say she still is, but it seems funny to say your best pard's ma is pretty.

"She's tough though. Her name is Molly. She's the one who made friends with the Indians in our area when she moved there in '68. I'm not sure if Broken Knife was their chief or just a head warrior, but he caused a lot of trouble before that.

"She married Lance somewhere back East, and they headed for Cheyenne. She helped Broken Knife's sister on that trip. They all became friends after that. In fact, Sam says Broken Knife is the reason his little brother, Paul, is alive.

"Molly had some trouble birthing him. Broken Knife brought an old woman out to help. She calmed Molly down and got things straightened out. Sam said that old squaw has helped Molly birth every baby since then.

"Her name is Nomi. I've never met her, but Sam said she's really old. Broken Knife brings her over to their place and drops her off when the Rankins put up the bear paw flag Broken Knife made for them. He picks her up when everything's done." Nate frowned slightly and shook his head.

"Sam said Broken Knife just seems to know when it is about time for the baby to come. Once that flag goes up, it doesn't take him long to get old Nomi over there."

"How much older is Sam than the other children?" Evelyn was watching Nate closely as she asked her questions.

"Sam's the oldest. He's adopted but you'd never know it. He looks like his ma to me. He's twenty. I think he's about three years older than Paul. Abbie is next. She's twelve, Henry is eleven, and Livvy is nine.

"Livvy is the same age as Merina's little sister, Emilia. Rollie, my little brother, is a year older so he's ten. Little Grace was the baby of our family. She was born right before I left home. She's four.

"Merina and Gabe had another little girl after I left home. Her name is Elena and she's two. I hope they have more kids. I like babies."

Isabelle leaned forward to ask, "How about Rowdy and Beth? Do they have children?"

"Yeah, they have six. Rudy is twenty-three and Mari is seventeen. Rowdy and Beth took them in when their folks died in an accident. I'm not sure how old they were but they were small.

"Sam told me the accident happened the day after Rowdy's wedding. Beth said they started their marriage with a ready-made family, but she never regretted it. She's a great mom.

"Rudy remembers his folks 'cause he was older—eight or nine I think, but Mari doesn't remember much about them.

"Ellie and Eli are twins. They are fourteen. Pauline is eight, and Emmalene is six."

Isabelle studied Nate's face a moment before she asked softly, "Is Mari the one who is at the college in Kansas where I'm going? Sam said he had a cousin who attended school there."

A slow blush creeped up Nate's neck, but he answered calmly, "Yeah, that's Mari. She wants to be a teacher. I reckon she'll be a good one too." He paused before he added quietly, "Mari makes the best bread I've ever eaten.

"In fact, all the women in our area are good cooks. That was one of my favorite things when we first settled there. 'Course, Gabe married

Merina shortly after we bought our ranch, and she's a good cook too. Now we have good food and lots of it all the time."

Nate was quiet as he stared to the west. "I mean, I did when I lived at home. I can make biscuits and beans, but my fixings aren't much compared to those ladies."

Isabelle studied Nate's profile before she asked, "Do you want to go back to Wyoming and settle down someday?"

Nate nodded slowly.

"That's always been my plan, and I don't reckon I'll change my mind. I'm saving my money. I hope to have enough to buy my own ranch in five years—or at least be able to put down some money on land of my own."

Evelyn's eyes pierced into Nate as she asked, "How about Sam? What are his plans?"

"Same as mine. We both want a place of our own. Our families both have little ones. One ranch can only support so many families. Sam and I figure we'll have to make our own way since we're both the oldest."

Evelyn's voice was sarcastic as she asked, "Doesn't Sam intend to marry a girl with a big ranch? After all, that would give him all you say he wants."

Isabelle's face turned pale and she gasped. "Mother!"

Nate jerked on the lines and the horses came to a stop. He turned in his seat to stare at Evelyn, and she felt the full force of his angry glare. His blue eyes were dark and cold when he spoke.

"Sam's not like that. He'd marry a gal who had nothing and be completely happy if he loved her. And he'd work hard to give her the best life he could.

"I know lots of moms who would be pleased to have Sam as a son-in-law. I don't have any sisters, and none of my nieces are old enough to court. If I did though, I'd be proud to have Sam marry one of them." Nate faced forward. His face was hard, and his voice was tight as he clucked at the horses.

"You have Sam all wrong, Mrs. Merrill. He's a fine man. He just likes to joke around. You took his teasing too seriously, and now you have judged him as unworthy.

"Your husband is lucky to have him as a rider. He's a top hand, a hard worker, and he rides for the brand."

Nate quit talking. He was angry and the stiffness of his shoulders told the two women riding with him just how he felt. Evelyn settled back against the seat and was quiet.

Isabelle fidgeted for a time. She finally asked, "So who is the better cowboy, you or Sam?"

Nate glanced over at Isabelle quickly. When he saw she was smiling, he chuckled.

"Sam's for sure a better rider than me. He can stick like a burr on anything with hair." His eyes crinkled as he added, "He's usually a better roper too—unless he gets distracted or mad."

Isabelle laughed. "And what can you do better than him?"

Nate's grin turned to a laugh.

"Shoot straighter. Sam talks with his hands, so I have to make him shut up when he shoots. Otherwise, he bobs his rifle around."

Isabelle laughed. "He is quite animated when he speaks."

Evelyn didn't talk any more, but Isabelle and Nate visited for several more hours.

Both women were stiff when they stopped for the night. Neither was looking forward to two more days in the buggy.

Nate wasn't either although he could understand why Sam had fallen so hard for Isabelle. He had enjoyed visiting with her.

Isabelle's a mighty nice little gal. Too bad her mother is so cantankerous. Makes me feel lucky that Beth is Mari's ma.

CHAPTER 23

A Fine Morning for a Ride

THE THIRD MORNING, ISABELLE APPEARED IN A RIDING skirt. "Mother said I could ride for a while this morning.

"Which horse do you want me to use? I can ride astride since Father sent my saddle along."

Nate stared at Isabelle for a moment and then frowned.

"You will have to ride Appy, but Demon is bad influence. He'll lead Appy off to who knows where, and you won't be able to stop him." As Isabelle stared at him, Nate added, "And nobody can ride Demon but me. He won't tolerate other people." He paused as he looked over at Evelyn.

"Go ahead and ride with Isabelle, Nate. I can drive the buggy for a time. Just don't get too far away." Evelyn's voice was firm as she spoke.

Nate frowned and shook his head.

"I don't think so. Jasper did tell me to drive the buggy and—"

"And I'm telling you I can drive it for a time. I'll wave at you when I get tired. Now go. I doubt you have ever spent this many hours in a buggy, and I'm guessing you are ready for a break."

Nate blushed and grinned as he nodded. "You are right about that. I was thinking of sitting on a blanket. In fact, I can still dig one out if you want to sit on one."

Nate saddled both horses quickly. He lifted Isabelle into the saddle and made sure Evelyn was comfortable before he mounted.

Demonio was spinning in circles as Nate held him down. He looked over at Isabelle.

"How well can you ride? Old Demon is ready to run."

Isabelle laughed and spurred Appy. The surprised horse leaped to a run.

Nate held Demonio back as he pointed at the trail in front of them.

"Just hold to that trail, Mrs. Merrill. We'll run some of the sass out of these horses and then we'll be back."

He leaned over Demonio and the horse took off. They soon caught Appy and the two horses ran side by side for a time before Nate slowed Demonio down.

Isabelle's eyes were sparkling, and she was laughing.

"Thank you for letting me ride. I was getting so bored in that buggy. Let's ride to the top of that big hill. I'd like to see what this area looks like from a higher point."

As they rode up the large hill, Isabelle looked sideways at Nate.

"Mother said she likes you, and she doesn't like any of the young men who want to come by to see me."

"I'm not that much different than most of the fellows out here. She'll see that. She'd like Sam too if she'd give him a chance."

They crested the knob and looked down on the rolling hills around them. The grass was turning brown and there were few trees. They could see for miles.

Some men below them had a group of cattle gathered in a small area. Two cowboys were branding a calf that was on the ground.

Nate cursed under his breath and whispered loudly, "Get off the top of this hill, Isabelle. Now!"

Nate wheeled Demonio around and raced him back toward the buggy. Isabelle followed without speaking. Her eyes were wide, and she stared as Nate strapped on his six-shooter.

"Pull up, Evelyn. I need to get my rifle out of the buggy." Nate looked hard at both women.

"Can you ladies shoot? If so, I may need some help."

When they both nodded, Nate jumped into the buggy beside Evelyn and whipped the horses to a run.

Evelyn's face was pale as she stared at him.

"Did you see something we should be worried about?"

Nate nodded grimly.

"Isabelle and I saw some riders branding a group of calves. They were using a cinch ring. That means they were most likely altering brands. If they saw us, we're in trouble.

"Once we get a little more distance between us, I'm going to slow down and ride like we are out for a picnic. Evelyn, I want you to keep this shotgun in the folds of your skirt." Nate handed her a double-barreled shotgun.

"Keep in mind that buckshot spreads, so don't shoot over the horses. Wait until someone is right beside you."

Appy was running beside the buggy and Nate stood. He shoved a rifle into the boot of Isabelle's saddle and passed her a small gun.

"Put that in your pocket.

"I might be worrying for nothing, but we are going to be ready."

CHAPTER 24

TROUBLE ALL AROUND

THE TRAIL DROPPED DOWN BETWEEN SOME HILLS AND
Nate slowed the buggy. He veered off the trail and took a path that
was less used.

He looked behind him for a time and then hissed at Isabelle.

"Put Appy on the other side of the buggy. I want Demon beside
me. And stay by the wagon. Don't take off running unless I tell you."

It wasn't long before four men appeared behind them. They rode up
on both sides of the buggy as they studied the three people.

"What ya runnin' yore hosses for? I seen from yore tracks that they
was a runnin' full out."

Nate's eyes were careful, but he laughed.

"They got away from my ma here. Sis an' me had to run 'er down."

"Where ya headed?"

"Down to Ogallala. Ma is meetin' some a her chatty friends this
evenin'. This is a pretty area, so we thought we'd see a little country 'fore
she flattens out an' gits browner."

The men studied Nate. They couldn't decide if he was telling the truth.

"Who are the women?"

"My ma, Mrs. Merrill, an' my sis, Isabelle."

"I think yore lyin'. Ol' Jasper don't have no son. I heard him an' his Missus only had one kid an' that was a daughter."

Nate grinned at them.

"Well, I've been away fer a time. 'Sides, when a man ain't so proud of his son, he don't go tellin' folks 'bout him…an' I ain't always been a son a man would be proud of." He bumped Evelyn and grinned at her. "'Course my ma likes me."

Evelyn said nothing as she stared from Nate to the men surrounding their buggy.

"Mebbie we'll ride along with ya fer a time. Keep ya company." The man who spoke leered at Isabelle as he edged his horse closer.

Nate dropped the lines. His rifle was in his hands, and it was pointed at the man in front of him.

"Fellers, I'm wanted by the law back East an' if they catch me, I'll hang. That means I don't much care how many of ya I shoot, an' I'm a losin' patience.

"Ya fellers drop yore guns, ever' one of 'em. Make it quick too.

"Ma, ya grab those lines an' wrap 'em 'round that brake beside ya. Then ya pull out that shotgun ya have in yore skirt. Ya shoot that man beside ya if he so much as flinches.

"Only use one barrel though—we might need the second one.

"Sis, ya pick up those guns an' toss 'em in the back a this buggy."

As the men stared at Nate in shock, he motioned with his rifle.

"Get down from those horses. Pull off yore boots. Socks too."

One man cursed Nate as he dropped to the ground.

"I ain't takin' off my boots. Ya shoot those guns and the rest of our outfit will be right here. Ya done bit off more than ya can chew, boy."

Nate gave the man a cold smile. He lifted a large knife from under the blanket on the wagon seat.

"This won't make any noise now, will it? Ya want to take a chance on how fast I cin throw this knife, or do ya want to take off those boots an' mebbie live another day?"

Nate's voice was soft as he pointed toward Demonio.

"Ya see that big, black horse? He belonged to Miguel Montero. Now Miguel an' me rode together fer a time, an' that horse claimed me after Miguel died. All I have to do is give the word an' he'll tear into ya fellers like the pack of coyotes ya are." Nate pretended to snap his fingers.

"Now pull off those boots."

Isabelle was on the ground beside the buggy and Nate motioned to her.

"Ya boys step back, an' Sis 'ill pick up yore boots. One wrong move an' things 'ill go south mighty fast."

Once the boots were in the wagon, Nate stepped down. He tied the four horses together and tied the first one to the back of the buggy.

"I'll leave yore hosses in Ogallala at the sheriff's office. If he ain't in town, I'll give 'em to those soldier boys who hang 'round there.

"An' I'll be sure to mention that I saw ya usin' a cinch ring on some cattle on the north end a John Kirkham's range.

"In fact, we jist might stop in an' make it a point to tell ol' John his own self. I'm a guessin' he'd be mighty pleased to have a necktie party fer a bunch a cattle rustlers."

Nate's eyes were cold and the smile he gave them was dangerous.

"Ya fellers think long an' hard 'bout yore future now 'cause if I spot *anyone* ridin' up behind me, I'm a goin' to start shootin'." He patted his rifle and added softly, "An' I don't often miss."

Nate lifted Isabelle into the wagon and mounted Demonio.

He stared at each man before he spoke.

"I know what each of ya looks like an' I'd better not ever see ya in this country again." A hard smiled filled his face as he added, "Unless yore hangin' from a tree."

Evelyn's face was white when Nate pointed toward the team.

"Wheel that team around, Ma, an' point 'em south."

CHAPTER 25

A FAST RIDE

ALL THREE PEOPLE WERE QUIET AS THEY LEFT THE outlaws behind. When they were nearly a half mile away, Nate let out a deep breath.

He grinned at the two women.

"Ma—Sis—you both did a fine job!"

Isabelle laughed and even Evelyn smiled a little. Her voice showed her worry when she spoke.

"Do you think they will come after us?" she asked nervously.

"Not those four but the rest could.

"We are on Kirkham's land now though, and I know this ranch like the back of my hand. His headquarters aren't too far from here. We might even run into some of his riders before long. Regardless, the farther we get inside his range, the safer we'll be."

Evelyn was quiet a moment. She finally looked up at Nate.

"Thank you, Nate. You handled that situation well."

"You ladies did too." He grinned at the older woman and added, "I guess you ain't the prissy tinhorn I thought you were."

Evelyn stared at Nate a moment. She sputtered several times before she finally laughed.

"Men out here are so blunt. You just say whatever is on your mind."

"I reckon so, ma'am. Mostly, we just don't have time to play word games. Decisions are made fast because folks have to rely on themselves."

Nate rode Demonio close to the buggy and climbed in. He took the lines from Evelyn. He pointed around them as he spoke.

"You ladies need to tell me when you want to take a break because we are going to move as fast as we can.

"We'll get a couple of horses from Kirkham since your team will be played out by the time we get there, but we aren't going to stop there long."

Isabelle listened intently. Her voice was quiet when she asked, "How did you know what to say? And who is Miguel Montero? Was that part of your story true?"

Nate looked over the hills before he answered. He smiled as he spoke quietly.

"Miguel was my brother-in-law. He died four years ago down in Kansas. He floated back and forth between good and bad, but mostly, he was a good man.

"He was deadly though, and his reputation followed him farther north than I knew. Sam and I ran into some fellows up here not long ago who knew him. That's why I took a chance on mentioning him to those outlaws." Nate pointed at his horse.

"Demonio was his horse.

"Old Demon and me are one now. I'm guessing he probably would kill someone to save me." He grinned at the two women.

"He won't let anyone on him if I'm not around, and to be honest, I don't really trust him around most folks."

Isabelle's eyes were large as she listened.

"He let Sam ride him."

"That's 'cause I was there at the rodeo. He'll let Sam catch him though. He can saddle him too. He just can't get on unless Demon can see me."

They pushed hard through the morning and into the afternoon, not even stopping to eat. Nate watched the trail behind them, but no horses appeared. They finally saw buildings just before five.

"Kirkham's ranch headquarters are in front of us. We'll let you rest up a bit while we change horses. We have to keep moving right along to get into Ogallala tonight though. We've gone some out of our way to stop here.

"Kirkham might send some men with us, and that would be just fine with me."

BAD NEWS

ISABELLE POINTED DOWN AT THE RAIL TRACKS AS THEY crossed them. "Why didn't we catch the train? Wouldn't it have been faster?"

"The tracks are torn up just outside of Ogallala, so no train north will run until they're fixed."

Nate pulled the team to a stop in front of the barn and jumped down. He helped the women out of the buggy and asked the cowboys walking toward him, "Kirkham around? We need to swap horses. These are played out.

"And if Ann's around, these women could use some refreshments. We've been on the trail for the better part of three days, and today was a long one."

Everyone turned around as John Kirkham hurried out of the house.

"Nate! Is there a problem? I figured you'd be in Ogallala by now. I was just getting ready to leave myself."

Nate pointed from the women to Kirkham.

"John, this is Evelyn and Isabelle Merrill, Jasper's family.

"He asked me to take these ladies down to Ogallala to catch the train. We ran across some rustlers just below Knob Hill. They were going to give us trouble, but they changed their minds.

"We left four of them on foot." Nate grinned as he added, "Their boots are in the back of the buggy if any of your riders want them." He nodded toward the horses. "Those are their horses too.

"No one followed us, but I saw eight men total. There could have been more because we didn't stay long to study the situation." Nate was unhitching the horses as he spoke.

"We could use a fresh team if you have a couple of horses you can spare. I pushed these two hard all day."

Kirkham gave quick orders, and two large bays were soon hitched to the buggy. A cowboy pulled the boots out of the back of the buggy and several hands were soon trying them on. Another cowboy untied the four horses. He looked over at his boss.

"What do you want me to do with these?"

"Put them in the barn. Give them a little grain and hay. They look like they could use a good rubdown so do that before you turn them out in the corral.

"I'll file a report with the sheriff when I get to Ogallala."

Ann appeared and Kirkham waved to her.

"Take Mrs. Merrill and Isabelle into the house. Get them something to eat and let them freshen up a little. Make it quick though. Nate wants to leave as soon as they are ready."

He pointed toward one of the cowboys who was hanging around the buggy.

"Bandy! Find Milt. Tell him to take some of the boys and find those rustlers. Try to bring them in alive. Shoot them if you have to, but don't hang anybody. I'll send the sheriff up when I get to town in case you have any prisoners." He turned around and faced Nate.

"How about I ride down with you? I'll take a couple of my hands along. They can bring Merrill's buggy back here.

"I'll send a rider up to let Jasper know his family is all right and that we have his team." He frowned and shook his head.

"Durn rustlers. They moved in last year and we haven't been able to catch them. They take little bunches, alter the brands, and move them out of the country." He chuckled as he stared toward the northeast.

"They might be a little easier to identify now since four of them will be missing their boots *and* their horses!"

He pointed at two of his riders.

"Biggs, you get Yankton. You two can ride down to Ogallala with us. And make it quick. We want to leave here in about twenty minutes. Tell Cookie to fix you a bait of food.

"Come on up to the house, Nate. Ann made supper. Let's eat a bite before we take off. I'll even drive the buggy so your backside can take a break."

CHAPTER 27

AN ORNERY OLD MAN

THE LITTLE GROUP WAS SOON BACK ON THE TRAIL. Nate and the other two cowboys were quiet, but Kirkham had lots to say. It wasn't long before he looked over at Isabelle and winked.

"So, you're the little gal Sam was in such a hurry to ride north and see? I guess he trusted Nate enough to let him spend three days on the trail with you. In fact, I'm guessing it was Nate's job to tell you what a good guy ol' Sam is!"

Isabelle blushed and Nate laughed. Evelyn frowned. She started to speak several times before she addressed Kirkham.

"My husband asked Nate to take us to Ogallala since he was already going there. Sam had nothing to do with this trip."

"Oh, Sam had everything to do with this trip. He's the reason Nate rode north in the first place.

"See, Nate's the voice of reason when it comes to those two. Sam is the dynamite and Nate is the fuse. They work together like a couple of old spinster sisters. And you can bet it was Nate's job to make Sam look good."

Evelyn's face grew pale as she looked from Nate to Kirkham. Nate blushed but said nothing.

Kirkham laughed as he studied Evelyn's face. He looked around at the three men riding beside the buggy.

"Why don't you fellows spread out a little. Maybe one of you can watch our back trail and the other two can ride ahead of us."

Nate studied the older man. He frowned slightly but dropped back.

"I'll scout our back trail if you fellows want to take the front."

Once they were gone, Kirkham looked over at Evelyn seriously.

"Let me tell you a little bit about Sam. Nate too, but since you are dead set against Sam, I want you to know what I've seen.

"I met Sam several years ago when he was a sprout—probably sixteen or so. He was already a top hand, and I would have hired him then. He needed to spread his wings a little before he settled down though. He was anxious to see some new country. He's grown up some since then, but he was always a good kid.

"He and Nate came riding up to my place with this little gal on Nate's Appaloosa. They had happened to be riding by her farm when they heard shots.

"I knew the family. They lived southwest of me quite a ways. Poor as church mice but good people.

"A couple of fellows had escaped jail in Julesburg. They were on the run and had worn their horses down to the bone.

"Now two old work horses weren't going to do them much good, but instead of moving on, they shot that little gal's ma and pa. They were trying to chase her down when Nate and Sam heard the shots.

"Not many words were spoken but a lot of guns talked. When it was all over, those two jailbirds were dead.

"'Course, now those boys had another problem on their hands. Two young, single fellows and a gal about their age out in the middle of nowhere and dark coming on. Those boys were gentlemen, but that little gal didn't know them.

"They decided to take her to my ranch. They were both real concerned about her reputation if they spent the night alone with her.

They put her on Nate's Appaloosa and headed for my place. Pushed their horses hard and made it just after dark.

"Now like I said, she lived southwest of here. Nate and Sam were headed toward Ogallala. It would have been easier for them not to backtrack, but it would have meant spending the night out on the prairie. They brought her up here. Once arrangements had been made for her, they headed out in the dark. They were in a hurry too because they had to be in Ogallala by daylight to pick up some cattle." John rubbed his chin and then looked over at Evelyn.

"That's just the kind of men those fellows are. Shoot—if I had another daughter, I'd *try* to marry her to one of them. Either of them. I only have one girl though, and my Ann found a man she loves. Even though he's a durn cattle buyer, I get along with him.

"And I love those little boys of theirs. Being a grandpa is the most fun I've ever had."

Evelyn was quiet. She frowned several times and finally cleared her throat.

"Jasper said you lost your wife several years ago. I'm sorry for your loss."

John was quiet for a moment. He rubbed his hand across his face before he answered.

"Lydia and I were married for over forty years. She was the love of my life and the best decision I ever made. Even so, I left her alone too much. I don't think I really appreciated her.

"She took sick in '76 and never did get completely well. She just kind of faded away. She passed in '78." He looked at Evelyn seriously.

"You take care of Jasper. The Good Lord gave you a fine man." He grinned as he added, "Even though we don't get along the best, I respect him." His voice was soft as he added, "You just don't know how much you'll miss that person you're married to until they aren't around anymore."

Evelyn listened closely but she never answered. Kirkham didn't talk much after that. Both women were tired, so the rest of the buggy ride was quiet.

CHAPTER 28

Good Company

ITWAS DARK WHEN THEY ARRIVED IN OGALLALA. MANY of the businesses on Front Street had burned over the summer and the blackened ruins of buildings showed between the new construction.

Kirkham waved his hand toward the remnants of burned walls as they passed.

"Don't you worry now, ladies. That fire didn't get past this street. Nate said you are staying in the Spofford House, and it is just fine. It had a little smoke damage but that has all been fixed." Kirkham pulled the buggy to a stop in front of a large hotel.

"Nate will get you all settled in, and my boys will take care of your buggy."

Nate nodded as Kirkham spoke.

"I can arrange for your tickets too if you'd like. It will be less rushed if we can take care of that tonight."

Isabelle jumped up.

"Let me go with Nate, Mother. I have never been to Ogallala. I'd like to see a little of the town before we leave in the morning."

Evelyn frowned but Isabelle was insistent.

"Please, Mother. I know you don't want to give our money to someone else to handle so let me do this. I could use some walking."

Evelyn reluctantly handed her bag to Isabelle.

"Now you stay right beside Nate." Her eyes moved to Nate as she added, "And I want her back at the hotel in an hour—and not a minute later."

Nate agreed with a grin. He helped both women out of the buggy while Kirkham and his men unloaded their bags.

The old man hollered after them, "Have that clerk arrange for a bath. He can have that water hauled right up to their room." He grinned at Isabelle and added with a chuckle, "Besides, if he knows bath water will have to be hauled up, he just might find you a room on the first floor."

Evelyn could feel herself blush, but she didn't turn around.

Once she was checked in and a bath arranged, Nate galloped back down the steps.

"Come on, Sis. We don't have much time. Let's get those tickets and then I'll put my horses up." He took Isabelle's arm, and they hurried toward the train station. The ticket agent was pulling his window closed. Nate pushed his hand between the window and the small opening.

"This lady needs to purchase tickets down to Kansas on tomorrow's train." The agent glared at Nate and started to speak when Nate added softly, "And I know you don't want to make her stand out here in the dark while we argue."

Isabelle stepped forward with a bright smile. "Please, sir. My mother and I have ridden in a buggy for three days to get here. It would be a great help for both of us if I could purchase our passage tonight."

The agent looked closely at Isabelle for a moment and then became very agreeable.

"I guess I can make an exception for you since you have traveled so far. Now tell me your names and where you want to go."

"Isabelle and Evelyn Merrill. To Manhattan down in Kansas." Isabelle slid a note through the window. "My father said that is the route we will need to take." Isabelle smiled and added, "We are from Georgia and just moved to Nebraska. This is my first time in Ogallala."

The man paused a moment as he stared at the note.

"Your pa fight in the war?"

Isabelle's smile became bigger as she nodded her head. "Yes, he was an officer for the Confederacy."

The man's face lost its smile. He slammed his book shut.

"You blasted Rebs. I lost my pa and a brother in that war. I wouldn't make an exception for no Reb, not even if you were the only folks on the train.

"You come back tomorrow morning and maybe there will be room for you. Not if I can help it though."

Nate reached through the booth and grabbed the agent by the shirt collar. He jerked him forward until their noses were inches apart.

"There is no call for that kind of rudeness. You sell the lady her tickets, or you and me will have a little altercation out there behind that train car. Maybe you will be more agreeable after we talk personal like."

"What's the problem here?" John Kirkham's voice was hard as he stepped up to the window.

Nate dropped the agent.

"This fellow doesn't want to sell Miss Merrill tickets since her pa was a Reb."

Kirkham glared at the agent.

"Ridge, you sell this lady her tickets. And you put both Miss Merrill and her mother in my car. There will be four of us in there when we leave tomorrow, so you make sure there is adequate food." He poked the book with a big finger and added, "And you be mighty civil, or I'll see to it that you don't have a job tomorrow."

"Yes sir, Mr. Kirkham. It's just that since we are a Yankee town and all, I didn't think—"

"You're right—you didn't think. That war ended nigh on twenty years ago. Besides, Jasper Merrill is a business associate of mine, and I won't have his family treated rudely.

"Now get that sale made. And make sure my car is at the back of the train. None of us want to be breathing all that smoke.

"While you are counting seats, put me down for two. Nate Hawkins and myself." Kirkham slapped a pass down on the counter. "Put those two seats on this pass." Kirkham waited until the tickets were purchased. Then he took Isabelle's arm.

"Miss Merrill, let me take you and Nate here out for supper. We'll eat at my favorite spot. It's not fancy but it has the best food around." He nodded toward Nate. "Meet us down the street as soon as you put your horses up. José's American Cantina."

Kirkham led Isabelle down the street to a small cantina. He pushed through the doors and held them open for Isabelle.

"José cooked for us on roundup several years, and I developed a fondness for his food. I tried to hire him as a cook, but he refused. He said he could make more money off me and all my cowboys if he opened his own eating place." Kirkham laughed. "He's right too."

A man poked his head out of the kitchen. He waved a large wooden scoop-like paddle.

"Señor Kirkham! I see you have come to see me tonight so I can take more of your money! Please, sit down, and I will bring you my best."

Kirkham held up three fingers. He laughed when Isabelle looked at him with confusion.

"You don't order here. José only makes one thing each night. Everyone eats the same thing. He told me once that his customers are like his family. He only fixes one meal for his family to share, so his customers are treated the same way. I promise it will be delicious.

"So tell me, Miss Merrill. What do you plan to study in college? I assume you are going to Kansas State Agricultural College since you and your mother are traveling down to Manhattan."

Isabelle looked at him quickly. She slowly blushed.

"I—I don't really know. This came up rather suddenly." Isabelle's blush became deeper as Kirkham waited for her to finish. She straightened her shoulders and looked the old man in the eyes.

"College was my mother's idea. She doesn't like Sam, and she is using it to keep us apart."

Kirkham studied Isabelle's face and he chuckled.

"There are worse things than college, Miss Merrill. I think you will enjoy yourself. Perhaps so much you won't want to come back home to Sam Rankin."

"We'll see. I promised Father that I would stay for two years. After that, it is my choice if I return."

"So what do you want to do?"

Nate pushed through the doors and dropped down in the open seat just in time to hear Isabelle's answer.

"I want to help Father manage the ranch. I want to make decisions with him, ride with him, and help buy cattle." Her face had regained its normal color, but she once again blushed as she added, "I want more of a life than to just be a helpless woman who sits around and waits for her man to come home."

Nate grinned while Kirkham threw back his head and laughed.

"Good for you, although I don't think you will find many helpless women out here. Women in the Sandhills—in fact all over the West— work hard, whether they are at home or out with the men.

"If that's the case though, you make sure you take classes that will benefit you—even if you have to argue with the powers that be over where a woman's place is."

José arrived with the food and Kirkham grinned at the small man.

"Enough of this talk. Let's enjoy whatever it is that José cooked up for us this evening."

CHAPTER 29

JUST FRIENDS

ONCE THEIR MEAL WAS COMPLETED, NATE ESCORTED Isabelle back to the Spofford House while Kirkham went to look for the sheriff.

"Mr. Kirkham is a nice man. He seems to be good friends with José too."

Nate was quiet for a moment and finally nodded.

"Rowdy talks about a fella who ran an eating house in Cheyenne for a time. Barney Ford. He said Mr. Ford offered the best food around. He was Colored, but that didn't bother the folks in Cheyenne and for sure not Rowdy. They were good friends. In fact, Beth and Rowdy make a trip to Denver once a year to see that feller.

"Beth told me Cheyenne even gave Mr. Ford a parade when he left, but that was before Gabe and I settled there.

"I've never met Mr. Ford, but I'd like to someday. Sam and I talked of stopping in Denver just to eat some of his grub and stay at his hotel, but we haven't made it yet." Nate gave Isabelle a quick grin. "Besides, he runs one of the swankiest hotels in Denver. I doubt we'd be able to afford it.

"Sam remembers him. He said the Rocking R riders always ate at his eating house, so Lance knew him long before Rowdy arrived in Cheyenne.

"Mr. Ford always brought Rowdy two plates of food. He never asked Rowdy a thing. He just did it. Ol' Rowdy liked that too because he likes to eat.

"Sam said Rowdy invited him to his wedding. He told Mr. Ford he didn't want him to cook that day—just come as a guest and enjoy himself. And he did too.

"He must have been just an all-around good guy because Beth told me he provided all the food for the family after Lance's best friend died. Slim was married less than two years. His wife's name was Sadie, and she was pregnant at the time. That's how she met her second husband. He was prosecuting lawyer at that trial.

"The neighbors had just moved Sadie to Cheyenne. In fact, the trial for the men who killed her husband was the day after she moved." Nate frowned a moment and shook his head. "I never met her first husband, but everyone says Young Levi—that's the boy Sadie was pregnant with when Slim died—is a lot like his pa. If that's the case, he was durn ornery.

"Anyway, Mr. Ford sent over a message that he would be by the evening of the trial with food." Nate was quiet as he looked out over the prairie. He finally added softly, "Sam told me some about Slim. He called him his uncle, and he said he cried when Slim died. 'Course, he was just a sprout when that happened.

"I wish I had known him. Sam said his pa gets real quiet when folks talk about Slim. They were pards before Lance bought his ranch, and they stayed good friends." Nate looked down and added, "'Course, Sadie was already married to Levi Parker when Gabe and I settled there. Levi is a heck of a nice guy too."

Isabelle listened closely to Nate. She smiled at him.

"No wonder you want to go back home. It sounds like a wonderful place to live. So much family." Isabelle looked away and added quietly,

"We don't have any family that I know of other than some distant cousins. Mother called herself a war widow when I was small since my first father died in that terrible war. I don't really remember my first father. I only remember being hungry all the time, and I remember my mother crying.

"My mother was beautiful, but she wouldn't walk out with men. Being a widow was difficult for her. It was even harder as the war progressed. After it ended, things didn't get any better.

"Mother always told me that a woman needed to marry for security before love. She said she married a poor man for love and look what it got her."

Nate pulled Isabelle's arm a little closer. He finally asked, "How did she meet Jasper?"

Isabelle laughed softly.

"In Atlanta, Georgia. That was after the war ended. My first father's cousin told Mother the owner of one of the dry goods stores in Atlanta was looking for help. He said Mother could easily get the job because she was so pretty. He said her looks would bring in lots of business, and she should tell the owner that when she applied.

"Mother was horrified but we made the move. That cousin loaned Mother the money for the train fare. I don't think he ever expected to get it back, but Mother saved and scrimped to do it. Everyone was hard up after the war. That cousin had a family of his own to take care of." Isabelle frowned.

"Before that, we lived in Columbus, Georgia. Some of the women there didn't like Mother. They whispered about her behind her back. I think it was because she was so pretty. They were afraid she would take one of their husbands." Isabelle had tears in her eyes when she looked up at Nate.

"Mother didn't tell me that. I heard some of them talk. They ignored me because I was so small and afraid of everyone. I listened all the time though, and some of them were just cruel.

"As I look back on it now, I think it was because we were all so afraid. Everyone was struggling to get by." Isabelle was quiet for a moment. She finally smiled softly.

"I remember the first day Father came into that store in Atlanta. Mother was trying to lift a large bag of flour onto the counter. He never asked if she needed help—he just lifted it up and smiled at her. Then he offered her his handkerchief to dust the flour off her face.

"He came in every day for a week and bought something small. He visited with everyone, making small talk until Mother was free. He always bought me a piece of hard candy too.

"At the end of that week, he came in just before closing time. He asked Mother to supper. She started to say no. She only agreed when he told her he had already asked me, and I said yes.

"He asked Mother to marry him the next day. She was in a tither. She said she didn't know him well enough. There were so many men who asked her the same thing every time they came in. She was going to say no.

"The owner of the store said, 'Jasper Merrill is a successful businessman, Evelyn. He's a mover and a shaker in this part of Georgia. You should accept his offer. Besides, you won't find a better man.'"

"When Father asked again the next day after church, Mother said yes. They were married that morning, and we moved that evening.

"Father's plantation had been destroyed but he was rebuilding everything. He had started on the house, but it wasn't finished. We lived in the chicken coop for nearly three months before we moved into the new house." Isabelle smiled at Nate again.

"My mother fell in love with Jasper while we lived in the chicken coop. He was so kind and so thoughtful. As she became more comfortable with their marriage, he started to tease her some.

"I adored him. I barely remember my first father, so I was excited to have a father who paid attention to me.

"Mother became pregnant that first year. She nearly died trying to have the baby. She was broken hearted when my little brother died. The surgeon in Atlanta told Father she would never be able to have children again. He said he had to take that part out to save her life." Isabelle wiped the tears from her eyes and Nate offered her his bandana. She took a deep breath.

"And that's why I'm an only child. Mother comes across as cranky and angry, but mostly, she is just afraid. I think there is still a part of her that thinks she will be poor and alone again someday." Isabelle's eyes were bright when she added, "And that's why she doesn't like Sam. She doesn't want me to struggle like she did. She is convinced I should marry a 'man of means,' and she is determined to make sure that happens."

Nate was quiet. He was almost ashamed of himself for judging Evelyn so harshly.

The Spofford House was in front of them. They had been talking so intently that Nate didn't even realize where they were. He took Isabelle's shoulders and smiled down at her.

"Sam is wild and ornery but he has a kind heart. He's a good man and your ma will see that someday." He grinned and added, "Besides, he inherited his pa's love of the land. If he has his way, he'll probably own an entire state someday. He'll need a woman like his ma to whoa him down and make sure he doesn't get so carried away."

Nate kissed her cheek. "Good night, Sis. I hope it works out between you and Sam." He waited until Isabelle was on her way up the stairs before he turned toward the livery.

"I'm going to sleep with my horse and save my money. I'll get up early and take a bath."

CHAPTER 30

A MOTHER'S FEAR

EVELYN WATCHED FROM HER FIRST-FLOOR WINDOW as Nate kissed her daughter's cheek. She frowned slightly and sat down on the bed. She was watching the door when Isabelle slipped in.

"You are nearly an hour late, Isabelle. You know you should not be out on the streets at night with so many rough men everywhere."

"Oh, Mother. I had such a good time. Mr. Kirkham took us out for supper. He's a kind and wonderful man. Nate is too."

Evelyn's voice was dry when she spoke.

"Yes, I saw him kiss you. That's not exactly how a good friend should behave."

Isabelle stared at her mother for a moment. The smile disappeared from her face and her blue eyes became angry.

"Nate *is* a good friend. We talked all the way back here about Sam, their home in Cheyenne, and even my life. He's good and kind, and he loves Sam like a brother." She glared at her mother before she added, "Besides, he calls me Sis.

"Nate would never do anything to hurt Sam or their friendship." She tossed her head as she added, "He has a girl he's sweet on anyway. She is in college down in Kansas and I hope I meet her. In fact, I hope we become friends." Isabelle placed her hands on her hips and stomped her foot as she spoke.

"I wish you could see Sam as I see him, Mother—as everyone else sees him. You haven't even given him a chance.

"And I doubt I'll like that old school. I am only going because you are forcing me to. After two years, I'm coming home, and if Sam asks me to marry, I am going to say yes." She glared at her mother and added softly, "If he asked me now, I would say yes. You don't know it, but he's the one who told me to do as you wanted me to and go to college." Tears filled Isabelle's eyes. "Please give Sam a chance, Mother."

Evelyn's eyes filled with tears, and she began to cry softly.

"I just see so much of me in you. I don't want you to make the same mistakes."

"Love is never a mistake, Mother."

"It is if it is love for the wrong man."

"Was my first father the wrong man? Tell me about him, Mother. Tell me about my first father. You have never talked about him."

Evelyn wiped her eyes. She smiled at her daughter and patted the bed beside her.

"His name was Ira, and he was a farmer. Oh my, but he was handsome. I was eighteen when we met, and I was taken by him immediately.

"His eyes were as blue as yours and his blond hair was curly. When he smiled, he ducked his head and gave this shy smile. That smile slowly filled his entire face.

"My father was a tenant on the big farm where we lived, and Ira owned a few acres next to it. He helped some on the big farm to pay bills.

"We married in 1860.

"Ira had all kinds of plans and was saving his money to buy more ground. I think he would have too, but that terrible war changed everything. He enlisted shortly after it began.

"I didn't want him to go. I begged him not to leave. He told me the Yanks had started that war and it was up to the South to end it.

"He gave me the tin of money he had saved to buy land and told me to head west. 'Don't stop until you cross the Mississippi," he said. "I'll find you when the fighting is over.

"I was terrified. I leased our small farm to the big farmer and made plans to leave the next day. I couldn't make myself go though. I moved back in with my parents and tried to wait the war out with them. That was in the spring of 1861.

"I didn't hear from Ira for nearly three years. My parents were convinced he had died. My mother told me I was blessed that we had no children. I cried every time she said that.

"And then one summer day in 1864, Ira rode in. His arm was in a sling, and he was so thin. That smile was the same though. We spent three wonderful days together and that's when you were conceived. I had no idea when he left that I would never see him again.

"He was killed right there outside our town in the Battle of Columbus and buried without me knowing. That fight took place on April 16, 1865. We didn't know it, Lee had already surrendered when the Columbus battle took place.

"You were born the next day. It was a difficult birth, but you were healthy and strong even though you were small.

"When we finally heard the war was over, we all celebrated. I made plans for us to leave. Of course, I didn't know your father was dead.

"The city of Columbus was planning a party for all the men who were returning home. When they arrived, they were so worn and tattered. Those who couldn't ride were in wagons. There were four wagons of wounded. Of course, the dead were buried on the field.

"Those of us who were waiting for our men ran to meet them. When I saw Ira wasn't among the mounted, I checked every wagon. By the time I reached the last one, a young soldier grabbed my arm.

"He said, 'Who are you looking for, ma'am? Maybe I can help you.'

"I replied, 'Ira Claining. Can you tell me where he is?'

"There was an officer riding close by. He dropped off his horse and said, 'I'm sorry, Mrs. Claining. Ira was killed in the last battle. He wanted me to give you this though.' He handed me Ira's bible and a letter.

"I was almost hysterical. My father finally found me and led me home. Mother cared for us both for the next year.

"When I was well enough to work, I took over things in the house and around our little homestead while Mother helped in the fields. I wanted to trade her places, but she said I needed to care for you. I think she said that because I was so frail. She was afraid the heavy labor would break me down completely." Tears filled Evelyn's eyes. "It killed her instead. Mother died two years later.

"I worked in Columbus another two years. You were five when we left there for Atlanta." Evelyn held Isabelle's hands as she smiled at her through her tears.

"Ira was wonderful, but my parents didn't like him. They said I needed to marry someone who could lift me above the poverty I was born into." Tears slid from Evelyn's eyes. "And now I am doing that to you. I'm sorry, Isabelle. I will try to become acquainted with young Sam. I will even try to like him. I just don't want you to struggle like I did. I want so much more for you. Jasper and I both do."

"Oh, Mother. Please don't cry. I know you are afraid for me. I'll be fine though. Thank you for telling me about my first father. And I promise I'll stay in college for two years. I doubt I will stay longer, but I'll try to learn and be a good student." Isabelle squeezed her mother's hands and smiled excitedly.

"Now let me share all the stories with you that Mr. Kirkham and Nate told tonight."

Monday, October 6, 1884
Kansas State
Agricultural College
Manhattan, Kansas

CHAPTER 31

College Life
and a New Friend

THE DRIVER EVELYN HIRED TO TAKE THEM TO THE college in Manhattan was a bent old man. His full name was Wilson Penny, but folks just called him Penny. Evelyn cocked an eyebrow at him when he said he would be glad to get them settled in.

"Mr. Penny, this trunk is quite heavy. Are you sure—?"

"Ma'am, I've been haulin' heavy bags 'round fer a number of years. I may look weak but I ain't found a trunk I cain't hoist yet." He grinned and winked at Isabelle, "'Sides, there's always lots a help jist a hangin' 'round a waitin' to be handy when a young lady is involved."

Both Isabelle and Evelyn were nervous when Penny stopped in front of the building that housed the administration. Jasper had sent a message with Nate to be delivered to the telegraph office in Ogallala. His wire announced the two women and requested late enrollment for Isabelle.

President Fairchild had the proper papers in front of him when they arrived, and the enrollment process was simple and painless. Once that was completed, he sent them to the women's dormitory to unload.

"I'm not sure what is available there. However, Miss Morton will see to it that you are settled in." He smiled at both women. "Welcome to Kansas State Agricultural College, Miss Merrill."

Three young men were gathered around Penny's buggy when the women returned. The ornery old man winked at the Merrills as he drawled, "These here fellers offered to carry Miss Isabelle's travelin' bags up to where she'll be a stayin'. I'll jist wait here by my buggy so's I'm ready when ya want to leave, Mrs. Merrill."

Evelyn rapped on the door to Holtz Hall. A tall, stern-looking woman jerked the door open. She stared at the Merrills without speaking. Isabelle smiled at the gruff women.

"Good afternoon. I'm Isabelle Merrill and this is my mother, Evelyn. I just enrolled today, and Mr. Fairchild said I should talk to you about a room."

Miss Morton crossed her arms and tapped her toe as she studied Isabelle.

"Enrollment ended last week. You are late and there are no spots available."

A young woman with a thick braid of brown hair wrapped around her head was standing behind Miss Morton. She cautiously touched the older woman's shoulder and almost jumped when Miss Morton whirled around.

"Actually, there is a spot available in my room. Miss Sexton withdrew from school yesterday. Her parents just collected her belongings an hour ago."

Miss Morton glared at the young woman before she turned to face the Merrills.

"Fine. You boys may put Miss Merrill's bags in Room Ten on the third floor. You have three minutes to get them up those stairs and be gone from here." She stopped to glare at the young woman who had spoken. "Miss Rankin, why are you not in class?"

"Miss Purdy became ill today. I covered her class for her and released the girls twenty minutes ago. I was just going to my room to study." She smiled at Isabelle.

"Come, Miss Merrill. I will show you where you will be staying." As they hurried toward the stairs, she added, "I'm Mari Rankin. I'm so pleased you are coming to school here. Miss Sexton left unexpectedly and—"

"Miss Rankin! You do not have to tell all you know. You wait right there until those young men come down those stairs. I won't have the five of you up there unsupervised." Miss Morton glared at Mari again as she added sarcastically, "Afterall, Miss Sexton *was* your roommate."

Mari stopped and took a deep breath before she turned around. Her voice was dripping with sugary sarcasm when she replied.

"Yes, she was. Of course, I just had the only room available." Mari smiled sweetly before she turned around. "Come, Isabelle. Let's get you settled in."

As the three young men rushed by them on their way out, they tipped their hats to the women.

"We hope to see you at the dance Saturday, Miss Rankin. You too, Miss Merrill!"

Evelyn turned around to watch the young men leave. Her face was thoughtful as she followed the two younger women.

Isabelle smiled at Mari as they hurried up the stairs. "Please call me Isabelle, and my mother is Evelyn."

Mari smiled as she shook their hands. "I'm Mari. Mari Rankin. It will be so nice to have a roommate. Sally Sexton was rarely here. She was so sick the last few months. I'm sure she's glad to be going home.

"Is this your first year here?" Isabelle's voice was curious as she looked around.

Mari shook her head. "It's my second year here but I'm in my third year of college. I helped the teacher at our little school back home for a year while I completed my Normal Teacher Training. I studied some on the side as well and was able to enter college last year as a sophomore." Mari's brown eyes were friendly as she added, "I love teaching. I wouldn't have come to college, but Mother insisted—both she and my Aunt Molly. They convinced me that I could help the children learn more if I had a broader education. Now here I am.

"It's been a wonderful experience though, and I'm glad I agreed. I love school. I have learned so much in just a year.

"Where are you from, Isabelle?"

"Originally, we lived in Georgia, just outside Atlanta. However, this past summer, we bought a ranch in the Sandhills. We moved there this past July."

Mari's face lit up.

"My cousin Sam is working in that area somewhere. His mother showed me a letter he wrote. He said he loves it there." Mari added softly, "Of course, he is with his best friend. He and Nate are inseparable."

Isabelle's face turned a light pink, and Mari cocked an eyebrow as she studied her new friend. Then she turned away and pointed at one of the beds.

"You may sleep there. Sally didn't take her bedding. We can wash it if you want to use it. Otherwise, we can fold it and store it away in case her parents come by to pick it up later."

Evelyn watched the two girls. She smiled slightly and shook her head. *Mari Rankin. I guess I am never going to be able to separate Isabelle from Sam. We travel nearly four hundred miles to take her to college in Kansas and her roommate is his cousin.*

"Isabelle, how about I let you unpack and maybe Mari can help you find your classes? Then I can pick you up for supper this evening. I'd like to spend a little time with you before I leave tomorrow."

Mari thought a moment before she agreed.

"I will find someone to do my part of the cooking. We have to be back here by eight though, or Miss Morton will lock us out." She smiled at Evelyn. "You might tell her as you leave what your plans are. She doesn't let us go out during the week unless our parents come to town."

Evelyn hugged her daughter. Her eyes searched Isabelle's excited face. *Here I am about to cry, and Isabelle is excited for me to leave.* Evelyn turned toward the door. She smiled as she looked back at the two young women.

"I will plan to pick you up at five. That should give us plenty of time to eat and get you back here."

Isabelle ran to hug her mother again.

"Oh, Mother. Thank you for bringing me down here. We will be waiting for you at the door." She kissed her mother quickly and rushed back into her room. She couldn't wait to talk to Mari about Sam and Nate.

CHAPTER 32

COMMON INTERESTS

THE TWO GIRLS QUICKLY STRIPPED THE BED AS THEY visited. They gathered the bedding and Isabelle followed Mari down the stairs. Her new friend showed her where the kitchen was as well as the laundry and a small waiting area.

"This is where gentlemen wait when they come to call. We are only allowed to have male visitors in the sitting room on Sunday afternoons though.

"Lots of girls leave for the weekends since many live around this area. Those of us from farther away are usually the only ones around.

"Life here is very structured. We can only leave for the weekend or an entire day with an approved family member. Saturday evening is when gentlemen are allowed to come to the dormitory and pick us up. They knock on the door and then wait until Miss Morton calls us. They are allowed to step inside to collect us at the bottom of the steps, but they can come in no further. We must be back inside by ten o'clock."

The two young women washed the bedding and hung it on the line in the courtyard to dry. The day was warm, and it was pleasant in the afternoon sun.

Mari's eyes were sparkling as she leaned toward Isabelle.

"You must know Sam and Nate since they are working up there. Please tell me how they are. I miss them both so much!"

Isabelle blushed furiously.

"I do. I met them this past spring when we were visiting the ranch where they were employed. They were so dirty when they arrived. Big beards and such shaggy hair too.

"They were friendly though. I think they were lonesome since had been out on the range by themselves all winter." She giggled and added, "They were good-looking too once they cleaned up.

"Nate brought my mother and I down to Ogallala. My father couldn't make the trip and since Nate was going with Mr. Kirkham to work for the railroad, my father asked if he would escort us that far."

Mari's face showed her confusion.

"So, Nate and Sam are not working together?"

Isabelle shook her head.

"No, Sam is going to work for my father. John Kirkham offered Nate a job with the railroad, and they left this morning for Omaha.

"Nate helped Mother and I with our train tickets. In fact, we were in the same car for a short time. Then we had to change trains to head down here." Isabelle smiled at Mari shyly. "I didn't want to come but Sam said I would like it here. I'm so glad we met."

"Nate knew you were coming here? Did he send a message or a letter?" Mari's eyes were hopeful as she waited for an answer.

Isabelle shook her head. "Nate didn't give me a message of any kind, but Sam said Nate wants to buy his own place. That's one of the reasons he took this railroad job. Maybe since he is traveling around, he will be able to stop in some. It is hard for them to get away when they are cowboying."

"I don't know why I expected anything. They left four years ago." Mari looked away. "We were just kids then. Nate gave me his bandana to wear while he was gone. He sent me a letter right after he left but that's all I've ever heard from him.

"He writes his family some, and they try to keep me updated." She wiped her eyes. "I'm being foolish. No one keeps promises they make when they're kids." Her smile returned and she leaned toward Isabelle.

"So you are sweet on Sam? Is he your fellow?"

Isabelle stuttered a little before she finally laughed.

"No, but I'd like him to be. Mother sent me down here to separate us. She doesn't like him much, although she might be coming around." Isabelle's eyes sparkled as she added, "When he told me you went to school here, I was hoping we'd meet."

Mari laughed as she jumped up.

"Get your schedule and let's see what classes we have together. I can show you where to go too. Hurry. We have just a little time. You run upstairs and I will find Miss Morton."

CHAPTER 33

ANOTHER GOODBYE

PENNY HAD GIVEN EVELYN THE NAME OF A RESTAURANT he thought they would enjoy. He even offered to wait outside so they didn't have to send for a ride. When Evelyn protested, Penny laughed.

"A feller up to Cheyenne told me to make sure any of his kinfolk who showed up here was cared fer proper. Now I know Mari here is a Rankin so that makes her kin to ol' Badger. Why he'd skin me alive if he knowed I made his womenfolks wait outside in the dark." He grinned at Mari and winked.

"'Sides, word is if ol' Sam Rankin has his way, Miss Merrill there might be kin too. Naw, I reckon I'll jist wait outside."

Isabelle blushed and Evelyn frowned while Penny laughed wickedly.

"Yessir, I like to do what I cin to help folks out when they's family.

"Now ya ladies jist go on in there an' have yore own selves a chatty little time. I'll be right here when you's ready to leave." Penny helped them down and was whistling off-tune when he jumped into the buggy.

"Yessir, that ol' Badger be a scallywag if there ever was one. He's one a the best friends I have though. In fact, I might take a little time off an' go see 'im one a these days. Martha too. I cin ride the rails all the way up there so that trip wouldn't take no time a'tall."

Evelyn was quiet as the girls chatted. She smiled from time to time but mostly she thought. She thought about how lonely the ranch was going to be with Isabelle gone. She worried too about Jasper and his stomach issues. They hadn't told Isabelle anything yet because they didn't know what it was. Jasper had an appointment with a surgeon in Cheyenne in November. They hoped to learn something then.

She smiled slightly. *Goodness, I could meet some of Sam's family there. I guess we will have to listen for names we know. I wonder what his parents are like.* She was jolted out of her thinking by Isabelle's question.

"What will I do for Thanksgiving, Mother? I might not have enough time to get home and back before school resumes."

"Your father and I have discussed that. He has an appointment that month in Cheyenne. We thought we'd come on down to visit you." She smiled at Mari. "You too, Mari, if your folks are coming down."

"My parents won't be here. One of my brothers invited me to come to Kansas City and visit him. He graduated from law school last year and has a job there."

Evelyn smiled at Mari.

"Why that's wonderful, Mari! Has he always wanted to be a lawyer?"

Mari nodded. "Since we came to live with the Rankins. They took us in when our folks died. Rudy interned with Levi Parker. He's a lawyer in Cheyenne. In fact, it was Levi's first trial there that piqued Rudy's interest."

"Well, I'm sure your parents are very proud of him. All four of them."

Mari nodded happily. "They are. But then, they are proud of all of us.

"Mother wanted me to go to college so I'd have a trade. She has always said that motherhood is a noble profession, but we must always be prepared for whatever life throws at us."

If the girls had noticed, they would have seen the tears that pooled in the corners of Evelyn's eyes. She blinked them away before she smiled and patted Mari's hand.

"Your parents sound like wonderful people," she commented softly.

CHAPTER 34

FAMILY HISTORY

IT WAS NOVEMBER AND ISABELLE HAD BEEN AT SCHOOL for nearly two months. She looked around their small room. It was cozy and tidy. They shared a desk but they each had their own bed. Down the hall, she could hear the rest of the girls in the large sleeping room. Beds were lined up along the walls two high. Another smaller room was designed for studying. Mari and Isabelle's room was the only individual bedroom that housed students. The other small bedroom belonged to Miss Morton.

Mari was reading a letter she had received. She was smiling and Isabelle waited until she flipped to the next page before she asked, "Why do you and I get a separate bedroom while the rest of the girls stay together in that big sleeping room?"

"I am a teaching assistant. Instead of paying me, they give me my own room. That way, I have a quiet place to prepare lessons." Mari's eyes crinkled with humor as she added, "My last roommate's parents paid extra so their daughter would have her own area. They didn't want her to share space with so many other girls."

Isabelle stared at Mari. "We didn't pay extra. Mr. Fairchild didn't even know what would be available. He said Miss Morton would find me a bed."

Mari shrugged her shoulders. "I don't know. You help around here like the rest of us so maybe that's why." She laughed and added, "Or maybe your folks will receive a bill. Who knows.

"Millie Sexton didn't do any work here. Quite frankly, I'm not sure why she even enrolled. Her parents didn't want her to socialize with any of us. They thought we were all below her social station." She laid the letter on her lap. "Millie was a sweet girl but so unhappy and terribly lonesome.

"She was already here when I came. Her parents had her tutored all summer before she started college.

"They thought it was the cowboy they saw hanging around here who put the bun in her oven. It wasn't him though. It was one of the men who made food deliveries. That man doesn't deliver here anymore so I am guessing Miss Morton knew.

"The first time I saw that cowboy down here was at church one Sunday. I recognized him. His name was Tobe Benson. He had worked for Gabe, Nate's brother, on their ranch in Cheyenne. He told me was restless and had decided to quit. He was tired of our long winters up north.

"Gabe sent him down here to manage their ranch south of Manhattan. Gabe's business partner, Rusty O'Brian, had been running it, but his wife's father was ailing. Rusty wanted his wife to be closer to her folks, so they moved down south of Dodge City. That left the ranch foreman job open.

"Tobe's pardner, Bart Black, came with him. He said Gabe didn't want to lose them as hands, so he offered them both jobs down here. It worked." Mari laughed.

"Tobe confessed that he didn't usually go to church, but he thought he'd try it once. He'd heard it was a good way to meet women." She rolled her eyes and laughed again. "I enjoyed talking to him. It was like visiting home. Tobe was funny and nice too. He came up the next Sunday afternoon to visit. While we were visiting, Millie walked through. I introduced them, and that's all it took for Tobe." Mari's brown eyes sparkled and she smiled at Isabelle.

"He kept coming every Sunday on the pretense of seeing me, but it was Millie he wanted to talk to. In fact, both Tobe and Bart used to show up every Sunday afternoon. Then Bart met a neighbor girl and he quit coming. After that, it was only Tobe.

"Tobe offered to marry Millie when he heard she was in a family way. I told her she should accept. She said her parents would never allow it—Tobe was just a cowboy, and they wanted her to marry a rich man." Mari frowned.

"Tobe was persistent though. When her parents were loading Millie's things, he was right there talking to her folks. Her father was yelling. Millie and her mother were both crying. I wanted to go outside but Miss Morton wouldn't let me. I watched out the window though.

"Every time they tried to put some of Millie's things in their wagon, Tobe would pull them out and put them in his. The last I saw, Millie had stopped crying. She was watching Tobe.

"Tobe wasn't mean or disrespectful to her parents either. He just matter-of-factly put her things in his wagon. When Miss Morton pulled me away from the window, Millie's father was still yelling. Tobe had his hand out to Millie. She was going to have to choose him or her folks.

"I hope she chose Tobe. I'm guessing I will see them in town sometime if she did. Tobe made her smile, and I think that is important when you marry."

Isabelle pondered on that. *Maybe that is why all the books I read say you should be friends before you court and marry. Mother and Father weren't though. They barely courted and hardly knew each other.*

Mari frowned as she looked up from her letter.

"Rudy has to go out of town to try a case. He is leaving on Friday."
Mari looked at the calendar on their wall. "That is November 21 and
Thanksgiving is just next week." Mari looked down at the letter again be-
fore she added, "He said he most likely won't be back before Thanksgiving.
Darn. That means I can't go to Kansas City for Thanksgiving."

Isabelle watched her friend for a moment. She leaned forward as
she smiled.

"Well, you can just spend it with my family. Of course, I have no
idea what Mother wants to do. She told me when I enrolled that Father
had some appointment and they would stop on their way home."

"Does your father travel a lot?"

"Not as much as he used to. When I was small, he was around but
as I became older, he traveled more. He loves to make business deals,
and from what Mother has told me, he's quite the businessman. The last
several years though, he hasn't traveled as much." Isabelle looked off in
the distance. She was smiling when she looked back at Mari.

"How about your father? Does he travel?"

"Heavens no. He loves Mother and horses. He said one time if he
had to choose between the two of them, it would be a hard choice."
Mari laughed.

"It wouldn't be though. Father adores Mother. He told me one time
that she still looks the same as she did the day he met her. That's not
true, of course. He met mother in 1870, and that was fourteen years ago.

"Father joined the Southern army when he was a teenager. He was an
excellent marksman and that became his job. He was a sharpshooter and
almost died in his last battle. In fact, a body was misidentified, and he
was pronounced dead. Mother met him looking at his own tombstone.

"They went back there several years after they married. The man
who was buried under Father's name was actually Mother's brother. He
had been listed as missing in action. They put up a new stone to mark
his grave and brought home the one with Father's name on it." Mari's
eyes sparkled and she laughed as she added, "Father put it in Mother's

flower garden. He said if it hadn't been for that old stone, he never would have met our mother."

Isabelle stared at Mari in surprise. She laughed with her friend. She became quiet as she looked out the window. When she spoke again, her voice was serious.

"Father was in that war too but he doesn't talk about it." She looked at Mari and asked quietly, "Do you ever feel sometimes that you know nothing about your parents? Like they have this secret life they led before you were old enough to pay attention?"

Mari shook her head. "No, but we live in a community surrounded by cousins and friends. Even though Father never talks about his time fighting for the South, I have picked up a little."

"Various men who worked for us called him Sarge. One time, one of those men became extremely sick. He was out of his head and talking crazy. Mother was gone so I sent my little brother for the doctor. I took care of that man until Doc arrived." Mari's face became pale, and she shivered before she continued.

"He talked a lot about the war and about my father. He told me things I have never told anyone. Later, I talked to Mother about it. I didn't tell her all he'd said. I just said he'd talked about the War of Southern Independence when he was out of his head, and his stories were frightening. Mother's face turned nearly white. She told me lots of men were wounded in that war, both inside and out. She said I should try to forget what he'd told me.

"He *was* out of his head so who knows if what he said was even true." Mari shivered. "I can't forget though. He screamed and cried. He talked about being in some terrible prison and then he begged for his life. He started shaking, and finally, he fainted. I thought he'd died. When his fever broke, he stared around terrified. Once he figured out where he was, he became quiet. He never talked like that again."

Just then, Miss Morton rapped loudly on their door.

"Miss Merrill, I have a wire for you."

CHAPTER 35

A Spontaneous Trip

ISABELLE HURRIED TO OPEN THE DOOR AND MISS Morton thrust a sealed envelope into her hand. Her eyes were almost kind when she spoke.

"I hope it's not bad news."

Isabelle unfolded the paper slowly. She looked up at Miss Morton in surprise.

"Mother and Father aren't coming here for Thanksgiving. Father's meeting was moved to this Wednesday, November 19." She smiled at the stern woman in front of her.

"Thank you, Miss Morton. I appreciate you getting this to me so quickly." Isabelle turned away from the door as she read the rest of the telegram slowly.

"Mother said she is going to wire me some money. She suggested I go with you to Kansas City for the holiday."

Isabelle's brows pulled down as she thought. She looked up at Mari and her eyes were shining.

"I think we should leave early and go to my home in Nebraska. Classes are in session until Wednesday afternoon, but if we leave the prior Friday, we will have over a week including travel time.

"You can come with me. That way you will be able to see Sam too. You said you'd never seen the Sandhills. Well, here's your chance."

"Skip classes?" Mari's eyes were big. "My parents would kill me if they even dreamed I would do such a thing!"

Isabelle tossed her head.

"Come on, Mari. Neither of us wants to be stuck here for the holiday. Besides, young women are not supposed to travel alone. Traveling in pairs is acceptable though. I'll pretend the wire I received said my father was ill and I must leave as soon as possible. I'll say my parents don't want me to travel by myself, so they offered to pay your way too." When Mari stared at her, Isabelle rolled her eyes.

"All of that is true except the part about my father." Isabelle stared down at the telegram and frowned. She reread it and her frown became deeper. Her breath caught a little. "Actually, that part could be true. Father didn't drive Mother and I down to Ogallala. He asked Nate to take us, and that is not like him at all. He would never send Mother off anywhere by herself. She is too timid.

"Mother would never tell me if Father was ill either. I think he had an appointment with a doctor." She grabbed Mari's hands.

"Please. Come with me. I must go home."

Mari shook her head. "I can't. I don't have the money to travel that far. I have just enough to get to Kansas City and back. No more."

Isabelle laughed. "Mother will send me more than the fare will cost. She is always concerned I won't have enough money when I travel. I'm sure there will be enough for the both of us." Isabelle's eyes were excited and pleading at the same time. "Please, Mari. Come with me. I am going and I'd love to have you along."

Mari stared at Isabelle. "We'll see. I'll wait until you receive the money your mother is sending. If there is enough, I'll consider it.

"I won't lie though, and you can't either. You have to tell the truth, or I won't go with you. In fact, you can't even *stretch* the truth. Deal?"

180

Isabelle stared at her friend. "Deal. Truth only." Her blue eyes sparkled as she whispered, "I guess I'd better practice pretend-crying then!"

Mari stared at her friend and shook her head.

"I declare, Isabelle. You are a pill. No wonder you find Sam so interesting. You are as ornery as he is!

"Fine. Cry all you want but only the truth. I won't be part of a lie to get out of school."

CHAPTER 36

A WISE DEAN

GEORGE FAIRCHILD'S VOICE WAS STERN AS HE SPOKE. As president of the college, it was his job to handle situations like this. He was a "rule man," and he didn't like college rules to be questioned.

"Miss Merrill, I see from the note my receptionist gave me that you want to talk to me about leaving school early for Thanksgiving break. That is not something we allow here."

"Mr. Fairchild, I believe my father is ill. My parents were planning to come here for the holiday. Mother canceled that visit. My father had an appointment near here and they were going to stop in after that appointment. She wired me and said my father's appointment date was changed so they wouldn't be able to come.

"I know I am assuming but you must understand. My mother is a true southern lady. She doesn't like to discuss delicate or private matters. My father's health would qualify as both to her." Isabelle's blue eyes were focused on Mr. Fairchild's face.

"I was surprised when my father didn't come with Mother and me when I enrolled. I am an only child, and he is quite doting. However, I didn't think any more of it until I received this wire." She held up the telegram. "You are welcome to read it if you'd like." When Mr. Fairchild did not reach for the telegram, Isabelle sat back in her chair.

"I do want to go home for the holiday but more than that, I am concerned about my father."

"When were you hoping to leave?"

"Originally, I thought Monday or Tuesday. However, if I left on Friday, I would only miss four days of class plus have an extra three days to travel and spend with my family."

"Who is going to escort you? You know I can't release you to travel by yourself."

Isabelle's face blushed slightly but she raised her chin higher.

"I would like to take Mari Rankin with me. Her cousin is employed on our ranch so she would be able to see family. Besides, she is more experienced in rail travel than I.

"Mr. Penny offered to ride with us as far as Ogallala. He has friends in Cheyenne."

Isabelle leaned forward and spoke earnestly, "Mr. Fairchild, Mari refused to go with me if I lied to you in any way. I swear all of this is the truth."

George Fairchild leaned back in his chair as he studied the young woman in front of him. He believed her and that surprised him. Moreover, he remembered how nervous Mrs. Merrill was when Isabelle enrolled. He also remembered the wire he had received from Isabelle's father. *The man certainly wanted to come down himself. He was very concerned about his wife and daughter traveling alone. Besides, Isabelle has been a model student in the few months she has been here, and Mari Rankin certainly is.*

"Miss Merrill, I am going to break protocol and give my permission for this." When Isabelle began to smile, Mr. Fairchild held up a hand. "However, I am leaving the final decision with your teachers. If they say you may go, I expect all necessary work to be completed before you leave. Again, any exceptions will be decided by your instructors."

He scratched out two notes and handed them to Isabelle. "You may be excused." His eyes twinkled slightly as he added, "And have a safe trip."

Isabelle was almost skipping when she left Mr. Fairchild's office. Mari was waiting for her outside and the two girls swung each other around before they raced toward the building that housed their classes.

George Fairchild watched the girls from his window and shook his head. "I suppose this set a precedent. So be it. I'm sure something like this will come up again. I certainly hope Miss Merrill uses her days at home to spend some extra time with her father. Regrets are a difficult thing to live with."

Once classes were out for the day, the two girls hurried downtown. Isabelle rushed into the First National Bank. She presented the wire with her mother's name at the bottom and signed quickly for the money. She slipped it into her handbag and nearly ran out of the bank.

"Let's hurry and get our tickets. We have to be back by five to peel potatoes for supper."

CHAPTER 37

A New Adventure

WILSON PENNY BROKE HIS LEG THE DAY BEFORE THEY were to leave. He wanted to go anyway but the girls insisted they would be all right.

"I'll send that feller what runs yore school a note. I'll tell 'im I made shore ya was all lined out." Penny winced as he tried to move his leg. "That durn wagon. I had it blocked up, but the wood slipped. The blasted axle landed on my leg. Now I don't get to take no trip or get any treats neither."

"Don't worry, Mr. Penny. We'll still bring you some goodies. The girls here all talk about Mari's bread, and I love to bake as well. We'll make sure you get your goodies." Isabelle patted his arm and Mari hugged him.

Penny had them write down the connections they needed as he explained them. He gave them estimated times and told them where the privies were at each station.

"I reckon ya better go ahead an' haul yore trunk down the night before. Miss Morton won't let no fellers in her buildin' and shore not of a mornin. Now once you's on the train, don't ya try to carry all them there bags yore own selves. Ya jist smile purty at some young fellers an' they'll haul 'em fer ya."

"We'll be fine, Mr. Penny. We aren't taking much since we won't be staying long. Besides, I left most of my clothes at home." Isabelle smiled at Penny before she continued. "Mari's a little taller than me but other than that, we are close to the same size." Both young women were bubbling with excitement and Penny grinned through his pain.

The two friends put in long hours and late nights to get their work completed before they left. They arranged with their friends to drop off their assignments at class on Friday.

The northbound train left at six on Friday, November 21. Penny had promised to have a buggy in front of their dormitory by five that morning. Mari and Isabelle were waiting by the door when the young man knocked.

Miss Morton jerked the door open and glared at the young man standing there. His smile faded as he backed up.

"I'm—uh—I—I'm here to pick up Miss Merrill and Miss Rankin. Wilson Penny sent me."

Miss Morton pulled the door fully open, and the two young women darted out. The rest of the girls were waving and calling as their friends were helped into the buggy. The wind was blowing, and the weather was cold. They pulled the quilts Miss Morton had insisted they take tighter around themselves.

The young man looked over at them and grinned.

"Percy is my name. Penny said I was to pick you gals up next Saturday when you get back. So, which one of you lives in the Sandhills? That's where my pa was raised."

Isabelle laughed. "That's where I live but I don't know very many people yet. We only moved there this past summer. I was raised in Georgia." She smiled over at Mari.

"Now, if you were from around Cheyenne in the Wyoming Territory, Mari would probably know your family. She has friends and relatives all over that area."

Percy looked at Mari in surprise.

"Do you know Bart Black? He rides for a ranch out south of here a ways. He cowboyed up north somewhere before he took this job."

Mari smiled and nodded. "I do know Bart. He rode for the ranch next to us. Both he and Tobe Benson."

"Well, I'll be. Bart is my cousin. Did you know he married? A little gal from Council Grove. He met her shortly after he moved down here, but it took him some time to get up the nerve to court her."

Mari laughed. "That sounds like Bart. He told me he was leaving Wyoming Territory because there just weren't enough women around Cheyenne. He said if he stayed there, he'd probably never get married.

"How about Tobe? Did he ever marry? I know he was sweet on someone."

Percy chuckled.

"He sure did. He married into the money too, but it likely won't do him any good. He ran off with Royal Sexton's daughter."

Mari's eyes opened wide and she giggled. "Good. I like Tobe. He will treat Millie well too. When did they marry?"

"They married in Council Grove a month or so ago. Her folks were fit to be tied. Millie's old man is a big dog lawyer from Lawrence. Folks call him Royal. I don't know if that's his name or if folks call him that because of how he acts. He sure thinks he's a king.

"Ol' Tobe stayed quiet when Millie's pa laid into him. When Royal finally ran out of air, Tobe smiled an' asked, 'Ya want us to let ya know when yore grandbaby comes, or do ya intend to carry this mad around the rest of yore life?'

"Missus Sexton started cryin' an' Royal started yellin' again. Tobe just lifted Millie up on her horse an' they rode away. Bart said Millie's folks had driven down to the Z Bar Ranch where Tobe worked in a fancy surrey to get her. She refused to go with them though. Tobe invited them to the weddin', an' that's what set old Royal off.

"Tobe is foreman on the Z Bar, an' Bart cowboys there. Bart said they had been pards a long time." Percy snapped the whip over the back of one of the horses before he continued.

"I like Millie. She's a sweet little gal. I'm glad she married Tobe. He's a lot nicer feller than her—than—well, he's just a heck of a nice guy."

Jasper Merrill's Rocking Chair Ranch
Unorganized Territory
West Central Nebraska

CHAPTER 38

No Cure

THE MERRILL'S ARRIVED HOME THURSDAY EVENING, November 20. Evelyn pulled off her cloak and dropped into a chair.

"Goodness, that was a cold ride. And we didn't even have bad weather to fight." She smiled at her husband. "I'm glad we made it home before the snow became heavy. Just look at the size of those flakes now." When she saw how pale Jasper's face was, she hurriedly stood.

"I'll start supper. I want you in bed early tonight. It's been a long trip." Jasper shook his head.

"You go ahead and start supper. I'm going to see if Sam is around." He paused and looked over at Evelyn as he added quietly, "I'm going to make him foreman. He's smart and cow savvy. The men like him too."

Evelyn's lips clamped shut and she turned away so Jasper wouldn't see her cry. Her voice was barely a whisper when she spoke.

"Jasper, that doctor said he might be able to remove the tumor in your stomach."

"Yes, and he also said he wouldn't recommend it." He took his wife by the shoulders and smiled down at her before he pulled her tight.

"I have cancer, Evelyn. Doc Williams said surgery wasn't effective and the treatments aren't either. I'm going to die before long and we need to accept that." He looked over her shoulder and added softly, "Maybe someday there will be a cure for this but one hasn't been found yet."

Evelyn began to cry. and Jasper sat down. He pulled his wife onto his lap.

"Ev, we have to be strong. We have a ranch to run and a daughter to care for."

Evelyn buried her face in Jasper's shoulder. Her sobs became harder, and Jasper patted her back.

"I can't stay here without you, Jasper. I won't. I'll sell this ranch and move east."

"No, Ev. That's why I'm going to make Sam foreman. He will run the ranch and someday, if Isabelle does love him, they can raise their family here."

Evelyn sobbed and shook her head.

"I can't go on without you. I just can't, Jasper."

"Ev, you will stay right here in this house. And when Isabelle marries, you will still live here. Sam would never turn a woman out, especially his wife's mother."

Jasper gently kissed Evelyn. He lifted her up as he stood.

"Why don't you lie down. I'm not hungry and you are exhausted. We'll talk more in the morning after you are rested." Evelyn started to shake her head and Jasper turned her toward their bedroom.

"Go on, Ev. Lie down and I'll join you later."

Once Evelyn had closed the door, Jasper pulled on his heavy coat and gloves. He was just walking toward the door when someone knocked loudly.

Jasper jerked the door open, and Sam grinned at him.

"Evenin', boss. I thought I might check in with you before that Norther hit. I think we are in for a lot of snow."

"Did you pick up the mail while I was gone?"

"Naw. Nobody got up that way. I can go get it now if you want."

"No, I'm sure there is nothing important in there."

"I'll catch me a bite and ride up that way." Sam grinned again before he turned away. "Maybe Isabelle wrote both of us a letter."

Jasper barely smiled. He studied the floor. When he looked up, Sam could see the sadness in his eyes.

"You go ahead. If the weather gets worse, turn around. Let me know either way. Knock even if it's dark in here." Jasper turned around slowly. "I think I'll lie down. It was a long trip."

Sam frowned as he watched his boss. *Jasper almost acts sick. I wonder if this trip was a visit with a doctor instead of a business trip like he told all of us.* He turned toward the door.

"I'll be back in a couple of hours. I'll see you then."

CHAPTER 39

A Horse Called Homer

SAM DIDN'T TAKE THE TIME TO EAT. HE WAS CONVINCED a blizzard was coming and he didn't want to get caught in it.

"Hard snow blowing around can confuse a man. Why I might get lost and end up in Omaha." He grinned to himself as he urged his horse to go faster.

The wind increased before he made it to the mailbox. By the time he turned around, the heavy snow was blowing. The wind made it almost impossible to see. Sam finally gave his horse its head. It was the horse Windeater had given him. It was sure-footed and strong.

"Take me home, old fellow. I'm just about lost, and I don't never get lost." The horse pulled to the right. Sam was sure that was wrong but let the horse lead.

"I hope you know where you're goin', Horse. If you don't, we could both end up frozen to death out here." The horse snorted and continued on into the night.

Sam's hands were numb. He pushed them deep into the pockets of his sheepskin coat, one at a time, to warm them. The wind blew harder and harder. The horse tripped a couple of times, but it maintained the same direction, only deviating when the drifts became too deep. Sam swayed in the saddle. Several times, when the horse staggered and almost went down, he nearly fell off.

Finally, the horse stopped. Sam looked around. At first, he couldn't see anything. Finally, he saw a flicker of light. He tapped the reins against the horses' neck, and they rode that way. It was a light inside the bunkhouse. He turned his horse the opposite direction. He stopped when the shadow of the barn loomed in front of him.

Sam was so cold he almost fell off the horse. He slid to the ground and staggered as he led the horse the last few feet to the barn. When they reached the barn, he pulled the door open. He turned the horse loose and rubbed his hands together. He couldn't feel his ears and gingerly touched one. It was almost hard. He breathed deeply on his hands and held them against his ears.

"Good thing I wrapped that scarf around my face and ears. I shore wouldn't be much to look at if both my ears fell off. I'd be like one of those bob-eared calves, and what would Izzy think then?"

His horse was standing with its head down, breathing heavily. Sam felt the horse's ears. They were hard. He slogged his way across to the bunkhouse. He grabbed the kettle they kept on the stove and poured it into a bucket. He filled the bucket with snow until the water was lukewarm and carried it back to the barn. He used his bandana to apply the warm water to the horse's ears and nose. He continued until the animal's ears were pliable. When he was satisfied, he pulled off the saddle and bridle.

"That's right, Horse. You just stand there. I'll get you warmed up here before long." He grabbed a saddle blanket off a nearby rack and began to rub the horse down. The longer he rubbed the horse, the warmer they both became. Once the horse was dry, he drew a bucket of water out of the well and carried it into the barn. When they had both drank their fill, Sam sat down on the bucket. He pointed at a stall that held grain and hay.

"You go on in there and eat. You can stay in the barn tonight." The horse stared at him. It pulled his hat off with its teeth and tossed it across the barn. Sam ran his hand through his tangled hair and grinned.

"I guess you ain't any worse for the wear. You shore earned yore keep tonight, Horse." He stared at the animal for a moment.

"I reckon you earned yourself a name. I think I'll call you Homer. You didn't get lost, and you brought me right home." The horse looked up and snorted before digging its nose deep in the pan of grain again. Sam chuckled.

He gingerly touched his face. His ears and face were still cold. He dabbed them gently with the wet bandana. "I'd better look in a mirror. If I have white spots, I'm in trouble.

"I'll get that mail in the house first though. Old Jasper might have given up on me—there aren't even any lights on."

Sam stumbled toward the house. He rapped softly on the door. No one came so he opened the door quietly. He pulled off his boots and tiptoed into the kitchen. He laid the mail on the table and dropped into a chair. He wiggled his cold toes and pulled off his socks. Evelyn had water heating, and he poured some into the basin, once again applying it to his cold feet with his bandana. He rubbed and flexed his toes before he put his socks back on.

"A feller just don't realize all the parts on him that can freeze if they get a chance," Sam muttered as he worked the circulation back into his feet. He leaned back in the chair as the wood heat warmed him and was soon asleep.

Jasper awoke around two in the morning. He slipped quietly out of bed and tiptoed into the kitchen. He was startled when he saw Sam asleep at the kitchen table. He added wood to the fire and lit the lamp. Sam was still sleeping so he sat down in the chair and began to pick through the mail. His hands held the telegram envelope a moment before he tore it open. His heart came up in his chest as he read the wire from his daughter.

"Oh, Lord," he whispered under his breath, "Dear Lord."

Sam stirred and opened his eyes. He looked around in confusion. He rubbed his eyes and ran his hand through his hair. When he finally realized where he was, his face turned red. He pulled his hat on.

"Sorry, boss. I guess I fell asleep. I'll be goin' now," and he started to stand.

Jasper's voice was strained when he spoke. Fear showed in his eyes as he looked at Sam.

"Izzy is on her way home. She should be here this evening."

Sam lunged to his feet.

"She can't! No one can get through. I got plumb lost last night. If it hadn't been for my horse, I wouldn't have made it home!" He stared at Jasper and shook his head. "That can't be right. They will shut down the tracks. No trains will run until this storm blows through. She'll be stranded somewhere."

"Well, she's farther south so maybe the snow hasn't started down there yet." Jasper cursed softly. "Izzy is headed into the heart of this blizzard, and we can't get to her."

Sam stood up and shook his head.

"I'll go back out. I'll go to Kirkham's ranch. He can send wires from there. I'll tell him to send one to stop that train."

Jasper stared at Sam. His eyes were bleak when he shook his head.

"You know you'd never make it, Sam. We just need to pray that the railroad and those who are riding it are aware of the weather conditions. Besides, the engineer would never allow women to be left at a siding if no one was waiting."

"Women? Who is coming with her?"

"She said she is bringing her roommate, a Mari Rankin." Jasper studied the telegram again before he looked up at Sam. "Rankin. Is she your relation?"

Sam leaned on the high back of the wooden chair and gave Jasper a slow grin.

"Izzy will be all right. Yeah, Mari is my cousin. She grew up around blizzards. She won't take any unnecessary risks.

"As soon as this storm clears, I'll ride down to Kirkham's. If the gals made it on the northbound train, they were probably dropped there because that rail line just fizzles out in the middle of nowhere." Sam straightened up. He started to say something else but changed his mind. He stared down at the small man in front of him. Jasper looked even frailer tonight. In fact, he looked almost sick.

Sam turned toward the door. He twisted his hat in his hands several times and finally turned around.

"You all right, boss? You look like you're ailin' this mornin'."

CHAPTER 40

Unexpected News

JASPER LOOKED UP. HE POINTED AT A CHAIR. "SIT down, Sam. There is something we need to talk about."

Sam moved slowly toward the table. He dropped down in a chair across from Jasper and looked quizzically at his boss.

"I have cancer, Sam. I know it's in my stomach, but that surgeon up in Cheyenne said it is likely all over." Jasper drummed his fingers on the table for a moment before he looked at Sam again.

"I'm dying. I likely won't live to see next years' hay taken off this place, and I surely won't make it to roundup."

Sam stared at Jasper in shock. "Does Isabelle know?"

"No. I didn't want to tell her anything until I met with that doctor in Cheyenne. And now that I know the prognosis, I don't want to tell her yet. Otherwise, she won't go back to school and this year will be wasted." He frowned and looked away before he continued softly, "Evelyn won't accept it. She wants me to see another doctor or at least have surgery to remove the tumors.

"Doc Williams up in Cheyenne said surgery won't do any good. He told me there aren't good treatments for cancer even though it's been around for a lot of years.

"He pushed and poked all over on me, and his face gave me my answer before he ever talked." Jasper's eyes were clear when he added, "This has been coming on for some time though. That's why I asked Nate to take Isabelle and Evelyn down to Ogallala. With the tracks torn up in places last summer and the train out of service, I knew it would be a three-day buggy ride. I just can't stand to be jostled around like that for very long, for sure not more than an hour or so."

Sam could feel his chest constrict. *This is going to be hard on both of those women. Evelyn leans on Jasper for everything.* He frowned as he thought about the relationship father and daughter had. *Isabelle dotes on her pa. She'll be plumb lost.*

"What can I do to help?"

Jasper smiled slightly as he looked at the earnest young man in front of him.

"I am going to make you foreman, but more than that, you are going to run this place. We can make decisions together for a time, but after I—after I can't, the future of this ranch is going to be in your hands.

"If Isabelle decides you are the man she wants, then you will move right into ownership." Jasper's eyes twinkled slightly as he added, "Of course, if she finds another fellow she likes better, you will be sent down the road."

Sam stared at Jasper in shock for a moment. Then he turned his head away. He rubbed his eyes before he looked back at this man he had hoped someday would be his father-in-law.

"Dadgummit, Jasper. This shore ain't the way I planned this here deal."

Jasper laughed quietly.

"Life is like that, Sam. We can plan all we want, but in the end, it is the Good Lord who moves the chess pieces of life where He wants them." He stood and put out his hand to Sam.

"So you'll accept my offer?"

Sam stepped around the table and gripped Jasper's hand.

"I'll run this place like it's my own but not because I want it to be someday. I'll do it for you and Izzy and Evelyn. I'll try to grow it so those two women have somethin' they can make a good livin' from. And I'll do it for you—for the love you have for your family."

Jasper smiled as he shook Sam's hand.

"You get some sleep." As Sam pulled the door open, Jasper added quietly, "And as soon as this storm breaks, I want you to find my daughter."

CHAPTER 41

A LITTLE REGRET

MARI PEERED OUT THE TRAIN WINDOW AT THE HEAVY snow falling around them. They had left Manhattan early Friday morning, November 21, and it started snowing shortly after the train left the station. She knew they should be close to Ogallala, but she couldn't see well enough to know where they were. She frowned as she turned back to Isabelle.

"You did send your folks a wire telling them we would arrive in Ogallala tonight, right?"

"Yes, but I didn't expect a return message because Father would have received it after he arrived home from his appointment. There is a box close to the railroad where messages and mail are left. Father has someone check it nearly every day. However, there would be no way for him to send a message back.

"He will be waiting at the mailbox though. The train stops there sometimes to refuel. They don't let passengers on, but people can get off. However, there isn't any place to wait so the train doesn't stop unless the flag is up. The engineer knows then that someone is there to meet a passenger and he will stop the train. The end of the tracks isn't much farther. They just stop in the middle of nowhere."

Mari pulled the quilt they were sharing closer as she shivered. Her stomach growled. Isabelle looked over at her and giggled.

"You probably will never come on a trip with me again."

Mari was quiet a moment. She looked over at her friend.

"I think maybe we shouldn't have been so spontaneous. What if your father didn't get the message? We didn't plan for bad weather like we should have. Like *I* should have. You haven't lived out here long, but I know how bad the weather can be this time of year. I should have thought ahead."

"Oh, Mari. We'll be fine. It will all work out." Isabelle pointed at a young family crowded together under a colorful quilt as she whispered, "Besides, we would have been warmer if you hadn't given your quilt to that cold little girl."

"And we wouldn't be hungry if you hadn't given them most of our food," Mari whispered back.

Both young women laughed softly.

"We will look back on this adventure someday and smile. We'll have something to tell our children. Let's rest a little. We should be in Ogallala before long. Penny said we would have about an hour wait before the northbound train leaves. It's going to be late when we meet Father." Isabelle laid her head back against the seat and smiled as she looked out the window.

"I love snow. It rarely snowed in Georgia. Maybe once or twice when I was growing up. Probably more than that but it wasn't often. There are just a few trees but look how beautiful they look. Even the fences have blankets of white covering them. Father bought a sleigh just for weather like this, and I can't wait to ride in it."

Mari stared out the window. The heavy snowfall was beautiful, but her stomach was twisting in knots. *What if Isabelle's parents didn't get the message? What if the train can't get through? Will we be stuck on a train that can't move?* She looked over at the little family in the seat across from them. The young mother and her three small children were clustered together under Mari's large quilt. *I'm glad we brought two quilts. At least that mother can get a little rest. What a long trip for all of them.*

Her mind went to Nate. *Where are you, Nate? Are you out in this weather or are you holed up in some town far away? Maybe getting ready to go dancing.* Tears filled Mari's eyes and she blinked them away. *I think of you often and you don't care enough to even send me a note.*

Friday, November 21
Manhattan, Kansas

CHAPTER 42

A Quick Visit

NATE RODE UP TO THE UNIVERSITY BUILDING HE WAS told housed the women. He was smiling when he knocked on the door. The older woman who jerked it open glared at him. He tipped his hat and grinned at her.

"Mornin', ma'am. I'm looking for Miss Mari Rankin and was told she lived here. I'm in town for a few days and I'd sure like to speak with her."

Miss Morton glared at him.

"Miss Rankin is not here. She left for the holiday."

Nate stared at her. He stuttered a little before he asked, "To Wyoming? She went home to Wyoming? When will she be back?"

"She's gone and that's all I'm going to tell you. You are welcome to leave her a note if you want."

Nate backed up and shook his head. "No, I don't reckon I will. Maybe I'll catch her on another trip." He tipped his hat to Miss Morton and turned to walk down the steps.

"Do you want to at least leave your name?"

"Naw. I'll just stop in another time."

Miss Morton watched the cowboy walk away. He slapped his hat against his leg several times before he jerked it onto his head. She muttered under her breath and finally called after him, "She went home with her roommate to some ranch in Nebraska. She won't be back until late next Saturday evening."

Nate turned around. His face slowly lit up in a grin.

"Isabelle Merrill is her roommate? Well, I'll be.

"I do thank you for that information, ma'am. That is the best news I've heard all day. And my name is Nate." He walked back to the door and handed Miss Morton the flowers he was carrying. "You just as well enjoy these. Please tell Miss Rankin I stopped by." He tipped his hat again and was soon riding away.

Miss Morton stared from the flowers in her hand to the cowboy's departing back. She shook her head as she muttered. "I don't know why that news made him happy." She slammed the door and hollered, "You ladies on lunch duty better have that meatloaf cooking."

Nate chuckled as he rode up the street. "Mari and Sis are roommates. That's just durn good news. And close enough friends that Mari went home with her. By George.

"I have to admit I was worried for a bit there. I thought maybe Mari had found a feller here and went home with him to meet the folks." Nate smiled again. "Yes sir. That was good news." He turned his horse toward one of the cheaper hotels in town.

"I didn't get to see Mari but her and Sis are friends." He grinned as he thought about Sam. "I reckon Sam will be pleased to see both of them."

Nate turned up the collar on his coat and pulled his hat down further when he felt the wind cut through him. "I hope those gals took some blankets along. Trains get cold in the winter and the old-timers are talking about a heavy snow. I for sure hope they make it north before this weather really cuts loose."

The longer Nate rode, the more concerned he became. He was almost to the hotel when he abruptly turned his horse toward the train station.

"I am going to do some checking on those gals. I sure don't want them to get stuck on a stalled train."

CHAPTER 43

"WHICH ONE ARE YOU COURTING?"

Nate laid his railroad pass on the counter.

"I need some information on some passengers. Mari Rankin and Isabelle Merrill. They would have been traveling on the northbound to Ogallala, Nebraska this morning."

The station agent checked his records. He nodded as he looked up at Nate.

"Yes, they boarded this morning. Is there a problem?"

"I'm concerned about the weather. Do you have any information on the status of that route?"

"Everything is good so far. The engineer reported heavy snowfall at his last stop, but he thought he would be able to make it all right."

"How about the northbound train from Ogallala? How do they handle things if the weather is bad?" Nate's face and voice showed his concern.

The agent stared at Nate a moment before he pulled out his manual.

"According to regulations, they have the option of leaving early if they think there is a chance they will have problems. It's more likely they would cancel all together though."

"Are there drop-offs along that route?"

"Yes, we have a passenger drop-off at John Kirkham's Ranch. He has a little shack there that folks wait in. They need special permission or a pass for the train to pick up there, but anyone can be dropped off." The agent looked hard at Nate.

"Kirkham has a telegraph wire right up to his house since he is connected to the railroad. You can send him a message if those gals are to get off there."

Nate nodded as he thought.

"They won't be planning on that, but I'm concerned no one from Merrill's Rocking Chair Ranch will be able to get out if this weather keeps getting worse. Does Merrill have a box you leave his mail in?"

"Yeah, we leave mail several places along that line but not regularly—more like once or twice a week. In weather like this, it could be a week or more before mail is even delivered."

"Can you have those ladies get off at Kirkham's stop and then leave a note for Merrill letting him know where they are?"

The agent frowned as he read the book in front of him.

"Our policy on messages is for railroad business only." He put up his hand and grinned when Nate glared at him. "I'll make an exception this time since the weather is bad." His grin became bigger. "Which one are you courting?" When Nate's face turned red, the agent laughed and pushed a paper toward him.

"You write out what you want sent to Kirkham. Write a second note to be left in the Rocking Chair box. 'Course that message to Merrill won't go through if the track is closed, but I'll make sure it is sent that way as soon as the train is running again."

Nate quickly wrote out two messages. He stared outside for a moment before he looked back at the ticket agent. "If I thought I could catch them, I'd go up there myself."

A machine against the wall clicked for several seconds. The agent rolled his chair over as he waited for it to finish. He read the message quickly and transcribed the morse code before he rolled his chair back.

He held up the message he had written down. "I don't reckon that will work. They are canceling all trains going north that aren't enroute. There won't be any more out today or tomorrow.

"You are sure welcome to check back tonight though. Maybe there will be an answer from Kirkham by then. I'll be here until seven or so, but I won't be in tomorrow morning until nine."

Nate nodded. He thanked the agent and slowly stepped outside. The snow was coming down in large flakes. It was blowing across the street and piling up against the raised boardwalks.

An older woman almost fell as she tried to step from the street to the raised boardwalk. Nate lunged and grabbed her arm.

"Here, let me help you." He looked around but he didn't see anyone waiting for her. "Where do you need to go?"

"I live several miles outside town, but my brother is only a few blocks away. I am going to walk over there. He broke his leg the other day and I want to check on him." She smiled at Nate as he let go of her arm. "My name is Elsie Smith. I guess I should have listened to my husband. He told me it was going to snow." Her smile became bigger, and her face wrinkled around dimples that age had turned to creases. "I told him I was coming in today anyway. I said I'd be home before the weather turned bad or else I'd stay with Penny."

Nate nodded as he held her arm. "The name is Nate Hawkins." He looked up the street and shook his head.

"How about you tell me where he lives and I'll give you a ride. I don't think you can walk in this wind."

The old woman grabbed her hat and tied the strings tighter. She eyed the big, black horse and looked back at Nate.

"Young man, I don't think you can lift me up there, so you are going to have to hoist me up. Help me get my foot in that stirrup and then give me a push. I'll just hike these skirts up."

Nate lined Demonio up against the boardwalk. He helped the woman get her foot in the stirrup. He was trying to figure out where to put his hands when Elsie looked around.

"Just lift the biggest part. There's no way to do this delicately."

Nate chuckled and heaved. Elsie fell across the saddle and finally was able to lift her right leg over the cantle. She settled herself in and put her hand down for the bags she had been carrying.

"You hand me those. You are going to have your hands full trying to walk into that wind. Just turn left at the next street. Penny's house is two blocks up on the left side."

Nate led Demonio up the street. He had his hat pulled down as far as it would come but the snow was still beating him in the face. He had left his gloves in his warbag, and he was regretting that. He beat his hands against his legs to warm them up. When they reached the house, he led Demonio up to the porch. He took the woman's bags and reached up his arms.

"If you can swing your right leg over in front of you and slip down, I'll catch you."

When the woman was once again on the ground, she laughed.

"Young man, would you like to come in and warm up? You can even stay for dinner. Penny is doing his best to get back to the livery, but the doctor wants him to stay off his leg for a time."

When Nate started to shake his head, Elsie nodded behind him.

"Whatever you had planned for the day isn't going to happen, but you still need to eat." She pointed to a shed behind the house.

"Penny keeps a little hay and grain in there if you want to put your horse up. Then come on inside and I'll make some coffee."

CHAPTER 44

WILSON PENNY

THE SNOW WAS BLOWING HARD WHEN NATE KNOCKED on Penny's door. The old man yelled, and Elsie opened the door quickly.

"Come inside, Nate. I think we are going to have a first-class blizzard if this snow keeps up. And you don't have to take your boots off."

Nate shook his head and grinned.

"I reckon I'd better. I'd never hear the end of it if my sister-in-law found out I tramped snow all over someone's house after I was invited in for a meal." After he pulled off his boots, he put out his hand to the old man sitting in a chair with his leg propped up.

"Penny, we've met before. Nate Hawkins. I ride that big black horse you like."

The old man peered at Nate and slowly grinned. He grimaced as he tried to move his leg and then the grin returned.

"Miguel Montero's horse. I recognized it when you rode in that first time. I didn't try to rub it down when Miguel rode it, and I still don't. Kind of like Badger McCune's mule. I never did mess with that animal either." His pale blue eyes were hard as they stared at Nate. "You must have been a mighty good friend. Miguel never would have given that horse away while he was alive."

"I always liked old Demon. When Miguel died, his sister gave me his horse." Penny didn't answer so Nate continued, "Miguel was my brother-in-law. His sister married my older brother in '79.

"I knew him before Merina and Gabe married though. Miguel helped trail a herd of John Kirkham's cattle north from Dodge City up to Ogallala, Nebraska. His brother, Angel, joined us south of here in the Indian Territory. Merina and her little sister, Emilia, were on that drive too.

When Penny raised an eyebrow, Nate shrugged.

"Merina is a top hand. She prefers working with Gabe over some of the things women are expected to do. He likes her help, so it works. She's a good cook too so that makes everyone happy."

Nate's face was curious as he asked Penny, "So how did you know Miguel? He got around some, but I didn't know he spent much time in Manhattan."

The old man shook his head.

"I didn't meet him here. I met him in Ellinwood. I used to run the harness shop there under the street. Miguel always stopped in when he was passin' through. I liked that kid too. I always hoped he'd settle down one day. Maybe find him a woman who would see the good inside him." Penny shook his head and frowned.

"Too bad about him dyin'. Just a fluke accident is what it was. Anybody who knew Miguel wouldn't believe he'd get runned over by horses. He did though. 'Course he saved those little kids who was crossin' the street. Funny thing was, they was one of his old pard's kids. Miguel would have done anything for a friend. Kids too. Put the two together an' he was determined to save their lives no matter what." Penny sat quietly for a time. He shook his head before he spoke again.

"Some of the folks who were there after Miguel died said he left a wife up north somewhere. I didn't figure that was true though. It would have taken a heck of a woman to slow that cowboy down. Besides, once he committed to a wife and marriage, he wouldn't a left her. That boy was wild, but he was true-blue on the inside."

Nate was quiet for a moment. He slowly nodded. His voice was a little sad when he spoke again.

"Miguel did marry. He was happy too. His wife was pregnant.

"I was driving the buggy she was riding in when we were attacked. We were headed out to my brothers and some fellows came up from behind. I tried to outrun them but we couldn't. I was hoping our riders would come up on us if we got farther down the road, but the buggy hit a rock and we had to jump. I tried to cushion Flory as much as I could, but we hit hard. Then those fellers who were chasing us rode right over the top of us. I threw myself over Flory, but she was hurt bad. Everybody, including the doc, thought she would die.

"Miguel left. He went after the man who was responsible. He got him too. He didn't know Flory was alive until he got to Ellinwood several weeks later."

Nate's voice was soft as he added, "He was on his way home when that accident happened. The three fellows with him brought him up to Cheyenne. They told us what happened."

"So the little gal lived?"

"She did but she lost the baby. She married again though. Nice fellow too. He was a friend of Miguel's.

"Merina said Miguel was watching over Flory. She said he picked the man he wanted his wife to spend the rest of her life with. In her last letter, Merina said they were mighty happy. They have a couple of kids now.

"I reckon Merina was right. Miguel is taking care of things from up there." Nate pointed toward the sky and grinned.

Mrs. Smith rushed into the room.

"Penny, I am going to feed you right here. And Nate, you can eat in here or come out to the table, your choice."

"I reckon I'll eat in here. I wouldn't mind chewing the fat a little longer with Penny here." He grinned and took the plate the older woman offered him. He smelled it before he set it on his lap.

"This sure smells good, Mrs. Smith. I do miss home-cooked food."

"You are welcome and call me Elsie."

CHAPTER 45

FRIENDS IN COMMON

THE TWO MEN ATE QUIETLY FOR A TIME. NATE FINALLY paused and looked over at Penny.

"You said you were familiar with Badger McCune's mule. I reckon you must know Badger too."

Penny chuckled and nodded.

"I've known Badger a long time, nigh as long as I've known Martha. I was sure surprised when they married up though. Never saw that comin'.

"I helped out some at the livery before I bought it from Cappy Livingston. I reckon your brother talked of him some. They was friends from way back."

Nate nodded. "I know Cappy well. He married a widow woman who lived east of Cheyenne by the name of Margaret Endicott. In fact, Merina and Angel bought her ranch when she moved to town. Angel lives there now with his wife. Her name is Anna, and she is Flory's sister."

Penny nodded. He stopped chewing and smiled as he looked out the window. Nate followed his eyes but could see nothing because of the blowing snow.

"Yep, I was there the day ol' Mule took care a Lumpy. Lumpy Smith he called himself but he warn't no Smith. He were a worthless turd who tooked that name. He were a Hollister. His kin made a livin' stealin' from folks when they left Saint Louis on their way West.

"I ain't sure how he lived as long as he did but ol' Mule took care of 'im in '68. That's the first time I met Lance an' Molly Rankin. I didn't actually meet 'em. I just knowed who they was 'cause they was pointed out to me." The old man turned his pale eyes back toward Nate.

"How is they? I reckon they have a passel of kids by now."

Nate laughed and nodded. "Five the last I knew. Sam is their oldest and he's my best friend. We met shortly after Gabe bought our place.

"We both like to fish, and we spent a lot of time together. In fact, we just parted company this year when we took different jobs." Nate's eyes were intense as he added, "He's sweet on a little gal who just moved down here to go to college. Isabelle Merrill. She's roommates with Sam's cousin, Mari Rankin.

"I stopped in to see them today and found out they'd headed for Nebraska. I wanted to make sure they stopped at John Kirkham's with the weather getting so bad. All the trains north were canceled shortly after they left, or I might have tried to catch them. I sure don't want them caught on a stalled train in one of those Nebraska northers.

"I was just leaving the train station when I met your sister."

Penny's old eyes twinkled as he stared at Nate.

"Sweet on that little Rankin gal, are ya?"

Nate turned a deep red and stuttered before he looked away. When he looked back at Penny, his face showed no expression.

"They are both my friends. I just wanted to make sure they were safe."

Penny laughed wickedly. "Shore ya did—'cause one is your pard's gal an' you is sweet on the other."

Nate finally laughed and shrugged. "She's not my girl but I wouldn't mind it if she was." He grinned as he added, "I s'pose you know the two of them well."

"Shore do. I make it point to know all the good-lookin' gals if they be nice. And those two little gals are cream of the crop. I stay away from the high steppers though." He frowned at Nate.

"Ya stopped in today? I hope ya left a note. Gals like that, ya know. They like letters 'cause they can read 'em time an' again.

"That little Mari is somethin' special. If I was fifty years younger, I'd spark her my own self." Penny grinned at Nate and both men laughed.

They visited a while longer before Nate stood.

"Elsie—Penny—thank you for the meal and the good visit. I need to get down to the train station and check on those girls again before I turn in for the night."

Friday, November 21
Ogallala, Nebraska

CHAPTER 46

GET OFF WHERE?

MARI AND ISABELLE GATHERED THEIR BAGS WHEN THE train blew its whistle. The conductor hollered, "Last Stop! Ogallala!"

The young mother across from them folded Mari's quilt and handed it back to her.

"Thank you so much for sharing your food and your wonderful quilt. It's beautiful. Did you make it?"

"I helped. The women in our neighborhood get together once a month and sew. Mother let me pick the colors and cut the fabric, but we all pieced and quilted it."

The woman smiled and put out her hand.

"I didn't even introduce myself. My name is Melva Boone. I went down to Kansas to visit my mother. She hadn't met our littlest one yet. This weather set in so quickly. I was completely unprepared."

"It was wonderful visiting with you too. I'm Mari Rankin and my friend is Isabelle Merrill. Where are you headed now? Is your husband meeting you here?"

"No, we live in North Platte. My husband works in a bank there. I'm hoping we can go on east this evening. Otherwise, I'll need to get a room here." Concern showed on Melva's face. "You should do that too.

That route north of Ogallala is quite desolate. There aren't any organized towns, and the rails just end in the country somewhere. You certainly don't want to get stuck out there in the hills."

Isabelle smiled. "Oh, my father is expecting us. We will be fine." She put out her hand. "It was nice to visit with you, Melva."

Just then, the doors were pulled open, and men stepped forward to help the women down the slippery steps. The snow was heavy, and drifts were everywhere. A man standing on the platform was shouting, "I have a message for Miss Mari Rankin and Miss Isabelle Merrill! Miss Rankin and Miss Merrill! You have changes in your travel plans!"

The two young women paused and Isabelle laughed.

"I told you it would all work out. Father is probably waiting for us somewhere. Hurry! Let's find out where he is!"

Mari and Isabelle rushed down the steps of the train and onto the platform.

"I am Miss Merrill and this is Miss Rankin. You have a message for us? Where is my father?"

"I don't know where your pa is, but I have a message here from a feller by the name of Hawkins. Ya both are to get on the northbound train pronto. It's leavin' shortly. And ya need to get off at Kirkham's rail shack. He'll have some men there to meet ya."

Isabelle stared at him for a moment and then shook her head.

"We can't do that. My father—"

"Isabelle, we should follow Nate's instructions. He would only send a message like this with good reason. Afterall, he now works for the railroad. Come, let's find that northbound train." Mari smiled at the man who had called to them.

"May I have that note, please?"

The surprised man thrust the note at her and turned away. As the women looked around the platform in confusion, the man looked over his shoulder.

"You need to head that way," he hollered as he pointed, "and make it quick. They held that train for you folks headed north."

As Mari and Isabelle ran the direction the man had pointed, they saw Melva Boone. She was looking up at a smiling man. He was holding one of their little girls. Mari heard him say, "When this weather started to move in, I caught the next train. I didn't want you out here by yourself."

Mari smiled as she ran. *Nate didn't meet us, but he made sure we were safe. Thank heavens for you, Nate Hawkins.*

Friday, November 21
Manhattan, Kansas

CHAPTER 47

A Full-Blown Blizzard

WHEN NATE STEPPED OUTSIDE, HE HAD TO HOLD the door to keep it from slamming back against the house. He could barely see the outline of the little shed and he picked his way carefully through the snow.

Demonio nickered at him when he pulled the door to the little lean-to open. Nate tightened the girth and petted the horse before he mounted.

"We don't have far to go, old fella, and then you will be in a nice, warm livery. And you'll probably be there for at least two days. I'm guessing it will be that long before the trains are running all their routes again. Who knows though. Those snow-busting plows can slog their way through some mighty deep drifts."

When Nate finally arrived at the train station, all the lights were off. However, a note pushed over a nail. He pulled it off to read it.

The gals made it to Ogallala. That train left early and was headed north. The fellow who was to pass on your note said he caught them. He said they agreed to get off at Kirkham's. Hope this is all good news. Jake

Nate stared at the note. He took a deep breath before he cursed softly.

"I'm glad they made it that far and that they got my note. Still, I wish they weren't out in this weather." His scowl became deeper and he muttered, "What was Mari thinking to run off like this? And to head north with a storm coming." Demonio snorted and Nate finally grinned. "At least she listened to me."

Nate brushed his horse down. He gave him feed and water as he talked to him. When he finished, he walked to the doorway of the livery.

"There is a hotel just across the street. I'm going to sleep in a warm bed tonight. Who knows what tomorrow will bring."

Nate grabbed his bedroll and forced his way across the street. He was out of breath when he finally made it to the stairs leading up to the hotel.

He was once again frowning when he finally made it inside.

"Those dadgum girls. It is plumb hair-brained to go out in this weather. And I don't care if the weather was good when they left. Traveling this time of year is always chancy." He was still frowning when he stomped up to the desk.

"I need a room. I'm alone so it can be your smallest one."

"I only have one room left and it is a small room. We normally keep it for staff, but I am allowed to rent it out in emergencies. Your name, sir?"

"Nate Hawkins. And I'll be here until the tracks north are open."

"Very well, Mr. Hawkins. I will make a note of that. The dining room is closed for the night. We usually open at six in the morning but the women who work here live out of town. The Wolf House Boarding House will be your best bet for breakfast.

"Oh, and no bathing facilities will be available here until we are fully staffed. Of course, the bath house down by the laundry will open early tomorrow as usual."

Nate nodded and paid the man. As he turned away, the clerk called after him, "Not to be rude, but I hope your stay here will be short, Mr. Hawkins."

"I hope so too," Nate replied with a chuckle. He waved at the smiling clerk as he climbed the stairs to the small room tucked behind a turn in the stairwell. The room was barely big enough for the bed that was squeezed inside it, but Nate didn't care. He dropped down on the bed and was soon asleep. He awoke at midnight and again at three in the morning. He was convinced the women were in trouble and there wasn't a thing he could do.

"Merina would tell me to say a prayer. I reckon that's all I can do from here." Nate followed her advice. By six the next morning, he was in the bathhouse and by six-thirty, he was eating at the Wolf House. The food was good, but he was too antsy to enjoy it.

Friday, November 21
Northbound Train
Ogallala, Nebraska

CHAPTER 48

AN UNPLANNED STOP

ISABELLE AND MARI WERE OUT OF BREATH WHEN THEY reached the northbound train. Several of the male passengers stood and grabbed the young women's bags as they climbed up the steps.

The cowboy who had taken Mari's bags smiled down at her.

"How far north are y'all goin'? I shore am glad I decided to take this here train."

Isabelle paused but Mari laughed.

"We are getting off at John Kirkham's rail shack wherever that is. Do you think we need to tell someone since we won't be going all the way to the end of the tracks?"

"You can but the engineer will know. Kirkham will have a lamp lit in the shack. 'Sides, you'll see his team an' sleigh there."

"What ranch do you ride for? Not that I will know it. I'm not familiar with the ranches in this area," Mari asked as she sat down with her valise on her lap.

"I ride for Bill Cassidy's CC Ranch. His place is on north of Kirkham's ranch a piece. In fact, I was thinkin' on gettin' off there with this bad weather." He grinned at the two young women. "I'm thinkin' harder on that now." He put out his hand.

"Windy Smith is my name. The three galoots grinnin' their fool heads off over there are Baker, Bixby, an' Tray.

"What are you ladies' names? We jist as well git acquainted since we have us a little time."

Isabelle smiled. "I'm Isabelle Merrill and this is Mari Rankin. Her family has a ranch up in Wyoming."

Windy's eyebrow shot up. "Rankin? I know a Sam Rankin from up that way. He be a relation of yours?"

Mari nodded happily. "Sam is my cousin. He works on the Rocking Chair now. Isabelle's pa owns that ranch."

Windy grinned as he looked from one woman to the other.

"Well, I'll be. Sam's girl cousin an' the gal he's sweet on, both on the same train—an' us to be snowed in alongside 'em."

Isabelle blushed. Even though it was dark inside the train, the men knew Windy had embarrassed her and they laughed.

Before long, every single man on the train was crowded around the two young women. They all vied for the open seats beside Mari and Isabelle. Windy dropped down by Isabelle and Tray won the other open seat by knocking his competition out of the way. The other men weren't deterred though. They were soon back and part of the conversation.

"So what other cowboys do you gals know who we might have ridden with?" Tray grinned as he leaned closer.

"Oh, I have friends and cousins all over who cowboy. Nate Hawkins was our neighbor south of Cheyenne. He used to cowboy for Cassidy and Kirkham so you probably all know him." All four cowboys nodded and grinned. Mari smiled and her brown eyes sparkled.

"As far as who else I know? Angel Montero, George Spurlach or Spur as we all call him, Tobe Benson, Bart Black—do you want me to go on?"

Windy leaned around Isabelle. His eyes were intense as he asked, "I heard Miguel Montero was run over by a horse and died down in Kansas. I knew that couldn't have happened. Miguel is a savvy horseman. How is he?"

Mari's voice was soft when she answered.

"I'm not sure what you heard, but he did die in Ellinwood, Kansas. He was trying to save some kids from being run over. The team he was holding spooked and ran over him."

The train screeched and jerked as the engineer applied the brakes. Both women nearly flew out of their seats. The cowboys grabbed their arms and held them until the train slowed enough for them to steady themselves. As they all looked around, the conductor appeared in their car.

"Sorry about that, folks. We are going to have to stop. The snow is too deep to push through, and we are starting to spin.

"Kirkham's rail shack isn't too far up the tracks." He looked at the cowboys. "Maybe these fellows will give you a ride. Otherwise, you can stay on the train and go back down to Ogallala. That's what the rest of the passengers are planning to do."

Both women stared at the conductor. Mari raised an eyebrow.

"How far is 'not too far?'"

"A half mile, maybe less. You'll want to bundle up though. That snow is deep and it's going to take some slogging to get through it. The wind is bad too.

"'Course these here fellows are used to this kind of weather. They know the lay of the land too." He looked around at the cowboys. "You fellows will make sure these ladies get to the rail shack, won't you?"

The men nodded in agreement and the rail car was soon a flurry of activity. The cowboys raced to the livestock cars and saddled their horses. Arrangements were made as to what horses the women would ride. It was decided to put them behind the two riders with the largest horses. That was Windy and Bixby. Bixby was the quietest of all the cowboys. He reminded Mari of her cousin, Paul.

Isabelle was concerned about riding astride in a dress. She whispered softly, "Our legs will show, Mari. My mother will be mortified when she hears of this."

Mari shrugged. "It can't be helped. We have on wool stockings, so they won't see much. Besides, it's dark. My biggest concern is getting cold."

Everyone was soon bundled up. Once Windy and Bixby were mounted, one of the riders lifted Isabelle up behind Windy's saddle. Mari held up a quilt and Tray wrapped it around Isabelle.

"Keep that wrapped tight. You southern gals get cold easy, and I don't want Sam mad at me just 'cause you are missin' some fingers!"

Mari laughed as Baker lifted her up. She grabbed the saddle strings and pulled until she was settled behind Bixby. Tray wrapped the second quilt around her.

Baker and Tray grabbed the women's travel bags, and the little group was on its way.

Windy called back to the conductor, "Send a message to Kirkham once you get back to Ogallala. He needs to know we have the women in case we don't make connections. And make sure you drop that letter in Merrill's box when this line gets broken open."

Isabelle looked over at Mari. She could barely see her face under the heavy scarf.

"My parents are going to be so worried," she whispered. Mari didn't hear her. The wind whistled and the snow blew wildly as the group moved out.

CHAPTER 49

Too Cold

ISABELLE WAS SHIVERING VIOLENTLY. WINDY TURNED around in his saddle.

"You all right, Miss Isabelle? You shore are shakin' back there." When Isabelle didn't answer, Windy pulled off his gloves and felt for her hands. She had no gloves on, and her hands were nearly frozen to the saddle strings. He hauled his horse to a stop abruptly.

"Where are yore gloves?" He lifted the quilt and grabbed her leg.

"For Pete's Sake, Miss Isabelle! You barely even have any stockings on! No wonder you're a freezin' back there.

"Tray! Haul her off the back of my horse and roll her up in that quilt. Then hand her up here to me."

Isabelle said nothing as Tray wound the heavy quilt around her. He handed her up to Windy and the worried cowboy opened his heavy coat before he pulled her close to his body.

"Now you hang on, Miss Isabelle. We don't have much farther to go."

Mari stared at her friend in surprise before she frowned. *I told her to put on wool stockings and heavy shoes. I guess I just assumed she would do it.*

The snow was coming down so hard they couldn't even see three feet in front of them. Tray and Baker rode close to the railroad tracks to keep everyone on course.

Tray raised his hand. He shouted over the wind, "The water tanks are just in front of us. That means the rail shack should be just west a ways."

The four riders turned their horses to the west. They almost ran into the shack when it appeared in front of them. Tray slid off his horse and put out his arms for Isabelle.

Baker dropped to the ground too. "I'll get that fire started," he hollered above the wind.

Bixby lifted Mari down. He gathered the reins of his and Baker's horses. He put out his hand to Windy.

"Give me your horse. I'll put them in the lean-to." He paused a moment as he looked toward the west. "Think we should pull the saddles off?"

Windy shook his head. "No. We don't have anything here to rub them down. Besides, the railroad should have sent Kirkham a message. He will be headed here with his sleigh." He frowned as he stared into the darkness. *If he got it. I don't see a sleigh, and I don't hear no sleigh bells neither. I sure hope we don't have to make a trip to Kirkham's on our own in this storm. I'm not sure we'll make it.*

"I'll make sure that big lamp is lit so he can see it."

When Windy opened the door, he could see Mari at work on Isabelle's arms and feet. She was softly scolding her friend as she cried.

She looked up at Windy as a tear ran down her face.

"This is my fault. I knew better than to leave with a storm coming in. And I should have made sure she was dressed warm enough." A sob caught in her throat as she added, "Isabelle doesn't own any wool stockings. She doesn't even know what they are." She stared down at her friend briefly before she looked over at Windy again.

"I need a pitcher of warm water. I need to warm her up slowly." All three men grabbed whatever they could find that would hold snow and rushed outside. They were soon back with buckets and pitchers of fresh snow. The fire was barely started so they set the smallest pitcher on the coals.

When the water was lukewarm, Mari dipped her bandana in it and touched the water to Isabelle's face, arms, and feet. She dipped Isabelle's limp hands into the pitcher and held them there until she could feel them getting warmer. Color slowly began to come back into Isabelle's face.

"Get that bucket just a little warmer. We need to warm her up gradually."

Isabelle finally opened her eyes. They were full of tears as she looked up at Mari.

"I'm sorry. I dropped my gloves as I was being lifted onto the horse. I thought they were just lost in the quilt. When I realized they were gone, I didn't want to say anything."

"No, it's my fault you weren't prepared. I forgot you aren't used to winter weather. Now hush while I warm your legs. Windy is making coffee. That will help warm you too." Mari's voice was soft as she dabbed water on her friend's feet and legs.

Friday, November 21
John Kirkham's
JK Connected Ranch
Kieth County, Nebraska

CHAPTER 50

AN URGENT MESSAGE

A COWBOY SLOGGED THROUGH THE SNOW AND BEAT on the door of John Kirkham's ranch headquarters.

"Boss, this message must have come through this afternoon. Wedge found it just now. The boys are hitching up the sleigh. We'll head over to the railroad shack as soon as you give the word."

John Kirkham unfolded the telegraph. He saw Nate's name at the bottom and read it quickly.

John, Isabelle Merrill and friend on northbound train. Weather bad. Will be left at your shack between 8 and 10 tonight. Message to be left in Jasper's box when train can make it that far. Not sure he knows daughter is coming.
  Nate Hawkins

Kirkham let out a low curse.

"Ann, get my coat! Milt, we are leaving as soon as I send out a message." He cursed again as he looked at his watch. "It's eight now! They could already be there!"

Kirkham punched out a message.

"Wedge, you wait for an answer. Hopefully, I'll have it before I leave. If not and plans have changed, run us down.

"Get those lamps lit on the sleigh." He turned around and hollered, "Ann, I need—"

Ann thrust some quilts into his hands along with a jar of coffee and some jerky.

"I'm not sure if those girls brought any food along with them. They may be hungry. In fact, I'm going to fix something now so they have a warm meal when they arrive." She waved her hands. "I'll have the men wrap some hot stones from the fireplace and put them on the floor of the sleigh.

"Go on now. I'll have things ready when you get back."

Kirkham tossed the quilts in the back seat of the sleigh. He carefully wrapped the coffee in the blanket on his lap. Two men dropped some heavy stones wrapped in blankets behind the seat.

"Milt, you drive. Bandy, you come along too. Let's go."

Some of the hands came out of the bunkhouse and watched the sleigh cut through the snow as Milt pushed the team up the lane.

"What's goin' on?" Ringer was one of the new hands. He had been trying to fix his socks when the message from Nate arrived.

Biggs grinned at him.

"That Merrill girl and one of her friends are headed this way. The train is dropping them at the rail shack. They are going to be snowed in here for a time. Our lucky day!"

"Well, shoot. I guess I'd better take a bath." Ringer turned toward the door and Biggs pushed by him.

"I get first water!"

The bunkhouse was loud for the next half hour as the hands hauled in snow to melt. Every tub of water was used three times before it was dumped and there was lots of negotiating about who went first. Ringer was low man on the totem pole, and he was the last one in line—with fourth water.

CHAPTER 51

Rescued!

THE STRANDED PASSENGERS HAD BEEN AT THE SHACK for almost an hour when Tray stepped to the dirty window and looked out. "I think I hear someone coming." He pulled the door open and peered toward the west. A voice could just barely be heard above the wind.

"Hello, the shack! Are there two gals in there? I have orders to get them back to the ranch pronto."

Tray hollered back in response.

Kirkham's sleigh swung around in front of the shack. He jumped down and rushed through the door. He leaned over Isabelle for a moment. His eyes were concerned but he smiled and patted her cheek.

"You'll be just fine, gal." He wheeled around to the men who were standing there. "Now don't stand around with your thumbs up your—don't—don't just stand there! Get these gals loaded. There are a couple of hot stones on the floor in the back seat. At least they were hot when we left home. Put the gals back there and get their feet on those rocks. Three of you fellows ride back there with them. Squeeze in close to keep them warm. Wrap them together in a quilt so they can use each other's body heat and throw more blankets over them.

"The rest of you fellows squeeze in up here. You'll be a little warmer in this sleigh than on horseback. Tie those horses on and let's get back to the ranch before we can't find our way." He looked from the shack to the lamp beside it and hollered, "Scatter those coals in the snow and put out that lamp before you leave."

It was over an hour back to the ranch. Isabelle finally quit shivering and went to sleep about fifteen minutes before they arrived.

The snow quit sometime during the night and the morning sun sparkled on the heavy blanket of snow. Kirkham's cowboys grumbled as they dug their way out of the bunkhouse and shoveled their way across to the barn. Cassidy's CC riders waved at the disgruntled cowboys as they rode out of the yard.

"See you fellers another time." Windy stopped and grinned at them. "Too bad you didn't get to take no midnight ride with those two little gals. We was all cuddled up, close-like in the back of that sleigh.

"Now you'll be out all day playin' nursemaid to Kirkham's cows, so you won't even see 'em. An' I'm a bettin' Sam will show up here tomorrow to take 'em both home with 'im."

One of the cowboys who was scooping snow cursed loudly. He made a snowball and pitched it at Windy. The ornery cowboy ducked. The four riders were laughing as they pushed their horses through the snow and headed north.

Kirkham appeared in the doorway. "Those CC cowboys gone?"

Milt nodded. "They just pulled out."

"Good. Sam will stop there to swap horses. He should get to Cassidy's about the same time as they do. After he talks with them, he'll know to come on down here." He looked toward the building that housed the telegraph machine. "Tell Wedge to check for new messages. I need to know when they expect the rail line to be open north of here. And leave a message saying we have the women here.

"If that train's not up and running by tomorrow, I don't know what I'll do. Those two little gals are going to want to get home, but I don't really want to send them all the way in a sleigh, especially as cold as Miss Merrill was."

Both men looked up at the sound of banging in the distance. Loud ramming noises as well as locomotives stopping and starting could be heard. Wedge grinned.

"No concern there, boss. The Bucker plows are out. They'll have that line open in no time. Shoot. Ol' Sam will be here tomorrow for sure."

"Get my sleigh cleaned up. I'll have Ann pull out some fresh quilts. I'll send that sleigh and a team with Sam. That way, he can take those gals the rest of the way home with no delays."

Kirkham stepped back inside and slammed the door.

Milt thought a moment. He shook his head and was soon headed to the barn. He hollered at Wedge as he passed the small building.

"Send a message. Let Ogallala know we picked up the women. The boss wants to make sure there's room in a car to haul his sleigh and a team of horses. If that operator argues with you, tell him to take it up with Kirkham."

Wedge chuckled and Milt continued on to the barn.

"Ol' Kirkham seems to pull a lot of weight with the rail company. That's not a bad thing neither. It is shore goin' to help us out with this deal."

Milt soon had the sleigh pulled out. He wiped off the seats and caught two fresh horses. He stared at them a moment before he turned them loose and caught two large mules.

"I think this here is going to be more of a mule trip. In fact, I might just catch the other two. That will give Sam four pulling in case the drifts are even worse than I think they'll be.

"You mules get on in the barn. You can take it easy and eat good today. I reckon Sam will be here by daylight if we have a moon tonight."

Milt was right. Sam rode in Sunday morning just as the hands were dragging out of the bunkhouse.

CHAPTER 52

A Sight for Sore Eyes

SAM PUT HIS HANDS ON THE HORN OF HIS SADDLE AS he grinned at the men in front of him.

"Mornin', boys! Whatcha doin' sleepin' in this mornin'? Ain't you got no work to get done or is Kirkham gettin' soft in his old age?"

Wedge tucked in his shirt as he stood in the bunkhouse door. He nodded to the east as he spoke.

"The snow is cleared partway north. The railroad boys said the first train would leave Ogallala tomorrow morning at seven. If all goes well, they'll be back on schedule by Tuesday afternoon."

Sam nodded and looked toward the house.

His eyes were concerned when he looked back at Wedge.

"Windy said they had a hard time of it gettin' to the rail shack. Ever'body alright this mornin'?"

Wedge shrugged. "I ain't seen those gals since they got here. Ann fussed over 'em all day yesterday, an' Kirkham ain't left the house.

"You'd think they was family the way he's actin'."

Sam grinned again at the cowboy in front of him.

"I don't know. I reckon I'd find a reason to stay in the house all day with a couple of good-lookin' women if I had the chance. You likely would too."

Wedge chuckled. "Yep, I shore would. We barely got a look at 'em since they come in late. Kirkham hustled 'em right into the house.

"Biggs said Miss Isabelle was mighty cold. I ain't heard if she got any frostbite but Kirkham was worried some accordin' to Bandy."

Sam slid off his horse and led it to the barn.

"I reckon I'll go see." He glanced back at Wedge. "I almost got stuck out in that storm my own self. It was a mean one. If my horse hadn't known the way home, I'm not sure I'd a made it."

He started to walk away but turned back slowly. "Does Bandy still keep that jar of leeches in the bunkhouse?"

"Yeah. We try to throw 'em out from time to time but he won't let us. We told 'im if those slimy worms ever get loose, we'll shoot *him* full a holes an' cover 'im up with 'em."

Sam chuckled and Wedge grinned back. Bandy appeared in the door bunkhouse door and Biggs was grinning over his shoulder. Sam nodded at them. He spoke quietly as he looked from them to Wedge.

"I appreciate what you fellers did. Those two little gals are mighty important to me."

"Aw, we didn't do nothin'. It was the CC riders. They's the ones who had the hard part on that ride. All we done was drive Kirkham's sleigh and make sure those hosses stayed on course.

"We couldn't foller our own tracks home though. They was covered in snow an' drifted over—an' we didn't waste no time loadin' those gals up neither. We let the hosses find their way.

"It's a mighty lucky thing those CC boys was on that train. That an' ol' Nate sendin' a message tellin' those gals to get off at the shack. Miss Isabelle didn't want to, but Miss Mari was mighty insistent. That's what Tray told me anyhow."

Sam listened closely and finally grinned.

"Nate sent a wire, did he? He's becomin' a regular railroad tycoon, ain't he?" He paused as he looked at Bandy.

"Why don't you hold up a bit before you head out. We might need your leeches today."

Bandy studied his friend and slowly nodded.

"I'll pull out my jar of hungry ones. Any idea how many you'll need?"

Sam shook his head. "I'm hopin' not any but I want to be ready. I'll leave the number up to you."

"I'll be ready whenever you holler." Bandy hurried back into the bunkhouse and began to rummage around under his bunk.

Sam pulled his saddle off his horse and rubbed it down. He dumped some grain into a trough and pitched a little hay.

"You rest up now. If we can catch that train, I might leave you here. Otherwise, we'll have some hard ridin' in front of us." Sam frowned and shook his head, "And I sure hope that ain't the case."

He patted the horse's back and tromped his way to the house. He had just put up his hand to knock on the door when it was jerked open.

Isabelle stood there with her hand on her chest. Her eyes were wide as she stared at Sam. He grinned at her.

"Hello, Izzy. You shore are a sight for sore eyes." He opened his arms and Isabelle rushed into them.

Mari appeared and Sam looked up. He held out one arm and Mari ran toward him.

He hugged them both as he murmured, "I shore am glad you gals are alright. I was plumb worried."

CHAPTER 53

FROSTBITE

MARI PULLED SAM INTO THE KITCHEN AND PUSHED him into a chair. Isabelle sat down beside him. Ann turned around from the stove.

"I almost have breakfast ready. I made extra in case you arrived this morning." She laughed softly and her eyes sparkled. "Father said you'd be here at first light, and he was right."

Sam grinned. He looked from Mari to Isabelle. His eyes lingered on Isabelle the longest.

"You gals are both okay? No frostbite?"

Isabelle blushed as she looked away.

"Not me but Isabelle has a little on her hands and feet. Ann treated her right away and her toes look much better today." Mari's voice was soft when she answered.

Sam's eyes dropped to Isabelle's legs, and she turned a deep red as she slid them under her chair.

Mari frowned slightly. "I didn't ask enough questions. I told Isabelle to wear wool stockings, but I didn't ask if she had any—which she didn't. She didn't even know what they were. Then she dropped her gloves.

"I'm glad we only had a short distance to ride. The wind was horrible. Windy and the rest of the CC riders had a hard time of it."

Sam turned Isabelle's hand over and studied the small blisters on the top of her hand. He was quiet as he looked at them. "How are your toes?"

Isabelle shrugged her shoulders. "They were cold, but they are fine."

Sam lifted the edge of Isabelle's dress and stared at her feet. He leaned over to look closer.

"One big toe looks swollen to me, but I can't tell with stockings." When Isabelle turned a bright red, Sam chuckled.

"I most certainly am not going to take off my stockings." Isabelle glared at Sam before she added, "Besides, Mari checked them already."

Sam glanced over at Mari and she nodded. "Her left big toe was the worst. Ann tried her best to warm her toes gradually. You might want to check them though."

"You are not looking at my feet." Isabelle glared again at Sam and tried to tuck her feet under her chair again. When her left toe bumped one of the chair legs, she winced.

Sam stood and nodded at Mari.

"Help her get those stockings off. We are going to treat that toe."

Mari led Isabelle toward the bedroom as she protested.

"What can he do? He's no doctor. So what if it's a little swollen. Maybe I bumped it during the ride."

Mari didn't answer as she pulled Isabelle's stockings down. When they were off, she looked up at her friend.

"Frostbite is serious, Isabelle. If it is not treated correctly, you could lose your toe.

"Let Sam do this. He's had lots of experience with frostbite. Besides, Doc Williams—he's my uncle—he gave us a first aid class at school. Trust me—Sam knows what to look for."

When the two women returned to the kitchen, Bandy was waiting there with Sam. He shoved the jar he was holding behind his back.

"Mornin', ladies. Which of you gals needs help with her big toe?"

CHAPTER 54

JUST A FEW LEECHES

SAM PUT TWO CHAIRS IN FRONT OF ISABELLE AND another beside her.

"Sit down and put your leg up on that chair in front there. This won't hurt at all, but you need to hold still."

Bandy sat down in front of her, and Sam was off to the side. He leaned across her leg as he held onto it.

"Lean up, Sam. I want to see what you are doing."

Sam ignored her. Isabelle tried to lean around him, but she couldn't see. The two men were quiet as they worked.

Isabelle looked over at Mari. "What are they doing? I can't feel anything other than Sam gripping my foot." She jerked her leg.

"Don't squeeze so hard, Sam! I'm going to have bruises on my ankle if you keep gripping it like that."

Sam looked back at Isabelle and grinned.

"You are goin' to have to sit here for about forty-five minutes, so you just as well relax."

When Isabelle tried to move her leg, Sam shook his head.

"Nope, it needs to stay right there. And I wouldn't even look at it if I was you."

Sam turned around and Isabelle leaned sideways. Her eyes opened wide, and she started jerking her foot to pull it toward her as she screamed.

Bandy grabbed her leg and Sam grabbed her shoulders.

"Isabelle! Trust me. This is what we need to do."

Isabelle squeezed her eyes shut and put her fist up to her mouth as she tried not to cry.

"What are those horrible slimy creatures attached to my toe?" she whispered.

"Leeches. They will pull out the swellin' and get your blood flowin' again. I don't know how it all works but freezin' damages folks on their insides—mostly toes and fingers." He picked up her hand and pointed at the blisters.

"That is what happens when it ain't too bad. You'll lose some skin, but you'll be alright 'cause it will grow back.

"Your toe was worse. If we don't get your blood movin' like it's supposed to, you could lose that toe."

"But I didn't even feel them bite me."

"They don't have teeth and they spit somethin' in you when they hook on. Whatever it is, it deadens the area where they attach. They're a painless way of pullin' out old blood, and they help the swellin' to go down."

"Have you ever had a leech on you?"

Sam grinned and nodded, "Yeah, but it was by accident. We were wadin' in some old water and I climbed out with 'em stuck all over me." He chuckled and added, "Ma's reaction was a lot like yours. She didn't want to touch 'em, and Pa wasn't around. She finally hauled me up to Doc's.

"Doc was excited to get fresh leeches. He called 'em 'fine specimens' and he intended to keep 'em once they were off. He even showed me how to remove 'em so's I didn't kill 'em. 'Course by that time, they was full and was startin' to fall off." Sam pointed at her foot. "Bandy has his leeches all sorted out. These here was his hungry ones. Once they come off, he'll put their jar to the back. They only eat ever' six months. They're like his pets." Sam pointed at Isabelle's toe.

"See? Your toe already looks smaller.

"Now once we take 'em off, you need to take it easy. We'll put more on tonight and maybe again in the mornin' 'fore we leave. And you need to prop that leg up some while we travel." Sam squeezed the fingers on Isabelle's hand that wasn't sore and added, "I cain't have my best gal missin' her big toe. She might step all over me when we dance!"

Isabelle watched as the worm-like creatures became fatter. She almost gagged when the first one fell off.

"Thank Heavens Mother isn't here. She'd have fainted by now. And, she'd have shot you when she came to."

Bandy had all three of the leeches off in less than forty minutes. He winked at Isabelle.

"I'll see you after supper, Miss Isabelle. We'll have your toe workin' proper in no time. Now just sit here for a time. You'll bleed a little, but it will stop soon enough. Make sure your sock is loose around that toe and try to keep your weight off it."

He hurried out the door holding the jar of leeches inside his coat. He waved and grinned at the chorus of thank yous.

Ann had been quiet the entire time. She looked from Sam to Mari and shook her head.

"Well. I certainly didn't know we had a leech-keeper on this ranch. That's good for future information."

Sam chuckled as he pulled his chair up to the table.

"Bandy is a curious kind of feller. You'd be amazed at all the things he's tried to grow in your bunkhouse.

"Now if that offer for breakfast is still good, I'll take you up on it. I need to keep my energy up so's I can talk to these two gals all mornin'."

Isabelle stared at him.

"Not before you wash your hands. I can still smell those slimy things, and you probably had them all over your hands."

Sam grinned at her as he sauntered over to the wash basin.

"Nope. The only thing I had my hands on was your foot. Well, a little bit of your leg too and it felt fine. Mostly though, my hands were all over your foot."

Isabelle slowly turned a deep red.

"You are a bold man, Sam Rankin."

Mari laughed. "That he is.

"How did you get here so fast, Sam? I thought the Merrill ranch was nearly forty miles from here. That would be a long ride in good weather."

"I left before daylight Saturday mornin' and pushed hard to the CC ranch. I changed horses there, ate a bite, and headed this way."

Isabelle stared at him.

"You rode all night? You must be exhausted! Did my father ask you to do that?"

Sam's eyes were a deep blue when he answered Isabelle.

"Your pa and me was both mighty worried. I told him I'd come as fast as I could. And I was glad to do it. You gals scared the livin' daylights out of ever'body." Sam's voice was soft when he added, "I'm glad you come home though. I just wish it had been an easier trip."

CHAPTER 55

QUESTIONS FROM A FRIEND

SAM HAD KIRKHAM'S MULE TEAM AND SLEIGH AT THE train shack by seven-thirty the next morning. The Ogallala dispatcher had sent a message to Kirkham when the train left there, and Sam planned his trip so the women wouldn't have to wait long.

Ann had given Isabelle a pair of her wool stockings along with some high-top shoes. She was dressed a little warmer, but Sam was still concerned about her getting too cold. Her toe looked much better though.

Mari was quiet as they waited for the train, but Isabelle chattered happily.

"I know it was reckless of us to leave but I am so glad we came. I just couldn't bear the thought of spending Thanksgiving alone in Manhattan. And Mari would have been stuck there as well. She was supposed to spend it with her brother in Kansas City, but his job took him out of town."

Sam looked over at Mari.

"How is Rudy? I haven't seen him in a long time. Maybe once or twice since he left for law school. Is he comin' back to Cheyenne or does he like the city life?"

Mari frowned slightly.

"I'm not sure. He doesn't make it home much. I think maybe he has a girl. He never says much to me about women let alone a specific one though.

"Mother thinks he is serious about the daughter of one of his professors from something he mentioned in one of his letters, but I don't know. Rudy has never talked about girls to me.

"I always hoped he'd come back to Cheyenne and work with Levi Parker. He enjoyed Levi when he was younger. He said he learned a lot from him too.

"Rusty told him last year he could find him a job just about anywhere. He said, 'Pick yore town, Rudy. I know folks all over the place.' He does too. You should hear some of his stories." Mari laughed as she looked at Sam. "You know Rusty. He loves to wheel and deal. He probably *could* get Rudy a job with all his contacts."

Sam grinned at the two women.

"There's an easy fix to that problem. Introduce him to a nice little gal he can't help but fall for. Make sure she lives around Cheyenne or at least would be willin' to move there."

Mari laughed. She was quiet a moment and then asked softly, "How is Nate? I know he is working for the railroad now. Does he travel all over?"

Sam nodded his head. "Yeah, but he doesn't intend to do it forever. He still plans to go back to Cheyenne and settle down. He is savin' his money to buy his own spread."

Mari's face showed her confusion.

"But he owns half of Gabe's operation!"

"Nate don't see it that way. He said Gabe has more kids comin' up. He wants to make it on his own. He will too. When we rode together, he took care of our money." Sam flashed Isabelle a smile. "He only gave me a little at a time. That was alright though. I would have just spent mine. Now it's in a bank in Ogallala." Sam's grin became bigger. "Nate set that up while we were pards." Sam looked across the shimmering snow and added, "Shoot, we are still pards. I reckon we always will be."

They didn't have to wait long for the train and the ride north went by quickly. Before long, they were back in the sleigh and headed east to Jasper Merrill's Rocking Chair Ranch.

Isabelle snuggled up next to Sam. It wasn't long before she was asleep. He looked down at her several times before he pulled the quilts tighter.

Mari watched her cousin and smiled.

"When did you know you loved Isabelle?"

Sam looked over at Mari in surprise before he looked ahead again. He was quiet for a time before he answered.

"I reckon it was love at first sight for me. Probably not for her though.

"Nate and me had been in a line shack all winter and had just gotten back. That was this past April. We was dirty and smelly and hungry. I didn't get to talk to her much till later that evenin'.

"We danced most of the dances that night and talked a lot. I knew after that evenin' she was the one for me. I told Nate on the way home I was goin' to marry her. He was a little surprised, probably 'cause I've had lots of gals over the years. No steady ones though—at least not longer than a month or so.

"I told him I asked her pa that night if I could court her. Nate laughed at me. He said, 'How's than goin' to work? She don't even live here.' Then he said she probably had a rich feller back East just a waitin' on her." Sam growled a little before he continued. "Nate acts all nice, but he has him a mean streak too. I couldn't believe my best pard would say that.

"'Course, she didn't live out here then. Her pa was thinkin' on buyin' but nothin' was final. I meant it though. I told Nate if she didn't come back, I was headed east to find 'er.

"Before they headed back to Georgia, her pa bought the Rockin' Chair Ranch. That's why Kirkham offered Nate the railroad job. We talked it over but we both knew he should take it. I wanted to stay up here to be close to Isabelle, and he wanted to make money to go back to Cheyenne.

"It pained both of us to think we'd be separated though. When he left in October, that was the first time we'd really been apart since he moved to Cheyenne in '79. Neither of us liked it much, but that's just the way it had to be.

"I miss him though. He's the best friend I ever did have. He whoaed me down lots of times and kept me out of trouble." Sam flashed Mari a grin and added, "'Course, there were times when he just joined me.

"I miss my old pard but we both knew if I had to choose him or Isabelle, I'd choose her."

Mari twisted the blanket she held in her hands. There were tears in her eyes when she looked at Sam.

"I miss him too. I don't understand why he never writes me. He has to have a little time, especially now with all his traveling."

Sam's voice was soft when he answered, "He does write you, Mari. His saddle bags are chock-full of letters to you. He just won't send 'em.

"I told him he should, and he said they was too mushy. He said you'd probably just laugh at 'em and read 'em to your girlfriends."

A tear leaked out of Mari's eye. "I would never do that. He doesn't know me very well if he even thinks it."

Sam shrugged his shoulders.

"That's just Nate. He says he has nothin' to offer you yet and he ain't goin' home till he does. I told him you might be married off by then. He just growled at me and wouldn't talk about it no more.

"He cares for you, Mari. Why, he ain't had a gal since we left home. Now don't get me wrong—we've gone to lotsa dances, but he never asks a gal out after it's over. I asked him one time how he was to know if you was the one if he never spends time with no other gals. He said if he found a gal purtier than you and easier to talk to, then he'd ask her out, but he ain't found one yet.

"Before he left, I made 'im promise to stop in and see you. I'm a guessin' he probably did last week and you was gone. I reckon that's how he knew you gals was headed up here."

Mari turned her head so Sam couldn't see her cry. He reached over to pat her hand.

"If you care for Nate, wait a little longer. He's a good man, and if he said he was a comin' back, he will." Sam leaned over and kissed his cousin's cheek.

"Smile, Mari. It was Nate who arranged for you gals to get off at Kirkham's. If he didn't care, he wouldn't have checked up on you."

Mari wiped her face and smiled.

"Thank you, Sam. Thank you for sharing all that with me. I miss you and I miss our talks."

Sam chuckled and pointed with his whip.

"There's Isabelle's place. The Rocking Chair Ranch—and here come her folks."

CHAPTER 56

CONCERNED PARENTS

BOTH OF ISABELLE'S PARENTS RUSHED OUT OF THE house to greet her. Her mother was crying and even Jasper's eyes were a little watery.

He shook Sam's hand and put his arm around the younger man's shoulders.

"Thank you, Sam. Thank you for bringing our daughter home."

Sam nodded. He stepped back with a smile as he watched Isabelle with her parents. Evelyn finally noticed Mari. She hugged the younger woman.

"Goodness, Mari. How rude of us. Welcome to our home. We are so pleased you were able to make the trip with Isabelle."

Evelyn turned to Sam. She tried to smile through her tears as she touched Sam's arm. She stepped away quickly and wiped her face.

Sam's face showed no emotion as he put an arm around Mari and pointed toward Isabelle.

"Let's get these gals in the house. Isabelle has a bad toe and if she don't take care of it, I'll have to put more leeches on it."

"You will not! Oh, Mother. You should have seen what Sam did to my toe. I had some frostbite, and he put these terrible, slimy—"

Jasper cleared his throat. He took Evelyn's arm and led her toward the house.

"Enough of that talk. Let's warm these girls up and eat. They must be hungry. Sam is for sure. Come on, ladies. Evelyn has been cooking all morning. It's early for dinner and late for breakfast but we are eating anyway."

Sam turned away at the door. He led the mule team to the barn and began to remove their harnesses. Dandy Dawson appeared in the doorway of the barn. He moved to the other side of the mules to loosen their harnesses.

"The boss told us you were going to be foremen. Guess you won't be chasin' no more wolves."

Sam looked up in surprise and then laughed.

"Yeah, he offered me the foreman job right before I left to get Isabelle. Caught me by surprise but I said yes."

Dandy lifted the harnesses off and led the two mules front mules to an open stall. He opened the door to another stall for Sam and then helped him pull the sleigh over to a corner of the barn. His eyes were serious when he spoke again.

"The boss ain't well. I'm new around here but my pop had a cancer in him. It took him mighty quick. The boss acts a lot like Pop did before he died."

Sam straightened up. His eyes were cool when he answered Dandy.

"The boss' health ain't any of our business. I reckon he will let us know when there are to be some changes. Till then, we work and we don't speak of it."

Dawson slowly nodded. He grinned and pointed toward the wall where a new wolf pelt hung.

"Chancy an' me did a little huntin' after that big snow. You are goin' to have to show us how you made yore pelts so soft though. Ours are mighty stiff."

Sam grinned and nodded. "I can do that." He looked out at the riders milling around in the yard.

"Why don't you gather the boys up. Tell them I need to see them right away. We'll have us a talk in the barn and get the day lined out."

Chancy nodded and headed for the bunkhouse. Sam put some feed and hay in the mangers for the mules as he talked to them.

"You mules did a fine job. We might have to add a mule team on this place one of these days. I just about forgot how much I liked driving mules." He grinned and turned around to walk to the front of the barn as he added softly, "Mules make me think of Badger and that makes me miss home."

The men were gathered around the doorway of the barn and Sam stopped in front of them.

"I'm your new foreman, boys. I don't intend to make lots of changes, but we are goin' to start earlier in the mornin'. There won't be no crawlin' out of yore bunks at six-thirty. Cookie don't have to make no changes. He has breakfast ready by six the way it is.

"And I want that bunkhouse cleaned up. It looks like a bunch a hogs live there." He gave the men their work orders for the day and slowly walked to the house.

"I think I'll eat some of that food ol' Jasper was talkin' about 'fore I leave...and talk to Miss Isabelle some."

CHAPTER 57

THE COWBOY'S PROMISE

WHEN JASPER OPENED THE DOOR, THE FIRST THING Sam heard were women's voices, happy voices as they laughed and talked. He grinned as he pulled his boots off.

"Jasper, this house sounds downright noisy. I reckon you'll get more sleep in the bunkhouse."

The older man chuckled softly and nodded.

"It is a good sound though. Ev needed this. She hasn't laughed this much in some time." His eyes were worried when he looked at Sam. He spoke softly.

"I'm counting on you to take care of her, Sam. Both her and Izzy. They are more important to me than my life, and I'll be leaving them in your hands."

Sam swallowed the lump in his throat.

"They will always be taken care of, Jasper. And Ev will have a place with Izzy and me as long as she lives." He grinned and added, "Provided we marry. I ain't even asked her."

"And I don't want you to ask her until she has two years of college under her belt. She'd quit tomorrow if you asked, and we both know it." He frowned and squeezed the back of a chair while he took deep breaths. When he looked up again, there was sweat around his hairline.

"After the girls leave, I want to go over our finances with you. Ev and I own quite a few properties in Georgia. I think we should liquidate some of those, maybe all of them. Ev isn't involved in any of my business decisions, and they will just cause her concern.

"And another thing. I can about guarantee you Ev will want to go East for a time after I pass. She doesn't have much family, but she has friends around Atlanta. She will want to spend some time away from here, and she will probably want to enroll Izzy in college wherever she goes.

"I want you to go along with Ev—regardless of where she wants Izzy to do her second year of college. Izzy will agree if you support Ev, and that is what I'm asking. After that second year, you can ask Izzy to marry. If she says yes, you bring her back out here. You give me your word on that."

Sam nodded. "You have my word, Jasper."

Jasper took a deep breath as he held his stomach. His voice broke when he spoke again.

"Izzy will be all right. She's strong and she'll have you. Ev—Ev is fearful. She lashes out at folks when she's afraid. She pushes them away too. You keep that in mind if she gets stubborn or angry. You treat my wife like the treasure she is to me."

Jasper leaned over the chair. His breath came quickly, and he groaned several times. He finally stood. He straightened his tie and smiled at Sam.

"Now let's go into the kitchen and join that happy conversation. I want to enjoy my daughter while she's home."

Sam followed Jasper into the kitchen. Both men were smiling and the noise the little room picked up as they were welcomed into the conversation.

"Father—Sam—we were just talking about how we should visit Mari's family next summer. I have never been to the Wyoming Territory and her stories are fascinating." Isabelle blushed slightly as she added, "And your family too, Sam. Mari has talked so much about all of them, I almost know their names."

Sam grinned and nodded.

"That would just be mighty fine. 'Course, I have a job here, so I don't reckon I'd be able to go. Not sure if the boss would let me off for a week with all the work around here."

Isabelle stared with surprise from Sam to her father.

"Of course he would. There are lots of cowboys around here to do the work. I'm sure you could take a little time off."

Jasper's eyes twinkled and he shook his head somberly.

"Probably not. I need my foreman to stick around. We can't both be gone at the same time. After all, I made Sam foreman so I wouldn't have to work so hard."

Mari jumped up and hugged Sam.

"Oh, Sam! That is so exciting. Congratulations! Your parents will be so proud of you."

Sam grinned and Jasper chuckled as he pointed toward a chair.

"Let's eat a bite and then my new foreman needs to get outside. He's been chasing girls all over this country for too long."

CHAPTER 58

A Fun Day

AFTER THE MEN LEFT, MARI TOLD EVELYN AND IZZY about their big family gatherings and suggested they feed the Rocking Chair cowboys on Thanksgiving.

"Most of your riders will be right here on Thanksgiving Day. Why don't we make extra food and invite all of them to eat with us? Neighbors too if you have any close enough."

Evelyn frowned.

"I'm not sure about that. I rode over to Freda Cassidy's once. One of the riders drove me in the buggy, but it was over a twenty-mile ride. The only homestead between Cassidy's and us belongs to a young farm couple. We don't have many neighbors."

Mari laughed and her eyes shined when she spoke.

"Maybe we should invite that young couple too. We can talk to Mr. Merrill and Sam when they come in. I'm sure they know where everyone lives."

Evelyn still wasn't convinced a big crowd was a good idea.

"But what do you feed so many people on Thanksgiving here? I know we have pork in the smokehouse, and we always have beef. I haven't seen any turkeys around here though."

"You have plenty of chickens and some of them look like cockerels with their big combs. We can catch some of those and butcher them." Mari laughed and added, "Fried chicken, potatoes, and white gravy will be a treat for everyone."

"You know how to butcher a chicken? I have never done that in my life!" Isabelle's eyes were wide as she stared at Mari.

Mari paused. She was surprised as she looked from mother to daughter. She shrugged.

"It's not so hard as it sounds. I'll show you. Now we just need to figure how many men to plan for."

Evelyn smiled at Mari's excitement.

"You take care of the chickens, and I will make some pies. I brought some canned pumpkin with me when we came out here. And there are potatoes in the cave. I won't go in there because I am afraid of snakes, but Jasper said they are still good. We can send one of the men out to the cave for the potatoes and five jars of pumpkin.

"Today though, I'd like you girls to help me with something else. That back room is packed full of things I brought from Georgia. I'd like you to go through everything. Sort by what to give away, what to keep, and what to throw out. I like to keep everything, so I won't be much help. Jasper really wants that room cleaned out though." Evelyn smiled at Isabelle as she touched her cheek.

"You used to love to go through my things. There is some jewelry in there too I'd like you to look at. Jasper has given me so many pretty things over the years. I need to share some of them with you."

Both girls were on their way to the back bedroom by the time Evelyn finished speaking. She could hear their happy chatter and she smiled.

"Perhaps if I get rid of some things now, it will be easier for Isabelle to leave." Her eyes filled with tears, and she turned toward the wash basin where the dirty dishes were stacked. "Jasper wants me to keep this place. He wants me to live here after he passes but I won't do it. I can't. This place is his dream, not mine."

Just then, Isabelle rushed into the kitchen with a pearl necklace in her hands.

"I remember when you used to wear this! Tell me about it, Mother." She took Evelyn's hand and pulled her toward the back room.

"You need to tell us about all these things. We can't sort them without your help."

Evelyn sat down on the bed. She took the necklace in her hands and smiled as she rubbed her fingers over the pearls. Her eyes had tears in them as she looked at Isabelle.

"This belonged to your grandmother, Ira's mother. It was her most treasured possession and she gave it to me as a wedding gift. I loved to wear it while Ira was alive. Once he died though..." Evelyn smiled at Isabelle as she held the string of pearls out to her.

"Perhaps one day, you will wear them on your wedding day."

Isabelle stared at the pearls. She hugged her mother.

"Oh, Mother. What a wonderful gift. Yes, I will be proud to wear it." She opened a wooden jewelry box with intricate carving on the top and sides. "Now tell me about the rest of the pieces in here."

CHAPTER 59

Thanksgiving in the Sandhills

ISABELLE WATCHED IN AMAZEMENT AS MARI SNARED the chickens with a bent wire. She was a little horrified at how quickly they were beheaded and then dipped in the boiling water to loosen their feathers. The butchering was fascinating to her because Mari showed her each part as she cleaned it or threw it away.

Evelyn watched them for a moment. Then she put on an old apron, caught a chicken, killed it, and began to clean it herself. Isabelle stared at her mother in shock.

"Mother, you never told me you knew how to butcher chickens! Why did you never show me?"

Evelyn threw the chicken offal in a bucket outside the door and answered calmly, "Because I never had to after I married Jasper. Before that, chickens were our main meat supply. Yes, I've butchered my share." She smiled at Isabelle and added, "But I never lost my taste for them. Fried chicken is still one of my favorite foods.

"You cut this one up, Isabelle. Place your knife on the joints and cut there. It is much easier than trying to saw through a bone."

Before long, they had six chickens cut into pieces and dipped in flour. Evelyn pulled out three big skillets, melted some lard and butter in them, and added the floured chicken to the hot grease. She smiled at the two young women.

"It won't take this chicken long to fry, and as soon as it's done, we'll make the gravy.

"The potatoes are cooked. I left a little water in the bottom of that big kettle so they'll stay warm. We'll use the rest of the water along with some milk to make the gravy. With Mari's bread, our canned green beans, and those pumpkin pies, we'll have a regular feast."

Isabelle lifted a fresh roll out of the bowl and popped a piece in her mouth.

"Mmm. These are good. So tender that they just melt in your mouth. Who taught you to make bread, Mari?"

"My mother but now she says my bread is better than hers." Mari laughed softly. "I don't think it is. I think she just wants me to make all the bread.

"I don't mind though. Baking is something I love to do, and Mother is busy. She works hard to keep everything going and the little kids under control too."

"How many children are in your family, Mari?" Evelyn set some butter on the table and helped herself to a roll. She slathered it in butter as she waited for Mari's answer.

"There are six of us now, but Mother is pregnant again. My little brother or sister should arrive around Christmas. My parents are both excited. They love babies.

"Rudy and I are the oldest. Mother and Father took us in when our first parents died. Sometimes people say we are adopted but mother doesn't like that word. She says we are a gift that God gave to her and Father.

"Ellie and Eli are twins. They are fourteen. Pauline is eight and Emmalene is six. Mother lost several babies between the twins and Pauline. That's why they are so far apart in age. I didn't know that until last year. She never told any of us.

"It must have been hard for her, because she cried when she told me." Mari was quiet as she looked away. When she looked at Evelyn again, she smiled.

"I think that's one of the reasons I love to teach. There have always been little ones around our house and cousins everywhere too. We have lots of cousins." She laughed again. "And some children we all call cousins who aren't even related."

Evelyn smiled at her.

"You are going to teach when you go back home?"

"Oh, yes. I would do it now, but Mother and Father said I needed to get away for a time. Education is important to Mother and to Aunt Molly. They both want to make sure we girls can provide for ourselves if we choose not to marry." Mari rolled her eyes. "Of course, Mother expects me to find a man and settle down someday."

"Well, I'm sure you have lots of beaus, Mari. You are a beautiful girl."

Mari blushed and looked away, but Isabelle laughed and bumped her friend.

"Only one, Mother. Mari has been sweet on Nate Hawkins her entire life. He's the standard she measures all men against, and no one else measures up."

Evelyn looked at Mari in surprise and then nodded.

"He's a fine man, Mari. He's the one who drove Isabelle and me down to Ogallala to catch the train when she started college. Yes, I think you have chosen well. It would be hard to find a man better than him."

Isabelle leaned over to Mari and whispered, "Unless it was Sam!"

Evelyn frowned slightly but Isabelle didn't notice. She stood quickly and clapped her hands.

"Enough chatter. It's time to turn that chicken.

"Isabelle, you and Mari put the extra leaves in that table. I'll set out the china. If we need more plates, use some from the cupboard. We will fit as many as we can around the table. The rest will have to find a seat on the stairway.

"Mari, when you are done, draw the milk up from the well. I put it in there to make it nice and cold. We will skim the cream off before we make gravy.

"Isabelle, whip up that bowl of cream by the wash basin and add a little sugar. No, not the fresh cream. I set some cream out this morning so it could warm a little. It whips easier that way. Quickly now. I see the men gathering in front of the bunkhouse."

CHAPTER 60

SLEDDING ON A SHOVEL

THE MEAL WAS DELICIOUS. ISABELLE WAS SURPRISED at how quiet the men were when they first started to eat. Before long though, they began to talk. Soon the house was filled with laughs and happy voices.

Freda and Bill Cassidy had come over along with the four hands who had helped Isabelle and Mari get to Kirkham's. The young farm couple, Jase and Stella Wilson, came with their baby. With the Merrill's hands, there were twenty-two people in the kitchen.

Evelyn was the ultimate hostess. She barely sat the entire meal as she refilled plates and set out more food. Once the men began to relax in their chairs, the women quickly cleared the table and brought out the pies.

The cowboys stared at the pie. Their eyes opened even wider when Evelyn dropped whipped cream on each piece. Sam was the first to speak.

"Ladies, this here is the best meal I've had since I left home." He looked around the table at the other riders as he added, "And I reckon we won't never have a hard time keepin' hands around here once the word on this here meal gets out."

One piece of pie was left when the meal was finished, and Evelyn beamed happily as the men complimented her on a fine meal.

"Thank you but I had lots of good help. Isabelle made a few pies while Mari made the bread. Freda Cassidy and Stella Wilson brought food, and we all worked on the meal. Many hands make light work, you know."

Dandy stood behind his chair while he twirled his hat in his hands. He was so tall he almost had to duck his head to get out the door.

"Ladies, some of us fellers found some old shovels in the barn. We wondered if you gals would like to go sledding this afternoon."

Isabelle stared at him incredulously.

"On a shovel?"

Mari nodded excitedly.

"We'd love to. We'll be out as soon as we get everything cleaned up."

Dandy grinned as he rolled up his sleeves.

"We'll make it quick then. I'll wash those dishes. My ol' ma would have a fit if she heard I walked out without helpin' after a meal like we just had." He looked around at the rest of the cowboys.

"In fact, we'll all help. You ladies just sit yourselves down. We'll have these plates scraped and cleaned in no time at all."

The kitchen was soon full of arguing cowboys. They banged pans and nearly dropped plates as they pushed and shoved each other out of the way. Every time something hit the floor, Evelyn jumped.

Bill Cassidy grinned. He took Freda's arm and led her to the living room.

"Let's sit in here. It will be easier to talk. Besides, someone could get stepped on out there." Evelyn and Jasper followed them as well as the Wilsons. Mari and Isabelle hurried to change clothes.

"What do you wear to ride on a shovel, Mari? I've never heard of such a thing," Isabelle whispered.

"Well, it's not too ladylike. You straddle the shovel. Most of the time, the shovels are too small to keep your feet and legs inside, so you stick them out straight beside the handle. A rider will tie one end of his rope to the handle and the other to his saddlehorn and off you go! It is wonderful fun, although you do get dumped sometimes.

"If you have any britches, we should put them on under our dresses. If not, we'll get cold sooner and won't be able to stay out as long."

"Father has some old britches. I'll get two pairs of those. We will look a sight and Mother certainly won't approve."

The young women were soon outside. Evelyn was wiping the spilled water off her floor when she heard excited laughing and screaming. She opened the door just in time to see Isabelle careen wildly up the lane on a shovel as the running horse she was tied to raced through the snow. Isabelle's dress was flapping well above her knees as her legs stuck out on either side of the shovel.

Evelyn grabbed her chest and whispered, "Oh my stars and garters! Those girls will be killed!"

Mari's shovel swung wildly around the side of the house as Dandy cut his horse back and forth. Before long, more horses were tied to shovels and the cowboys began to race each other.

Evelyn backed away from the door. She shut it silently and leaned against it for a moment as she closed her eyes.

"That child is not going to make it to her twentieth birthday," she whispered to herself as she joined the other adults in the living room.

CHAPTER 61

A RIDE IN THE MOONLIGHT

FRIDAY, NOVEMBER 28 CAME TOO SOON. SAM WOULD be taking them to catch the southbound train at nine the next morning. They should arrive in Manhattan around ten that same night if no trains were late and all went well.

Sam wanted to take Isabelle on a sleigh ride that evening. He said there would be a full moon, and he wanted her to experience a snowy night in the Sandhills.

Mari watched them go from the doorway. She was just ready to close the door when Dandy appeared.

"Want to go for a ride, Mari? There's no wind tonight and that's a rare thing. It would be a mighty nice night for a moonlight ride." He smiled down at her as he waited for her reply.

Mari hesitated. She wanted to go but she wasn't sure she should.

Dandy's smile became bigger.

"As friends. Just a ride with a friend."

Mari slowly nodded. "All right but let me change. I'll be out in a bit." She hurried into the room she shared with Isabelle and pulled a riding skirt out of her valise. She added a heavy shirt, coat, scarf, gloves, and a cowboy hat with stampede strings that she tied under her chin.

She rushed into the kitchen where Evelyn was sitting at the table.

"I'm going riding with Dandy. I should be back in an hour or so."

Evelyn opened her mouth to reply but Mari was already gone. She looked out the window in time to see Dandy give Mari a leg up on her horse. He was pointing down the valley and talking as they rode away.

Jasper walked into the kitchen and Evelyn smiled.

"Both girls are out tonight. Mari is riding with Dandy and Sam took Isabelle for a sleigh ride. Those kids just never seem to get tired."

Jasper laughed. "That's youth, Evelyn. I remember when we played until the late hours too." He smiled down at her.

"Dance with me tonight, Ev. I'll sing to you like old times."

Evelyn let Jasper pull her up and they danced slowly across the kitchen floor while he sang softly, "I'll Take You Home Again, Kathleen." When he finished, they stood quietly together. Jasper felt Evelyn shake as she cried silently.

"Don't cry, sweetheart. This world is temporary for all of us. You know that. Let's enjoy our time and not waste a moment mourning about what could have been."

Evelyn didn't answer. They went to bed before the girls came home but she didn't sleep. She listened for them and smiled when she heard their happy whispers as they hurried to their shared room.

"I'm so happy Isabelle found a friend. Mari is such a wonderful girl. I wonder if she will wait for Nate or if she will give her heart to another man before he goes back home."

She held her breath and listened closely to Jasper's quiet breathing. He didn't struggle or moan in his sleep that night and she finally fell asleep.

CHAPTER 62

HARD GOODBYES

EVERYONE WAS UP EARLY THE NEXT MORNING. EVELYN fussed over breakfast and fluttered around as the girls set their small bags outside the front door. Sam wanted to leave at seven-thirty so they would have plenty of time to reach the train tracks. He had sent a rider down to Kirkham's two days before requesting a ride for two passengers on the southbound train to Ogallala.

Sam grinned as he tossed the women's bags in the back seat of the sleigh.

"Ol' Kirkham is a good man to know. He arranged for that train to stop at our mailbox. Trains on this line don't normally pick up passengers who don't have a ticket. Shoot, they don't even come this far north unless they are dropping someone off. He must have twisted some big arms."

"Lucky for us too. Now we only have an hour's ride to get to the train. That beats riding forty miles to Kirkham's to catch it there."

Sam was knocking on the front door by seven-fifteen.

Isabelle pulled it open with a smile.

"How about a cup of coffee and a cinnamon roll before we go, Sam? Mari and I promised the old hostler in Manhattan some treats for helping us arrange this trip. We are taking him chocolate cake and cinnamon rolls."

Sam stared down at her for a moment. He grinned and nodded.

"I reckon that would be jist fine. I like sweet things."

Isabelle blushed and Mari shook her head.

"Sam, you just love embarrassing people." She turned to Evelyn and gave her a hug.

"Thank you for a wonderful time, Evelyn. It was worth all the effort to get here. And, Mr. Merrill, thank you as well. I hope you will let me show both of you our Wyoming hospitality someday."

"You come back any time, Mari. We loved having you here. And have a wonderful Christmas with your family. I hope the new baby arrives before you get there so you'll be able to meet him or her." Evelyn smiled as she hugged Mari.

They were in the sleigh and ready to leave when Dandy appeared.

"So long, ladies. I'll look forward to your next visit." His eyes lingered on Mari and he asked softly, "Can I write you, Miss Mari? I sure enjoyed your company." His eyes twinkled as he added, "As friends, I mean."

Mari blushed softly and laughed.

"A friendly letter from you would be fine, Mr. Dawson. And thank you again for the beautiful ride last night."

Sam wheeled the sleigh around and everyone waved. Isabelle cuddled up next to Sam and Mari sat back in her seat as she smiled.

It was a wonderful trip. I so enjoyed myself. She started to think about Nate but shook her head. *No, I won't let him spoil this moment. I am going to savor this week and enjoy it again in my mind.*

CHAPTER 63

WILTED FLOWERS

I T WAS LATE SATURDAY NIGHT, NOVEMBER 29, WHEN
Mari knocked on the door of Holtz Hall. Miss Morton jerked it
open with her typical frown. The girls had sent Penny a wire from
Ogallala telling him when they would arrive. They also asked him to
let Miss Morton know they'd be arriving late. *Apparently, that was not
good enough,* Isabelle thought. Her smile was bright though when she
walked through the door.

"Thank you for waiting up for us, Miss Morton. We had a most
wonderful time. We—"

"Save your chatter for tomorrow, Miss Merrill. You ladies need to
get to bed." Miss Morton turned her hard eyes on Mari.

"And Miss Rankin, a cowboy came by while you were gone. He left
flowers for you. They are in your room." She locked the front door and
turned abruptly towards her room. She paused and looked back at Mari
as she added, "He was disappointed you weren't here. Good night."

Mari stared from Miss Morton's closed door to Isabelle. She raced
upstairs.

"Did Nate come by? Who would have left me flowers?" She jerked
open the door to their room and ran to the small table that held some

wilted flowers. A note in Miss Morton's neat handwriting was sitting under the flowers.

Miss Rankin,

A young man by the name of Nate Hawkins left these on November 21, the same day you left. He was disappointed you were not here but seemed pleased you were with Miss Merrill. He left no message, only his name.

Miss Morton

Mari stared at the flowers. Most of the blooms had fallen off and the rest were dried on the stem. She lifted them to her nose. Only a faint scent remained on the faded blooms and that was overwhelmed by the smell of decaying leaves and stale water. Mari stared at them a little longer before she picked up the vase and dropped everything into the small trash bucket by her desk.

Isabelle watched her friend but said nothing. She could hear Mari crying that night.

Oh, Mari. I wish I knew the words to tell you. Nate does care for you—I know he does. And he tried to see you. Please don't be sad.

Mari was gone Sunday morning when Isabelle awakened. She hurried downstairs and asked some of the girls who were eating if they knew where she was.

"She said something about going to church this morning, but she left really early. Services at the church she usually goes to don't start until ten so she must have gone somewhere else first."

Isabelle left for Mass. Sometimes, Mari met her there, but her friend was nowhere to be seen. Isabelle hurried home when Mass was over. Mari wasn't back yet so she unpacked both of their bags and took the dirty clothes down to the laundry area to wash them. When they were hung on the line, she went back up to their room. She studied the flowers for a moment. She finally pulled them out of the trash, dumped the water, and set them on the table.

"Maybe Mari will feel differently when she gets back today," she whispered.

Mari didn't appear until after dinner. She went up to their room without speaking and was asleep when Isabelle slipped in. However, the flowers were laid out on some papers to dry. Isabelle lay down quietly beside her friend to take a nap as well.

"I guess she will talk to me when she's ready."

Monday, November 24, 1884
Cheyenne
Wyoming Territory

CHAPTER 64

HEADED WEST

B Y THE MONDAY BEFORE THANKSGIVING, NATE WAS headed to California. He didn't have time to visit anyone in Cheyenne on his way through because the stopover was short, but he looked around as he stepped off the train.

"This is my town," he muttered to himself, "and I can't wait to get back home." He picked up his messages at the rail office and smiled. The first message was from Kirkham.

"Everybody is safe, and Sam is already there. That's good. I'm glad he stayed and is working for Jasper. Shoot, he'll be foreman in no time. And maybe Jasper's missus will even get to like him."

He read and then reread his work messages. His boss wanted him to go to Blackfoot in the Idaho Territory first. From there, he was to take the train north into Butte. That line was a three-foot narrow-gauge track and Union Pacific wanted to convert it to standard gauge. It wouldn't happen immediately, but they wanted it completed within six years.

Nate read through the list of people he was to meet with in Blackfoot as well as the specific times. After he made the necessary changes to his schedule, he smiled. "I need to be in Blackfoot tomorrow, but I don't have to be in Butte until December 2. I guess I will plan to take a trip to the Bitter Root Valley for a surprise visit with Spur and Clare. And over Thanksgiving too." He grinned as he hurried back to the train. Just as he started to climb inside, he heard someone call his name.

"Nate Hawkins! How are you, boy?"

Nate turned around. He dropped back onto the platform as Rowdy Rankin came toward him with a grin.

"By all that's mighty, I sure didn't expect to see you today." Rowdy's grin was friendly, and Nate put out his hand.

"I just arrived and am leaving right away. I had to stop and pick up my work orders." He held them up as he smiled. "It looks like I might have enough time to spend Thanksgiving with Spur and Clare though."

Rowdy nodded as he watched the young man in front of him.

"Say, thanks for the arrangements you made for the girls during that blizzard in Nebraska. Mari wired us. It was a long message too. She said a fellow by the name of John Kirkham told her to let us know she was all right." He chuckled and added, "She even told how Sam used leeches to save Isabelle's frostbitten toe." Rowdy's grin became bigger. "I guess Miss Merrill was a little horrified about slimy worms being put on her foot—kind of like Molly the first time leeches got all over Sam when he was just a little tyke."

Rowdy laughed out loud, and Nate chuckled.

"You should have seen Sam. Why, I'm guessing he had fifteen or twenty of those things on him. Molly told him to stay out of that water. He didn't, of course. Instead, he took off all his clothes. He figgered if his clothes were dry, he wouldn't get in trouble.

"Rudy was with him. He told Sam to stay out of the water too, but Sam didn't listen to him either. I was fixing fence not far from there. I ran down to the creek when I heard all the squalling. I tried to pull some of them off, but Sam wiggled away and took off running.

"'Course leeches attach to anything that sticks out, so you can guess where a bunch of them were on his naked little body. Sam ran a bellering back to the house. I think he was four or five at the time. Molly told Beth later she almost fainted.

"Lance wasn't around so Molly loaded Sam up in the buggy and headed for Cheyenne. By the time they got to Doc's, the full leeches had started to fall off.

"Badger showed up just as Molly was trying to pick Sam up. Paul was just a baby at the time, so Badger offered to carry Sam. Molly stepped on one of those full leeches as it dropped to the ground. It shot out from under her foot and splattered all over the wagon wheel. She lost her dinner right there in front of Doc's office."

Both men laughed. The train whistle blew, and they shook hands again.

"I'm going to try to make a trip home this next year," Nate called as the train pulled away. "Tell Mari hello for me."

Rowdy waved as the train pulled away.

"I'll tell her, but it would be better if you told her yourself," Rowdy muttered as he waved. "I sure like that boy though." He shrugged and turned away. "I reckon if it's meant to be, it will work out." Rowdy was whistling by the time he reached the street. He chuckled again as he thought about Sam and the leeches.

"I sure hope we get to meet Sam's little gal sometime. According to Mari, Sam is mighty sweet on her."

Wednesday, November 26
Bitter Root Valley
Southwestern Montana
Territory

CHAPTER 65

ADVICE FROM A CHILD

NATE RODE INTO THE HEADQUARTERS OF THE DOUBLE Spur on Wednesday evening. He looked around in surprise. The ranch house was large and looked like some of the big houses he had seen in the southern states. Two young girls were carrying a milk bucket between them. A little boy around four or five was hiding in the bushes. He jumped out just as they reached him. Both girls dropped the bucket when they jumped. One screamed while the other one dived to keep the bucket upright. Once it was stabilized, she chased after the boy. He ran laughing and shouting as he slid down a hill and disappeared.

Nate rode toward the girls with a smile on his face.

"Howdy. Are your folks around close?"

The shortest girl stared up at him before she pointed toward the house.

"They both are. Pop has a horse buyer coming by after supper so he's eating early." She looked back at the stranger. "Are you a friend of Pop's?"

Nate chuckled and nodded.

"I sure am. I knew your pa before he married your ma. I'm from down south." Nate reached out his hand to the girl. "Nate Hawkins. And who might you be?"

"I'm Annie and this is Nora. That bratty little boy is Chas. Our older brother is out with the men today. His name is Zeke. Eddie is in the house with Mama. You can come in if you want."

"Let me put up my horses and I'll be in. Do you reckon it would be all right to put them up in your barn?"

Annie nodded.

"Here, Nora. You carry the milk in and tell Pop who's here. I'll show Mr. Hawkins where to put his horses.

"Where do you live, Mr. Hawkins?"

"I live down by Cheyenne in the Wyoming Territory, but my job takes me all over. Rollie is my little brother. I'm sure you remember him."

Annie stopped suddenly.

"Rollie Rabbit is your brother!" she exclaimed. "He is our cousin! We are going to go see him next summer. Pop said we could."

Nate chuckled.

"I reckon Rollie would like that just fine. I haven't been home for some time, but he sure missed you when I was there."

"Do you have any kids, Mr. Hawkins?"

"Nope. Maybe someday but not yet."

"Do you have a wife?"

Nate grinned and shook his head.

"Do you at least have a girl? Most fellows your age have a girl. Mama says Pop had lots of girls before her. Pop just laughs, but I think Mama is right."

Nate chuckled "I think your ma is probably right about your pa. As far as a gal of my own, I kind of did when I left home, but I've been gone so long I doubt she remembers me."

Annie was quiet as she watched Nate rub down Demonio.

"Your horse is pretty. What's his name?"

"I call him Demon and I don't want you kids to get too close to him. He isn't always so friendly, especially if I'm not around."

Annie nodded. "Pop has a few horses like that. Mostly studs but we have a mare that's mean. We call her Maybelle. Every year, Pop says he's going to get rid of her but then she throws a nice foal, and he keeps her around.

"I like horses. I almost like them better than cows. Pop likes horses and cows, but he says he likes Mama most of all. All of us kids too."

Nate grinned and nodded.

"I reckon that's a good way to be if you're married."

Annie was quiet for a time. Her voice was soft when she continued.

"My first pa died. He didn't come home from that trail drive he went on. Sometimes I think about him, and I get kind of sad. I wish he hadn't died. But then, we wouldn't have Pop and I like him a lot too."

Nate nodded somberly.

"I was on that drive, and I remember your pa. He was a good man. Spur is too. I reckon that makes you one special girl. You have two pops who love you. Most folks aren't that lucky."

Annie stared up at Nate. She frowned a little but slowly nodded.

"I guess so. Do you have a pop?"

"No, both my ma and pa are gone. I have other family though—two brothers, a sister, plus nieces. That's quite a bit of family."

Annie's face was serious as she studied Nate.

"You should probably go home and find that girl. If she's nice, maybe you should marry her. Pop says marrying our mama was the best thing he ever did. He said he's never been as happy as he is now.

"I think that's true. He sure laughs a lot. Mama does too. I think she likes Pop as much as she liked my first pa.

"Now, we have another little brother named Eddie. He's not very old but Mama says he's a stinker. I like him though. I like babies and little bitty kids. I don't like brothers Chas' size so much though. He's a pest. I hope Eddie doesn't act like him when he gets bigger."

Annie leaned toward Nate and whispered, "I think Mama is going to have another baby. She was smiling all sweet-like at Pop, and he was patting her tummy. Mama loves babies. Pop does too."

Nate coughed and hid his grin. He patted Demonio and pulled the stall door closed.

"Well, let's go up to the house. I haven't seen your folks for four years and I'm looking forward to a good visit."

CHAPTER 66

"No Clothes on Eddie!"

SPUR POKED HIS HEAD INTO THE BARN. HE GRINNED as he walked toward Nate with his hand out.

"Nate Hawkins! It's good to see you. Why, you are all grown up. And darn if you aren't a spittin' image of Gabe!" He shook Nate's hand and pointed over his shoulder.

"Come on up to the house. We are just sitting down to an early supper. Clare always fixes extra so there's plenty.

"Are you just passing through or can you stay for Thanksgiving?"

Nate grinned back at the smiling man who was pumping his hand.

"I have a few free days. I'll even trade you work for room and board. It's been some time since I had home cooking and I sure do miss it."

"Well, come on up to the house. You don't know Clare well, but you will by the time you leave." Spur turned toward Annie.

"Go find Zeke, Annie. He can eat with us tonight instead of playing poker with a bunch of cussing cowboys."

As Annie ran off, Spur grinned.

"Zeke is our oldest. He has always wanted to be a cowboy. I'm letting him ride out more with the men. He's doing all right too. Now, he's decided he'd just as soon stay in the bunkhouse at night. He figures if he doesn't come in the house at night, he won't have to scrap with his sisters—and that doesn't make his mama too happy." Spur shook his head and added, "She doesn't think much of his cursing either."

Nate laughed. "And I'm guessing his sisters tell on him."

"They sure do. Annie repeats everything he says, word for word. Loudly. Nora whispers the words in my ear.

"Those two little girls are like day and night, but I love them to pieces." He added softly, "I guess the Good Lord knew what he was doing when he sent me on that drive. I sure didn't see my life turning out this way—I—"

The kitchen door flew open, and a naked little boy came tearing out of the house. He had black curls, and his eyes were so dark they almost looked black. He was laughing and giggling as his mother tried to catch him.

"Edwin George, you get back in here right now. I won't have you running around naked in front of company!"

She stopped when she saw the two men. Spur was laughing and Nate joined him.

Clare blushed and shook her head.

"Eddie hates to wear clothes. Sometimes I just get tired of fighting him. Spur says he might potty train himself this way, but I don't know.

"Besides, it's cold outside—not that it bothers him. He'll stay a few minutes before he comes charging back into the house, red as a beet, shivering and laughing." Clare shook her head. "He's just wild." She looked sideways at Spur and added dryly, "Like his father."

Spur was still grinning when he put his arm around his wife. He winked and commented softly, "Maybe, but at least I don't run around naked—at least not in front of company!" When Clare's face turned pink, Spur laughed.

"Nate, you met my wife four years ago. Clare, this is Nate Hawkins. He was just a sprout the last time he was up here."

Clare smiled and reached out her hand.

314

"I remember Nate. Besides, Merina and I have been writing back and forth since Spur and I married. After all her talk about you, I feel like I know you well."

"That sounds like Merina. I don't know how she gets so much done but she does. She works outside with Gabe a lot besides all her work in the house."

Spur chuckled as he spoke, "Ol' Gabe was my first pard when I left New Orleans. He's a fine man. Little Rollie even thinks our wild kids are his cousins.

"We have visited down there several times. We are hoping to make another trip this next summer." Spur smiled down at Clare.

"Let's go on up to the house. What brings you up this way, Nate? Kind of chancy weather to just leisurely ride around and visit folks."

"I'm working for the railroad now and have a little time between jobs. The railroad wants to work on the line between Blackfoot in the Utah Territory and Butte up here. They are slowly getting rid of that narrow-gage line. I don't have to be in Butte until next Tuesday morning, so I do have time to visit some."

"That will be just fine. We'll have a big Thanksgiving meal here tomorrow at noon. Then Friday night, we'll get things ready for the After Harvest Dance.

"Clare started an organization two years ago in this area to help out families who lost their fathers. She calls it The Ladies' Aid Foundation.

"We didn't realize the number of women and families around who were struggling to survive after the father died. The lawyer here in town put the bug in Clare's ear and she took off with it." He smiled at Clare again and gave her a squeeze.

"My wife is kind of a bleeding heart. That's good though. It made her marry me." Spur winked at Clare, and she rolled her eyes.

Nate stared from Spur to Clare in surprise.

"So how do you help those families?"

"We do community things people like to take part in. We ask for a small donation or sometimes, we ask for food. Before Christmas, we have a big meal and a dance. We charge $1 for each adult to get in. Children get in free. If someone brings one of the widows, they both get in free." Clare laughed as she looked at Spur. "That was Spur's idea."

"We have even managed to marry off a few of the younger women. Spur supports us because married cowhands stay around longer."

Spur chuckled. "Father Ravalli is right in the middle of it. He usually paints a picture or carves something to be given away. We donate an Angus heifer or a cow each year. People donate what they can. Tickets are sold and the person whose name is drawn wins that prize.

"We have good community support. We can do something good for folks who have less than we do, and everyone has a good time."

Just then, Eddie tried to dart by them. Clare caught him and carried him into the house while he hollered at the top of his voice what sounded like, "No clothes! No clothes on Eddie!"

Spur grinned and shrugged.

"I kind of agree with him. He is mighty ornery though. He keeps Clare on her toes."

CHAPTER 67

TOO MANY WOMEN

NATE WAS UP EARLY ON THANKSGIVING MORNING. Clare had insisted he sleep in the house. He carried his boots downstairs as quietly as he could. He heard voices in the kitchen and headed that way.

Clare was sitting on Spur's lap, and she and Spur were laughing as he kissed her stomach. She slid off quickly when Nate appeared. She blushed when he grinned.

"No need to be embarrassed. The married folks in our community cuddle all the time. It used to embarrass Merina, but I reckon she is used to it by now."

Spur grinned and pointed at a chair.

"Let's eat quick and get out of here. This house will be full of women in no time at all." His grin became bigger when he added, "I had to help peel potatoes the first year we were married, but now enough women show up to help that us cowboys are out of a job. Besides, Clare thought we wasted too many potatoes with all the men carving critters out of them as well as eating them raw."

Nate laughed. "I can see that. So do all the widows help with this too?"

"Sure do. Most of them don't have family so this has become quite the production. Anyone with no place to go is invited. The first year, we just had the hands from our ranch. Word got out about the pumpkin pie though, and this shindig has grown every year.

"We built another barn last summer. The loft is full of hay, and we use the bottom for livestock and for calving." Spur grinned when he added, "I take out the ladders to the loft before folks get here. That keeps most of the kids out of the hay. We use it for our social gatherings. We made it big so there is plenty of room.

"'Course, this whole deal is Clare's idea. She's just a regular little butterfly when it comes to socializing." Spur laughed and Clare shook her head.

"I think you know better than that, Nate. I do enjoy it though. Even more now that there are so many people helping. Some come early to help prepare the meal while others fix their food at home and bring it with them." She smiled at him and her eyes sparkled as she added, "The younger women will be so excited to see a new bachelor. We're so glad you came this week."

Nate's eyes opened wide and for a moment he almost panicked. He looked quickly at Spur and the cowboy laughed.

"You have to keep an eye on Clare. She acts all innocent, but she always has a plan."

The men were nearly done eating when the first surrey pulled into the yard. Eddie had once again taken all his clothes off and escaped out the door before Clare could catch him. Three young women and a bevy of children piled out of the surrey.

Nate shoveled the last bite of food in his mouth and rushed for the door.

"Thanks, Clare. That was mighty good." He pulled his hat on and nodded at Spur. "I'll be in the barn."

Clare began laughing and Spur shook his head.

"Now there's a man who is plumb afraid of women. That's what he is."

Nate tipped his hat to the smiling women, but he didn't slow down. Only when he reached the barn and pulled the door partway shut did he start breathing normally.

"I should ride out of here right now. Why in a few hours, this place will be plumb full of women looking for husbands. There had better be lots of cowboys here today or I am going to miss a good meal."

Nate grabbed a currycomb and a brush off the wall. He brushed Demonio down as he talked softly to him. A little boy popped his head out of Demonio's hay.

"Howdy, mister. Is this your horse?"

CHAPTER 68

A WISE LITTLE MAN

NATE ALMOST DROPPED HIS CURRYCOMB. "YOU HAD better come out of there, young fella. And stay away from this horse's head. He doesn't like people much."

The little boy climbed out of the hay. He almost fell against Demonio and Nate grabbed him.

"Easy there. This horse isn't a plaything. In fact, he doesn't like most folks at all. Now you stay away from him."

The little boy nodded. He watched Nate quietly for a few minutes. Finally, he asked, "Are you a cowboy?"

Nate thought a moment and then laughed. "I reckon I am."

"My pa was a cowboy, but he died. He drowned in a big ol' river."

Nate's hands went still. He took a deep breath and turned his head to look down at the little boy.

"I'm sorry to hear that. Is it just you and your ma now?"

"Yeah. She's sick though. She don't talk about it with me, but I listen when the doctor comes. That doc told her last week that she needed to get her ducks in a row. I don't know what that means 'cause we ain't got no ducks.

"We used to have some chickens, but the coyotes took 'em. Ma says the chicken coop has some holes in it that need fixed, but she can't do it."

Nate listened quietly. His face tightened as he straightened up.

"What's your name, son?"

"Jackson David Boyce but folks mostly call me Beaner. My pa used to call me that. He said it was 'cause I weren't no bigger than a bean when I was born.

"What's your name?"

"Nate Hawkins." Nate put out his hand as he smiled. "It's nice to meet you, Jackson David Boyce."

The little boy smiled. He nodded at Demonio.

"I ain't afraid of horses. They like me. Can I sit up on your big horse? I promise I won't kick him none."

Nate slowly nodded.

"I'll let him smell you first so hold really still." He lifted the small boy and held him in front of Demonio as he talked to the horse softly.

"Now you be nice, Demon. I'm going to let this boy sit on you for a little bit. And don't you start snorting or crowhopping."

The big horse sniffed Jackson. It looked around at Nate and then buried its nose in the pan of oats in front of it. Appy was on the other side of the fence, and he was trying to push his head through to get to the pan as well.

Nate set Jackson on Demonio's back. He held onto one leg while he watched his horse carefully.

Demonio blew through his nose and switched his tail, but he didn't seem to mind.

Nate stepped back and looked at his horse in surprise.

"Jackson, I believe you do have a way with horses. Old Demon here seems to like you. You sit still now while I comb out his tail."

Jackson laid over Demonio's neck. He hummed softly and patted the horse's shoulders. He eventually began to sing while he wrapped his fingers in the horse's black mane. He finally sat up and looked back at Nate.

"Did you know I'm four? Ma says that's big."

"Four is big."

"I don't remember my pa much. Ma has a picture of him by her bed. She tells me stories about him every night. She says that way I will remember. I talk to him some before I go to sleep...after I say my prayers. Ma says we can pray for him.

"Sometimes I hear Ma cry at night. That makes me sad.

"Do you have a pa?"

Nate shook his head. "Nope. He died when I was a little tyke, just a little older than you. I have a big brother though, and he took care of me."

"You didn't have no ma?"

"I did. She was sick for a long time too. She was a good ma."

"I have a good ma. I wish she wasn't sick. Sometimes that priest comes by. I like it when he comes. He always brings us some food and a little candy.

"Ma used to work at the dry goods store. She can't walk no more though."

"Is your ma coming today?"

"Naw. One of the neighbor ladies picked me up. Ma says she might come to the dance, but she probably won't. Dances make her sad. She said she remembers when Pa and her used to dance. She said they just twirled all over the floor. She ain't danced since he died. 'Course now she can't 'cause she can't walk."

A boy just a little older than Jackson popped his head in the barn door.

"Come on, Beaner. We have some explorin' to do!"

Jackson slid down Demonio's front leg before Nate could catch him. He petted the big horse one more time and hollered as he raced out of the barn, "Thanks for letting me sit on your horse, Nate Hawkins. I don't think he's so mean as you say."

Nate stared after Jackson. He shook his head and muttered under his breath as he moved over to brush and curry Appy.

"Sometimes being a kid is just hard. I think this deal Clare started is a good thing. And I hope Jackson's mother does come. Maybe I will have to make a trip out their way. I could fix her chicken coop while I'm here."

CHAPTER 69

A BAD ACCIDENT

NATE HEARD CHILDREN SCREAMING. HE TURNED around to look just as Annie rushed into the barn.

"Beaner fell in the swimming hole! He can't swim and we can't get him out because of the ice!"

Nate grabbed his rope and raced toward the sound of the screaming. The ice was thin around the edges of the pool but was a little thicker in the middle. He could see a hole in the ice but couldn't see Jackson's head.

He slipped the loop over his chest and tied the rope to a large tree nearby. He kicked off his boots as he ran toward the water. Just before he dove in, he heard men's voices coming toward the swimming hole.

Nate swam underneath the ice and felt with one hand for the hole. When he found it, he came up for air and then dove down again. The water was murky and bitterly cold.

His hand touched something, and he grabbed it. It was a small leg. Nate didn't know where the hole was, so he pulled himself back to the shore with the rope. As he staggered out of the water, Spur grabbed the little boy. Father Ravalli was there. He helped Spur lay Jackson down on the ground. He began to push on his chest and breathe into his mouth.

Nate began to shiver. His clothes were freezing to him. Clare rushed toward him with some blankets. She tried to wrap the blanket around him. Nate grabbed the blanket and staggered to where the little boy lay on the ground. Just then, Jackson coughed. He coughed again and spit up some water. He began to cry, and Father Ravalli lifted him up. Clare handed Father Ravalli another blanket and the priest wrapped it around Jackson. He made a sign of the cross over him and handed him to Spur.

"Get him in the house. Take off his wet clothes and rub him gently. Make sure he doesn't have any frozen spots on his skin. I'll be up in a minute." Father Ravalli turned to Nate.

Before he could speak, Nate growled, "I heard what you said but nobody is taking my clothes."

Father Ravalli laughed. He made a sign of the cross quickly on Nate's head.

"Get up to the house and get dried out. Here are your boots unless you can walk barefooted."

The priest was still chuckling when Nate pulled his boots on over wet socks. He staggered as he tried to climb the hill and two of the riders grabbed his arms.

"Here, hero—we can help you. That was a mighty brave thing you did there. How did you know to tie that rope on? I'd never have thought to do that, and we'd have both drowned."

Nate didn't answer. He was too cold to talk. Besides, if he opened his mouth, he was afraid his teeth would clatter so hard he'd break a tooth.

A bevy of women met the men at the door. They had Jackson's clothes off. He was wrapped in a blanket in front of the fireplace. When Nate slid down in a chair, two women pulled off his boots. They pushed his chair close to the fire and handed him another blanket. When two of them offered to help him dry off, he shook his head.

He started with his hair and worked his way down to his feet. His soggy socks were leaking water all over Clare's floor and he tried to sop it up with a blanket that was by his feet.

Clare pulled off his socks and grabbed the blanket.

"For Pete's Sake, Nate. Let me help you. Now stand up while I get some of the ice and water off you."

Slowly, the feeling came back into Nate's feet and arms. He flexed his fingers and they felt fine. He dropped back down in the chair and scooted it closer to the fire. He looked over at Jackson and grinned.

"Next time you decide to go for a swim, try to pick a pond that isn't so cold."

Jackson's blue eyes were wide when he answered Nate.

"I didn't mean to go for a swim. I was just trying to climb that big tree. My feet slipped and I fell in." He stared at Nate before he asked, "Did you fall in too?"

Nate grinned and shook his head.

"No, I pulled you out. I didn't want Demon's new friend to drown." Nate chuckled and added, "Ol' Demon doesn't have many friends."

Jackson stared at Nate and slowly smiled. He leaned toward him and whispered, "I saw my pa down there. He said, 'Keep movin' an' don't give up. We'll get you out of here,' so that's what I did. I thought it was Pa who grabbed hold of me."

Nate stared at the serious little boy. His voice was soft when he replied, "I reckon we both owe your pa a thank you then." He ruffled Jackson's hair before he stood.

"I am going to find some dry clothes. I'll see you afterwhile." Nate changed and lay down on the bed. He was still cold, but he didn't want to be in the middle of so many helpful women. Suddenly, he frowned.

"I can't sneak outside. My boots are by the fire."

CHAPTER 70

BEANER'S MOTHER

NATE FINALLY EASED DOWNSTAIRS. HE GRABBED HIS boots, hat, and coat and headed for the back door. He was still shivering, but he made his way to the barn. He was burrowed in the hay with a couple of saddle blankets over him when Spur strolled in. The ornery cowboy started to laugh.

"Too many women in there for you, hero? You know, I'm sure several of them would love to warm you up. You should take advantage of this situation."

Nate grinned and shook his head as he stood.

"I don't think so. I don't like crowds. Besides, too many women scare me. I like to observe them from a distance, not be in the middle of them."

Spur laughed. His face became somber, and he nodded toward the house.

"It was lucky for little Beaner that you were handy. I don't think we'd have gotten him out in time."

Nate was quiet. He nodded slowly.

"He's a fine little boy. What's his story?"

"His pa's name was Davy. He died crossing the Yellowstone River with some cattle several years ago. It was a fluke accident like so many are. His horse went down in a hole. It landed on Davy's leg and then caught his foot in the stirrup. Davy couldn't get loose and the horse drug him down the river in a panic. By the time his friends got to him, he was dead.

"Davy was a good man. Little Beaner's ma is too. Her name is Alice. I'm not sure what she has, but she is now in one of those rolling chairs. She can't walk and she is losing the strength in her arms too.

"Father Ravalli goes to see her quite a bit. She doesn't like charity, so he just leaves food on her table without asking. The word is she won't make it much longer. No family that we know of. We helped her sell her little farm and get a small house in town. She was hoping to rent the farm out, but she didn't have enough acres. It couldn't even support her and Beaner with the rent income let alone buy or rent a house. 'Course, lots of folks have volunteered to help out. Clare got that wagon rolling.

"Alice wants to keep Beaner as long as she can. We told her we'd take him in when she can no longer take care of him. In fact, we offered to bring both of them out here, but Alice refused. She's a strong woman and is fighting to hold onto her independence. I'm guessing we'll have Beaner before long though.

"Just a darn shame. They were a happy couple. They went to all the dances and always had a good time. Davy was always laughing, and he adored his family.

"Alice rarely comes to dances now. Folks mean well but they treat her differently. She hates sympathy and is almost fierce about staying independent." Spur pointed over his shoulder.

"Ready to take a ride? I'd like to show you around a little. We can't go too far and be back in time for dinner, but we can ride down the valley a little ways."

Nate nodded. He brushed the hay off his clothes, saddled Demonio, and they were soon riding south.

CHAPTER 71

A Big Cowboy and a Little Cowboy

THE THANKSGIVING MEAL WAS DELICIOUS AND LOUD. Nate had never seen so many people together outside of weddings. He kept to the back of the cluster of cowboys and was able to eat mostly undisturbed. He was almost done eating when Jackson found him.

"Hi again, Nate Hawkins. Is that your first or second piece of pie? I only ate one piece, but I'm thinkin' on gettin' another."

Nate grinned at the little boy.

"I tell you what. You go get another piece. If you can't eat all of it, I'll clean up the rest. How's that?"

Jackson nodded excitedly. He rushed up to the pie table and came back with a large piece of pumpkin pie.

"This is sure good pie. My ma used to make pie. She can't roll out the dough anymore though. It hurts her arms."

Nate nodded somberly, but his eyes twinkled when he answered.

"I can't roll out pie dough either. My arms hurt and then the dough gets stuck all over my fingers. By the time I'm done, I have a big blob of sticky dough stuck all over my hands, on my shirt, on the floor—and none in the pan." Nate waved his arm around dramatically as he spoke.

"No sir, I think pie making takes a lot of skill."

Jackson stared at Nate. He grinned and then started laughing. Soon they were both laughing as Jackson rolled on the floor.

He was smiling when he looked up at Nate.

"I wish you were my pa. Then we could go ridin' every day. You could be a big cowboy and I could be a little cowboy. And we could both ride your big Demon horse."

Nate didn't know what to say. He finally ruffled Jackson's hair.

"I tell you what. If it's all right with your ma, I'll take you riding on Sunday after church. How does that sound?"

Jackson nodded excitedly. "That sounds fine. I'll ask her when I get home today." He set most of his pie on Nate's plate and waved back at him before he ran off to play.

CHAPTER 72

An Enjoyable Dance

NATE THOUGHT ABOUT SKIPPING THE DANCE. IN THE end, he decided to go. He was hoping Jackson's mother would be there and he wanted to meet her.

Spur's barn was large. One end had barrels and boards piled high with food. The band was on the other end, and they weren't bad.

Nate danced with Clare and a few of her friends. He was just about to fill his plate when he spotted a pretty woman in a wheeled chair. Jackson was pushing her as he talked excitedly. When he saw Nate, he waved wildly.

"Come over here and meet my ma, Nate Hawkins. I told her all about you!"

Nate strolled over to Alice Boyce. He bowed and tipped his hat.

"Mrs. Boyce—it's nice to meet you. Jackson here told me all about you."

Alice laughed and blushed prettily.

"I'm sure he told you something. Jackson is a little uninhibited." Her smile faded and she looked at Nate seriously.

"I want to thank you for saving Jackson. He might have drowned if it hadn't been for you."

Nate shrugged. "I was just the closest one. Any of those fellows would have jumped in that water. Father Ravalli is who you need to thank. He breathed life back into your son."

The musicians were tuning their instruments for a waltz. Nate grinned at Jackson and winked.

"I understand you and your husband were quite the dancers in your day, Mrs. Boyce."

Alice laughed and nodded.

"We tried to make every dance and barely sat down."

"Would you allow me to dance this one with you?"

Alice stared up at Nate in confusion.

"Mr. Hawkins, as you know, I can't—"

"You can't walk. I know. But I can dance, and I am asking if you will allow me to carry you through this song. You don't look as heavy as some of the gals I have swung around. How about it—one dance?"

Alice looked from Nate to the dance floor. Her eyes sparkled with excitement.

"I accept but you have to promise to put me down when you become tired. I don't want to make a scene when you stagger and drop me."

Nate leaned over the wheeled chair. Alice put her left arm around his neck and grabbed his vest with her right. He picked her up easily. She was lighter than he expected.

"Now you hang on, Mrs. Boyce. I reckon I'll only have the energy to do this one time."

Nate moved to the middle of the dance floor. He swooped and whirled as Alice hung on. By the time the dance was nearly over, she was leaning her head back and laughing. Nate strolled to her wheeled chair and sat her down carefully.

"There you are, Mrs. Boyce. Now you can say you danced tonight." Nate backed away and Alice was soon surrounded by her friends.

The muscles in Nate's arms were burning but he resisted the temptation to stretch them.

"I think I'll have that plate of food now. And maybe a drink if Spur has something he can share."

He danced with lots of women that night but rarely more than one dance. When he wasn't dancing, he sat with Spur and Clare. They danced often and danced well together. Nate grinned when he thought of Clare's marriage contract and Spur's additions.

"I guess that means if you marry the right person, love can grow even if it's not there to start with. I don't think I want to chance it though."

Watching the couples as they laughed and talked almost made Nate homesick.

"I miss my family and all the people in our little community. And I miss Mari most of all. I guess I'll write her another letter tonight."

CHAPTER 73

THE END OF A FUN WEEK

NATE ENJOYED HIMSELF SO MUCH WITH SPUR AND Clare that it was hard to leave. He received at least three hugs from the little girls before he finally dragged himself away.

Clare shook her finger at him.

"Now you come back and visit, Nate. You made lots of friends here who want to see you again, including Alice and Jackson."

Nate laughed and waved.

"I'll be back this way when I get some time. Shoot, maybe I'll even come up with Gabe and Merina the next time they visit."

He waved again and turned his horses north. Going south would have been shorter, but Skalkaho Pass was high and difficult. Nate didn't think he wanted to attempt it with the snow they'd had there.

"Going north will be a few more miles but I'll still be in Missoula by noon. I can catch the afternoon train to Butte and spend the night there. That way, I'll be in town and ready for that afternoon meeting.

Nate smiled as he thought about Jackson and his mother.

He had danced a second dance with Alice. That time it was a polka. She had protested but enjoyed herself.

Nate wrote Mari when it was over. He felt like he was talking to her in his letters. He told her all about the dance as well as about Alice and little Jackson too.

Sunday Mass with Spur and his family at the little mission church had been entertaining too. Nate chuckled as he remembered all the antics Eddie pulled. *At least he kept his clothes on.*

It had been a long time since Nate had gone to church, and he made it a point to talk to Father Ravalli afterwards. He had some questions for the priest and was pleased by the answers.

"Jackson enjoyed his ride on Demonio Sunday afternoon too." Nate reached down and slapped Demonio's neck. "I have never seen you be so tolerant of anyone let alone a kid. What was the deal there? Are you turning over a new leaf?" Demonio just tossed his head and snorted.

"Jackson and I fixed their chicken coup and Father Ravalli helped me out with some chickens. Now they'll be able to have fresh eggs again. Yep, it was a busy week and one I surely did enjoy."

Nate wound Appy's lead rope around the saddle horn and turned the gelding loose. The spotted horse wouldn't go anywhere without Demonio so it would be a relaxing ride. He leaned back in the saddle and began to whistle.

His whistle faded away as he thought about his conversation with Spur.

"When do you plan to go home, Nate? You know, traveling around like you are—it can get in a man's blood. It might not be as easy to quit as you think. If I hadn't married Clare, I'd probably still be roaming all over." Nate frowned and shook his head.

"I don't think so. I'm looking forward to going home. Nope, I don't think it will be hard for me to settle down."

SUNDAY, MAY 3, 1885
ROCKING CHAIR RANCH
UNORGANIZED TERRITORY,
NEBRASKA

CHAPTER 74

A FRIGHTENED WIFE

JASPER'S FACE WAS PALE AS HE GASPED FOR AIR. "GET Sam in here." He gripped Evelyn's hand as he groaned. "Now."

Evelyn's eyes filled with tears.

"He's gone. He left to get Isabelle yesterday morning. I told him to wait until he talked to you but he refused." She leaned over Jasper as she whispered, "Hang on, Jasper. He will be back with her as soon as he can."

Jasper's smile was more of a grimace.

"He's a good man, Ev. He will be a good husband for our daughter. They will make fine-looking grandchildren.

"You lean on him now. Don't try to be tough to protect Izzy. You let folks help you."

When Evelyn started to cry, Jasper squeezed her hand. "Lay down here beside me, Ev. Let's both rest a little."

Evelyn moved close to her husband. Jasper could no longer hug her, and it hurt him when she put her arm around him. Tears leaked from her eyes as she thought about what was to come.

What will we do? I don't want to stay here, and Izzy should experience more culture than she will get on this Godforsaken ranch. I will take her back to Georgia. Maybe we will travel even farther east. I can enroll her in a girl's college on the East Coast.

Sam can run this place. He doesn't need me in his way. Jasper doesn't want me to sell, but if I can convince Izzy to leave...

Evelyn was almost asleep when she heard banging on her door.

"Open up, Evelyn. It's John Kirkham."

Evelyn sat up quickly. Jasper was asleep and she rushed toward the door as she pushed her hair into place. She rubbed her cheeks to make sure the tear tracks were gone. She pinched them to push some color into them. She was smiling when she opened the door.

"Good evening, John. Please come in. To what do we owe this surprise visit?"

"I came to check on you and Jasper. I met Sam in Ogallala yesterday. In fact, I traded my horse for one of his. He had pushed hard to be there in time to catch the train. He said he was going to get Isabelle.

"Sam made that eighty-mile ride in less than twenty-four hours, changing horses at the CC Ranch and my place. Darn trains. We just can't count on them up this way—not yet anyway.

"I thought I'd better check on you." John's face was concerned as he spoke. Evelyn's forced composure cracked, and she started to cry.

"Jasper's dying, John. We were told he had cancer a year ago although he was sick before then. I wanted him to have surgery but that doctor in Cheyenne said it would do no good. He told us to get our lives in order." She was sobbing by the time she finished, and John Kirkham pulled her close. He patted her back awkwardly.

"We'll all help you, Evelyn. I went by Cassidy's ranch on my way here. Freda will be over tomorrow. She said she could stay with you for a time.

"Let's sit down." He studied her face a moment and asked softly, "When was the last time you ate?"

Evelyn was startled. She looked up quickly and stuttered, "I—ate? I—I don't remember. Jasper hasn't been able to eat much of anything for nearly three days. Probably then but I don't remember."

342

Kirkham grinned at her.

"I'm not much of a chef but I make mean biscuits. I know you have some side pork out there in the smokehouse. You just stay put and I'll fix us a bite to eat."

Kirkham soon had the side pork frying and biscuits in the oven. Evelyn watched him in surprise.

"I had no idea you could cook, John. Did your wife teach you?"

Kirkham chuckled and shook his head.

"Nope. This is the only thing I know how to make, and I learned when I was trailing cows. My wife was a good cook, and she didn't like me messing up her kitchen. That was fine with me because I liked her food a whole lot better than mine.

"Every once in a while though, I just get a hankering for biscuits and side pork. The wife used to tell me it was my 'happy food.'

"I don't know about that, but I do enjoy it.

"Ann says I make better biscuits than her, so I make them more often now that my Lydia is gone." He checked the biscuits before he pulled them out of the oven.

"And there you are. Hot biscuits and pork. Tell me where your butter is, and I'll slather some of that on a biscuit for you."

They ate quietly for several minutes before Evelyn commented softly, "I know your wife passed in '78 but you never said what she had."

"I reckon it was the cancer, but the doctor in Ogallala couldn't give us an answer. I wanted to take her to Denver, but she hurt too bad to ride for that long." John cleared his throat and forced a smile. "She suffered those last two years. It was hard to watch that and not be able to help her. Before she died, she took my hand and told me forty years with me was enough. Then she laughed." Kirkham rubbed a big hand across his face and shook his head. "That woman said the darndest things."

"Lydia was a good wife. A strong woman too. I don't think I appreciated her as much as I should have but we were happy."

"Do you have other children besides Ann?"

John shook his head slowly.

"Only in our little cemetery. We lost our two little boys at three and five. A sickness came through and folks all over took sick.

"Ann and the boys were mighty sick. Lydia was down for a time too. Ann and Lydia came out of it, but our boys didn't. We buried one in July and the other in September. Losing our boys almost broke Lydia. That was in '57, almost thirty years ago. It doesn't seem that long though.

"Ann was a happy little girl. She was almost one when her brothers died, and we just dumped all our love on her. Now she has three little boys and two of them look just like her brothers. She even gave them the same names. Jake and Luke. The third one is the orneriest and she calls him Johnny."

Kirkham's eyes were soft, and he put his hand over Evelyn's.

"It won't be easy, Evelyn, but you will get through it. You'll get through it because you are stronger than you think. Besides, the Good Lord don't give us more than we can handle." He smiled at her and stood.

"I'm going to check on your riders. I reckon Sam lined them out before he left, but I just can't help myself." He grinned and patted Evelyn gruffly on the back again.

Evelyn didn't answer. She was quiet until the door closed after John.

"Get over it? I'm not sure about that. I'm not sure my heart healed completely after Ira's death, and now I'm going to lose Jasper.

"The one thing I do know is that I will *never* marry again. If what John said was true, the Good Lord has too much confidence in my strength."

She picked up the plates and carried them to the wash basin. As she began to clean up the mess John had made, she laughed.

"I think I know why Lydia didn't want him cooking. Goodness, he made a mess—and just for a few biscuits and fried pork."

Evelyn washed the dishes and cleaned her table quickly. She was surprised when she heard herself humming. "Working is good for the soul. I think I will wash the bedding today. Then Isabelle will have fresh sheets to sleep on."

CHAPTER 75

A TIRED COWBOY

SAM ARRIVED IN MANHATTAN AT TEN-THIRTY ON Saturday night, May 2. He stopped by the livery to get some oats. The old hostler offered to let him stay the night in the barn.

"Naw. I need to get up to that house where the gal students live. I have a message for one of them."

Penny looked at Sam carefully before he nodded.

"If yore aimin' to pick up one of 'em, ya jist as well wait till tomorrow. That train headed north don't leave till six in the mornin'."

Sam cursed and shook his head.

"That don't work. I need to get Izzy home as quick as I can."

Penny shook his head.

"Frettin' won't help ya none an' neither will leavin' tonight. The train will catch ya 'fore yore a third of the way there. 'Sides, that little blonde gal ain't used to ridin' like ya are. You'd have the skin plumb wore off her legs.

"Nope, ya need to take ya a bath an' eat a good meal. Be at that door by five-thirty tomorrow mornin'. 'Course the cranky ol' gal what runs that place won't let ya in, but I reckon ya can figger somethin' out." He grinned at Sam.

"Git on down to that wash area an' I'll take care a yore horses. Then come on home with me an' I'll get ya somethin' to eat." His grin became large as he added, "I reckon ya be Miss Mari's cousin from up in Nebrasky. Her an' Miss Isabelle be mighty close to my heart. I'll give ya a clean bed an' some vittles too, an' ya can be out a here on that first train."

Sam looked at the old man in surprise. He slowly grinned as he put out his hand. "Yeah, I'm Sam Rankin. I reckon you must be Penny. Izzy and Mari spoke of you. I had to smell those rolls and cake they brung down here the whole time we was ridin' in the sleigh on the way to the train."

Penny chuckled as he shook Sam's hand.

"Sam Rankin, ya get that bath so ya smell an' look purty fer yore little gal in the mornin'. Then we'll eat us a bite while we chew the fat."

Sam was back quickly. He had shaved, bathed, and changed clothes. Penny winked at him and chuckled.

"Yore a site better lookin' now." He pointed up the street.

"I don't live far. We can walk it in no time. My leg pains me some but the doc here said walkin' was good fer it. I broke it last fall." He was quiet for a time. He finally looked sideways at Sam and asked, "Izzy's pa dyin'?"

Sam looked at Penny in surprise and the old man shrugged.

"Miss Mari an' me talk some. She tells me all her troubles an' I jist listen." He grinned and added, "Yore ol' pard better pick up his spurs if he intends fer her to be his gal. She's been gettin' letters from a Dawson feller most ever' week. He's from up in Nebrasky too."

Sam didn't answer until the old man pointed at a little house in front of them.

"That's my place. Yore buddy Nate spent an evenin' with me the night those gals left fer Thanksgivin'. He was mighty concerned 'bout the weather." He grinned and added, "Miss Mari an' me had a long talk 'bout that trip the day after she come back. That an' Nate."

Sam almost tripped and Penny winked at him.

"I don't look like much, but the young gals like me."

Sam laughed out loud.

"Well, that's just fine, Penny. You just keep a talkin'. I told Nate he needed to mail some of those letters he writes to Mari all the time, but he won't do it. He thinks she'll laugh at them. Instead, he just dreams about Mari, and she never hears a word from 'im."

Penny nodded. He opened the door and pointed at the table.

"Go ahead an' sit down. My sis was in over the weekend an' brung me some vittles. We'll have us a cold beef sandwich an' then ya cin sleep in that far room. I keep a bed in there fer my sis. She likes to come to town ever' week er so an' she stays with me."

Penny soon had thick sandwiches in front of them. He looked hard at Sam and asked again, "Izzy's pa a dyin'?

Sam nodded slowly and answered after he swallowed a big bite of sandwich.

"Yeah, her folks found out last winter. They didn't want to say anything to Izzy for fear she wouldn't go back to school. Now we're a pullin' her out 'fore the year is finished so I don't reckon it would have mattered."

Penny chewed in silence before he looked at Sam.

"Miss Mari will take care of her studies. Shoot, she'd probably do them her own self if she thought it would help." He paused briefly before he shook his head, "Naw, I don't reckon she would. She'd say that was cheatin', an' that gal has a mighty straight rod in her back when it comes to right an' wrong."

Sam laughed. "She gets that from my Uncle Rowdy. He's about as honest a man as you'll ever meet. My pa says when they bury Uncle Rowdy, they should put on his marker, 'He never skinned a man in his life,' and that's quite a compliment comin' from my pa." Sam shoved his last bite in and stood up as he swallowed. He almost tripped from exhaustion as he turned around.

"Thanks for the meal and the bed, Penny—and for all the help you give to Izzy and Mari. If I don't see ya—"

Penny interrupted him. "I'll have my buggy in front of that house fer girls by five-thirty in the mornin' to give Miss Isabelle a ride to the station." He grinned at Sam. "I don't think ya should give 'er a ride on yore lap all the way to the train station even if it would be enjoyable." He added, "I reckon ya have the tickets a'ready?"

"Bought 'em in Ogallala. Thanks, Penny. I'll see you in the mornin'."

Penny watched Sam go. He was muttering to himself as he dumped the dishes in the wash pan.

"I think I'll send a wire to Nate. I'll tell him what's a goin' on. Mebbie him or Kirkham can get that train to drop Sam farther north an' make that trip jist a little quicker."

CHAPTER 76

AN ANGRY BEAU

SAM BEAT ON THE DOOR OF HOLTZ HALL THE NEXT morning at five. The angry woman who jerked it open didn't intimidate Sam when she snapped at him.

"Young man, we only receive male visitors on Sunday afternoons between one and four. Come back then." She tried to slam the door, but Sam pushed his boot into the opening.

"Lady, I need to see Isabelle Merrill. I have ridden a long ways, and I'd appreciate it if you'd call her for me. Her folks sent me."

The woman glared at him.

"I will ask you kindly to remove your foot. Miss Merrill will not be available until this afternoon. Good day, sir." She kicked his boot to remove it from the doorway. As she slammed the door, Sam heard the lock click.

"Lady," he shouted, "I'll wake this whole damn place if you don't call her!"

Miss Morton didn't answer. She smiled grimly when she heard his boots retreating down the walk. Her eyes opened wide when she heard him shouting.

"Isabelle! Isabelle Merrill! It's Sam Rankin. I've come to take you home. Tell me where you are!"

Windows opened quickly and soon many young women were peering out. They looked shocked at first but smiled and waved when Sam tipped his hat.

"Sorry to wake you ladies but I need to speak to Isabelle Merrill. Anybody know what room she's in?"

One of the girls called, "Go around the back. She's on the other side. I will tell her you are here!" The girl disappeared and Sam could hear her calling. He could hear the old bat who slammed the door in his face yelling as well.

"Get back in your room! Miss Merrill is going nowhere." The woman appeared in the window, but the shouting cowboy was nowhere to be seen.

She soon heard him yelling again, "Isabelle, throw open your window! I need to talk to you!"

Isabelle appeared in a second story window.

"Sam! What are you doing here?"

"Izzy, grab your things. You need to come with me now."

Isabelle stared at Sam. "I—I have classes tomorrow and studies today. I can't leave."

"Now, Isabelle. We're leavin' on the six o'clock train. Pack a bag fast and meet me out front."

Isabelle disappeared from the window. Sam could hear her arguing with someone, and a door slammed loudly.

Isabelle was crying when she appeared again.

"Miss Morton locked the door! I can't get out!"

Sam's voice was soft when he spoke.

"Izzy, hold your pillow out the window. When my rope catches it, pull it in and have Mari hitch it to your bed. You are goin' to have to climb down the rope so throw your bag down first. We are goin' home fast so pack light."

There was a flurry of footsteps in the room. Soon, a bag sailed out the window. Isabelle appeared again with a pillow in her hand.

"Kneel down, Izzy. I don't want this rope to jerk you out that window.

"Here it comes. Now grab the loop and hand it to Mari. Put the loop around the leg of the bed, Mari. Dally it twice. And you need to sit on that bed to keep it on the floor while Isabelle climbs down."

Isabelle looked from Sam to the rope.

"I—I don't think I can, Sam. I'm afraid of heights." Isabelle's breath was coming quickly. She was almost gasping for air.

Sam's voice was soft.

"You have to, Izzy. We've got to catch that train today. I'll stand up on my horse and hold onto the rope. I'll be right here if you slip. Come on now. Lower yourself, one hand at a time."

Isabelle stepped onto the windowsill. She grabbed the rope and squeezed her eyes shut. "Dear God, please don't let me fall," she whispered as she moved her feet off the ledge.

"Just like that, Izzy. Keep comin'. You're halfway. Almost here. There, I've got you." He kissed Isabelle and lowered her to the ground.

"Throw my rope down, Mari. And you'd better get back in bed. Why, I doubt you even know what just happened!"

Mari flashed Sam a smile and his rope soon dropped to the ground. They both heard the bed slide and Mari waved before she closed the window.

Sam grabbed Isabelle's bag and swung her up in the saddle in front of him. He waved at the girls who were still staring out the windows.

"So long, ladies. Y'all have a real fine day now!" He swung Isabelle into Penny's waiting wagon and dropped the bag beside her. They left on a run for the train station.

Miss Morton jerked open the front door and shook her fist as she shouted, "I'll send the sheriff for you, young man! And you too, Penny! How dare you take that girl from here!" She stomped up the stairs and unlocked Mari's door. When she jerked it open, Mari sat up in bed as she rubbed her eyes.

"Did something happen? I just had a dream that Isabelle jumped out the window! Oh my gosh! She's gone!" Mari ran to the window and threw it open.

"Isabelle! Where are you? Isabelle!" Mari was leaning out the window as she called, and Miss Morton jerked her back.

"Don't you act all innocent with me, Mari Rankin! I know Miss Merrill ran off with that cowboy, and I know you helped her. You are going to be reported, and I hope you are ejected from this school."

Mari straightened her back and walked back to her bed. Her voice was cool when she answered.

"Miss Morton, that door was locked, remember? And Isabelle certainly didn't jump. How do you know if she was in this room at all? Now, if you don't mind, I have classes to prepare for."

Miss Morton stared at Mari. She crossed her arms as she tapped her foot.

"This is the last year you are going to be staying here. I am going to have you removed, and I hope Mr. Fairchild kicks you out of school as well."

Mari stood. She clenched her fists at her side and took a deep breath. She slowly walked toward Miss Morton. Her voice was low, and her eyes snapped as she spoke.

"You go right ahead. And while we're sharing stories, I have a few of my own to tell—starting with Millie Sexton and how she managed to get in a motherly way with a delivery driver—and while she was under your watch. She was here all summer, remember?"

Miss Morton's eyes opened wide. She stuttered a few times before she backed out of the room, slamming the door as she left. Mari threw the tin cup that was sitting on her desk at the door and dropped into her chair.

"And I don't even know why Sam came for Isabelle. I'm guessing it was a family emergency, but he never said.

"Oh dear. I hope her father is all right." Mari frowned as she tapped her fingers on her desk. She finally sighed.

"I think I had better find a different place to stay next year. I'm sure Miss Morton won't let me back in here.

"Maybe I can find a family in town who will let me have a room in return for helping around the house." She frowned. "Or maybe I *will* be kicked out of college."

Mari stood and began to pack Isabelle's belongings in the large trunk she had brought with her.

"I will have Penny help me ship Isabelle's things up to her. I doubt she'll be back next year. I had better talk to her teachers too. Maybe they can send work so she can complete this year."

Mari's hands stopped and she whispered, "Our little school back home needs a teacher. This just might be my last year. I have two years of formal training and that is more than most teachers have. Yes, I think that is what I will do. Mother probably won't like it, but Father won't argue with me.

"If I only knew Isabelle's family was all right."

Sunday, May 3, 1885
Rocking Chair Ranch
Unorganized Territory
Nebraska

CHAPTER 77

FOR LOVE OF A DAUGHTER

ISABELLE SOBBED AS SHE LEANED AGAINST SAM. "WHY didn't Father tell me he was sick when I was home for Christmas? He could have told me then."

Sam squeezed her shoulders.

"Your folks wanted you to finish the school year. They didn't think you would go back if you knew."

"I wouldn't have. I would have chosen one more year with my father over school. Besides, I didn't finish. This entire year is wasted anyhow."

Sam laughed as he shook his head.

"I doubt it. I'm guessin' Mari is already talkin' to all your teachers. They will probably send a whole passel of work for you to complete, and you'll get credit once it's done."

Isabelle sat back in the buggy.

"Mari is a wonderful friend. I wish we lived closer. I am going to miss her terribly."

Sam squeezed her again as Dandy wheeled the team into the Rocking Chair yard.

"Pull as close to the house as you can get, Dandy. See if you can drop Isabelle right on her porch."

Isabelle burst through the door.

"Father! Mother! I'm home!"

Evelyn rushed into the kitchen. Although it was after midnight, she was fully dressed. Isabelle hugged her and ran to the bedroom.

"Father! I'm home!" The bedroom barely showed any light, but Isabelle could see her father had lost weight. The frail man lying there looked nothing like the vigorous man her father had always been.

"Why didn't you tell me," Isabelle sobbed. "I would have stayed here."

Jasper smiled up at his daughter.

"Isabelle, how much luggage did you bring home with you?"

"Only a small bag. Sam told me to pack light, so I only brought what I had to have."

Jasper smiled and barely nodded.

"Just what you needed because you were traveling quickly."

Isabelle was confused but she nodded.

Jasper pointed his arm around the room.

"I too am leaving on a trip, Isabelle. I will only take what I need. That is nothing but a clear conscience and full heart.

"Don't worry about me, sweetheart. I have had some time to make my peace with leaving. A traveling priest stopped by the other day as well. Your mother and I both had some time to talk to him.

"He said if you look at your life as a series of mountains, I am cresting my last one. The valley below is welcoming me."

"But Father, we need you. Mother and I—"

"This life is temporary, Isabelle. We aren't the ones who make the decisions of when we leave or when we arrive either, for that matter.

"Now you go to bed and get some rest. I'm looking forward to a long visit when I wake up."

CHAPTER 78

A Few Good Days

ISABELLE HEARD LAUGHTER THE NEXT MORNING AND she rushed to get ready. When she hurried into the kitchen, she saw her parents, John Kirkham, Freda and Bill Cassidy, Red Valentine, and Sam. Freda was cooking, and everyone was talking.

Sam stood and pulled out the chair between him and her father as he grinned.

"Have a chair, Isabelle. I was just tellin' these folks how you shimmied down that rope to escape that old bat who runs your girl's house down in Kansas."

Isabelle blushed and then laughed.

"I wasn't quite that brave. Besides, Sam stood on his horse and promised to catch me."

Sam scratched his head, and his grin became bigger.

"I was hopin' that wouldn't happen 'cause we'd a both hit the ground. It'd be mighty hard to catch a gal, even as small as you, standin' on a horse like that. I reckon I stretched the truth some."

Isabelle stared at Sam and then hit him with her elbow.

"How dare you tell me that, Sam Rankin. If I'd known the truth, I would never have climbed out that window."

Everyone began to laugh. Just then, there was a knock at the door. Freda opened it quickly, paused, and pulled it wide.

"Nate Hawkins, you get in here!"

Nate pulled off his hat and left his boots by the door. He nodded around the room and his eyes twinkled when they rested on Isabelle.

"You're looking good, Sis." His grin was wide as he nodded at Evelyn. "You too, Ma. Your prodigal son is here for a visit."

Isabelle rushed to give him a hug and Evelyn followed quietly. Nate reached out his hand to Jasper.

"Jasper. Good to see you." He punched Sam in the shoulder as he chuckled.

"Don't you look all purty this mornin'? Amazing how a cute little gal gets you to shave and comb your hair!"

Sam growled at him before he laughed.

"You ride in? Is ol' Demon in the barn?"

"I rode in but Demon's out front. I figured you could tell me where to put him. I have Appy too, but I don't pen them together."

"I'll come out and show you." Sam called back as they left the kitchen, "Save some eggs for Nate and me. We'll be right back."

As the door closed, Nate looked over at his friend.

"Penny sent me a wire. I got it in Salt Lake. I was going to stop in Cheyenne, but I came here instead." He nodded toward the house. "I had a wire from Kirkham when I got to Ogallala. I caught the train north as far as it went and rode the rest of the way." He was quiet as they led the horses toward the barn. "Kirkham said the train made a special run last night to get you and Sis up here—not sure how he arranged that." He added softly, "Jasper looks mighty tough."

Sam nodded.

"I was afraid he'd be gone by the time I got back with Isabelle. He kind of held his own for a time there, but he really went downhill these last few weeks.

360

"He wanted me to wait until the school term was finished, but I figured I'd better get her home. Today is the best he's looked in over a month."

The two men grabbed some blankets and rubbed the horses down. Sam brushed Appy while Nate combed out Demonio's tail.

"How long can you stay?"

"Until Thursday evening. That gives me almost four days. Kirkham said the train was making a special run to deliver freight at the end of the tracks. It will be back through here around six that evening. I'll be at Kirkham's shack by five just to play it safe. That will save me a lot of riding hours if I can catch that train."

"I need to be in Omaha Saturday morning. Big meeting there with all the top dogs."

Sam gave him a long look.

"Think you'll ever quit that job? You sound like you're enjoying it more all the time."

Nate shrugged.

"I like what I'm doing. It isn't hard and it's interesting. Besides, I've been able to see lots of country and meet up with old friends." He added with a grin, "And the money's good."

"How close are you to getting that ranch?"

"I figure I'll have enough money to go home in '88. That's three years from now."

"Think Mari will wait that long? Without hearin' from you, I mean."

"Dadgummit, Sam. I've tried. She's hard to catch. Even this week, when I had the time to stop by home, she was still going to be in school."

Sam kicked one of Nate's full saddlebags.

"Send her a letter, Nate! How hard is that?" He stared at his friend and shrugged.

"It's your funeral. Dandy Dawson don't have trouble writin' letters. There's been one from him goin' south ever' week since Thanksgivin'." He grinned at Nate's irritated face.

"You missed a fine party. We had us a mighty good time. And the last night 'fore the girls left, Dandy and me took Mari and Isabelle for a moonlight ride. We—"

Nate swung his fist at Sam and his friend jumped backwards, almost going down. Sam was grinning when he stood up.

"I'm just sayin' you shouldn't take nothin' for granted."

CHAPTER 79

HE CLIMBED HIS LAST MOUNTAIN

JASPER LIVED THREE MORE DAYS. NATE HAD HEARD about people seeming to get better before they died. He had never seen it though. Of course, most of the people he knew who died were the result of an accident or a fight.

Isabelle was broken-hearted but Evelyn never shed a tear. In fact, she acted like she was made of wood. Nate mentioned it to Sam who just shrugged.

"Evelyn is all cried out. She watched Jasper die a little each day. Now that he is finally gone, she doesn't have any more tears.

"She will crack though. She is goin' to break down and I hope she does it here."

Jasper's hands made him a casket. They brought it up to the house the day he died. Dandy showed it to Sam.

"The fellers all helped build this. Jasper had some wood stored in the barn and we used a little of that. We didn't make no marker but we can."

Sam was quiet as he looked at the coffin. Someone had carved a rocking chair in the lid along with Jasper's name.

His eyes were red when he looked up.

"It's a fine coffin, Dandy. A mighty fine one. I reckon Evelyn and Isabelle will both be mighty pleased."

They laid Jasper down on Saturday morning, May 9. Sam had carved a marker. It read,

JASPER MERRILL
DIED MAY 7, 1885
HE CLIMBED HIS LAST MOUNTAIN

No priest or preacher was available, so John Kirkham conducted the funeral. Sam thought he did a fine job. Jasper was laid down in the little cemetery Sam started. The men built a fence around the small plot, and Sam promised Isabelle he would paint it.

When it was over, a meal was provided by the Merrill's camp cook. The women who attended each brought a little something too.

When the last person left at two that afternoon, Evelyn asked Sam to come with her into the house. She led him to the bedroom she shared with Jasper and pointed toward a large chest.

"I want you to load that in the buggy for me. Isabelle and I will be leaving on the same train that Nate is taking."

Sam stared at her. His face became almost white.

"Evelyn, I don't think that's is a good idea. Let's talk about this. You have plenty of time to leave."

She shook her head stubbornly.

"We are leaving today. Isabelle's trunk is to arrive on the train today, so she is already packed. Mine is ready to load.

"I know Jasper asked you to support me if I wanted to leave. Well, I do. I'm not sure when or if I'll come back but what I do is irrelevant.

"Your name is on all our accounts. As far as I'm concerned, this ranch is yours whether Isabelle marries you or not. I have watched you for the last year. I listened when Jasper discussed our business and finances with you. I know you will run this ranch like it's your own.

"If Isabelle wants to come back after a year, she can. However, during that year, I don't want you to contact her or try to find us. If she writes to you, I don't want you to write back. If she decides not to come back or if she marries another man, I will gift the ranch to you." Evelyn's eyes were hard and angry when she looked at Sam.

Sam looked away and said nothing. His body was stiff, and he clenched the hat he held in his hands. When he finally looked at Evelyn, his blue eyes were hard and angry.

"I'll agree to all that except the writin' part. If Isabelle sends me a letter, I reckon I'll write back. And no one can stop me.

"And I want you to know that leavin' like this ain't right. You ain't givin' Isabelle no time to grieve her pa. She needs to be able to walk out to his grave and talk to 'im. She needs time, Evelyn. I think yore bein' selfish and I'm a tellin' you straight up."

Evelyn's chin came up and she glared back at Sam.

"I'm sure it appears that way to you, but I am doing this for Isabelle. Now please, load this trunk in the buggy for me."

Sam grabbed the trunk and jerked it across the floor. It gouged the wood in several places, but he didn't slow down. He pulled the door open and drug it out the door before he stomped across the yard.

"Belt, Sawyer. Catch the team and hook up the surrey. Put four horses on it. I don't think we'll need them, but we had a little shower and some of the draws might be boggy."

As the men hurried to comply, Sam grabbed Isabelle's arm.

"We are goin' for a ride. Put on somethin' comfortable.

"And pack your travel bag. You and your ma are takin' a trip."

CHAPTER 80

A Hard Goodbye

SABELLE STARED FROM SAM TO HER MOTHER. EVELYN said nothing. She just turned around and shut the door.

Isabelle ran into the house. She followed her mother into her room. Evelyn began to pack Isabelle's valise, the one she had brought from Kansas just a few days ago.

"Mother, what is Sam talking about? What trip?" When Evelyn didn't answer, Isabelle stomped her foot. "I don't know what is going on, but I am not taking a trip. We just buried Father!"

When Evelyn still didn't answer, Isabelle stepped in front of her.

"All my life you have been trying to mold me into this little miniature of you. I'm not you, Mother. I don't want to travel all over and see the world. I'm perfectly happy here."

Isabelle dropped her skirt on the floor and pulled on a riding skirt. She looked at her mother one more time before she stomped out of the room, slamming the door behind her.

Sam was waiting in front of the house. He gave her a hand up and turned their horses toward a little creek. It was the only place around that had a few trees.

They stopped there and Sam put his coat down on the ground for Isabelle to sit.

"Sam Rankin, you had better tell me what is going on."

"I will, Izzy. Now sit down here beside me."

Isabelle dropped down on the ground. She could tell Sam was angry and his anger diffused some of her own.

"Izzy, your pa and me had some long talks this past year. He asked me to promise some things. I didn't want to, but I did because he was your pa."

"What things? What did you promise him?"

"He said your ma would probably want to leave here after he died, and he asked me to support her in that decision."

"What does that have to do with me?"

"He asked me to not to try and stop her from takin' you. He said if I didn't get in the way, you would go and that's what he wanted."

Isabelle turned to face Sam. Her blue eyes were snapping with anger, and she was trying not to cry.

"What about me? Was what I wanted an issue at all? I love you, Sam. I don't want to leave here." Sam didn't answer and Isabelle pulled him around to face her.

"Do you love me, Sam Rankin?"

"You know I do, with my whole heart and all that's in me."

"Then why don't you ask me to marry you? If we marry, Mother can't force me to leave."

"Because I gave your pa my word that I wouldn't ask you for two years, and that was a year ago."

"That was because he wanted me to go to college for two years. Did he even know he was sick when he asked you that? I can't believe you had these conversations without talking to me first." Isabelle began to sob, and Sam pulled her onto his lap.

"Please don't cry, Izzy. I'll be right here waitin' for you," Sam whispered. His chest hurt. He wanted to ask Isabelle to stay more than anything in the world.

Isabelle looked up at him. "And if I don't come back in a year? Will you come and get me?"

Sam slowly shook his head. "I reckon not. If you don't come back, that will mean you went and found some fancy feller back East and you ain't interested in no cowboy."

"If I write you letters, will you answer them?"

Sam pulled Isabelle close and kissed her before he nodded.

"Ever' single one of 'em."

"And if I don't write?"

Sam touched his chest. "Then I reckon this ol' heart will be broke in more pieces than it is right now."

Isabelle took Sam's face in her hands and whispered, "Sam, ask me to marry. I will say yes. I'll say it right now. All those promises don't matter. They were made a year ago to a man who is no longer alive."

Sam's hands trembled as he kissed her, but he shook his head.

"They matter to me, Izzy. A man's word is the most important thing he owns. I promised your pa and I won't go back on my word."

Isabelle began to sob. "I don't understand. Why would he ask you to promise such things? None of this makes any sense to me."

Sam wrapped Isabelle up in his arms as he spoke softly.

"He was worried about your ma. He said she might get unreasonable, but he wanted me to support her in whatever she asked.

"I shore didn't expect her to leave the day of your pa's funeral though. I told her it was a bad idea and I tried to talk her out of it.

"She's a confoundedly determined woman though, and there ain't no changin' her mind. And that means I have to agree."

Isabelle sat up and wiped her eyes. She pulled away from Sam and slid off his lap. Her voice was flat and hard when she spoke.

"Sam, if I leave, I may never come back. Do you understand that? Mother will make sure I am in places where there are many men, men who fit her expectations of marriage. And just maybe, one will turn my head. Knowing that, you are still sending me away?"

Sam stood and looked down at Isabelle. He pushed his hat back and ran his hand through his hair. He took a shaky breath before he replied.

"Izzy, if I'm that easy to walk away from, then your love for me ain't that deep. Mebbie that's what your pa wanted to see.

"If you come back next May, I'll ask you to marry. If you ain't back in two years…" Sam's voice trailed off and he shrugged. "I guess I'll see then. If I ain't heard nothin' from you, I'll know you went and found yourself some other feller. If that happens, I ain't fer certain what I'll do."

Sam put his hand down to help Isabelle up, but she stood without taking it.

"And I think if you can't forget about some silly old promises—well then, you don't love me that much either." Isabelle stomped to her horse and mounted without Sam's help. She spurred it in the direction of her home and left Sam standing by the tree.

Sam slowly rode back toward the ranch.

"Jasper, I reckon those promises I made you will be the hardest ones I've ever had to keep." Sam cursed as he slapped the reins against his leg and pushed his horse to a lope.

CHAPTER 81

SAD HEARTS ALL AROUND

NATE WATCHED ISABELLE RACE HER HORSE INTO THE yard. She dropped the reins by the house and ran inside crying. He picked up the reins and led the animal to the barn. He rubbed it down and saddled Demonio. He cursed softly and shook his head.

"This deal sure didn't play out the way I thought it would."

Sam rode in just as Nate finished saddling his horse. He slid off and stood beside the horse without looking up. He finally pulled the saddle off and threw it on the ground. He led his horse to the pasture and turned it loose.

Nate picked up the trophy saddle and set it up on the holder Sam had made for it. He waited for his friend to come into the barn before he spoke.

"You want to talk?"

"Nope."

"You going to drive Isabelle to the train?"

"Don't reckon she wants me to."

Nate fiddled with Demonio's saddle. He looked over at his friend, but Sam wouldn't look at him.

"I'll make sure they get their tickets to wherever Evelyn is going."

Sam cursed long and low. He walked to the doorway of the barn and stared out before he looked back at Nate.

"If I hadn't promised Jasper I'd stay, I'd ride out today."

"If you hadn't promised Jasper you'd wait to ask Isabelle to marry, you wouldn't be in this predicament."

"Yeah, well mebbie that wasn't such a bad idea. Any woman who can forget a feller as fast as Izzy plans to forget me didn't love me that much to start with."

"Sam—"

"I don't want to talk about it." He kicked a pile of dry manure. He finally looked up at Nate and spoke softly.

"You said you have three more years with the railroad. Well, I'll give it three years here. We just might be fishin' together back home after that 'cause neither of us will have wives."

Nate stared at his friend and finally laughed.

"It won't be all bad then, will it? We'll always be pards." He punched Sam's arm, and they walked out of the barn together.

Belt and Sawyer had the women's bags loaded. Sam waved at them.

"Belt, you drive the women up to the train stop. Put the surrey in the back of the barn when you get back. We won't be needin' it for a time." He walked toward the surrey.

"Evelyn, Nate will help you get your tickets lined out and make sure your bags get loaded. He can arrange a room for you tonight since he'll be stayin' in Ogallala too. The bank won't be open so you'd better take some bank drafts with you."

Evelyn didn't respond as she hurried toward the surrey. Belt helped her in, and she sat down without speaking.

Sam offered Isabelle his hand, but she climbed in without taking it. His face was a little paler as he backed away.

"You gals have a good trip. I guess we'll see you when we see you." He shook Nate's hand and walked to the barn without looking back.

May 5, 1887
Cheyenne
Wyoming Territory

CHAPTER 82

A Quick Visit

NATE PULLED THE DOOR TO THE PASSENGER CAR OPEN and stepped down on the platform.

"I think I'll stop at the express office and see if there is any mail for me there. It's been nearly two years since Jasper died and over six months since I heard from Sam."

There was a letter waiting for Nate and it was from Sam.

Nate—Just a few lines to let you know what's going on. Got the place fixed up a little. The fellers thought we needed to put a big porch on the house for sitting of an evening. We built it last summer—wrapped it around on three sides of the house. Dandy made a couple of rocking chairs. He said any ranch called the Rocking Chair should have a couple of them on the porch. They sit nice and it's pleasant out there of an evening.

Ain't heard a word from Izzy since she left and it's been almost two years. If she ain't back by next spring,

I'm headed home. Maybe you'll be ready to go by then too. Say hello to the folks for me if you see them.

Sam

Nate stared at the letter and shook his head.

"I sure didn't think Sis would leave all mad like she did—and never send a letter for two years either." He read Sam's letter again and frowned. "Women. They just mess with your head all the time."

Nate turned west on Rankin Ranch Road. It was a little wider and smoother than it had been when he left. He stared at the wires running from Lance's barn to his house and shook his head.

"I reckon the whole durn neighborhood is hooked up by telephone now. Not me though. I don't like all the noise they make."

Two teenage girls and several smaller children were running down the road toward Lance's place. They stopped as Nate rode toward them. One of the older girls walked toward him with a smile.

Nate tipped his hat at her. He stared from her to the young lady beside her.

"I know you are both Rankin gals, but you sure aren't kids anymore!"

Both girls giggled. The taller one pointed toward herself.

"Hi, Nate. Yes, I'm Abbie and this is Ellie. I'm fifteen and she's seventeen. She's older but I'm taller.

"Are you back to stay?"

"No, I just have a couple of hours, so I thought I'd stop at a few places and say hello." He paused and asked Ellie casually, "Do you think anyone will be around if I go by your place?"

"Probably. Mari is teaching at our school now. She let school out about fifteen minutes ago so she should be around. She was in a hurry to get home.

"I doubt Pa will be there but Mother rarely leaves. Somebody will be around for sure."

Nate rode his horse beside the kids and talked to them as they hurried toward Lance's house. Everyone was talking at the same time and Nate was grinning. Molly called to him, and he rode his horse up to where she was hanging clothes on the line.

When she asked about Sam, Nate replied, "Just got a letter from him. He said hello. He's doing fine. Built a big porch on the ranch house and one of the hands built some rocking chairs." Nate grinned and added, "He said he likes to sit out there of an evening. He's getting mighty domestic."

They talked a little longer and Molly finally asked softly, "Have Isabelle and Evelyn come back home or are they still traveling?"

Nate shrugged. "I don't know where they are. I don't think anyone has heard from them unless John Kirkham has. He seems to know everything that goes on. He hasn't mentioned them to me though."

Just as he turned his horse to leave, a flashy buckboard went by. Nate couldn't see who was driving but the man in a bowler hat was sitting close to Mari. She held onto his arm and smiled as she looked up and talked excitedly.

Nate felt a pang go through him, but he said nothing. Instead, he waved at the Rankins before he turned his horse south.

"I'll make a quick visit home. It will be good to see everyone."

He hollered back at the happy group behind him, "You kids be good now. And, Ellie, tell your folks hello for me." He rode out of the yard. His feelings were all mixed up inside.

"Well, Demonio, we took a chance when we left. We knew something like this could happen."

The horse snorted loudly and pulled on the reins. Nate laughed.

"You go ahead and run, you ornery cuss. We haven't had enough exercise lately, and it will be good for both of us." He leaned over Demonio's neck, and they raced south down the road toward the Diamond H Ranch.

Rollie and Emilia were just putting their horses in the corral when Nate rode into the yard.

He stepped off Demonio and Emilia charged him.

"Nate! I've missed you! You need to stay home now. I'm tired of you being gone!"

Nate grabbed Emilia as she jumped. He hugged her before he put her down.

"Dang, Emilia. You went and grew up. You too, Rollie. I guess there aren't any little kids left in this house anymore."

Emilia pointed toward the house. Merina was in the doorway, and she was smiling. Her stomach was large, and a little girl peeked out from behind her skirts. "Grace? Is that you? And Elena—look how big you are!" Nate's smile was big as he hugged Merina. He pointed at her stomach.

"It's about time you kicked out another Hawkins, Merina. You make mighty pretty little girls." He leaned over and kissed the two little girls quickly.

Merina took his arm and led him into the house.

"Can you stay for supper? We can eat a little early."

"No, I just have enough time to stop in and say hello. I need to be back on a train headed west in two hours."

"Then have a piece of this pie while I pack you a lunch. You can at least eat something decent while you travel." She paused in her rushing and added softly, "We all miss you, Nate. Don't wait too much longer to come home. Seven years is a long time to be gone." Her dark eyes were soft as she added, "The Rankins miss you too."

A dark blush climbed up Nate's neck, but he shook his head. "I don't think I'm missed as much as I'd hoped." He shoved the last bite of pie into his mouth and stood.

He hugged everyone again and grinned at all of them. "Tell that brother of mine he's a lucky man. I'll see you all the next time I'm through."

Nate turned Demonio north toward Cheyenne.

"One more year. That's all I need to save enough money for my ranch." He frowned as he muttered, "Mari waited seven years, but I guess she's done waiting."

The ride to Cheyenne seemed a little longer to Nate than he remembered. He loaded his horses on the train and dropped down on the hay beside them.

"Mari, you are all I want. You and a ranch we can work together. Maybe I'll have to settle for ranching alone."

December 24, 1887
Los Angeles, California

CHAPTER 83

A LONELY CHRISTMAS

NATE PICKED UP HIS WORK ORDERS AS SOON AS HE stepped off the train. There was a wire from John Kirkham as well. He shoved everything in his saddle bags to read later.

Los Angeles was a bustling city. He rode by groups of men who were arguing loudly, and he heard shots behind him. Nate shook his head. "For a town that means 'the angels' in Spanish, this place is plenty rough."

As he rode his horse down the busy main street, people called gaily to each other. Shoppers were hurrying to grab last-minute gifts. Nate had to stop his horses several times to avoid running over people who rushed into the street without looking.

He rode by an old Spanish church. Its bells were tolling, and Nate pulled Demonio to a stop.

"I haven't been to church in six months. I think I'll go to Midnight Mass tonight. I'll put the horses up and grab a bite to eat first. I don't know a soul here, but someone at the eating house can probably tell me what churches have a service at that time."

He was smiling when he rode into the livery.

"Howdy. I need stalls for two horses. I'd like some oats and fresh hay as well."

The hostler was a young man. He nodded as he hurried to get the feed.

"You want me to rub those horses down?"

"No, I'll do it myself. And stay out of this black horse's pen. He's touchy around strangers." When the man hurried by again, Nate asked, "Any place you'd recommend for food tonight? I mean with this being Christmas Eve and all."

The man pointed down the street. "If you hurry, that first cantina will still be open. They'll be closing in an hour though."

Nate thanked the man and hurried to finish rubbing the horses down. He slapped Demonio as he walked out of the stall.

"You be good now. No kicking at folks or trying to bite someone who gets too close to you." Demonio snorted and pushed his nose into his grain pan.

Nate chuckled and hurried up the street.

The cantina was painted in bright colors, and there was a feeling of festivity inside. People turned to look at him for a moment before they continued their conversations. Nate listened absently and almost didn't hear the young woman who stopped in front of him.

"Do you want to eat, señor, or are you just here for a drink? Perhaps some tequila?"

Nate looked up. For a moment he thought Merina was in front of him. The young woman cocked an eyebrow when he stared but said nothing.

"I'm sorry. You reminded me of my sister-in-law for a moment there. Yes, I want to eat. Just bring me whatever you are serving this evening." He smiled and added, "Thanks."

The young woman was back quickly with some food and Nate began to eat. He could understand just a little Spanish and he listened quietly as he ate.

When he finished, he asked the waitress, "Can you tell me where the closest Midnight Mass is? I don't want to take my horse so I'd like to go to one I can walk to from here."

She answered quickly and Nate strolled outside. He glanced up and then down the street. He narrowed his eyes and looked closer.

"Well, I'll be."

He strolled down the street and tapped a young woman on the shoulder. When she turned around, Nate grinned.

"Hello, Sis. Mighty far from home, aren't you?"

Isabelle stared and then quickly hugged him.

"Nate! It is so good to see you! What are you doing out here?"

"Railroad business but this is my last Christmas away from home. How about you?"

Isabelle's face colored slightly as she answered, "Mother and I are visiting a friend."

Nate looked around. He saw Evelyn talking to a stiff-backed young man who gripped a cane in his right hand. He peered down at the people rushing by with disdain. *That's who Sis traded Sam for? Why his nose is so high in the air that he'd drown if it rained.*

"That fellow over there? He looks like he has starch in his long johns," Nate commented sarcastically.

Isabelle's hands gripped her bag, but she didn't reply.

"Why didn't you write Sam, Sis? It's been over two years and not a single letter from you."

"That's rich coming from you." Isabelle glared at Nate. "I wrote him. I wrote lots of letters—almost one a day that first year. He never answered any of them."

Nate gripped Isabelle's shoulders and pulled her toward him.

"Sam never received any letters." He jerked Sam's latest letter from his wallet and thrust it into her hands.

"I received this last May. Read it for yourself. Hell, I'll quote it for you. 'Ain't heard a word from Izzy since she left. If she ain't back by next spring, I'm headed home. Say hello to the folks for me if you see them.'

"Does that sound like a man who received any letters?" Nate was mad and his voice expressed that anger.

Isabelle's hands shook as she held the letter. She stared from the crumpled paper in her hands to Nate.

"You keep that letter, Isabelle. You keep it as a reminder of the man whose love you threw away."

Evelyn turned around at the sound of Nate's voice. She stared in shock. Her face was pale as she hurried toward her daughter. The haughty young man followed them.

"What's going on here?" he demanded. "Are you bothering my fiancé?"

Nate looked from Isabelle to the stranger. His face broke into a slow grin.

"Nate, no!" Isabelle screamed.

It was too late. Nate's fist made direct connection with the man's long nose. All the anger he felt for his best friend went into that punch, and the man dropped without a sound.

Isabelle leaned over to look at him. She stared up at Nate in horror.

"You killed him," she whispered.

Nate's blue eyes were cold when he looked at Isabelle.

"I didn't kill him, but that long nose won't be so purty when it heals up. Maybe he won't stick it so high in the air now.

"So long, Isabelle." Nate's eyes moved to Evelyn. They narrowed down at the look on her face. "You and your daughter should have a talk, Evelyn. Either she's a liar or you are. Sam didn't get any letters." Nate turned away with no other words.

He shoved his hands deep in his vest pockets and strolled away from the sound of police whistles behind him. He stepped into the nearest church and sat down in the back pew. His hands were trembling, and he wiped the blood off his knuckles with his bandana.

A priest hurried into the church. He approached Nate with a smile.

"I am hearing confessions now if you are waiting." His smile was friendly and Nate grinned as he stood.

"Padre, I ain't been to confession in over seven years. I reckon I will at that. But just so you know, this may take some time."

Friday, May 11, 1888
Cheyenne
Wyoming Territory

CHAPTER 84

Eight Long Years

NATE CLIMBED OFF THE TRAIN AND STRETCHED HIS legs. It had been a long ride from St. Louis, Missouri and his back ached. He pulled off his black hat and ran his fingers through a thick mess of curly, black hair. He smiled and his blue eyes sparkled as he looked around.

He sauntered back to the car that held his horses and led them out. Demonio was excited to be back on solid ground, and both animals sniffed the air. Their ears pricked forward, and they pulled to the south.

"I think you two are as happy as I am to be back. Well, don't worry. It won't be long before we're home.

"I want to clean up first though. I'll get you some grain and hay. Then we'll all be ready to head out."

He rode the big black horse and the leopard appaloosa with a lot of white around its eyes followed along behind. Nate looked around as he rode through Cheyenne. The town had grown while he was gone.

"Streetlights! When did Cheyenne get streetlights? And look at all those trees!" Nate muttered as he stared. He looked from one end of the main street to the other. Nearly all the buildings had businesses in them plus there were new buildings as well. Still, there were "For Sale" signs in some of the windows too. He frowned.

"I reckon these last two years have been hard on folks. Gabe for sure. I almost came home last year but after the drought here and then the Big Freeze, I figured he had enough problems without me getting in the middle of things.

"I have a little money in my pocket now though, and I'm ready to settle down." He stared toward the southwest and grinned.

"And if Mari's not married off, maybe she will be happy to see me."

An old man hobbled out of the livery. When he spotted the smiling young man riding toward him, he pulled the straw out of his mouth and rushed toward him with his hand outstretched.

"By all that's mighty, Nate—it shore is good to see ya! An' I reckon ol' Gabe 'ill feel the same way.

"Ya stoppin' by Rowdy's? That durn Jack Presley's been a hangin' 'round out there, an' Beth is the only reason Rowdy ain't shot 'im yet.

"You's a goin' by there, ain't ya?"

Nate grinned as he shook Rooster's hand.

"I am as soon as I wash some of this dirt off. I swear I get dirtier riding on a train than I do a horse—and I sure would rather be on a horse."

"I heard ya worked some fer the railroad. That true?"

"I did. John Kirkham down by Ogallala, Nebraska set me up mighty nice. I worked for the railroad for three and a half years. Got me a little nest egg so I decided to come home." Nate slid off his horse and wrapped the old man up in a hug as he lifted him off the ground.

"It's mighty good to see you, Rooster. Now if you can point me to the bathhouse, I'd sure like to clean up."

"You jist go on up to where Barney Ford had his eatin' place. That's a bath house now. Hot water, your own room, an' ever'thing.

"I'll rub yore hosses down an' give 'em a bait a grain. Some hay too. They'll be ready fer ya to ride south in two shakes."

Nate nodded and laughed. "Be careful of Demon there. He's a little calmer than he used to be, but If he lays his ears back, just leave him."

"Say, be sure to stop down to the express office 'fore ya leave town. They's a letter there waitin' on ya. It come a month ago, but no one knowed where ya was. I told 'em jist to hang onto it." Rooster's old eyes twinkled and he added, "I said you'd be through some time to check on yore gal an' we'd catch ya then."

Rooster watched Nate walk away before he rushed into the livery. He talked to the animals as he rubbed them down. Demonio looked back at the old man several times, but the brushing felt good and he behaved.

When he finished, Rooster scratched a note on a piece of paper and handed it to the boy who was mucking out the stalls.

"Ya take this on down to Badger. Tell 'im Nate is back an' headed out to Rowdy's. An' it's 'bout time!"

The young man took off on the run and Rooster grinned.

"By cracky, I'm plumb glad that kid is back. Little Mari waited on him a long time, but she done give up this year. I'm afeared she went an' decided to marry that durn Jack Presley. I sure hope that ain't right. Lookin' at Nate though, I'm a guessin' he's a goin' to work on that there deal right away."

Rooster grabbed a pitchfork when he finished with the horses. Forks of manure flew out of the empty stalls and he whistled as he worked. He felt better and spryer than he had in a long time.

"Yessir, things is lookin' up 'round here."

CHAPTER 85

A Letter from Sam

NATE STOPPED BY THE EXPRESS OFFICE FIRST THING. He didn't know who he would get a letter from unless it was Sam telling him when he was quitting.

He stared at the letter. It was from Sam all right. Nate cursed low in his throat.

"I reckon I'll read this tonight when there aren't so many folks around." He shoved it into his pocket. Curiosity got the best of him though. He slipped around the building and dropped down behind a fence. He tore open the letter and began to read.

Friday, January 27, 1888

Nate,

I reckon this here will be the longest and happiest letter I've ever written in my life. Course, what I mostly want to say can be said in three words. IZZY COME BACK!

Yep, you read that right. She showed up at the ranch shortly after Christmas last year. She got Kirkham to stop the train at her pa's mailbox.

Old Kirkham brung his sleigh and drove them the rest of the way home. When I come in from breaking ice and checking cattle, there Izzy was, all bundled up and waiting for me on the porch in one of those rocking chairs. I reckon seeing her there was the happiest day of my life, or it will be till our wedding day. Yep, I asked her and she said yes.

Izzy's ma was mighty quiet when I come in the house. She finally cried and said she was sorry. Izzy wrote me a passel of letters after she left, and Evelyn burned all of them. I thought about throwing her out but I didn't do it. I knowed old Jasper was a watching from up above, and I did promise him I would take care of Izzy and her ma. I wanted to though. What a thing to do to your own girl just cause you don't like the feller she is sweet on.

Kirkham was acting mighty funny too. Izzy told me later he is sweet on her ma. He even asked Izzy if it would be all right with her if he called on Evelyn from time to time. Well, that kind of excited me. Maybe she'll marry him, and she won't be living with us for the rest of her life.

Now here is the second reason I wrote you this long letter. Seeing as how Izzy and me are going to marry and I want to take her home to meet the folks, we decided to get married back home. I thought maybe her ma would argue some but she didn't. I guess she figgered if Izzy warn't to be married to some feller with starch in his long johns (Izzy told me what you did to that feller and it made me plumb happy!) then she just didn't care no more. Well, that is just fine with us. Izzy don't care much about a wedding, and I sure don't.

We figger we will just let Ma take care of it. She will tell everybody what to do, including Evelyn, so that will work out just fine.

That brings me to my third reason for this here letter. Izzy and me want you and Mari to stand up with us. And since you will both be there, how about we all get married at the same time? I don't know how your plans with that are coming along but we will be out in June. I ain't telling Ma before we come so you have a little time to plan on your own time. But you better hurry it up cause Izzy and me are doing this with or without you and Mari hitching up alongside us.

Well, I done said all I need to say. I want to thank you for the talk you give Izzy in California. She said that was what brung her home. I reckon you are the best pard a feller ever did have.

Yore pard and best fishing pal,
Sam Rankin

Nate sat still for a time after he read Sam's letter. His smile was wide when he stood. He folded the letter and put it in his pocket.

"I reckon that was the best news I've had in some long time." He shook his head in surprise at the idea of Kirkham courting Evelyn.

"I sure never saw that coming. Old John is just plumb full of surprises. Shoot, he probably has some moldy money just sitting around somewhere and will even build Evelyn a new house. I doubt Ann will want that testy old woman underfoot all the time." Nate chuckled as he walked out to the street.

"Sam marrying and coming home to do it. I don't know. May is half over and June is mighty soon to marry a gal you haven't seen in eight years."

CHAPTER 86

A FATHER'S BLESSING

NATE STROLLED OUT OF THE MERCANTILE. HE TIED one new bandana around his neck and shoved the other one in his vest pocket. Then he took the rope halter off the appaloosa. He turned him loose and slapped him on his rump.

"You go on home, boy. I'll be there later. Demonio and me have some business to take care of first."

The appaloosa stood still a moment. It turned its head to look at Nate and the big, black horse. Then it bucked and snorted as it raced south out of town, dodging people trying to cross the street.

A man waved a walking cane at Nate.

"You darn cowboys need to hang onto your horses. Why that animal could have killed me!"

Nate rode toward the man. He pulled off his hat and scratched his head.

"You mean that appaloosa? He ain't mine."

"He's a rough one though. Those railroad boys put 'im in the same car as this little hoss. He pertineer killed old Fred here," Nate drawled as he patted Demonio's neck. The big horse snorted.

"No, sir. He ain't mine. I sure hope he gets out a town 'fore he hurts someone though. Y'all keep an eye on 'im if ya see him again—and get outta the way. He's a killer, that's fer shore."

The man stared at Nate's sincere face before he turned to stare at the appaloosa's rapidly departing hind end.

Nate pulled his hat back on his head and tipped it at the older woman who was trying to dodge the piles of horse dung the appaloosa had dropped as it ran.

"Ma'am," he drawled, and he rode out of town with a grin on his face.

The whitened skeletons of cattle were scattered across the pastures. There weren't as many as he had seen in some places. Still, it was more than any stockman would want.

"That blizzard of '86 was a killer, and it killed from Montana all the way south to Texas. Put a lot of ranchers out of business, and it broke more who refused to quit. Gabe said the ranches around here weathered it better than some in other places. He said the smaller operators did the best. They were able to scatter hay for more of their livestock. He and Angel lost nearly a fourth of their cattle though and that's tough. Lance and Rowdy lost livestock too, but they weathered it as well. He never mentioned how Tex and Flory held up."

Nate was quiet as he rode farther south. The whitened bones made him sad. By the time he turned west though, excitement at being home took over.

"I sure am looking forward to seeing Mari. According to Rooster, she's not married yet so that means I still have a chance."

Rowdy stomped out of the barn just as Nate rode into the yard. He stopped to stare a moment and then strode toward the younger man with a huge smile on his face. He stretched out his hand.

"Nate Hawkins! By George, it's good to see you! You step on down from that horse, and I'll have one of the kids put it in the barn."

Nate dismounted and looked around. He counted three little people he didn't recognize.

"It looks like you added a few more little faces to your family," he commented with a grin.

"We sure did. Beth makes good lookin' kids and we both like babies. Besides, we need the help around here," Rowdy replied with a grin. "No more twins though…yet." Rowdy winked at Nate and pointed toward the house.

"Mari is out behind the house hanging up clothes. I'm guessing you didn't ride over here to visit with me."

Nate looked toward the house. He twisted his hat in his hand a moment before he replied.

"Actually, I do want to talk to you. I'd like your permission to court Mari."

Rowdy frowned at him.

"You have my permission. When it comes right down to it though, it's up to Mari, and she's a little testy these days." A growl rose from Rowdy's throat. He shook his head as he stared toward the house. His voice was hard when he finally answered. "You were gone a mighty long time, Nate. She waited seven long years for you to come back with barely a word from you. This winter, she started seeing Jack Presley."

Nate held back the scowl that tried to cover his face. He kept his expression bland and listened as Rowdy continued to talk.

"I'd like to shoot the sidewinder, but Beth says we need to be nice to him. If Mari is to wed him, he'll be part of the family." Rowdy cursed and shook his head.

"I didn't like him when he was growing up, and I don't like him now that he's full grown. Well, he's sort of full grown.

"He has money though. I think Mari has decided if she can't find love, then she just as well marry for money." Rowdy's brow furrowed and he kicked at a clod in front of him.

He looked up at Nate and slowly grinned.

"You know, Nate, you should stay for supper. That smart aleck Jack is coming out for the evening." Rowdy snorted and added, "He's always trying to impress us with his fancy rigs and prissy ways.

"He'll sit beside Mari, but we'll put you across from her, kind of accidental like." Rowdy winked at Nate. "Mari won't like it, but I reckon the rest of us will enjoy the show. That's as much help as I can give you." Rowdy looked out over his ranch before he looked back at Nate.

"You might have to work a little harder than you think though. Mari's sweet but she's stubborn as a mule. I reckon she'll marry someday—when she's good and ready.

"She didn't go back to college after Isabelle left, you know. She came home and took over the teacher position at our little school.

"Beth wasn't too happy. She wanted Mari to graduate but Mari talked to me some." Rowdy grinned and added, "That little deal with Sam sneaking his gal out the window was going to get her kicked out of the place she lived. I offered to go down there and straighten things out, but Mari said she was ready to come home. She said one year of college was enough to certify her and she had two—three actually since she was in her second year when she enrolled down in Kansas.

"She always wanted to be a teacher and that's what she is.

"She's had all kinds of suitors out here since she came back but she didn't pay them much attention…till Presley started coming around." Rowdy jerked off his hat and ran rough fingers through his hair. He snorted disgustedly before he jerked it back on.

"I just don't understand it. Presley's not much of a man.

"Beth told me if Mari wants him, then I have to give them my blessing. Well, I won't. I don't like him and if I said I did, it would be a lie.

"I'll tolerate him for as long as I can, but I'll be danged if I'll give him my blessing." He scowled at Nate again and shook his head.

"In the end though, it's her choice. I reckon if she wants to settle down with a fellow like him, I just need to keep my mouth shut and resist the urge to hit 'im. And shooting him would be my first choice."

Nate listened quietly and didn't respond. Rowdy looked hard at the younger man before he spoke again.

"So, if your intentions are permanent, then get on up to the house. You ever run off again though and you'll answer to me." Rowdy glared at Nate as he spoke. He finally grinned.

"Oh, Hell's Bells, Nate. I like you too much to be mad at you. Get on up to that house and win your girl back."

CHAPTER 87

An Old Bandana

MARI WAS FACING AWAY FROM NATE WHEN HE STEPPED around the house. She was singing and he could see his old bandana in her hair. He watched her for a moment before he spoke.

"Hello, Mari."

Mari's body went still and then she spun around. She stared at Nate for a moment. Emotions flashed across her face faster than he could track. He slowly walked toward her with a crooked grin and pointed at her hair.

"You are even prettier now than the day I gave you that bandana."

Mari's breath was coming quickly. She touched her hair. Then she pulled the bandana off and shoved it into her apron pocket. She put her hand on her chest and tried to slow down her breathing.

"Eight years and only one letter, Nate Hawkins. And that one just two months after you left. I had to find out where you were from Merina," Mari's voice was angry, and she had tears in her eyes.

"I guess you thought one letter was enough to keep stringing me along."

Nate shook his head.

"I wrote you a lot more letters than that. I even brought them home with me. I wrote them when I thought of you and that was a lot. After I finished them though, I just couldn't mail them. They were too lovesick, and it was embarrassing."

Mari stared at Nate. He was a full head taller than he had been when he left. His eyes were the same deep blue she remembered, and the crooked grin was the same too. Yet he was different. He was more sure of himself. His arms and shoulders had filled out. The boy she had been waiting for had returned as a man.

"You've changed."

"You have too. You were mighty pretty when I left, and you are even prettier now."

"You already said that." She frowned and cocked her head. "What am I supposed to do? Run and throw myself at you because I'm so grateful you came back?"

"Well, that would be fine. I reckon I won't hold my breath though." Nate grinned and stepped closer to her. "You want me to help you hang these things up?"

He started to reach into the basket, but Mari jerked it away from him.

"I don't need your help."

Nate stared at her before he turned to look at the long line full of women's undergarments. His smile became bigger, and he started to laugh.

"Well, if you don't want any help, I reckon I can just squat down here and visit while you hang them. I'm going to see them either way though."

Mari glared at Nate before she grabbed the basket and rushed into the house. Nate could hear her talking angrily, and he followed her to the door. When he knocked, Beth answered with confusion on her face. Mari slammed the basket down on the table and rushed out of the room.

Nate blushed slightly.

"Hello, Beth." He grinned at her and nodded toward the door Mari had slammed. "That didn't go exactly as I had hoped."

Beth grabbed Nate and hugged him.

"Come in here, Nate. I want to hear all about what you have been doing these last eight years! Did Sam come home with you? My, how we have missed you boys.

"And look at you. Why you are at least six inches taller than you were when you left. You might even be taller than Gabe!

"Does your family know you are home yet?"

"They know but I haven't been there yet. I turned Appy loose in town and he headed south on the run. They'll know I'm back when he shows up. He was mighty pleased to be home. I am too but I wanted to stop by here first."

He grinned at Beth and nodded his head toward the outside door.

"So how many kids do you have now? I saw three running around outside that I didn't recognize."

"We have nine now. I can't believe how time just races by.

"Rudy is working as a lawyer in Kansas City. He's twenty-seven now. He met a woman some time ago. Her father was one of his teachers at the law school he attended. She was in Kansas City and stopped by her father's law office for a visit. Rudy works for him now and seems to be quite taken with the daughter. Of course, he hasn't told us that. In fact, he barely tells us anything.

"We were all hoping Rudy would come back here and practice law with Levi. He hasn't mentioned that though.

"The twins are eighteen. Ellie is going to Georgia this summer to stay with some of my relation. She will be attending college this fall in Kansas. She thinks she might want to be a nurse.

"Eli will be in for supper—he never misses a meal. He hates school. He barely passed eighth grade. All he wants to do is ride and break horses. Rowdy needs the help so I guess that's what he will do.

"Pauline is twelve now and Emmaline is ten. The three youngest are the ones you haven't met yet, but you will soon. Betsy is four. Rowdy says she looks like the picture Lance has of their mother. Fred is two and a half. His siblings call him Fritz. He's a little stinker. He's every bit as ornery as Molly's Livvy and Henry are. Callie is one and she is just precious." Beth paused and added softly with a smile. "I so love babies." She laughed when Nate laughed and added, "Of course, you know Mari is twenty-one—almost twenty-two.

"Yes, it's a full house. Rowdy has added on twice. He pretends to complain but he loves little ones too." Beth giggled and added softly, "He's an old softie at heart."

The bedroom door opened, and Mari hurried out. She refused to look at Nate. He looked at her though. She had changed her dress and fixed her hair.

Mari grew up. She always was pretty, but she is downright beautiful now. Better looking than all the women I have seen since I left here. She filled out too and in all the right places. Nate colored slightly under his tan when he realized he was staring. He looked away for a moment. His eyes returned to Beth when he realized she was talking.

"Would you like a glass of water or milk, Nate? If you just arrived today, you must be starving. And please, sit down. Make yourself comfortable. Take this end chair and stretch out your legs.

"Mari, get Nate a glass of milk and maybe one of those rolls you just made. I'm sure he's hungry and a little bread might hold him over until supper." Her green eyes were wide when she asked, "You will stay for supper, won't you, Nate?"

Nate pulled out a chair and dropped into it. He leaned over to smell the bread and gave Mari that smile that always made her melt.

"Beth, I would never willingly miss one of your meals. You bet I will. And, Mari, I dreamed of your bread every time I ate hard biscuits…and that was a lot of times."

Nate's smile became bigger as he took a bite of the bread in his hand. He chewed contentedly.

Mari said nothing. She was nervous and kept looking out the open door. Nate pretended not to notice.

CHAPTER 88

"ONE MORE WORD..."

BETH CHATTERED WHILE NATE ATE. SOON THEY ALL heard a buggy driving into the yard.

Nate leaned back and looked out the door.

Jack Presley jumped out of a smart-looking buggy and tied his team in front of the house. He hurried up the steps. He stopped suddenly when he saw Nate.

"I—uh—I came to take Mari for a buggy ride."

Rowdy stepped through the door and bumped the smaller man out of the way.

"You will have to wait on that buggy ride, Jack. We eat as a family here. You are welcome to join us though.

"Nate showed up a while ago and he is staying too. Beth always manages to have enough, even when we're not expecting extras." He hit the back of the chair where Nate was sitting.

"I won't give up my chair though. You go sit over on that side of the table," he growled at Nate as he pointed toward a chair.

Nate stood hurriedly as he grabbed the last bite of roll off his plate. Mari looked suspiciously from her father to Nate. The younger man didn't look up. He quickly moved to the new spot Rowdy had directed him.

Rowdy grabbed Jack's arm and pointed at a chair across the table from Nate.

"Sit down so you're out of the way, Jack. This kitchen isn't big enough for people to stand around and do nothing while the women are trying to get food on the table."

Jack hurried to the other side of the table. He started to sit down across from Nate but moved down one chair.

Nate almost laughed. *For a man who is gruff and tough, old Rowdy orchestrated that like a music director.*

The children tumbled through the door and Mari finally sat down. She was beside Jack and directly across from Nate, just as her father had planned.

Rowdy led the grace. When it was finished, the bowls of food were passed around.

The table was almost quiet as everyone ate. Jack finally cleared his throat and looked over at Nate.

"What ranch have you been riding for these past eight years, Nate?"

Nate chewed for a moment before he answered.

"I've been a little bit of everywhere. I worked on ranches from Texas to Colorado, and one up in the Dakotas. Sam and I took several herds north too. By the end of '83 we were working in the Sandhills in Nebraska.

"John Kirkham has a ranch north of Ogallala, and he hooked me up with a railroad job. I spent most of the last four years running all over the country platting out train routes and negotiating land purchases." He looked at Rowdy and chuckled softly as he added, "I even spent a few days with Clare and Spur up in the Bitter Root Valley in Montana Territory several years ago. They have five little ones now, or at least they did then.

"Ol' Spur is downright contented. He settled into married life mighty easy. He told me he was happier than he ever had been, and I reckon that's true.

"Clare is happy too. Spur teases her all the time, and she laughs a lot."

Mari listened closely. She finally leaned forward and asked excitedly, "Were you ever in Charleston in South Carolina? I have read so many books about that area. I would love to visit there."

Nate nodded as he looked at Mari.

"I spent several days there last year. I didn't look around much because I was working. I reckon it would be a nice place to spend some time…if a fellow was with the right person."

Nate's voice was innocent, but his eyes were intense. Mari blushed and Jack looked suspiciously from her to Nate.

"It doesn't sound like you worked too hard if you had that much time to gad around and visit with people. And on the company dime too," Jack commented sarcastically.

Mari's face lost its color, and she ducked her head. Nate stared at Jack. His eyes were hard, but before he could reply, Beth spoke.

"What was your most favorite activity while you were gone, Nate? What did you do during your off time?"

"When I was bumping all over with the railroad, we worked crazy hours. Sometimes, we worked twelve or fifteen days in a row with barely any sleep. The food wasn't bad if you had time to eat—I missed a lot of meals though. Besides, even good food was nothing like this.

"Then there would be a time when we were off for three or maybe five days. I loved those days. I rode Demonio all over the place. I met ranchers everywhere I worked, and I did day work for them when I had time.

"My best times were working on those ranches and seeing how they did things. I have always wanted to make my living as a cattleman, and that hasn't changed."

Nate grinned at Beth, and she smiled back. He looked to her just like the young man she had hugged goodbye eight years ago. Before she could reply, Jack spoke up.

"Well, lots of cattlemen up here went broke in the last two years. I'm guessing if you were here during that time, you would have been one of them. Your brother certainly lost his share. He is not much of a rancher, and I doubt you are either."

Nate laid his fork down and stared at Jack. The man fidgeted in his chair and sank lower as Nate continued to stare.

"Jack, out of respect for this family, I won't hit you for that comment. But if you speak one more time during this meal, I am going to forget my manners."

Jack glanced up with a startled look on his face. He opened his mouth and Nate pointed at him.

"One more word."

The man sank lower in his chair and began to eat with a surly look on his face. Nate's eyes moved to Mari and the total disgust she saw in them made her blush.

The meal was quieter after that. Even the children were afraid to talk. Nate was irritated with himself. He finished his pie quickly and stood.

"Rowdy. Beth. That was a mighty fine meal. I'd best get on home before it gets too late." He paused a moment and looked at Mari. When she didn't look up, he pulled his hat on and strode toward the door. He stopped there and turned around.

"Thanks again, ladies, for one of the best meals I have had in eight years. And I'm sorry I lost my temper."

His shoulders filled the doorway for a moment and then he was gone. No one spoke until Mari stood.

"I—may I—may I be excused?"

Rowdy growled an answer. Mari rushed out the door and Jack started to stand. Rowdy pointed at him.

"Sit down, Jack." He glared around the table. "You kids go outside. You can play for five minutes. Then get back in here to help your mother clean up this mess." His frown became deeper when he added, "And stay out of the barn. Nate's black horse isn't used to kids."

When the kids were gone, Rowdy looked over at Jack. His eyes were glinting with anger, and he tried to control his voice.

"Jack, I don't like you. I never have but I tried to tolerate you for Mari's sake." He pointed a big finger at Jack and his voice was almost shaking. "I won't have anyone insult a guest at this table the way you did today.

"Now, get out. I don't want to ever see you on this ranch again." When Jack started to speak, Rowdy stood. He leaned both huge hands on the table as he glared at Jack. Then he pointed at the door.

"Get! If Mari wants to see you, she can meet you in town, but don't you *ever* come to this house again."

Jack fairly ran out the door. Rowdy ran a shaky hand through his hair. He looked over at Beth and she covered her mouth. Soon her giggles were leaking out in spite of her attempt to control them.

"What I really wanted to do was wring his scrawny neck. That little weasel caused more ranchers to lose their places than any banker around. Instead of working with them, he took great pride in calling in their notes.

"I can't believe Mari even tolerated him."

Beth walked over to Rowdy. She smiled up at him and put her arms around his waist.

"Rowdy Rankin, I love you. I have loved you since I met you in front of your own tombstone. I am so pleased you threw Jack out.

"And don't worry. Mari didn't like him. It was more like she was seeing him to spite Nate's memory." She laughed softly.

"Thank Heavens Nate came home."

413

CHAPTER 89

NOT LIKE HE PLANNED

NATE HAD DEMONIO SADDLED AND WAS TIGHTENING the cinch when Mari rushed into the barn. Her brown eyes were wet, and she blinked to keep the tears back.

"Nate, I'm sorry. I'm sorry Jack was so rude."

Nate dropped the stirrup he held and turned to face her.

"Mari, you don't have to like me. You don't even have to see me, but for the love of Pete, pick a *man* to spend time with!"

Tears leaked out of Mari's eyes, and she shook her head.

"I don't want to spend time with Jack or with any other man. I was mad at you for not writing and for staying away so long. I told myself that by picking someone I knew you would despise, I could get even with you for not coming home." Her voice caught in her throat as she whispered, "Please don't go."

Nate stared at Mari in stunned surprise. He slowly shook his head.

"Mari, that makes as much sense as putting a bucket under a bull and expecting milk.

"I am going to leave. I'm tired and I'm mad. I need to go before I say something I'll regret."

Mari's body stiffened and she glared at Nate.

"You were gone nearly eight years, Nate. *Eight years.* What did you expect would happen when you rode in here? You left as a boy and came back as a man. I don't know you anymore." She was quiet a moment and then whispered, "We don't know each other as adults, Nate. We only have our memories as children. You've never even courted me."

Nate looked at her and then looked over her head before he answered.

"I thought of you every day. I talked to you before I went to sleep at night. I wrote you letters and told you how I felt."

"But you never mailed them! *You* might know how you feel but *I* don't know!"

"I'm telling you now."

"It's not enough."

"What do you want from me, Mari? Do you want me to ride out and leave you alone? Is that what you want? I have plenty of work to keep me busy if you do. Just say the word and I'll be gone."

"Nate, please. Don't say that."

"Then tell me what you want!" Nate was nearly shouting. He jerked his hat off and pushed his hand through his hair.

"I'm sorry, Mari. I'm headed home. I need to get some sleep and clear my head. You have me all twisted up inside. Maybe things will look different for both of us on another day."

He mounted Demonio and held him still while he looked down at her.

"Goodbye, Mari," he said quietly as he turned his horse toward the lane.

Mari watched Nate ride away and something inside her broke. She sobbed as she sank down in the hay. She curled up tightly as she cried. She was still there when Rowdy walked into the barn. He lifted his sobbing daughter and patted her back as he held her on his lap. She buried her head against his shoulder and cried some more.

"Talk to me, Mari. Tell me what Nate said that broke your heart."

"He came back. Before that, I had my memories, and I could move my life around to make it work exactly as I wanted. He didn't behave like I expected him to, like I dreamed he would.

"He came back all grown up and handsome. I realized he hadn't just sat around and missed me for eight years. He continued to live and work. He probably even met girls and went dancing. The thought of that made me mad.

"I am mad I waited for eight years. What is so wonderful about Nate that I would wait that long?" She sobbed as she added, "What is wrong with me?"

Rowdy didn't know what to say. He wasn't sure if he should laugh or try to comfort his daughter. *She is completely unreasonable. 'Course, Mari has always been stubborn. So sweet but mighty stubborn.*

"Why did you wait, Mari? You had plenty of chances to date other fellas. Boys and men. Lots of them came out here and tried to court you. You sent them all away. You even told that Dawson fellow in Nebraska not to come up here.

"You went to plenty of dances too. You just never let any of the young men take you home. Now why didn't you?"

"Because none of them measured up to Nate. He was my standard and no one else compared," she sobbed.

"Well then, maybe you should let him court you. See if he meets the high mark you set. Maybe even he won't measure up to the Nate of your dreams.

"See, that's the problem with arranging dreams. They aren't realistic. We can make them fly as high and be as perfect as we want. No real fellow can measure up to that perfect man.

"Still, I think courting would be a good start. There's a dance tomorrow night at the Rollins House. Maybe you will see him there."

He patted her back and added quietly, "I ran Jack off. I told him to never come back."

Mari started crying again. "I am so ashamed of myself. I never liked Jack. He was rude and self-centered. I only let him court me because I knew it would make Nate mad." She sobbed as she added, "I'm a terrible person."

Rowdy grinned over her head, but he said, "Come on, Mari. Let's go on up to the house. You can take a nap, or you can go fishing with the little kids. Your choice. Personally, I think a nap sounds better."

He led his daughter up to the house. She went into the bedroom she shared with her sisters and closed the door. She didn't come out for supper and was still asleep when Beth went to check on her at seven that evening.

Beth quietly shut the door. She raised a quizzical eyebrow at Rowdy. He just shrugged.

"High emotions take a lot of energy. Let her sleep and we'll all feel better."

CHAPTER 90

A WARM HOMECOMING

DEMONIO WANTED TO RUN, AND NATE LET HIM. HE could feel the tension seep out of him when he rode his horse into the Diamond H yard. It was hard to tell who was more excited to be home, Nate or Demonio.

Gabe jerked the door open with a rifle in his hand when he heard a strange horse neighing. When he saw Nate, he laid the gun down and walked out with a smile on his face.

"Hello, little brother. Appy showed up here hours ago. It's about time you came home." He turned around and hollered, "Merina! Nate's home!"

Just then, Rollie and Emilia appeared in the doorway. Nate shook his head as he laughed.

"Holy smokes. You are both almost grown." He studied Rollie a little longer and ruffled his hair. "Dang, Rollie. You are like looking in the mirror. You are a Hawkins through and through!"

Rollie grinned and Nate hugged Emilia.

"And Emilia, you are as pretty as your sister. I'll bet ol' Gabe has to beat back the fellows who hang around you at the dances."

He stared at the little girl peeking from behind Merina's skirt.

"Hello, Grace. You have grown some too." When another little girl dashed out of the house, Nate looked at his brother and laughed.

"Elena looks just like her pretty sisters." He looked behind Merina and then at Gabe. "Where's the little one Merina was—" Gabe shook his head and Nate stopped talking.

Gabe scooped up his littlest girl.

"Elena, remember your Uncle Nate?" Gabe winked at Merina as Elena slid down and ran off to play. "Elena is six and as wild as her mother."

One of the hands carefully took Demonio's reins, and Nate's family pulled him into the house. He was pushed into a kitchen chair, and everyone began to ply him with questions.

Nate finally waved his hands and laughed.

"Yes, I am home to stay, but no, I'm not moving back. I've saved enough to put some land together. I thought I might look at some ranches tomorrow."

Gabe nodded slowly.

"That's a good plan but the only available land I know of that's selling is north or west of town."

Nate nodded.

"Badger gave me the names of three ranches. One is north of Angel and the other two are northwest of Cheyenne, out closer to where Tex and Flory bought.

"How are they anyway?"

"Happy as clams. They were married shortly after you left. Frieder and Dot were married at the same time. That was the first double wedding I ever attended, and it was darn efficient. Now Tex and Flory live in the main house. Dot and Frieder live in the smaller house.

"Pop bought Flory's house in town. Chet and Nancy Reith live with him. Pop has even made a couple of friends. Several other old fellows live fairly close, and they walk to each other's houses nearly every day.

They play checkers and shoot the breeze. One of them likes to make root beer so they test that on a regular basis.

"Ol' Pop threw out his canes. All that walking is doing him good. He's happier too. And he just loves Flory. She and Tex have two little boys, and Pop considers himself their grandpa. Chet has to take him out at least once a week to see them."

"Do Frieder and Dot have any kids?"

"Not yet. That Dot is something else. If any of the older women ask her when she intends to have children, she tells them she doesn't know but it sure is fun trying."

Gabe shook his head. "Dot's bold and brassy but Frieder adores her. They work side by side every day. She's good help too. She usually comes with Frieder to help during roundups.

"Flory and Dot have become close. They are like sisters which makes it nice for both couples. I think Flory was almost afraid of Dot in the beginning, but they are best friends now. It's not so lonely for Flory either."

The three adults visited until late in the night. Nate finally stood. "I'm calling it a night." Merina wanted him to sleep inside, but he shook his head. "I'll sleep in the bunkhouse. I don't want to mess up sleeping arrangements."

Gabe offered to go with him in the morning to look at ranches and Nate was smiling as he climbed into his bunk. His smile slowly disappeared when he thought about his conversation with Mari. He shook his head as he muttered, "I will never understand women. They just don't track in a straight line." He grinned to himself and added, "But they sure are fun when they're happy."

CHAPTER 91

JUST BETWEEN BROTHERS

NATE SADDLED APPY AND GABE'S HORSE, WATIE, before he knocked on the kitchen door. He opened it and stepped through just as Merina backed away from Gabe, shaking her spoon.

Gabe grinned at his brother as he sat down.

"I was just telling Merina she should come with us today. She said she has too much gardening to do though. Besides, there is a dance in town tonight. She informed me that we are going, so we had better not be late today."

"Sí, you had better be back in time. You have found a reason to miss every dance for the last six months, and to this one we are going."

Gabe winked at Nate and the two men ate hurriedly. Nate looked up with a smile as he pointed at Gabe's old, rundown boots.

"Remember when you told me the story of your first pair of cowboy boots? You said you ordered them from a cobbler while you were in Kansas City one time."

Gabe nodded. "I remember. His name was C.H. Hyer and those were the best boots I ever owned. I stopped in Olathe on the way home from a drive. It was a little berg close to Kansas City. I told him what I needed—a boot toe that would slide into a stirrup, a raised heel to keep it there, and a curved top to give more room to pull the boot off and on. The boots I was wearing were a pair of old army boots, but they didn't cost me anything." Gabe grinned and winked at Merina. "I traded a feller a song on my harmonica for those boots.

"I hid and played a sweet song under the window at his gal's house. When she came outside, he asked her to marry. It worked too." Gabe and Nate both chuckled.

"Those army boots were durned uncomfortable though. My feet hurt when I walked because they didn't fit right. Shoot, they hurt all the time. I didn't like to spend money, but I decided if that cobbler could make me something more comfortable, it would be worth it.

"Hyer said he'd never made anything like that before, but he was game to try. I was headed back to Texas to bring another herd north, so he measured my feet and said he'd have them ready when I came back. I forgot to give him my name before I left."

"It was nearly four months before I made it back in there. He had them setting up on a shelf and pulled them down when I walked in." He grinned at Nate and added, "I even took a bath and put on new socks before I tried them on.

"Now you talk about boots. Those were the best boots I ever owned. I wore them for nearly eight years. By that time, they'd been patched so many times that there wasn't a place on either boot that was original. I don't know how many soles I had put on them. At the last place, the cobbler just laughed at me. He threw my boots out the window onto his trash pile and handed me a pair he made.

"They were all right, but they were nothing like those Hyer boots. I've often wished I had stopped in and gotten another pair, but I just never took the time. 'Course, I was rarely that far east again. The drives kept getting pushed farther west because of tick fever, so we didn't take any more herds into Kansas City." Gabe's grin was bigger when he added, "I bought that cobbler's new boots, but I pulled my old ones out of his trash pile before I left. I was hoping to get me another pair someday."

Nate's eyes twinkled as he asked, "Merina, is that package I mailed you handy? I'd like to show something to Gabe this morning."

Merina nodded and hurried into the bedroom. She returned with a large box. Nate took it from her and set it in front of his brother.

When Gabe stared at him, Nate grinned and nodded at the box. "Open it."

Gabe pulled out his knife and cut the cord that held the box closed. He was quiet when he lifted the lid. He stared for a moment before he lifted out a new pair of boots.

"I'll be darned. Do you think they'll fit?"

"Hyer still had the last he made for you—that was the form he made of your feet. It was labeled 'Texas Cow boy, First Cow Boy Boots,' so it didn't take him any time at all to find it. He even put a note in the box for you."

Gabe pulled out the note. He was quiet as he studied it. Merina finally took it from his hands and read it aloud.

Mr. Hawkins,

You were the first cow boy to ask me for a special design of boots—boots that worked for a cow boy's way of life. You must have told everyone you knew because orders came in from ranchers and riders everywhere. Why only last week, a rather well-known outlaw hid out while we made him a new pair of cow boy boots!

Mr. Hawkins, you changed the course of my life from a simple teacher and cobbler to a craftsman—a craftsman who makes boots for men (and even some women) who live on horseback.

When I opened my shop in 1874, I employed some of my past students from the School of the Deaf. They are excellent craftsmen, and thanks to you, we are all staying busy. Because of your vision, I now have a lucrative business.

Your brother ordered these for you. I added to his simple design and signed my name inside them.

Please enjoy this gift from me and know that I will always be thankful for the wandering cow boy who happened to walk into my cobbler shop that hot summer day in 1875. And if you are ever this way, do stop in and say hello. I call my business Hyer Boot Company, and we are located on main street in Olathe, Kansas.

Again, I thank you for your vision and for all the business your riding boots sent my way.

Sincerely, C.H. Hyer
Hyer Boot Company

Merina was quiet when she finished.

"What a wonderful note. I am going to save this." Her face was somber, but her eyes sparkled as she added, "Perhaps now Gabe will let me throw away that pair of stinky old boots. This letter will be much easier to store—and it smells better too."

Gabe pulled off his boots and slid the new ones on. He stood and walked around the room before he wrapped Nate up in a bear hug.

"Little Brother, you're all right. This was a fine gift, and I do thank you." He pulled the new boots off and slid his feet into the old pair as he looked from Merina to Nate with a sheepish grin.

"I'll save them for good. I might be able to get a few more years out of this old pair."

Merina rolled her eyes while Nate laughed.

CHAPTER 92

OF WOMEN AND LAND

AS THE TWO BROTHERS RODE OUT OF THE YARD, GABE asked, "Which way—north or west? We can cut through the pasture here if you want to go north. We own everything from here up past Angel's place now. We are adding more wooden windmills and water tanks on his place since the water holes are so far apart."

"Let's go north. I'd like to connect with you if possible."

Gabe was quiet for a time. He finally commented softly, "Half of all we have is yours, Nate. This was never all mine."

"I know, but with Angel, you have two families already trying to make a living off this ranch. I don't think you need one more.

"I'll share Gallagher's investments and the profit off that, but the ranch is yours and Merina's. You have more kids coming up too. You are going to need every bit of land you have."

"You have enough saved to put some land together or are you going to have to borrow money?" Gabe's face showed a mixture of concern and curiosity.

"I have some money put aside. I did all right trailing cattle and cowboying, but where I made most of my money was with my railroad job. I even invested a little in that industry.

"John Kirkham has been a good friend. He's the one who made all that happen for me. That man has his fingers in all kinds of pies. I learned a lot from him."

Gabe listened as Nate talked. He finally looked over at his brother.

"You never said how your visit with the Rankins went. Did you get to see Mari?"

Nate tapped the reins on his horse's neck and stared out over the pasture for a time. He finally looked over at Gabe.

"I think my expectations were too high. I thought she'd be glad to see me, but she was mad. I was mad too by the time I left. Jack Presley showed up while I was there." He frowned at Gabe. "Why would a gal let a man like that court her?"

Gabe grinned at him.

"Because she was mad at you. You didn't come back, and she knew you despised him. Kind of a jealousy thing."

"Mari said the same thing when we were arguing, but that makes no sense. How could I be jealous? I wasn't even around!"

Gabe laughed and shrugged.

"I suggest you get all dandied up and try to court her a little tonight. Mari didn't exactly sit around and twiddle her thumbs while you were gone, but she certainly didn't encourage any men to stick around.

"She waited on you, Nate. She's almost twenty-two years old and she's mad at herself for expecting you to return."

He laughed when his brother glared at him. "And don't think those are my words—Merina told me what to say. That doesn't make any more sense to me than it does to you.

"Except for the letter part. Why you didn't just mail those letters, I don't know."

Nate looked over at Gabe carefully.

"How do you know about my letters?"

"I had Rollie bring your saddlebags in. One side came open and a couple of letters fell out. I just naturally took out the rest to see if they were all to the same gal." Gabe whistled softly.

"Now that was a pile of writing." He smacked Nate and began to laugh. "You are one lovesick fool!"

"And that right there is why I didn't send them. I was afraid she would laugh at them and show them to all her friends. I should have burned them. In fact, I will have Merina do that when we get back. She can burn them when she burns the trash.

"Now let's talk about this land. Tell me what piece you think is the best."

CHAPTER 93

ONE LITTLE DANCE

GABE AND MERINA TOOK THEIR SURREY TO THE DANCE since all the kids were going too. Nate rode beside them.

He had brushed Demonio until he gleamed. The conchos on Miguel's saddle and bridle sparkled in the light. The new shirt Nate wore was a dark blue. His vest was brushed, and his boots were new.

Gabe looked him over and whistled.

"You took that gussying up part to heart. You are almost purty!" He paused and asked, "You have Hyer make you a pair of boots too?"

Nate grinned and nodded. "Sure did. I'm glad I did too since he only charged me for one pair."

As they pulled up in front of the Rollins House, Gabe looked back at Emilia.

"You stay inside once the dance starts. Even if your girlfriends go outside, you aren't to go." He waited as he watched her. When Emilia didn't answer, he asked, "Understand?"

Emilia muttered an answer before she jumped down. Gabe watched with a frown as a trail of boys fell in behind her.

"I liked it better when she was little and thought I was the best fellow around," he growled as he lifted Elena down.

"Oh, you are still her favorite fellow. She just doesn't like to play by all the rules you have. She'll stay inside though because she knows someone will see her if she goes outside…and you will find out." Merina was laughing as she watched Gabe.

"Come, my husband. Let's dance some before these kids get too tired.

"Nate, would you carry that big pot in? Just put it on the table with all the other food.

"Come now, girls. And don't walk so close to me. You might trip both of us. If I fall down, I could hurt the baby in my tummy."

Nate looked over at Gabe and grinned. Gabe puffed himself up and nodded proudly as he smiled. "Yep, another little one is cooking. This one should be done in about five months. I'm kind of hoping for a boy this time, but Merina makes mighty special little girls. Pretty ones too."

Merina slowed down to walk with them.

"Which piece of land did you like the best, Nate? And how many acres?"

"There's a parcel northwest of town. William Sturgis owns it. It doesn't have as much grass right now after the dry years you had and the hard winter too. Still, I remember the year we took Rock Beckler's black cattle north. Sturgis had those cattle all grazing in one of those valleys when we picked them up, and it was some of the nicest grass I had ever seen.

"He has twenty thousand acres in there and I made him an offer. There's a house on it too. It's not much but it will do for me."

They stepped through the door and the first person Nate saw was Mari. Her long hair was in a loose knot at the nape of her neck and little curls were trailing around her face.

Yep, she's still the prettiest gal I have ever seen. And she probably has a date tonight just to see if she can make me mad again.

Mari looked up and smiled before she looked away. Nate blushed and Gabe laughed.

"Just ask her to dance. You love to dance or at least you did unless that has changed."

"Nope, I still do. I danced every chance I had while I was gone. It was always fun, but I like to dance with women I know. It's easier to have a conversation. It's too much work to think of things to talk about if you don't know the gal."

Gabe laughed and shook his head.

"Dang, Nate. You left all friendly and came back acting like me! Well, I have a woman I like to talk to *and* dance with. And I had better do it or I will hear about it tonight."

"Gracie, why don't you take Elena and go sit with Molly. Let me dance with your mama and then I'll dance some with you girls."

Nate sauntered over to where Mari was talking with some other girls.

"Miss Rankin? Would you do me the honor of this first dance?" He bowed in front of Mari and waited for her answer.

Mari smiled and held out her hand. Nate spun her around before he pulled her into the waltz.

"I'd say you have been dancing some while you were gone." Mari smiled up at him and Nate grinned.

"Every chance I got. I stepped on a lot of toes. I moved around enough though that I stayed ahead of my bad-dancing reputation." He spun Mari in circles as they kept up with the lilting music. He twirled her around when the dance ended and then pulled her back in before he let her go.

"Want to dance another one or is your dance card all filled up?"

Mari looked up at him and slowly nodded her head. As they moved across the floor, she asked, "Do women still use dance cards?"

"Some places they do, mostly in the South. It's all mighty exhausting for us fellows though. Hard to keep track if you ask them all!" He grinned at her and added, "I prefer to be the first one to ask the prettiest gal there. Then I just hog her for the rest of the night." He laughed down at Mari. "Kind of like I'm doing with you."

Mari laughed and they danced six dances before she sat down.

Nate danced with Merina, Grace, and Emilia. He carried Elena through a couple as well. Then he asked Molly, Beth, and Flory. He was headed back across the floor to ask Mari again when another man led her onto the dance floor. Instead, he danced with Abigail, one of Lance's daughters. She was almost sixteen and as pretty as could be.

"What are you going to do this fall now that you are out of high school, Abbie? Are you headed to Manhattan to attend Kansas State Agricultural College? Molly always said all her girls were going to college."

Abbie nodded excitedly. Her hair was silky black. She had Molly's blue eyes with the intensity of Lance's. *All the little girls around here have grown up, and dang! They are all pretty.* Nate smiled as he listened to Abbie talk.

"Mari has been teaching at our little school for almost three years now. She loves to teach. She's an excellent teacher too. She went to college for two years in Kansas plus she usually takes some teacher training classes in the summer to get ready for the next year.

"She reads all the time too. She tries to make sure we are all prepared for college…or for whatever we want to do for a living. Not everyone wants to go to college.

"Classes begin in mid-August. I'm scared and excited too.

"My cousin, Ellie Rankin, left for Georgia today to visit Beth's family. She will be back next month, and we will travel down to Manhattan together."

"I didn't know Beth still had family there. Does Rowdy as well? I've heard both of them talk about Georgia from time to time."

"Uncle Rowdy's family is gone but Aunt Beth has some cousins and old aunts in Columbus, Georgia. They just love Ellie.

"She said she is going to ask her aunts if she can take me along next summer. I would love that. She has such a good time and gets to see so many things. I love history and fashion. I can't wait until Ellie gets back each year so she can fill me in on all she did while she was gone.

"Mari is fascinated with Charleston in South Carolina. Every year, she does a section on the history of the War Between the States and the significance of Fort Sumter. She said she would like to go there someday."

"I hope she gets to do that. Charleston is a beautiful town." Nate smiled as he listened.

"I've never been there but Ellie and I are making plans. We have lots of places we want to go." Abigail gave Nate a quick smile before she continued talking.

"Pa said he is sending Paul down to Manhattan with us because he doesn't want us on the train by ourselves." Abbie wrinkled her nose. "We don't think that's necessary." She frowned and was silent a moment before she added, "Mother isn't saying anything, and she is usually all for us being independent." The frown was still on Abbie's face when she looked up at Nate. "I really don't like all the rules that go with being a girl."

Nate laughed as he swung her around.

"Well, maybe you should look at it this way. I doubt you will be traveling all that light. Paul might be kind of handy. He can drag your heavy trunks down those rough streets."

Abbie's blue eyes were sparkling when she looked up at Nate, but she tried to look serious.

"Ellie and I have never had trouble finding someone to help us carry anything. I doubt that would be a problem."

Nate threw back his head and laughed.

"Yep, and that right there is why Lance is sending your brother. Your pa's a smart man."

"Slim Parker offered to go with us." When Nate looked at Abbie in question, she added, "His name is Levi but since his pa has the same name, he goes by Slim now. He works on a ranch south of Manhattan somewhere. He came back this weekend and is headed back down there in a few days.

"I wouldn't mind spending some time on a train with him. He is so funny. I just laugh all the time when he is around." She glanced toward the side of the room where some young men were talking and laughing loudly.

Abbie looked up at Nate again and asked, "You remember Slim, don't you? He is Sadie and Levi Parker's son. He has wanted to be called Slim since he was five or six. That's what everyone called his first pa before he died. That was before I was born.

"Pa talks about him from time to time. They were pards and best friends.

"Some of the adults call his son Young Levi. We kids just call him Slim."

"I do remember him, but I doubt I'd even recognize him. You kids were all a lot younger when I left."

Abbie sighed. Her voice was soft when she continued.

"Slim is wild and so much fun. He went to high school in town here for about a week before he was kicked out. His first warning came after he rode his horse into the classroom and tied it to the chalkboard. He was giving a lesson on horsemanship when the instructor arrived. That teacher kicked him out of class.

"Then he organized a rodeo on the front lawn of the school. When the bulls got loose and ran through the door of the library, the principal threw the book at him." Abbie watched Nate closely and then added, "That was a pun on words. Mari taught us about puns."

Nate chuckled. "Good one. I didn't even catch it."

Abbie laughed and continued, "Slim didn't care though. He didn't want to be there. All he wanted to do was be a cowboy. He told me that the day before he left for Kansas.

"Rusty, Gabe's partner, lives in Kansas now. He offered Slim a riding job on a ranch he and Gabe own somewhere south of Manhattan. He got Slim out of Cheyenne and made him work off the cost of the damage. That is probably the only reason the school didn't press charges.

"What they don't know is that Slim was behind all the goats that were turned loose at the high school just a few days ago. I don't know how he managed it, but they showed up on Thursday night. By yesterday morning, they were in half the buildings and had eaten everything green they could find. They chewed on a lot of other things too. Thank Heavens they didn't get in the library.

"The principal was furious. He went to see Levi and Sadie, but Slim could prove he was working with Angel that day." Abbie laughed softly and added, "Slim attended our little school from third grade through eighth. He did well there. I always sat by him even though he was a year behind me in school. The teacher thought he behaved better when he was beside me.

"He has always been our friend. I can't remember a function I've been to that the Parkers haven't attended, so none of us were surprised that he wanted to go to school with us.

"His pa didn't care but Sadie thought it was too far for Slim to ride every day. They finally gave in when he started third grade. Besides, he was in trouble all the time in the town school.

"Pa found him a riding job the summer after his eighth grade, but it wasn't with us. I don't know why Pa didn't hire him. Slim was a good hand even then. He's been cowboying down in Kansas ever since Rusty hired him." She smiled up at Nate and added, "I hope I get to see him some while I'm in school. We have so much fun together."

Just then a young man appeared beside them. He danced by himself but kept the beat as he grinned at Abbie.

"Hello, Abbie. You goin' to save a dance for me or are you goin' to break my heart after I came all this way to dance with you?"

Nate chuckled as he looked at the young cowboy. Blond hair curled over his forehead and his blue eyes twinkled with orneriness.

"Slim, I didn't know if I'd recognize you after eight years, but you haven't changed." He swung Abbie away and called over his shoulder,

"You'll have to get a turn on your own though. I don't share pretty girls." He shook his head as he looked down at Abbie.

"He's trouble, Abbie. If you tie onto him, you had better be prepared for a wild ride!"

They were both laughing when Nate led her back to her seat.

Molly scowled as she watched her daughter.

"Just look at Abbie swoosh her hips. She is pretty and she knows it."

Lance laughed down at his wife. He spun her close to him and whispered, "She looks like my mother, but she walks just like you, Molly girl. And I have always liked that swooshy walk."

Molly blushed but they both laughed as Lance spun her around again. They danced another dance and were just walking to their table when Young Levi appeared in front of them.

"Lance, can I have a word with you? Outside if you have a little time. I'm headed back to Kansas in a few days, and I was hoping to catch you before I left."

Molly looked startled but Lance nodded.

"Let me take Molly back to our table and I'll meet you behind the hotel."

The young cowboy strolled toward the door, joking with his friends as he passed them. Molly frowned.

"Why in the world does Young Levi need to talk to you in private? That boy hasn't done anything quietly in his life."

Lance just grinned and headed for the door.

CHAPTER 94

JUST LIKE MY OLD PARD

LANCE PAUSED IN THE DOORWAY AND WATCHED THE young man in front of him for a moment. Young Levi was twisting his hat nervously in his hands as he stood with his back to the door.

"He looks just like my old pard," Lance muttered. "Slim was as wild as a March hare, but he settled down after he met Sadie. I think I might know where this conversation is going."

Lance strode through the door and stopped beside the younger man. They both stared out across the prairie.

"There is nothing like a summer night around Cheyenne. I love my job in Kansas, but my heart will always be here." Slim's voice was soft as he spoke. Then he cleared his throat and looked at Lance nervously.

"Lance—I mean, Mr. Rankin, I'd like your permission to court Abbie. I have been thinking on this for some time, but I thought I had better ask you first."

Levi's blue eyes were steady and direct even though Lance could see his shirt moving as his heart beat wildly in his chest.

Lance looked away and tried not to smile. He forced himself to look irritated and was frowning when he looked back at the young man.

"Levi, you haven't exactly been the model of maturity. You were kicked out of high school. Even now, you would rather play than work from what I can see."

"Mr. Rankin, I didn't want to go to high school. All I have ever wanted to do was run cows and ride horses. I told Ma that too, but she was sure I would like high school once I got there. She said I might even want to be a banker like Paul wants to be." Slim snorted before he continued.

"Well, I didn't like it. Those stuffy rooms and all those pointy-headed people walking around and telling me things I didn't need to know—and them acting all important. I *wanted* to get kicked out of school. I couldn't believe they didn't do it when I took my horse to class." Levi grinned at Lance and shrugged.

"The rodeo was just something fun a few of us fellows decided to organize." Levi's eyes twinkled when he added, "We just didn't intend for the bulls to get loose."

"And the goats?"

Levi caught his breath and let it out slowly. He looked sideways at Lance. "That was only partly me—well, maybe a little more than half.

"That principal told me I would never amount to anything. I told him that was a compliment coming from an old goat like him. Then several weeks ago, one of my friends found out about a bunch of goats some feller was going to sell. They were going to be all penned up and handy-like this week and…well, it just kind of went from there." Levi looked down at his hat. He tried not to grin when he looked up at Lance, but his face became somber before he spoke again.

"I heard you were maybe looking for a hand, and I'd like to apply. I know I don't always do what folks think I should, but I know cows and I'll work hard." He grinned at Lance and added, "Besides, I'll be mighty tempted to go to Manhattan every Saturday night if I stay where I am. It's not that far, and I'll have even more reason to head that way this fall."

Lance's eyes almost bored through him and Levi stuttered a little. He worked hard not to back up before he looked Lance squarely in the eyes.

"Now don't get me wrong—I'd enjoy that, but Abbie should get a taste of college without me interfering all the time. Besides, with Sam staying in Nebraska and Paul moving up to Stevensville in Montana Territory to work with that banker up there, I was hoping maybe you would need to take on a permanent hand."

Lance stared at the young man in front of him. *Paul headed north? When did that come about?* He cleared his throat and looked away as he pondered what Slim had said.

His first reaction was to laugh. Levi had him over a barrel and they both knew it. *He negotiates like his pa, and I sure miss my old pard.* Lance's eyes drilled into the young man again before he answered.

"Levi, I'll hire you on, but I won't put up with all the shenanigans you have pulled in the past. I'll fire you fast if you get out of line."

Levi's face turned red, but he didn't look away.

"And don't even ask about the foreman's job. It's not available and even if it was, you aren't qualified. The foreman is the leader, and he's usually one of the more experienced hands. He has to be responsible and mature, someone the men look up to.

"I understand practical jokes, but you are going to keep your boots pointed in a straight line if you work for me. Understand?"

The young man grinned and nodded. "Understood." He cleared his throat and asked carefully, "And about courting Abbie?"

"You can court her when she's home but no going south to see her. And I want her home by eleven tonight. If she's late, you're fired before you start."

Slim grinned and grabbed Lance's hand. "Thanks, Lance. You won't be sorry! I'll tell Rusty I'll work through the end of the month. I even know a fellow who needs a job down there. He was hoping I'd leave so he could apply. I'll be back up here on June 1."

Lance's voice followed the young man as he turned away. "One more thing. What do you want to be called?"

Levi looked back at Lance in surprise and his face lit up.

"Why I reckon I would like to be called Slim. That was my first pa's name and folks say I look like him. You can call me Slim."

Slim rushed back inside, and Lance followed him slowly. "And you act like him too," he muttered. He watched as Paul met Slim and the two of them talked for a moment. They laughed and Paul shook his hand. Then they strolled across the floor to where Abbie was seated with some of her friends.

Lance was quiet as he walked back to Molly's table. She watched him closely and frowned when she looked from him to Young Levi.

"What did Young Levi want? You didn't hire him, did you?"

"I did. It was either that or have him in Manhattan every weekend once Abbie moves down there." He paused and looked over at Abbie. She was listening to Levi's animated talk with a smile on her face. It wasn't long before the two of them were dancing.

"He reminds me so much of his pa. I miss Slim—some days more than others—but I miss him. He was a good man and the best friend I ever had. Talking to Young Levi tonight was like talking to my old pard back when we were young and bulletproof. I could feel him smiling when we finished. And now his son wants to be called Slim." Lance pulled Molly up.

"Let's go dance. Let me hug you a little and shake off this sadness. Our kids are growing up and things are changing fast."

"I love Young Levi, but I can't believe you hired him," Molly said as Lance twirled her close. "I know he's a good hand but he's wild and reckless."

Lance nodded as he swung his wife around.

"He is, but he'll grow up. And I'd rather him be here where our hands will keep him from getting too cocky. Besides, I don't think we want him and Abbie to court unsupervised."

Molly stared up at Lance a moment as she pulled her brows together. Lance squeezed her and chuckled.

"Your daughters are too pretty, Molly. Now they are all growing up, and we have more trouble than we can handle."

Lance and Molly danced a full circle around the room. They both frowned as they watched Livvy bat her eyes at the group of young men who surrounded her and Emilia.

Molly muttered, "That girl. She is going to be the death of me."

However, they both smiled when Paul pushed through the group and escorted both young girls to the other side of the room.

Molly's face was soft as she watched.

"Every mother needs a sweet child. Paul was always such a precious little boy. And now he is a wonderful big brother." She looked up at Lance and gave him a wistful smile.

"I'm going to miss him when he leaves." When Lance pulled his brows together, Molly laughed softly.

"Yes, I knew he was leaving. And don't frown at me—he is planning to talk to you this week." Molly sighed.

"First Sam and now Paul." Her eyes were wet as she whispered, "Our little boys have grown up and now we have to share them."

CHAPTER 95

FIRE!

A MAN RUSHED ONTO THE DANCE FLOOR. HIS FACE was dirty, and his clothes were covered with soot.

He shouted, "There's a fire northwest of town! It's burning fast and headed this way. We need every available man to help!"

There was a rush of activity as families tried to organize rides home. Nate looked around for Rowdy but didn't see him. He ran toward Mari and grabbed her arm.

"Where are your mom and dad?"

"They went home earlier. I am planning to spend the night in town with a friend."

Nate shook his head. "Go home with Molly or Merina. If that fire breaks through, part of the town could burn too."

Mari started to argue. However, Nate's face was so intense that she agreed. She spoke quickly to the girl next to her and hurried to follow Molly out of the Rollins House.

Nate raced out behind her hollering, "Get the fire lit in the steam engine!" While men rushed to hitch the team, Nate jumped into the firebox to help the fireman.

Demonio raced after the fire engine. He didn't like all the noise or the people rushing around, but where Nate went, Demonio followed.

The two men worked to get the fire hot enough. The steam created pressure, and it took a lot of power to pump the water. Soon another fireman climbed in, and Nate jumped off the steam truck.

Men were starting backfires and he joined them. He couldn't see Lance or Gabe, but he knew they were somewhere to his right. He could see the wall of fire rushing toward them. Nate looked behind him. The steam engine still didn't have enough power to operate the pumps. Several men moved farther out on the prairie to start more fires and he rushed to join them. Everyone's fear was that the fire would jump the burned ground and get into the town.

The backfires caught and slowly began to burn. As they grew larger, they combined and the two fires raced toward each other.

A man yelled, "Everybody down! Cover your ears and open your mouth!" The men dropped flat on the ground as the two huge fires met with a whoosh followed by the sound of an explosion. The fire sucked the air around it before it collapsed into ashes.

About that time, the steam built high enough to power the pump, and the fire engine began spraying water.

Men arose from the ground all around Nate. They rushed to beat out the small fires that were still going.

Nate slowly climbed to his feet. He waved his hand toward the huge swath of burnt ground.

"Where did that fire start? How far did it burn?"

"It started northwest of here, up by Sturgis' ranch. I'm not sure if it was a campfire that got away or just dry grass that caught a spark from something. It burned everything south of Sturgis though, almost down to the tracks. Then the wind changed direction and pushed it this way.

"Rowdy Rankin left the dance early. He was backfiring north of his place. It's a good thing he was around and some of his hands too. Who knows how far south it would have gone if he hadn't gotten it stopped!"

Nate stared to the northwest and scowled. *Well, I'm guessing that fire wiped out a good share of the grass I planned to buy and likely my little house too. Dad-blamed fires. Maybe I should take a ride up there. The moon is bright tonight and I'm this much closer.*

He stopped when a horse nickered and pushed through the smoke.

"Demonio, you old devil. How did you find me? I for sure will take that ride since you are here." He grabbed a couple of sacks and dipped them in some water tubs in the back of a wagon. He wrung them out and tied them behind his saddle before he mounted.

A cowboy was walking back toward the steam engine. He stopped and stared for a moment at Nate.

"Are you riding out yet tonight to see where the fire started?"

"I want to see what the damage is and make sure there are no small fires that might kick back up." Nate pointed to the northwest. "I thought I'd check on Sturgis too."

The cowboy nodded. "If you'll wait a minute, I'll go with you. My horse is tied to a wagon back there."

CHAPTER 96

A Durn Fool

THE TWO MEN WERE SOON HEADED NORTHWEST IN the moonlight. Nate reached his hand over to the man.

"Nate Hawkins. My brother ranches south of Cheyenne."

"Roscoe Reed. My pard and me ride for Angel. Temple went over to help at Rowdy's today, so he was probably one of the fellows fighting fire on that end. I came in to the dance." He pointed at Nate's horse. "I recognize that horse. That's old Demon. He was Miguel Montero's horse." Reed grinned.

"Temple and me met him in Kansas City." Reed shook his head. "That Miguel was somethin'. He hit trouble head on. Looked for it and that's a fact. He found it too but always came out with nary a scratch.

"I couldn't believe it when he died." Reed looked over the burned prairie. He nodded his head as his eyes followed the charred ground south. He finally chuckled.

"I tried to court Rowdy's oldest daughter. In fact, I'm guessing she is why Temple was so eager to help over there today.

"She shut me down mighty fast. She's a looker too." Recognition slowly came over Reed's face. "Nate Hawkins. I remember you now.

You were a gangly kid when you left here some time back." He looked at Nate curiously. "Are you back to stay now?"

Nate nodded and laughed ruefully. "I just made an offer on some land of Sturgis'. I'm thinking it is probably what burned. The house wasn't much but it's most likely gone too."

Reed listened as Nate spoke. He pointed toward the southwest.

"You might talk to Rowdy. One of the places he owns up that way has a little house on it. In fact, it's the old Hatch place. Angel said that's where Rowdy's two oldest kids were born. I guess Beth and Rowdy took them in when their folks died.

"I didn't know Mari was adopted till Angel told me that. I always thought she looked like a purty version of ol' Rowdy."

Nate listened closely. Sam had mentioned the Hatch family, but he didn't say where they had lived. He remembered Sam telling him about how Mari and Rudy came to live with Beth and Rowdy too, but he had forgotten they were adopted. *We never really spoke of it. All the folks I know treat their adopted kids just like the rest. That's how it should be too.*

"If the land you are wanting to buy is where I think it is, it's just north of the old Hatch house. The house ain't much but it might work, at least until you can build you something."

The two men visited more as they rode. They topped a small hill and stopped to stare at the devastation caused by the fire. Several cows were standing with their heads down. Their ears were burned off and large patches of hair were gone. Their feet and legs were burned as well.

Nate cursed quietly as he pulled out his rifle. He shot both of them and the two men continued on. Dead cattle were scattered across the prairie. In some places, their bodies were still smoldering. The two men didn't speak as they rode by. They finally reached the place where Nate's house had once stood.

Nothing was left but cinders and some pieces of charred wood. They started to ride on when they heard a weak voice.

"If somebody's out there, I'd sure appreciate a little help gettin' outta here."

Nate and Reed jumped off their horses and raced toward the house.

"Where are you? Are you under the house?"

"In the cellar, not far to the left of the house."

The men pushed the charred wood away from the cellar opening. The door was burned off and the opening was filled with smoldering shards of wood, ash, and half-burnt timbers. The two men beat at the smoldering timbers with their wet sacks. They were finally able to clear the opening and saw a man lying on the floor. Several large beams had fallen on him, pinning him on his back.

Reed and Nate climbed over the rubble and lifted the beams off.

The man's voice was weak when he spoke.

"Hicks Johnson is my name. I sure am happy to see you fellers. I thought I was a goner fer a time there." He coughed as he tried to sit up and groaned as he held his side. Nate and Reed helped him to stand.

"A fool drunk was out here shootin' at empty whiskey bottles. I heard the shots an' pulled out my spyglass to see what was goin' on. I was about a quarter of a mile away when I spotted 'im. This is all private land, but that didn't make him no never mind. Most of the time he missed the bottles an' those bullets ricocheted off the rocks. Ever' time one hit a rock, it would throw up sparks. He was too durn drunk to see he was startin' fires. When he did notice, instead of tryin' to put 'em out, he took off on his horse." The man snorted in disgust before he continued. "He probably could have stomped out those first fires since they was so small.

"The sparks caught that grass an' the wind took it from there. I headed over here to try to put 'em out. By the time I made it this far though, it was one fire an' too big to stop. I could see it was goin' to burn over the top a me, so I climbed in that cellar an' said my prayers. I tried to get my horse in too, but he spooked an' took off. I hope he made it." The man winced again as he held out his hand.

"I didn't get a real good look at that feller's face, but he looked like that tinhorn banker by the name of Presley or Presser—somethin' like that."

Hicks nodded at the two riders and added, "I'm mighty appreciatin' of ya stoppin' to help."

Nate studied the man in front of him.

"I think maybe you should see a doctor. You might have crushed something."

Hicks shook his head. "Naw. I might of broke a few ribs, but they'll heal. Those beams was on my chest, an' my big ol' chest is mighty strong." He grinned at them. His smile slowly faded as he looked across the burned prairie.

"Did we lose lots of cows?"

"Some but we haven't made it far yet."

"If you fellers don't mind, I could sure use a ride back to headquarters. Ol' Sturgis'll be roundin' up the boys. I want to tell 'im I'm alright 'fore he wastes time sendin' some of my friends out to look fer me."

CHAPTER 97

MOTHER NATURE IS CRUEL

THE THREE MEN RODE NORTH TOWARD STURGIS'S ranch, and Nate was almost sick by the time they arrived. They had to shoot more cattle as they rode. Some cows had their udders burned off while others were going to lose their hooves. He shook his head and cursed under his breath. *I had better not catch the fellow who started this. I just might have to beat him within an inch of his life. And if it was Jack Presley...* Nate glowered and shook his head.

Hicks pointed at the small groups of cattle clustered together.

"Did you notice how many more burned cows there are than calves? Those ol' gurls musta put their babies in the center to keep 'em safe."

Nate looked closely. Hicks was right. Sturgis was going to lose more cows than calves. *And how is he going to feed all those orphan calves? Bucket calves take a lot of time not to mention milk. Sturgis doesn't have any milk cows or kids. He's got no way to feed them.*

When they arrived at Sturgis' ranch headquarters, Hicks slid off Reed's horse. He limped as he walked toward the bunkhouse. Sturgis was just walking out of the main house. Nate thought he had aged quite a bit from when they first met in '79. Today he just looked beaten. *Well, why wouldn't he? First a drought and a killing winter, and now a devastating fire.*

Nate and Reed waited while Hicks talked to his boss. About that time, Stub and Tuff rode in. They stopped beside Sturgis and the four visited a moment before the older man headed back to the house. He hollered as he walked, "Saddle my horse, Stub. Bring him up here after you get things lined out."

Nate grinned and rode his horse toward the two brothers. Tuff spotted Nate and began to grin as well. The two old friends slid to the ground and shook each other's hand.

"Dang, Nate. You make me look all runty. You are even taller than when you left. I think you put on a hundred pounds too.

"You back for good or just for a visit?"

"I'm back for good. How about you? Think you'll stay in the Wyoming Territory now that you've been down here awhile?"

Tuff chuckled and shrugged. "I don't know. Both of my buddies left after I moved here just to be closer to them.

"One didn't come back at all and the other one was gone eight years," he added sarcastically as he punched Nate in the shoulder.

"It's been a good eight years though." He blushed and added, "Nora Spurlach wrote me a month ago. Well, longer ago than that. I received her post a month ago.

"She invited me to come up and visit. She was always such a sweet little gal. She had been on my mind before I received her letter, and I've decided to accept her invite. If she ain't decided to become a nun, I just might talk to Spur about courting her. She should be about fifteen now."

When Nate looked at Tuff in surprise, the rawboned cowboy grinned.

"Nora always talked some about doing that, so I guess we'll see. Stub ain't happy about it but I told him I was goin'. I said he could give me the time off or I'd quit." Tuff's grin became bigger. "'Course, I might quit anyhow once I get up there. I always liked Clare, and Spur too.

"Nora said they were lookin' for help. A bunch of their riders quit after the last couple of bad winters, and they are shorthanded."

Nate smiled as he listened to his friend. Tuff had filled out some, but he was still lanky. He was now much taller than his brother. His face still held the boyish grin that Nate remembered though.

"I reckon that's a good idea. Nora is a sweet gal. Now that Annie is a whole 'nother story!"

The two friends stopped talking as they listened to Stub.

He was all business as he organized the men. He told them what to look for in the injured cattle. Each cowboy carried a rifle, and they rode out in groups of two.

Tuff waved and called back as he followed Hicks out of the yard.

"Let's have a beer in Cheyenne this next week, maybe Friday night. I'm headed north a week from tomorrow. That's next Sunday, May 20. I want to be in Stevensville in time to help move cattle to summer grass, but I'd sure like to catch up before I leave if you have time."

Nate grinned and waved. Tuff waved back before he spurred his horse to catch up with Hicks.

After everyone left, Stub turned back to Nate and the cowboy beside him.

"Reed. Nate. Good to see you fellows. Did you see a lot of dead cattle?"

Nate frowned and slowly nodded. "More than we had hoped to. We shot quite a few too. Some that weren't as bad we left, but you may end up putting them down." He nodded toward the south. "Most of them were scattered around in that pocket in the hills south of here."

"Yeah, there was no way for them to get away from the fire. No creeks close enough to get to. Just lots of dry grass." He pulled his hat off and ran his fingers through his black hair.

"I think we're going to have a passel of orphan calves and I just don't know what to do with them. I hate to put them down."

Nate had been thinking about that.

"Do you have a wagon with high enough sides to hold them? Maybe we could take some down to Rowdy and Lance. They both have milk cows and a passel of kids too. They might help you out. I'd even drive them down there for you."

Stub nodded slowly. "I'll talk to Sturgis. We have a hay wagon that might work. I told the boys to bring back any calves they could tell were orphans. We'll see how many they show up with." Stub started to turn away. He stopped as he pointed toward the house.

"Sturgis wants to talk to you. He said to ask you to come on up to the house." Stub's eyes were worried. "This fire was another hard hit he just didn't need." His face became angry and he added, "You didn't see a drunk fellow riding around out there by himself, did you? Hicks told us what he saw."

"No, we didn't see him or his horse either." Nate's eyes were intense as he looked over the burned grass. "Did you have any horses out there?"

"We did but we gathered them yesterday and moved them to one of the north pastures. We were going to gather the cows today." Stub cursed under his breath again.

"I'll find that wagon while you talk to Sturgis. We'll see what we end up with for babies today. I reckon we'll find more tomorrow but we can only do so much."

CHAPTER 98

So Many Orphan Calves

WILLIAM STURGIS HOLLERED WHEN NATE KNOCKED. "Come on in, Nate. Grab yourself a cup of coffee. I'll be out in a minute."

Nate poured himself a cup of the strong coffee and stretched out in the chair. He was tired but he would stay and help. "Last night was a long night and today will be worse," he muttered as he looked out the window.

Sturgis walked slowly into the kitchen. His face was drawn down in deep lines, and worry was all over his face.

"There's no grass left on that piece you wanted to buy. It won't do you much good now." Sturgis's gaze was direct as he spoke. He cursed softly as he looked away. "I won't hold you to that offer, Nate. The cattleman in me just can't do that."

Nate shook his head.

"No, I am still going to buy it. That grass will come back and will be better than before. I'll have to figure out where I'll live though. Maybe I can find something close to rent until I'm ready to build my house." He looked at the worn-down man and added softly, "If I can help you out somehow, just let me know."

Sturgis looked up at Nate and smiled for the first time that day.

"Thanks, Nate. I appreciate that.

"I caught a little of your talk with Tuff about the calves. If you'll haul off my orphan calves, I think that will be help enough. I hate to put an animal down, and I think we'll be doing a lot of that over the next few days."

Nate worked with Stub all day. They found twenty-six calves that were for sure orphans as they were trying to nurse dead mothers. The men brought them back to the headquarters two and three at a time. They were loaded in the hay wagon as they were dropped off at the ranch. It had been a long day already when Nate finally headed south with the wagonful of bawling caves. It was after dark when he arrived at Rowdy's ranch.

The door flew open and all the kids poured out of the house to see what all the commotion was. Every calf in the wagon was bawling and bawling loudly. Nate's ears were ringing.

He staggered when he stepped off the wagon, and Rowdy could see the exhaustion all over the younger man. He listened closely as Nate explained the situation.

"Why don't you let my kids unload those babies. We have some milk cows and the kids know how to bottle-feed calves. In fact, Beth insisted on getting a couple of goats for this very reason. I guess we'll see if they work like she promised." Rowdy grinned and added, "If they don't, we are eating them because they sure aren't going to run loose on this ranch.

"I'll keep twenty calves here and Eli can take the rest over to Lance's tomorrow. I don't think he'll have as much extra milk as we have.

"Lance is going to take some of his riders over to help Sturgis tomorrow. In fact, he sent four up today. I'm taking four of my cowboys too. We'll take that wagon back and see if he needs us to pick up more orphans.

"You come on up to the house, Nate, and Beth will get you something to eat. We can take care of your horse."

Nate shook his head. "I think I'll just bed down in your barn. That hay looks mighty inviting." He looked back at his horse standing behind the wagon. The saddle and bridle were both dirty, and the silver conchos barely showed.

"Demonio, you let Rowdy unsaddle you." The horse snorted and Nate walked toward the barn. He tripped several times before he disappeared through the door.

Rowdy led the horse to water before taking it to the barn. He unsaddled it and rubbed it down. Demonio would not go in a stall though and Rowdy laughed.

"Yep, you intend to stand guard tonight. Well, you just do that." He poured some grain into a tub and forked some hay in front of the horse. Then he left quietly.

"You kids stay out of that barn until morning. Let that man get some sleep. And stay away from that horse. He's had a long day too. I'm guessing he'll be a little protective until he knows Nate is all right."

Rowdy walked up to the house. Mari and her mother were washing dishes. He looked over at Beth as he washed his hands.

"Nate worked all night and today too. He's plumb worn down. Maybe someone can take him some breakfast first thing in the morning. I'm guessing he is going to be mighty hungry." He winked at Beth before he added, "I'm headed to bed."

Mari started pulling ingredients out of the cabinet and Beth looked at her in surprise.

"You don't have to make that bread tonight, Mari. As long as it is done by noon, that's plenty early enough."

Mari blushed and shook her head.

"I want it done by breakfast. Tomorrow is going to be a busy day." She pulled Nate's old bandana out of her apron pocket and tied it over her hair. She was soon singing softly as she kneaded the bread.

CHAPTER 99

JUST A LITTLE PRIVACY

MARI WAS THE FIRST ONE UP. SHE HAD GRIDDLE CAKES and sausage cooking when Beth hurried into the kitchen. She had just cracked some eggs into a skillet, and fresh bread sat on the counter under a towel.

Beth smiled. She kissed her daughter and whispered, "Nate's a fine man, Mari. You fix him a plate and sit with him while he eats. I can finish up here…and I'll keep the little kids inside as long as I can."

Mari smiled at her mother. She pushed some loose curls into the braid that was hanging down her back. She fixed a huge plate of food and hurried toward the barn.

Rowdy strolled into the kitchen and watched their daughter from the doorway.

He was grinning when he looked back at Beth.

"How long?"

When Beth looked at him in confusion, he nodded toward the barn.

"How long before a wedding?"

Tears filled Beth's green eyes. "Oh, Rowdy. I am so happy, but I'm a little sad too. I don't want Mari to leave even though I know that's selfish of me. I still see that sweet little girl we took in so many years ago. How I love it when she sits on your lap to talk to you."

Rowdy wrapped his arms around his wife and rested his chin on her head.

"She will always be our little girl, but I think she will be leaving before long. Nate is going to ask her to marry, and she is going to say yes. And I'm guessing the wedding will be soon."

The kids were soon tumbling into the kitchen and Rowdy pointed toward their chairs.

"You all sit down and be polite." He winked at Beth and added, "Your mother has worked hard on this meal. Let's see if we can eat once with no messes."

Eli looked at Mari's empty chair.

"Where's Mari? I can go wake her up."

"You just leave Mari alone. Now fold your hands and let's pray."

As soon as they finished praying, Betsy began to gobble her breakfast.

Rowdy cocked an eyebrow at her.

"Since when have you been so excited to get out and do your chores?"

"I want to see if Nate is still sleeping in the barn. If he is, I'm going to wake him up. I want to see if I can ride his horse. I want to sit on his saddle too. It has shiny things all over it. It's real purty."

Emalene frowned at her. "You tried to sneak out last night after everyone went to bed. I saw you and I told you Pa would whoop your bottom." She turned her green eyes on Rowdy and asked with a pout, "Why does Betsy get to wake Nate up? I want to help too."

Rowdy laid his fork down and stared around the table.

"Nobody is going to wake Nate up. That fellow was up all night helping a neighbor, so you kids leave him alone."

Eli poked at his food before he asked, "Then how are we going to get our chores done? We can't even milk the cows."

"Criminently! Will you just eat and stop worrying about Nate? I'm sure he'll be up before long. He'll be hungry too so if you don't eat your breakfast, you might not get anything." Rowdy didn't know whether to laugh or be irritated. "Go milk those goats and try to feed each calf just a little."

When they were gone, he looked over at Beth and she began to laugh.

"It's pretty hard to have privacy in any family, let alone one this big."

Rowdy pulled her onto his lap as he chuckled.

"Then we had better take advantage of it."

CHAPTER 100

BREAKFAST IN THE BARN

MARI PULLED THE BARN DOOR OPEN AND CALLED softly, "Nate, are you up yet? I have breakfast for you."

She heard some stirring, but Nate's horse stood in the doorway of the barn and wouldn't let her in.

"Demonio. Back." Nate's voice was quiet as he talked to his horse.

The horse snorted and backed up. Nate stood and brushed off his clothes. He rubbed his face. His beard was rough, and he felt dirty. He knew he looked as bad as he felt.

He walked toward the barn door just as Mari stepped through with a big plate of food.

She was smiling. She smelled fresh and looked pretty. Nate slowly smiled as he took the plate from her.

"Good morning, Mari. You look as fresh as a new rain on a spring day." He bit into the thick slice of bread. He chewed contentedly as he stared at it.

"This bread is fresh. Did you make it this morning?"

"I made it last night after you came in. I had to bake today anyway, and that way, we could have it for breakfast."

Nate grinned at her around his food.

"I guess that means you don't hate me—but do you like me?"

Mari blushed and pulled out his old bandana.

"I missed you so much. I wore your bandana every day. I watched the road for you for so many years. And then when you came back, I was mad at you for staying away so long."

Nate chewed for a moment. He swallowed and spoke quietly, "I tried to see you several times. I even rode as far as Lance's place last year. I had just a little time before I had to be on the next train.

"While I was talking to Molly, you rode by in a shiny buggy with your arm around a tall fellow. He had on one of those bowler hats.

"I decided not to holler at you. I stopped in to see Merina instead and went back to Cheyenne. I got on that train, and I didn't even get off when I came back through town."

Mari stared incredulously at Nate for a moment.

"That was Rudy! He was working for a law firm in Kansas City, and he came home for a visit. He was leaving that morning. Of course I was hugging him. I missed my brother!" She stared at Nate and asked in surprise, "You thought he was my beau?"

Nate slowly turned red. He finally nodded his head.

"I never have understood women and Gabe is no help. He doesn't even understand Merina most of the time. I'm sorry, Mari. I should have waved you down. I just didn't want you to break my heart."

Mari's eyes were sparkling and she laughed. She pulled an open letter from her apron pocket and held it up.

"By the way, I have your letters. I've read all of them too."

Nate stared at her in surprise, but he shook his head.

"Not my letters. Merina burned them. I gave her the whole kit and kaboodle before the dance the other night. She agreed to burn them when she burned the trash."

"Merina didn't burn them. She said if you didn't want them and considered them trash, then she could do whatever she wanted with them. My name was on all of them so she gave them to me.

"She brought them over to Molly's yesterday morning. I was there since I stayed Saturday night after the dance."

Nate's neck began to turn red.

"You read them?"

"Every single one."

"I reckon you laughed some too."

Mari leaned forward and shook her head. Her eyes were wet when she spoke. "Nate, they were wonderful. They were sweet and honest just like I remembered you. I read them from the oldest to the most recent. I was able to see you grow from a boy to a man. You were a shy, sweet boy and you grew into a kind and honest man.

"Why didn't you mail them? They were wonderful letters."

Nate stared at Mari and then looked away. His eyes were a deep blue when he looked back at her.

"I was afraid you would have another beau. It was easier to dream you loved me than to face the thought of you loving someone else.

"That's it. That's why. I'm a big coward. I couldn't bear the idea of sharing my heart and then having you toss my letters away or laugh at them with your girlfriends."

Mari's breath caught in her chest. It almost sounded like a sob. Nate set down his plate and climbed to his feet.

"Mari—"

Mari rushed into his arms. She was laughing and crying as she said, "Nate Hawkins, you had better be here to stay because I am done waiting."

Nate smiled down at her. "Now look at you. You are as dirty as me."

"I don't care. You just keep hugging me."

"You might have to kiss me, Mari, to make up for reading my letters." Nate tipped her head back and smiled down at her. "What do you think? How many kisses will it take?"

He wiped her tears away with his thumbs and kissed her. After the third long kiss, Mari pulled away. She stepped back unsteadily.

"I don't think we should be in here alone. You aren't shy anymore and I have missed you too much."

Nate stepped toward her. He pulled the new bandana from his pocket and tied it around her neck as he smiled.

"This time, I will be the one waiting. How long will I have to wait until you marry me? A week? Two weeks? It can't be more than three."

Mari stared at Nate. "You planned this? You expected me to say yes so quickly?"

Nate's grin became bigger, and he laughed softly as he pulled a letter from his pocket.

"Here. You can add this to your collection. It's from Sam. He's bringing Izzy home. They are going to be married here. He can only come in June though, and he wants us to marry at the same time."

"The timing was Sam's idea. I was a little nervous about it working out. After the first night I stopped in to see you, I figured nothing would pan out. So yes and no."

Nate dropped down on one knee and put his hat over his heart.

"So, will you? Will you marry me, Mari? Will you make me the happiest cowboy in the Wyoming Territory?"

Before Mari could answer, they both heard a voice they recognized.

"Did I interrupt somethin' important, pard? Hello, Mari! How is my favorite gal cousin?"

Mari turned and squealed. She threw herself at Sam.

Nate stood up. His face was red as he grinned at his friend.

"Howdy, Sam. You showed up at exactly the wrong time. What are you doing here? I thought you weren't coming till June."

Sam reached through the doorway of the barn and pulled a smiling Isabelle up beside him.

Mari squealed and the two women hugged each other. When their excited chatter died down, Sam grinned.

"Izzy, Nate here was just workin' up the courage to ask your best friend to marry." He pulled Isabelle closer. "Courage has never been a problem for me though." His blue eyes twinkled, and he jabbed Nate.

"So, Mari, you on board for a double weddin'? Izzy and me can only be gone till this next Sunday. We have to be back on the ranch Monday morning. That's time enough though, ain't it? Her ma and John Kirkham will be here tomorrow or the next day.

"And no, I ain't been home yet. I figured I'd better find out what you said before I got Ma all worked up."

Mari looked from Nate to Sam and laughed.

"Well, I don't know. We were just getting to that. Besides, Nate has to ask Father yet, and he threw the last fellow out."

Nate grinned and shook his head.

"I already talked to your pa. In fact, he's the one who set up that seating arrangement at supper the first night I was here." When Mari stared at him, Nate laughed. "I think your pa likes me almost as much as you do." He reached out to take her hand. "Is that a yes, or do I need to get down on my knee again?" He pulled Mari close to him.

Mari smiled up at Nate.

"It was always a yes. It was yes before you even tried to ask me."

"You want to tell your family now? We just as well get it done."

Just then, Rowdy stepped out of the house and hollered, "You kids get away from that barn. Nate is still sleeping!"

"No he's not, Pa. He was kissin' on Mari, and now Sam is in there with some gal!"

Mari rushed out of the barn. Her face was pink, but she was laughing.

"Come over here, all of you. I want you to meet Isabelle. She was my roommate in college and is my best friend. She and Sam are getting married, and Nate and I are too!"

CHAPTER 101

THE PLANNING IS DONE!

ROWDY GRINNED. HE SHOOK NATE'S HAND AND slapped him on the back.

"I can't think of another man I would rather my little Mari pick for a husband. Welcome to the family, Nate."

Beth sobbed as she tried to talk. "I'm not crying because I'm sad. Well, I'm sort of sad but I'm happy too. I remember the sweet little girl we brought home eighteen years ago. I knew you'd grow up and marry someday, but it's hard to let you go." She kissed Mari. "I'll miss you terribly.

"When are you thinking? A November wedding might be nice."

Nate's grin became bigger. Mari's voice shook a little as she looked from her mother to her father.

"This week. We want to have a double wedding with Sam and Isabelle, and they can only be here until Sunday."

Rowdy started laughing. He looked over at Beth.

"Told you," was all he said.

Beth patted her chest. "I—I'm not sure we can make it happen that quickly. There is a lot to think about. And plan. And where will you live?"

Rowdy chuckled.

"Beth, we married about a week after we became engaged. Let the kids marry when they want. Molly will be all over this. All you'll have to do is what she tells you.

"So, what day? Friday or Saturday?"

Nate's smile became bigger.

"Let's do Saturday if that works for Father Cummiskey."

Rowdy grinned.

"Saturday, May 19, at three in the afternoon. That way, we can feed folks before they go back home. You four decide if you want a dance, and Beth will work out the meal with Molly." He looked over at his wife and chuckled as he added, "There. It's all planned. Now, Nate, you get on out of here. I have work to do."

Beth was alternating between laughing and crying when Nate rode out of the yard. She was talking about Mari's wedding dress.

"You may wear my wedding dress if you want, Mari. We can alter it some. I know you are chestier than me."

Nate turned red as he listened. He spurred Demonio to catch up with Sam and Isabelle. He rode with them as he talked.

"I'll see you this afternoon. I am going to tell Gabe and then clean up.

"Want to go fishing today? I'll stop after I pick up Mari. We can do it a little different this time and bring the girls." Nate winked at Isabelle and she laughed.

She leaned across her horse and kissed his cheek. She whispered, "That's for the scolding you gave me last Christmas, Nate. I bought my ticket home the next morning."

Nate grinned as he squeezed her shoulder.

"I did it for Sam." His grin became bigger when he spoke again. "I hid in the back of a church after I popped that fellow. A priest found me and thought I was there for confession. I decided to take him up on his offer." He winked at his friends and added, "I think my confession was close to an hour long." Isabelle's eyes opened wide, and Sam began to laugh.

Nate bumped Sam with his elbow. "Glad it worked out for you and Sis. See you both later." He turned his horse south and headed for home.

Gabe was in the barn when he heard a horse running. He stepped out and stared down the road. He said something over his shoulder and grinned as he waited for his brother to arrive.

Nate pulled Demonio to a stop. He looped one leg over the saddle horn and leaned back.

"Don't make any plans for Saturday."

Gabe stared for a moment and finally laughed. He hollered at Merina.

"Mark this Saturday off. We are going to have plans."

Merina's surprised face showed in the doorway. She looked from one brother to the other. When Nate laughed, she hugged him.

"Mari said yes! And what time is the wedding?"

"It's at three. I still need to talk to Father Cummiskey but that is the plan." He spoke over his shoulder as he dismounted, "Sam is back. He's marrying his sweetheart at the same time, so we'll have a double wedding."

He dropped the reins and hugged Merina. He smiled at her as his neck turned red. "And thanks for not burning my letters, Merina," he whispered. "You helped me to win Mari over."

CHAPTER 102

SAM'S GIRL

SAM SQUEEZED ISABELLE'S HAND AND DRAWLED, "I sure am glad it worked out with Mari. Nate has been sweet on her since we was kids." He leaned over and whispered, "'Course, he wasn't as slick with the ladies as me."

Isabelle pulled her hand away and rolled her eyes. Sam laughed and grabbed it again. "My ma is goin' to love you," he said softly as they turned toward his home.

Sam and Isabelle rode their horses into the Rocking R yard. Molly shaded her eyes to see who the newcomers were. When she recognized Sam, she ran toward the barn.

"Lance! It's Sam and he brought his girl home for us to meet!"

Lance stepped out of the barn and the rest of the family soon appeared. They all stood silently and watched their brother ride toward them with the girl their parents had whispered about for four years.

Sam pulled his horse to a stop and grinned at his family. "Ma. Pa. This here is Isabelle Merrill. She is goin' to be my Mrs. Rankin."

Molly put her hand over her mouth. Her eyes were trying to cry but she wouldn't let them. She touched Lance's arm and hurried toward Sam.

"Oh, Sam!"

Sam slid off his horse. He hugged Molly before he gave Isabelle a hand down.

"Izzy, this is my ma, Molly. That's my pa, Lance. My sisters Abbie and Livvy and my little brother, Henry." He looked around in surprise. "Where's Paul?"

Lance nodded his head northwest.

"Paul took a crew of hands to help Sturgis gather cows. They are scattered all over after that fire Saturday night. I'm headed up there to help build fence as soon as I get saddled." He reached for Isabelle's hand as he grinned at her.

"It's nice to meet you, Isabelle. We thought sure Sam would be moving home this spring. I'm not sure if I'm glad this deal worked out or not. I could sure use his help around here."

Isabelle's breath caught in her throat, and she slid closer to Sam.

Molly pushed Lance aside.

"Good grief, Lance. Scare the poor girl the first time we meet her.

"Welcome to the family, Isabelle. Sam mentioned you often…in the few letters we received from him.

"Would you like to come inside and have a glass of lemonade? I just made some. Lance loves it. I can't always get lemons though, so it's somewhat of a treat." Molly was still chattering as she led Isabelle toward the house.

Lance grinned at his oldest son.

"So you found a little gal who would put up with you, huh? Your ma seems to like her already, so that's a good sign."

Sam nodded and laughed.

"I knew she was the one for me when I met her four years ago, but it took a little time to win her over." He frowned and added, "Her ma didn't like me much in the beginning. In fact, I don't think she does yet.

"Izzy's pa died three years ago and Evelyn—that's Izzy's ma—she just went a little haywire. She took Izzy away the day of his funeral. They didn't come back till the end of last year. She even burned all the letters Izzy wrote me just to keep us apart.

"Now, she'll probably be livin' with us." He started to say something else but frowned. He shrugged his shoulders and added, "An old feller who lost his wife wants to court her. I hope they get married. I'm just not sure I can deal with her ever' day."

Lance put his arm around Sam's shoulders. He grabbed the reins of Isabelle's horse, and they walked toward the barn.

"Son, in-laws aren't always easy to deal with, but you need to get along for your gal's sake. Isabelle loves her mother, crazy or not. You love her too. And every time she does or says something that makes you mad, you think of your Grandpa Samuel."

When Sam stared at his father in surprise, Lance nodded.

"I didn't like Samuel much before I got to know him. I didn't like him because of how he treated your mother after—after something bad happened to her. In fact, I wanted to hurt him.

"But then I met him. He was just a lost man trying to raise a girl by himself after losing his wife. It was a difficult time. He wasn't a bad man. He just made some mistakes.

"Your ma cut ties with him when she left home. She talked a lot about growing up after we married though, and her father was part of every story. I knew she missed him. I invited Samuel out here so they could make amends. He stayed and he has been a blessing to this family—to all of Cheyenne for that matter. Samuel is a fine man. In fact, he's one of the finest men I know.

"So you love Izzy's ma. And you *invite* her to live with you." Lance's eyes twinkled as he added, "Then have lots of kids. She'll move out soon enough when she gets tired of a wet bed every night."

CHAPTER 103

LET'S GO TALK TO THAT PRIEST

SAM WAS JUST COMING OUT OF THE BUNKHOUSE THE next morning when Nate rode into the ranch yard. He was riding Demonio and Appy followed behind. Nate laughed.

His friend's hair poked out in every direction, and he was rubbing the sleep out of his eyes.

"Pard, you are downright ugly in the morning. I hope Izzy knows what she's tying onto."

Sam pointed at the house and grinned.

"Ma said no way was I sleepin' in that house with my future wife in there. She threw me out—my own mother! She also said I was gettin' a haircut whether I liked it or not. Sadie always cut our hair when I lived at home. I guess I'd better talk to her.

"Eight years and Ma is just as bossy as ever. I don't know how Pa puts up with her."

Lance was just walking by the bunkhouse, and he smacked Sam on the back of his head.

"And you are just as mouthy as you were when you left.

"You two fellas playing all day, or do you intend to do a little work around here? Sturgis could use some help too."

Nate grinned at Lance and shook his head.

"Not today. Sturgis told me to stay home. I told him I'd be over tomorrow to help build fence." His grin became bigger and he added, "You old timers can handle things today.

"And while you're working, Sam and I are going to ride into Cheyenne and talk to that priest about marrying us on Saturday. I'm inviting Mari to ride along, and I'm guessing Isabelle will want to come too.

"Besides, I wouldn't count on getting any work out of Sam at all while Isabelle's around. He's so pie-eyed around her that he can barely think. I'm not sure how he runs their ranch a'tall."

Sam snorted and Nate turned Demonio away before his friend could reply.

"I'm headed over to pick up Mari. I'll be back here in a couple of hours."

Sam eyed Nate's back and shook his head before he hollered, "I ain't the only one who is pie-eyed. It sure don't take no two hours to ride there and back."

Nate pulled his horse around and chuckled as Sam continued talking.

"Go on over there, but if Ma don't make breakfast, I might join you. She's so busy makin' plans for this weddin' that we will most likely all starve between now and then unless I eat with the hands. And Gus ain't even around anymore.

"That durn cookie Pa has workin' for 'im can't..." Sam's voice died out when the cook poked his head out of the camp kitchen. Sam winked at Nate and added, "Say, since we're headed to Cheyenne to talk to that priest, we can eat dinner in town. And if that priest ain't around, we can wire 'im."

Nate held Demonio still as he listened to his friend.

"Ma said all the neighbor women are goin' to be makin' food today for the fellers who are helpin' out over to Sturgis'. I told her we could pack that over this evenin' if they need us to.

"Then tomorrow we'll help ol' Sturgis. That sound all right to you?"

"Sounds good to me."

Nate turned his horse to the west as he smiled. "I am going to spend the day with the prettiest, sweetest gal in Wyoming Territory.

"I guess I should have mailed those letters. Oh well. It all worked out. Now I just need to find us a place to live while I build a house. Wouldn't it be something if we could live in Mari's folks' old house. I think she'd like that. 'Course, it might take some fixing up. Maybe I'll talk to my future father-in-law about renting it for a time."

When he arrived at Rowdy's, Mari rushed out to meet him. She had his new bandana over her hair and Nate grinned. He swung his leg over the pommel of his saddle.

"Want to ride into Cheyenne today with Sam and me and Izzy? We need to talk to that priest about marrying. Then we might treat you gals to a meal at some swanky eating place like the Tin House." Nate's grin was big, and Mari laughed as she nodded excitedly.

Rowdy stuck his head out the door and hollered, "Come in, Nate. We are just finishing breakfast if you are hungry."

Nate pulled off his hat as he stepped through the door. The children all talked over each other, and Nate grinned.

"Howdy, kids. You ready to go to a big party? I'm going to marry your sister and we'll make it a humdinger. We might need a little help if any of you want to be part of it." A chorus of voices volunteered, and Nate laughed. He looked over at Rowdy as he pulled out a chair.

"What kind of shape is the old Hatch house in? The place I planned to move into burned and I need to rent a place for my new bride."

Rowdy chewed as he thought.

"It might work for a time. I sure wouldn't want to spend the winter there unless you do a lot of fixing. It's not real tight, but it will do for the summer.

"Mari can show you where it is. She's the one who goes over there the most often anyway." He eyed Nate as he held a piece of side pork on his fork.

"You planning to build, are you? Have a place in mind?"

Nate nodded.

"I do. I'd like to show it to Mari today if we have time. Sam and I will be helping at Sturgis' tomorrow. Probably the next day too." He flashed Beth a grin as he added, "This deal came together a little quicker than I thought it would—not that I'm complaining though."

Mari rushed into the room. She had on a riding skirt and stood nervously as she looked at Nate.

"You going to eat, Mari?" Rowdy asked. "It sounds like you have a busy day."

"I ate while I fixed breakfast so I'm ready to leave when Nate finishes."

Nate shoved the last bite of side pork into his mouth and stood.

"We can leave now. I ate earlier." He grinned at Beth again. "I just never turn down good food." He grabbed Mari's hand.

"I'll have her back this afternoon sometime or maybe this evening." Mari waved and they were gone.

Beth looked over at Rowdy and sighed.

"In just a few days, our little girl will be gone. And I doubt we will see her much before then either."

Rowdy chuckled and stood.

"Yeah, but she will be close if they move into the Hatch place. Now you kids get out there and do your chores."

CHAPTER 104

A Surprise Visit from Leo

NATE SHOOK THE EXPRESS AGENT'S HAND. "GOOD TO see you, Elmer. You know Mari. This is Isabelle Merrill. She is Sam's fiancé."

Elmer Tinley smiled and nodded. "I heard you fellows were getting married on Saturday. You need to send Father Cummiskey a wire? He is in Laramie and likely won't be back here until Friday night or later unless someone needs him.

"Oh, and I have wire here for you, Sam. It's from John Kirkham."

Mari grabbed Isabelle's arm. "Let's go down the street, Isabelle. I want to introduce you to more of our friends." The men were still talking as Mari hurried Isabelle toward Martha McCune's little dress shop.

"Sadie, this is Isabelle. She is Sam's girl. Her family has a ranch in the Sandhills of Nebraska. That's where Sam has been working most of these last four years." The women visited for a time before Isabelle walked around Sadie's shop. She stared at the labels on some of the dresses hanging there. She looked at Sadie in surprise.

"I recognize your label! In fact, I have several of your dresses. My mother ordered my wedding dress several months ago, and I believe it is one of your creations as well. If I had known you were located in Cheyenne, I would have waited and purchased it here.

"I'm not sure how it will fit. I wasn't around when Mother ordered it, so I don't even know what it looks like." Isabelle blushed slightly as she looked back at the two women. "My mother is fussier than I am. I hope it's not too frilly."

Sadie smiled and nodded. "I would be glad to alter it, Isabelle. Just bring it in when she arrives. We can change anything you want, including frills and ruffles."

Sam stepped through the door followed by Nate, and Sadie hurried to hug them.

"It is so good to see you boys. I'm sorry. I guess I should say men. You will always be boys to me though. And you are both getting married! Badger told us just yesterday."

"Badger still knows what goes on almost before it happens." Sam laughed and shook his head. He thrust a paper toward Isabelle.

"That wire just came in. Your ma and John Kirkham will be arrivin' tomorrow. This town is startin' to get crowded."

Sadie laughed as she looked from Sam to Isabelle.

"Leo surprised us with a visit on Monday. He said he was on the same train as the two of you from Ogallala." Sadie's eyes were curious as she added, "He had a nice young lady with him who is looking for work." She smiled. "Levi and I have so missed Leo. I hope he has time to stay for a while."

Nate looked curiously from Sam to Sadie. He raised an eyebrow, but Sam wouldn't look at him. Sadie continued, "Levi is conducting interviews this morning, and he told Leo's friend to apply."

Sam asked with surprise, "So is Levi hirin' a new receptionist? Annie doesn't work there anymore?"

"Annie is resigning. She has been parttime for several years now. She has her hands full at home with two little ones, and besides, she doesn't need the extra work.

"Tiny's carpentry business has grown so much that he put up a large building. Annie does all the books for that business plus they are planning to adopt another baby." Sadie smiled. "So, Levi is looking for a receptionist although it will be hard to replace Annie." She looked from Nate to Sam. "The girl who arrived with Leo is Sarah Wilson. She said she knew both of you."

Nate frowned slightly as he looked at Sam again. He slowly nodded.

"Isn't that the little gal we picked up some time back northwest of Ogallala? We found her after those outlaws hit her place. The one who lost her folks?"

Sam nodded. "That's the one." His face was overly innocent, and Nate watched his friend carefully. Sam winked at him when Sadie looked away.

"I thought Leo had some highfalutin' lawyer job in Saint Louis." Sam's eyes were twinkling, and he was working hard not to smile as he listened for an answer from Sadie.

"He does or he did anyway. He hasn't said much to us, just that he was taking some time off.

"Levi is excited to have him back. He is convinced that Leo is home to stay. I hope he's right. Levi is so busy he can barely keep up with all his cases let alone his legal work.

"As far as for good though, neither of us knows." Sadie frowned slightly. "Leo didn't bring anything with him—no clothes, no books, not even a travel bag. Regardless, it is wonderful to have him home."

Sadie smiled at the young people in front of her.

"Hug Martha on your way out. I heard her come in and I know she will want to see you." She hugged each of them again and added, "Enjoy the rest of your day."

They had just turned to leave when Sam paused.

"Sadie, do you have time to lower my ears some? Ma wants me to get a haircut 'fore the weddin'."

"Any evening this week will be fine, Sam. Just come by the ranch."

The two couples visited with Martha a moment before they mounted their horses. As they rode away, Nate looked over at Sam.

"What's the story with Leo?"

Isabelle began to laugh.

"Leo was waiting for a train to Kansas City when we arrived in Ogallala. He was with a most unpleasant young woman."

Sam snorted. "Unpleasant don't even come close to describin' that gal. She was meaner than the hind leg of a rabid cow. She stood there and gave Leo all kinds of orders. He didn't say nothin' neither…till she took in after little Sarah Wilson.

"That little gal was just a standin' there, waitin' on a train to Cheyenne, same as Izzy and me.

"First, Leo's gal made fun of Sarah's clothes. Then she made a few comments 'bout her character. That's when Leo had enough. He grabbed that nasty gal's skinny arm and told her to go sit down.

"She left alright, but when she walked by Sarah, she smacked her with that fancy little umbrella she carried. Racked little Sarah right across the shins.

"There was no call for that kind of behavior, so I bumped that nasty gal, accidental like. Knocked her into a pile of horse—horse dung. She sat there just a screamin' for Leo to help her up.

"Leo, he looked at me and grinned. He said, 'I don't have anything in Saint Louis I can't live without. I believe I'll go home with you fellows.' He took hold of Sarah's arm and asked if she was all right. Then he changed his tickets and we all got on the train to Cheyenne.

"That crazy gal beat on the train with her umbrella as we pulled out of the station. She was screamin' all kinds of threats. I looked over at Leo and said, 'Gals must be in mighty short supply in Saint Louis if that's the best you could come up with.' Leo didn't say nothin' but he was smilin' by the time we got to Cheyenne. Had him a real nice visit with Sarah too.

"He took her over to Badger's place to see if she could stay with them for a time till she got her feet under her. That's the last we saw of either one of 'em.

"I hope he stays. Leo is a fine fellow—way too good a man for that nasty gal. I think maybe she was his boss' daughter. At least it sounded that way from some of the things she was a yellin'. Could be that's why he took up with her." Sam shook his head. "Ain't no job in the world worth puttin' up with a gal like that though, and I told 'im so."

He grinned as he looked from Isabelle to Mari. He winked at Nate.

"I reckon that makes us mighty lucky fellers."

Nate nodded seriously. "It sure does and I'm glad this wedding is soon. They don't have much time to change their minds."

The women laughed and the four of them rode northwest to look at Nate and Mari's new ranch.

CHAPTER 105

JACKSON DAVID BOYCE

WHEN THEY RETURNED TO CHEYENNE, NATE GAVE the women their choice of eating at the Tin House in Dyer's Hotel or the Rollins House.

"You choose, Mari. I don't know either place," Isabelle stated. "I'm hungry so I'll eat wherever you want."

"Let's eat at the Tin House. It's cheaper and we don't need to spend extra money." Mari led the way across the street.

They had just sat down when Elmer Tinley hurried in.

"Nate, I have a message for you from Spur—George Spurlach that is. He asked if you'd stop by Levi Parker's place. He wants to talk to you." He hesitated and added, "Sorry to bother you. I don't know that it's urgent, but I saw you ride in and wanted to catch you before you left for home." Elmer patted Nate's back and hurried out.

Sam raised an eyebrow. "Spur's in town? That musta been a fast trip. Ma didn't say nothin' 'bout him comin' to visit. What do you reckon he wants?"

"I don't know but I guess I'll find out."

The four friends enjoyed their meal. Lots of folks stopped by to say hello and to welcome the two young men home. Of course, they were all smiling at Isabelle and Mari too. Weddings were always exciting because they usually meant a big party.

"You all right with riding out to Levi's now, Mari? I don't know how long we'll be there. Hopefully, we can make it to Sam's in time to help him deliver supper."

Sam studied his friend's face and slowly nodded.

"I'll keep an eye out. If you ain't out there by three-thirty, we'll head on up here with the wagon. We can meet in front of the Rollins House 'round five or so."

Nate nodded and waved. As Mari and he turned their horses to the east, she looked at him curiously.

"Why do you think Spur made a trip down here?"

"I'm not sure. I'm wondering if it could have something to do with a little boy I met four years ago when I was visiting them. His ma was sickly. Maybe she died." Nate frowned and shook his head as he added, "But even if that happened, Spur wouldn't come down here. He'd send me a wire or Clare would write a letter."

"His name is Jackson David Boyce, isn't it?" When Nate stared at Mari in surprise, she laughed.

"You wrote about him in one of your letters."

Nate grinned and took Mari's hand.

"Mari, I sure am glad you agreed to marry me. Talking to you in person is a lot more fun than writing letters.

"Now I want you to be thinking about what you want in your new house. I'd like to have it up by the time cold weather moves in so that doesn't give us much time to plan.

"My needs are a little slim, but I want my new wife to be able to make me lots of bread." He grinned at her again and squeezed her hand. "And we need to allow room for all the kids we are going to have."

Mari blushed prettily but she laughed. They were both smiling when they reached Levi's ranch.

Spur was outside when Nate and Mari rode in. Levi waved at them from the house and Clare hurried out to give them hugs. Spur grinned as he walked across the yard.

"Nate! I thought you were Gabe for a minute there. Hello, Mari. You went and grew up."

They visited for a time and Spur finally pointed toward the kids. "See a fellow out there who goes by the name of Beaner?"

Nate stared and nodded slowly. "Why is Jackson with you? I'm guessing Alice passed away, but why are you down here? Not that I'm complaining—we are marrying on Saturday and would love for you to come."

Spur grinned and nodded. "We'd like that." His smile faded and he frowned before he spoke again.

"Alice passed just a few days ago. I'm not sure exactly what happened, but some folks came out from Missoula a little over a week ago and moved her into the hospital there. They put Beaner in an orphanage.

"We didn't know a thing about it, or we would have brought them both home with us. A hospital wouldn't do anything for Alice that we couldn't do.

"Father Ravalli is the one who told us. He didn't find out until after Alice died. 'Course she was only in Missoula a week before she passed so this all happened mighty quick."

Spur growled under his breath and shook his head.

"We had told Alice we'd take Jackson in whenever she needed us to—her as well—but since she passed in a different county, things got all mixed up. We weren't notified and Jackson was passed off to a family he didn't know. He tried to tell the folks who ran the orphanage where he was supposed to go but no one listened.

"He thought we didn't want him, so he ran away. Sneaked onto a train and headed out to find you."

Nate stared at Spur.

"To find me? I'm a long way from Missoula!"

"Yeah, Clare and I weren't too happy when we were informed. We headed to Missoula right away and booked tickets to Cheyenne. Clare was a wreck. She just knew something had happened to him. We stopped in Helena to see if he had made it that far.

"We found him trying to steal some food in a mercantile there. He was mighty upset and wanted to see you.

"We already had tickets to Cheyenne and had the whole family along, so we decided to come on down." Spur grinned and bumped Nate. "It wasn't a planned trip but here we are. And since you and Sam are marrying Saturday, I reckon we will stay long enough to take part in that party."

Nate laughed and agreed. His face became serious again when a little boy looked their way. The boy walked slowly toward Nate. His eyes were wide, but he held himself stiff and tried not to show any emotion.

Nate sauntered toward him with a grin and held out his hand.

"Jackson David Boyce. It's good to see you again."

The little boy gripped Nate's hand and tear leaked out of his eye. Clare put her hand across her heart and Nate dropped down beside Jackson.

"Did your ma pass, Jackson?"

The little boy nodded.

"And the county wanted to give you to a family you didn't know?"

Jackson nodded. "Some folks moved us to Missoula. We didn't want to go but they said Ma couldn't take care of me. That wasn't true though. She told me what to do an' I did it.

"They hauled us off an' put her in a big house with lots of folks in white. Then they put me in an orphanage.

"When she died, they started lookin' for a family for me. I tried to tell 'em Clare an' Spur would take me in, but..." Jackson slid his eyes past Nate to Spur and then back to Nate.

"The next day they said they were takin' me to meet my new folks. I saw a train close by. It was just sittin' in the station. Steam was comin' out of it so I knew it would be leavin' soon. I got away from 'em an' ran toward some houses. Then I doubled back and climbed up in a livestock car. I picked one that was crowded with horses so they wouldn't check too close."

Nate winced as he thought of Jackson around all those hooves.

Jackson gave Nate a small smile.

"No one checked the car I was in. Those horses was mighty nervous but they give me a little room in one of the corners. I made it to Helena 'fore I got kicked off." He grinned at Nate. "Those railroad fellers was some surprised when they hauled me out of that car after the horses was unloaded.

"Spur and Clare found me in Helena."

Nate took Jackson's hand and led him over to a bench under some trees. He sat down and Jackson sat down beside him.

"Why didn't you head south to find Spur and Clare?"

"No trains run that way an' I knew I couldn't sneak onto a stage. Since the train was there handy-like, I took it." His breath caught in his chest, and he whispered, "Besides, Spur and Clare don't want me."

Nate frowned and shook his head.

"That's not right, Jackson. Clare and Spur worked mighty hard to find you. I know for a fact they'd like you to be their kid."

Jackson looked up at Nate and a big tear rolled down his cheek.

"The old lady who was draggin' me to the wagon there in Missoula, she said there wasn't *nobody* who wanted me. She said I needed to be grateful she had found some folks who would take me in even if it was just for a time." Jackson sobbed and Nate lifted the little boy onto his lap. He almost cursed but he took a deep breath.

"Jackson, that old lady was talking out of the side of her mouth. Why, if I told the folks I know around here that you needed a home, you'd have so many offers you wouldn't know what to do. And Clare and Spur would be the first ones in line." Nate gave the little boy a hug as he watched him closely.

"Where do you want to live, Jackson?"

"I want to live with you, Nate Hawkins."

Nate studied Jackson's face before he nodded solemnly. "I reckon that would be all right, but I don't have any kids for you to play with—not yet anyway. You might be kind of lonesome." He nodded toward the kids playing behind the house. "You'd have lots more kids to play with if you lived with Clare and Spur."

Jackson looked over to where Spur's and Levi's kids were playing. He listened for a moment as they called back and forth to each other. His eyes were big when he looked up at Nate.

"Do you really think Clare and Spur want me?"

"I know they do, but I'll make a deal with you.

"You walk toward Clare. If she doesn't put out her arms to hug you, you just turn right around and come back here to me. But if she cries and wants to hug you, then you'll know she wants you.

"Now Spur, he won't cry. He'll just rub his chin and smile." Nate slid Jackson off his lap and turned him toward Spur and Clare. "Go on now. You see if I'm right."

Jackson turned and slowly walked toward Clare.

Clare didn't wait. She ran toward the little boy with her arms held out. She picked him up and hugged him as she cried.

Spur patted his back. He rubbed his hand across his face a couple of times and Jackson smiled. He hugged Clare hard and slid down before he ran back to Nate. His eyes were shining as he looked up at him.

"I reckon I'll live with Clare and Spur. But you'll come and see me sometime won't you, Nate Hawkins?"

"I sure will, Jackson. I think I'll pair old Demon to some fancy mare, and if we get a colt that looks like him, I'll bring him along with me."

Jackson's face was happy, and he nodded excitedly. As he ran by Clare, he yelled, "Nate Hawkins is going to give me a Demon colt all my own!

"I'm going to play with all my cousins now." He raced away yelling for the group of kids to wait for him.

Spur put his arm around Clare and smiled at her. His eyes were red when he looked at Nate.

"Thanks, Nate. Clare's heart was going to break if we didn't take that boy home with us. But then, I reckon she'd take in every lost child she could find."

Clare wiped her eyes and smiled at Spur.

"Of course I would," she said softly. She reached out her hand to Mari.

"Let's go sit on that bench for a little while and talk. Tell me about Sam and Isabelle and how you all became friends."

Spur watched the women walk away. He was quiet for a time. He finally looked at Nate and pointed toward his heart as he spoke softly.

"That woman makes my old heart just tingle. I love her with everything I have."

Nate didn't answer but he thought about what Spur had said. *I sure hope Mari and I can say that after we've been married for a time. I think we will. Gabe feels that way about Merina so I reckon Mari and I will too.*

CHAPTER 106

Two Brides and Four Best Friends

ISABELLE WAS LAUGHING AS SHE SLID HER CORSET over her head.

"You'll have to lace this up for me, Mari. I can't get the strings pulled tight enough. I will tie yours for you too."

"I'm not wearing one. I never have and I'm not going to make an exception for one day." Mari blushed as she looked at her surprised friend's face. "Besides, Nate would never be able to get it off me. I doubt he has ever even seen a corset."

"You've never worn one?" Isabelle's face was shocked as she turned around to stare at Mari. "But doesn't your mother wear one?"

Mari shook her head and laughed. "None of the women in our community wear them. Mother said she did before she met father, but she dumped hers after her wedding. Anna, Angel Montero's wife, might still wear one in public—I don't really know—but none of the rest of us do."

When Isabelle continued to stare at her, Mari laughed.

"Make it easier on Sam, Isabelle! I can hear him now. 'For the love of Pete, Izzy—how do I get this thing off you? I reckon my knife 'ill be faster. Now hold still so's ya don't git cut!'" Mari's voice mimicked Sam's almost perfectly.

Isabelle giggled and pulled the heavy bone and cord contraption off her waist. She wiggled and tugged as she pulled her dress on.

"Don't mention this to Mother. She will probably swoon when I walk up the aisle. She'll say, 'Why, Isabelle Merrill, every inch of you moves when you walk. That is most inappropriate!' And I *know* she'll be bound up tighter than a tick.

"My poor mother. She worries so about what other people think."

Mari laughed again. "Well, I'm just glad she ordered a wedding dress for you with all those ruffles. Once you had Sadie take them off, I had some extra lace to add to the bottom of my dress to make it longer. Good thing too because I am quite a bit taller than Mother. We were both worried about making her dress fit me though the chest and hips. We totally forgot about the length."

Isabelle nodded as she smoothed her dress over her hips. She spoke softly as she looked in the mirror Martha McCune had placed in the room where they were dressing.

"This dress is just lovely. I have several of Sadie Parker's dresses in my closet back in Nebraska. I had no idea I would meet the designer someday let alone learn that her family is close friends of Sam's parents.

"Mother offered to buy me a couple more dresses while we were both here, but I told her I didn't need any. I'm afraid I will not be able to wear them for a time and I don't want them to just hang in my closet." Isabelle's face blushed a deep red. "Sam is hoping we get pregnant right away. He thinks being a daddy will be a lot of fun.

"Of course, he assumes our first child will be a boy. I'm not sure what he'll do if we have a house full of little girls who are as wild as he is!" As both women laughed, Isabelle asked, "Have you and Nate talked about children?"

"Not a lot. I know he wants them because he talked about all the little ones he met in his letters. He loves children and they seem to love him.

"Mother is almost giddy about becoming a grandmother. She is hoping we have one our first year too. Father hasn't said much, but he's an old softie around kids."

Both brides heard horses outside and Mari pulled the curtain aside.

"Why, it's Nate and Sam! They aren't even supposed to be here!"

Isabelle's eyes sparkled and she ran for the door. "You are the one who started breaking rules first thing this morning with no corsets. Who says we can't give our fellows a kiss before our wedding?" She darted out the door followed closely by Mari.

CHAPTER 107

More Broken Rules

SAM AND NATE PULLED THEIR HORSES TO A STOP. SAM slipped off quickly and raced toward the house as he yelled, "I'm a goin' to kiss Mari first. I reckon you'll hog her for the rest of the day, so I'd best say goodbye to my favorite gal cousin now."

Nate chuckled and followed his friend. He hugged Isabelle and kissed her cheek.

"I sure am glad it worked out between you and Sam, Sis. I reckon he's happier than he's been since we left home together."

Isabelle's eyes had tears in them, but she laughed.

"And I am so glad you and I happened to be on the same street in the same city at the same time—let alone in a state neither of us had visited before." She kissed Nate's cheek as she smiled up at him.

"You and Mari had better visit from time to time or I'm not sure I will ever keep Sam in Nebraska."

Sam grabbed Isabelle and swung her around before he bent her backwards to kiss her. Nate wrapped Mari up. He had just finished a long kiss when he heard a man's voice.

"I told Beth we'd better get in here and supervise you two fellows. I knew you'd both be over here before the wedding."

Beth bumped Rowdy as she laughed. "Like he was before ours!

"Now come, ladies. Let's get your hair done. The wedding starts in forty minutes." She gave Sam and Nate each a hug before she pushed them toward their horses.

"And you fellows had better have buggies arranged for your brides. They are not riding astride in their wedding dresses."

Nate and Sam kissed their future brides one more time before they strolled toward their horses. Sam turned around and hollered, "We'll see you gals at the church. And don't nobody cry. You know I don't like women gettin' all sappy on me."

Evelyn and John Kirkham arrived as the two cowboys were leaving. Evelyn looked at them in surprise. She frowned and glanced quickly toward the two young women waving from the front steps. She started to speak, but John patted her hand.

"Just wave, Evelyn. They are good boys. If they weren't, Mari's pa wouldn't be smiling. You relax now and enjoy this day. Your only daughter is marrying a fine man, and we both have cause to be happy."

Evelyn slowly nodded. Her eyes had tears in them, and she dabbed at them with an embroidered handkerchief. She sighed as she smiled at John.

"That's what Sadie Parker told me yesterday when I asked her if she knew Sam well. She laughed and said, 'A very long time.'

"She said she met Sam shortly after Lance and Molly adopted him, and he was a busy, ornery little boy. She also told me that she would be delighted to have Sam as a son-in-law. She said, 'I only hope when my daughters are old enough that they will marry men as fine as Sam and Nate.'

"Isabelle saw that when she first met Sam, but I didn't. It has been hard for me to like him. He's wild and brash, and I so wanted Isabelle to marry someone more cultured." Evelyn dabbed at her eyes again as she whispered, "My daughter is more like Jasper than she ever was like me."

John patted Evelyn's hand and smiled at her.

"They will be fine, Ev. Isabelle found a good man, and he will take care of her. And you helped her to do that when you chose Jasper to be her father.

"You don't have to worry about Isabelle being loved by the man she is marrying today, and that is the most important thing."

A small sob came up in Evelyn's chest and she worked to push it down. She smiled at the man beside her again.

"Thank you, John. You have been a good friend. You seem to know how to calm me down."

John smiled as he lifted Evelyn out of the buggy.

"Now you get on inside and help Isabelle finish getting ready. I see Badger coming up the street, and I'm guessing Martha has been cooking all morning. I'm going to see if they have anything to eat before we get this shindig started."

CHAPTER 108

A DOUBLE WEDDING

THE YOUNG WOMEN FINISHED DRESSING QUICKLY AND hurried to the waiting buggies. John Kirkham was stepping in for Isabelle's father, and he was proud to help.

Mari wore her grandmother's wedding dress, the same dress Beth had worn. The lovely old gown was fitted to a young bride's body again, this time with a layer of ruffled lace around the bottom. Mari had Nate's old bandana wrapped around the stems of the flowers she carried, and she wore a simple cross necklace Rowdy had found when he cleaned out the old Hatch house.

Isabelle's dress was a simple satin design with long sleeves of lace. Evelyn frowned slightly when she saw that all the rows of ruffled lace had been removed. She smiled when she saw that Isabelle wore the pearls she had worn on her wedding day. She kissed her daughter and handed her the small bouquet of flowers Martha had arranged.

Both women looked beautiful.

Sam and Nate were at the front of the church. They both looked nervous and happy. Sadie had cut Sam's hair, and his blond curls were a little calmer than normal. Paul stood beside Sam while Gabe was beside Nate.

Gabe kept an eye on his brother. He remembered fainting at his own wedding, and he did not want Nate to go down.

Just before Josie Williams started to play the "Ave Maria," the doors in the back of the church flew open. Badger's voice could be heard by everyone as he whispered loudly, "We made it on time, Penny. Nothin's even happened yet."

Nearly everyone turned around to look in surprise. They smiled at Wilson Penny as he kissed Mari's and Isabelle's cheeks and nodded at the smiling guests.

Spur and Clare both grabbed for Eddie when the ornery little boy made a break for the open aisle in front of him. They turned into the closest pew and were pleased when they saw Stub and Kit's smiling faces.

Tuff arrived shortly after the Spurlachs, and he blushed slightly when he saw Annie and Nora. He nodded at Spur and slid into the seat beside them. Clare hugged him and he grinned.

When the music started, the two fathers moved forward. John Kirkham held Isabelle's arm while Rowdy walked with Mari. They led the two young brides to the front and gave them to their future husbands.

Rowdy whispered to John just before they walked up the aisle, "Now, when we get up there, I'm going to step to the right. You move to the left and we'll see if we can't confuse those two fellows."

It didn't work though. Sam and Nate were ready. They quickly changed places and the guests laughed.

Beth and Molly cried during most of the wedding while Evelyn dabbed her eyes. Merina frowned at Emilia when Slim Parker winked at her and Abbie.

When the wedding was over, the two couples waited outside to greet their friends. Mule and Demonio even made an appearance.

Spur was the first in line to shake hands. He grinned at the two young men.

"You fellers will like this marryin' business. It's a fine thing to come home to a hot meal and a warm woman." He winked at Clare and added in a loud whisper, "'Course, it's good the other way around too."

Clare blushed. "Good grief, Spur. You have no muzzle at all."

Spur's grin became bigger, and he kissed his wife. "Well, it's true, and it's a fine thing too. No reason to be embarrassed about bein' happy."

Clare smiled as she congratulated the young couple.

"We wish all of you the best. Spur is right though. Marriage is a wonderful thing when you marry the one you love. And children are a blessing too." Her eyes teared up a little when she thought about the baby she and Spur had lost shortly after Nate's visit there. Spur could feel Clare's body tense and he moved his family out of the way so the next in line could congratulate the young couples.

He kissed Clare's cheek and whispered, "We'll have lots more babies, Clare. You just wait and see." His eyes twinkled when he added, "And maybe they will all be as wild as Eddie."

Clare laughed around her tears as she smiled at Spur.

"He's wild like his daddy and I love him to pieces."

CHAPTER 109

A WILD WEDDING DANCE

SAM GRABBED NATE WHEN THEY ARRIVED AT THE Rollins House.

"How about we show these folks how to do that Weddin' March we learned down in Kansas at all those weddin' dances we busted into." Sam grinned at the women and added, "We went to every weddin' dance in every town we passed through. We'd find out just enough about one side of the family before we went, and then we'd pretend to be guests. Ate lots of good food too.

"Shoot, we even sat at the front table at several of those shindigs. Had us a good ol' time."

Nate chuckled and blushed slightly when Mari stared at him. "That's true, but we did just about anything for a free meal when we first left home. That's been some time back though." He slowly shook his head.

"I don't think so on the Wedding March though. We probably need two couples to lead since there are two of us newlyweds, and we don't even have one."

"Kirkham said he could lead. I asked him last night. He thought he could find someone to help him. He didn't tell me who he had in mind, but he didn't seem too concerned.

"Come on. Let's make an announcement before folks get out on the floor." Sam held Isabelle's hand and led the way to the front of the room.

"Folks, we want to share somethin' with you tonight. They have a dance they call the Weddin' March down south in Kansas and Nebraska." His grin became bigger as he added, "After we left home, Nate here drug me to every dance he could find. 'Course, once we found out that folks down there fed all their friends at weddin' parties too, we hit every one we could." He waved at John Kirkham and the old man led Evelyn to the front of the room.

"This here is my new mother-in-law, Evelyn Merrill." He waited until people stopped clapping before he pointed to the man next to her.

"That feller is John Kirkham. He is from Ogallala, Nebraska. He has been a friend to Nate and me for a long while. He offered to lead this dance, so we'll just turn it over to him."

Kirkham smiled and waved toward the back of the room.

"Slim Parker, grab you a gal and get up here. We'll show this crowd how we dance down south."

Slim grabbed Abbie's hand and drug her toward the front of the room. When she protested, he just laughed. "It ain't hard, Abbie. Just move yore feet to the music an' hang onto me. I'll do the leadin'."

John directed everyone to gather in a big circle and grab hands.

"Now follow the person in front of you. We'll circle this room and twist around some. When we finish, those two young couples will be right smack in the center of the room."

A large circle was quickly formed, and the music began. Sadie and Levi watched in surprise as their son led half of the room in a winding dance that circled a smaller and smaller space.

Everyone laughed when a barefooted little boy darted into the circle. Spur made a grab for him, but John Kirkham grabbed Eddie's hand and held onto him for the rest of the dance. Before long, the two newlywed couples were in the middle of the dancers and the circle began to unwind.

When it was over, Slim grinned at Abbie as he led her off the floor.

"See how easy that was, Abbie? Maybe we'll have to be part of one of these dances again someday, you an' me together." Abbie blushed and Slim chuckled. He left her with her parents and joined the other loud young men clustered on one side of the room.

The two newlyweds enjoyed one dance on an open floor before the rest of the guests joined them. The room was soon loud with happy laughter and little children everywhere.

Angel Montero, Nate and Gabe's brother-in-law, and Rusty O'Brian, their business partner, were to "supervise" the many children. Of course, neither man cared much about control or noise. They did let every child who wanted to scatter sawdust on the dance floor have a turn with their own bucket once the "Wedding March" was over. The first dances were extremely slow as the dancers maneuvered carefully on the slick floor, trying to avoid the piles of sawdust.

The guests laughed when Rusty's twins introduced their new cousin, Jackson, to everyone as "Uncle Spur's son he just found out about."

Eddie took a liking to Evelyn Merrill and to the surprise of many, he fell asleep in her arms. Evelyn was the most surprised of all. She smiled and kissed his face as she pushed back his black curls.

Clare frowned and whispered to Spur, "He likes how she smells. That's why he wanted to sit on her lap. I declare that child is just like you."

Spur grinned and chuckled.

"I used to smell everything too. And to his defense, there is nothing like a sweet-smelling woman." He tried to sniff Clare's neck and she pushed him away.

"Stop it, Spur. You are making a scene."

"No one even noticed, Clare. They are all having too much fun. Now let's go dance before that wild son of yours wakes up and we need to take him out to Angel's."

CHAPTER 110

SPECIAL FRIENDS

CLARE SMILED AS SHE WATCHED TUFF AND NORA dance. *Tuff was always a sweet boy, and lately, Nora has been mentioning him more. I wonder…* She frowned when Annie joined a group of boys close to her age.

Spur laughed as he whispered, "Tuff and Nora—they have been friends since they were little tykes. We are going to Kit's for dinner tomorrow, and we need more hands. Maybe we can hire Tuff away from his brother.

"Then Nora will have to decide if she still wants to be a nun or if she wants to spend time with Tuff.

"And as far as Annie goes, she's a little tomboy. I doubt she is interested in any of those boys. She just finds them more entertaining than girls."

They both watched in surprise when Paul Rankin strolled across the room and stopped in front of Annie with a smile.

Paul bowed and gave Annie a friendly smile.

"Would you like to dance, Annie Spurlach?"

Annie frowned at him.

"I don't particularly like to dance, and I certainly don't want to dance slow." She paused when the song changed to a lively polka.

"Fine. I'll dance one dance but don't think I'm doing it because I like you. I don't need a beau."

Paul glanced at her in surprise and then laughed as he shook his head.

"I would think no such thing, Annie." He was still smiling when he led her onto the dance floor and began to spin her in circles.

Annie was quick on her feet and they both enjoyed themselves. When the dance finished, Paul guided her back to where she had been standing. He pointed toward her feet and chuckled.

"I think your moccasins helped you to dance. You are light on your feet and mighty easy to dance with."

Annie looked at her feet and her cheeks slowly turned pink. However, her face was defiant when she looked up at Paul.

"I don't like shoes—or dresses either for that matter. Mother made me wear a dress, but Papa said I could wear my moccasins." Her eyes sparkled with orneriness, and she added, "It was either these or my old boots." She added quietly, "Papa made my first pair of moccasins but now I make my own."

Paul leaned over to study her feet before he looked up at Annie in surprise.

"You made them yourself? The beadwork too?"

Annie blushed again but nodded.

"I made friends with an old Indian woman back home and she taught me. Beading was kind of hard to learn but now I enjoy it."

Paul smiled down at her. He bowed as he backed away.

"It was a pleasure to dance with you, Annie Spurlach. You are plumb full of surprises. I hope we get to dance again sometime."

Annie said nothing but she watched him walk away. She looked over her shoulder and saw that a seat beside her parents was empty. She strolled over and dropped down beside Spur. Her dark hair was trying to slip out of the knot on the back of her head, and she shoved a curl behind her ear.

"You and Paul danced mighty smooth out there."

Annie scowled at Spur and slid down in her chair.

"Did he tell you his middle name?"

Annie looked at her father in surprise but shook her head.

"Broken Knife. Paul Broken Knife Rankin. He was named for the brave who is his father's blood brother." Spur smiled at his daughter and whispered, "Paul wears moccasins sometimes too. He told me once that he almost prefers them over his boots. Of course, his boots work better for cowboying."

Annie stared at Spur for a moment and then turned in her chair to watch Paul as he joked with the group of men he was standing with. Spur patted her leg before he grabbed Clare's hand.

"Let's dance one more time before we head out, Clare. I think we need to get these kids home. We have a long day planned for tomorrow, and then we leave on Monday."

CHAPTER 111

THREE WEDDINGS IN TWO DAYS

KIRKHAM SMILED AS HE WATCHED THE NEWLYWEDS dance and talk with their friends. He looked at the woman beside him and the little boy asleep on her lap. He touched her arm.

"Evelyn, Martha and Badger told me they invited you to stay a few days with them. I think you should do it. It will be a nice vacation for you. I wouldn't mind staying an extra day or two as well. Gabe Hawkins and Merina invited me to stay out there."

Evelyn nodded. "That would be nice. I have enjoyed getting to know Martha. All the people here actually."

"How about the two of us get hitched before we leave here, Evelyn? We talked to that pastor from the Rankins' church through most of the meal tonight and he seems like a nice fellow.

"You and I get along well, and we make each other smile. Besides, I think it's time we both move out of our kids' houses and give them a little space. We just as well build one house as two and have some companionship while we get old.

"What do you think?"

Evelyn was surprised.

"I—I—why, John, I never thought about us marrying. This is quite sudden. Don't you think we are a little old to start over?"

"Nonsense. I've been thinking on this for nearly two years. Besides, there is no sense in wasting around. We don't know how many good years we have left.

"When we get back, I'd like to show you a place on the south edge of my property I think you'd like. It's closer to town and a mighty pretty place. We can even live in Ogallala if you want. I own a couple of houses there. I have a good foreman, and I'm not outside every day as much as I was."

He leaned closer to her and whispered, "Martha and Badger offered to stand up with us." When Evelyn looked at John in shock, he grinned at her. "I asked them yesterday. We can keep it private and quiet so there is nothing to plan.

"The McCunes married late in life and look how happy they are. You and I both had good marriages. We loved our spouses and would still be with them if the Good Lord hadn't taken them away. I reckon we know what it takes to make a happy life with someone.

"It will be a new adventure. Besides, Isabelle and Sam will most likely have a passel of little ones. It would be fun for both of us to be part of that."

"I—I will have to think about that, John. Marriage isn't something we should rush into." Still, Evelyn felt a tingle of excitement when John smiled at her and squeezed her hand.

Evelyn was nervous and excited when she agreed to marry John the next day. They were married Sunday afternoon in the little church that Rowdy and Beth attended. Martha and Badger were the only guests at their private ceremony.

Cheyenne was treated to three happy weddings in two days, and the little community of friends continued to grow. While one son left with his new bride, another young man settled in an old house that had been home to his bride as a child. The old walls had known much love.

CHAPTER 112

YOU ARE MY ROCK

THE STILLNESS OF THE LITTLE HATCH HOUSE WAS broken by Mari's voice.

"Have you ever seen that tree that grows in the middle of a big rock, Nate? It's five or ten miles from here."

"I know where it is. Folks call it Tree Rock and it marks the southwest corner of our property."

"Do you think we can build our house there? I'd like to see that tree every day."

Nate leaned up on an elbow and looked down at his wife.

"Now why would you want that?"

"I've always loved that old tree. I love how it is determined to survive in the most impossible of locations. Winds and storms blow it around. Snow beats on it too, but it keeps its roots planted firmly in the ground."

Nate stared down at Mari as the moonlight flickered across her face. He chuckled.

"Like us? I'm the big, clueless rock and you are the little tree who broke me?"

Mari pulled him back down.

"No, because you are my rock. You are the one I waited for. Our love grew over the years even though it could have died. Now there are two parts, but the rock is still one and the tree is still alive. That's why, Nate."

"Maybe we should talk about that a little more. That and the trip I am taking you on to Charleston, South Carolina."

Mari's eyes opened wide, and she hugged Nate tightly.

"Nate Hawkins, I'm so glad I waited eight years for you!"

The little house became quiet as the moon shined its light through the bedroom window.

No one would know for a time, but two babies were conceived that night...children who were destined to be lifelong friends.

The old tree lifted its branches to drink the sprinkle of rain that showered it. It held itself proudly as the wind jerked it from side to side. Its roots were buried deep in the ground and the rock where it grew hugged it tightly. Together, they would withstand the many storms to come.

Printed in the USA
CPSIA information can be obtained
at www.ICGtesting.com
CBHW021150300924
15101CB00003BA/4

9 781958 227350